KASEY MICHAELS

THE TAMING OF THE RAKE

Recycling programs
for this product may
not exist in your area.

ISBN-13: 978-0-373-77591-0

THE TAMING OF THE RAKE

Copyright © 2011 by Kathryn Seidick

All rights reserved. Except for use in any review, the reproduction or
utilization of this work in whole or in part in any form by any electronic,
mechanical or other means, now known or hereafter invented, including
xerography, photocopying and recording, or in any information storage
or retrieval system, is forbidden without the written permission of the
publisher, Harlequin Enterprises Limited, 225 Duncan Mill Road,
Don Mills, Ontario M3B 3K9, Canada.

This is a work of fiction. Names, characters, places and incidents are
either the product of the author's imagination or are used fictitiously,
and any resemblance to actual persons, living or dead, business
establishments, events or locales is entirely coincidental.

This edition published by arrangement with Harlequin Books S.A.

For questions and comments about the quality of this book
please contact us at Customer_eCare@Harlequin.ca.

® and TM are trademarks of the publisher. Trademarks indicated with
® are registered in the United States Patent and Trademark Office, the
Canadian Trade Marks Office and in other countries.

www.HQNBooks.com

Printed in U.S.A.

Dear Reader,

In the more than thirty years I've been spinning stories, and with the more than one hundred heroes I've created, I've written about a few who have not qualified as "angels." But none of them were bastards. Well, at least not according to the legal definition.

Then I had this idea about three bastard sons of an English marquess and an actress mother. Loved by their father, educated "above their station," rigged out, with scads of money in their pockets and, of course, handsome as sin. Where do they fit in an age and a society that stakes so much on pristine lineage? Certainly no papa would hand his daughter over to a bastard, no matter how wealthy or civilized that suitor might be. No, the bastard would be relegated to the very fringes of society, caught between two worlds, belonging to neither.

Well, that couldn't happen, not in *my* world! Love simply has to conquer all! But it would take three very special young ladies to defy convention and their families, and sacrifice their own place in society, all for the love of a brash, or a fun-loving, or a brooding and secretive Blackthorn brother.

Come along, meet Beau Blackthorn and the woman who will risk everything—not to defy her brother as she thought, but for the love of a most unacceptable yet irresistible man. Then, please, watch for *A Midsummer Night's Sin* and *Much Ado about Rogues*, coming soon.

The Blackthorn Brothers. You're going to love them!

Happy reading,

Kasey Michaels

To my daughters and best friends, Anne and Megan,
with love

THE TAMING OF THE RAKE

PROLOGUE

"Men have died from time to time,
and worms have eaten them, but not for love."

—*As You Like It*, William Shakespeare

OLIVER LE BEAU BLACKTHORN was young and in love,
which made him a candidate for less than intelligent
behavior on two counts.

And so it was that, with the clouded vision of a man
besotted, that same Oliver Le Beau Blackthorn, raised
to think quite highly of himself, the equal to all men,
did, with hat figuratively in hand, hope in his heart and
a bunch of posies clutched to his breast, bound up the
marble steps to the mansion in Portland Place one fine
spring morning and smartly rap the massive door with
the lion's head brass knocker.

Oliver, known to his family as Beau, performed a
quick mental inventory of his appearance, one he'd
worked over for a full two hours, crumpling both a
half dozen neck cloths and his valet's abused nerves in
the process.

He was presenting himself in a morning rigout of
finest tan buckskins, dazzlingly white linen, a stunning

yet unobtrusive waistcoat of marvelously brushed silk
shot through with cleverly designed stripes made of
the lightest tan thread and a darkest blue jacket that so
closely followed the lines of his young, leanly muscled
body that he could not manage to get his arms in or out
of the sleeves without assistance.

He'd practiced the jaunty positioning of his curly
brimmed beaver in front of the pier glass in his dressing room for a full ten minutes before pronouncing the
angle satisfactory; showing off his thick crop of sun-
streaked blond hair rather than crushing it, providing
just enough cover from the brim that his bright blue
eyes were not cast into the shade.

It only just now occurred to him that the hat would
be handed over to the Brean footman, along with his
new tan kid gloves and walking stick, and Lady Madelyn would never see them.

Hmm, no one had as yet answered his knock. Shabby,
that's what that was. He lifted his hand to the knocker
once more, just as the door opened, and very nearly
tapped on the footman's nose.

Beau glared at the fellow, who stepped back quickly,
and the well-tailored Mr. Blackthorn sauntered into the
black-and-white marble-tiled foyer, feeling his cheeks
growing hot and damning his lifelong tendency to blush.

Shortly thereafter he was admitted to the Grand
Drawing Room by the family butler, who seemed
disapproving in some way as he looked at the flowers, to await the appearance of Lady Madelyn Mills-

Beckman, elder daughter of the Earl of Brean, and Beau Blackthorn's beloved.

"Quite a lot of Bs in there," he murmured to himself, an outward sign of the nervousness he felt but had thus far managed to conceal. There had been that small slip with the footman, but by and large, Beau was still feeling quite confident.

Or he was until a young female voice interrupted his thoughts.

"Talking to oneself is considered by some to be an indication of madness. At least that's what Mama said once about Aunt Harriet, and she was mad as a hatter. Aunt Harriet, that is. Mama was simply silly. I once saw Aunt Harriet with her clothes on backward. Are those flowers for Madelyn? Should I tell you that she loathes flowers? They make her sneeze, and her eyes water, and then her nose begins to drip…"

Beau had already turned about smartly, to see Lady Chelsea Mills-Beckman, a rather pernicious brat of no more than fourteen, ensconced on a flowered chaise near the window. She had her bent legs tucked up under the skirts of her sprigged muslin gown, and an open book was perched on her lap.

His reluctant scrutiny took in her long and messily wavy blond hair that had half escaped its ribbon, the eyes that were neither gray nor quite blue below flyaway eyebrows that could make her look devilish and pixyish at the same time, the budding young body that should certainly be positioned with more circumspection.

The wide, teasing grin on her face, he ignored.

Beau had suffered the misfortune of Lady Chelsea's presence twice before in the past month, always with a book in her hand and a too-smart tongue in her head, and he was as loath to see her this morning as he'd been either of those other times.

"Your father should order a lock put on the nursery door," he drawled now, even as he strode to the French doors and unceremoniously tossed the posies out into the garden.

Lady Chelsea laughed at this obvious silliness, be it directed at his statement or the flowers he couldn't be certain. But then she told him, drat her anyway.

"I'd only find another way out. I'm motherless, you understand, and allowances must be made for me. Too young for a Come-out, too prone to mischief to be left with my governess in the country while Madelyn is being popped off. I suppose you want me to vacate the room now, before Madelyn makes her grand entrance and you delight her by drooling all over her shoe tops. Oh, look at that, you've got a wet spot from the stems on that odiously homely waistcoat. I'll wager that's put a crimp in your airs of consequence."

Beau hastily brushed at his waistcoat before his brain could inform his pride that the blasted girl was making a May game out of him. Had he really only considered the nursery for her banishment? He would rather the cheeky child left the continent, perhaps even the universe, but refrained from that particular honesty. "I would like to converse with Lady Madelyn in private, yes."

"Oh, very well, if you're going to be all starchy about

the thing." Lady Chelsea got to her feet and smoothed down her gown. She was a rather attractive child, he supposed. She'd probably break a dozen hearts in a few years. But she didn't hold a patch on her sister, she of the ice-blue eyes and nearly white-blond hair, her mouth a pouty pink, her skin so creamy and flawless above the low bodice of her gowns.

Beau inserted a finger beneath his collar and gave a small tug, as it had suddenly become difficult to swallow. That action then turned impossible as the object of his affection entered the room.

"Mr. Blackthorn, what a lovely surprise. I hadn't thought to see you so soon after our dance at Lady Cowper's ball. Naughty man, showing up uninvited as you did. Quite shocking, really. And just to dance with me and then take your leave? It was all quite romantic and daring." Lady Madelyn tipped her head to one side as if trying to somehow see behind his back. "Did you bring me a gift? I adore gifts."

Beau bowed to the love of his life and apologized for his sad lack of manners.

Lady Madelyn looked crestfallen for a moment but then brightened. "Very well, I accept your apology. Next time, perhaps you'll bring me flowers. I do love flowers."

A giggle from the corner alerted Beau to the fact that the brat was enjoying another small joke at his expense, but he refused to look at her or acknowledge the hit. "I will buy you an entire hothouse full of flowers," he promised Lady Madelyn earnestly, bowing yet again.

"And now, if I might have a word with you in private? There is something of great personal importance I wish to ask you. After the events of last night, I should think you know what that is."

She didn't move, didn't blink, and yet something changed in Lady Madelyn's ice-blue eyes. Her smile became frozen in place, and her creamy-white skin seemed to pale even more, all the way to porcelain, and looked just as cold and hard.

"Now, Mr. Blackthorn, you know that is quite impossible. No young lady of quality is ever without a chaperone in the presence of a gentleman, as we both know. I do believe, if I am interpreting your statement correctly, that it is my absent father you should be asking for, not me," she scolded in a rather strangled tone. "Chelsea, would you be a dear and ask our brother to step in here for a moment? Mrs. Wickham is still dressing, I'm afraid."

"But I saw her earlier on the stairs, and she was completely—"

Lady Madelyn whirled about to glare at her sister. "Do as I say!"

"You're such a snob," Chelsea said as she flounced out of the room.

Oliver Le Beau Blackthorn was young and in love, and like many of his similarly afflicted brethren, not thinking too clearly. But it didn't take a clear thinker to recognize that the rosy scenario he'd pictured in his brain and the scene playing out in front of him now were poles apart.

She was probably nervous. Women tended to be nervous at times like these; they couldn't seem to help themselves. He'd make allowances.

"Lady Madelyn...and if I might be so bold, dear, *dear* Madelyn," he said, taking quick advantage while they were still alone, dropping to one knee in front of her and clasping her right hand in his, just as he had practiced the move on Sidney, his horribly embarrassed valet. "It can be no secret that I have admired you greatly since the moment we first met. With each new meeting my affection has grown, and I believe it has been reciprocated, most especially after our walk together the other evening when I so dared as to kiss you and you did me the great honor of allowing me to—"

"Not another word! How *provokingly common* of you to speak of such things! No gentleman would ever be so crass as to throw a moment's folly into a lady's face. A single kiss? It was a lark, a dare, no more than that. Get up! You're a dreadful creature."

A single kiss? It had been considerably more than a single kiss. She'd allowed him to cup her breast through the thin fabric of her gown, moaned delightfully against his mouth as he'd run his thumb across her hard, pert nipple. If not for the sound of approaching footsteps, there would have been much more. He'd nearly been bursting, had come within moments of thoroughly embarrassing himself, for God's sake.

He would have thought her a cold, heartless tease if he'd been in his right mind. But no, he was in love. And she was clearly upset.

"I know I'm being forward," Beau persisted—he'd been up all night rehearsing this speech. "I ask only that I have your permission to address your father. I would not wish to do so if my affection truly wasn't returned."

"Well, it isn't," Lady Madelyn responded hotly, pulling her hand free. "You overreaching nobody. Just because your father is one of us, and you've been accepted in some quarters because of him and because of that ridiculous fortune he's bestowed on you, doesn't mean you'll truly ever be one of us. Don't you even know when someone is making a May game of you? You're a joke, Beau Blackthorn, a laughingstock to everyone in Mayfair, and you're the only one who doesn't know it. As if I or any female of decency in the *ton* would deign to align herself with a—a *bastard* like you."

Beau would later remember that the lady's brother entered the drawing room at some point during this heart-shredding declaration, along with two burly footmen who quickly grabbed hold of Beau's arms and hauled him to his feet and beyond, so that he was dangling between them, his boots a good two inches off the floor.

He called out his beloved's name, but she had already turned her back and was walking away from him, holding up the hem of her skirts as if to avoid stepping in something vile.

A dare? A joke? That's all he'd been? She—and God only knew who else—had been encouraging him, yet secretly *laughing* at him? Is that how Society really saw him? As some sort of monkey they could watch dance?

A performing bear they could prod with a stick, just to see how he'd react? Here, bastard, kiss me, touch what you'll never have. And then go away. *You're not one of us.*

His mother had warned him, warned all three of her sons. Beau had never believed the dire predictions that she ascribed to the ridiculous notions and actions of their father. The world had to have been better than she'd painted it. But she'd been right, and he and his father had been wrong.

At last Beau, his dreams, all of the assumptions and hopes of his young life shattering at his feet, came to his senses. He struggled violently to be free, to no avail, until he was carried out the way he had come in and been thrown down the marble steps to the flagway. He could hear as well as feel the crack of a bone in his left forearm as it made sharp contact with the edge of one of the steps even as all the air left his lungs in a painful *whoosh.*

Then the first snap of the whip hit him across his back, and he could do nothing more than curl himself into a ball and take each blow, trying to protect his face, his eyes, his injured arm.

"Insult my sister, will you? Take advantage of her innocence?" The viscount flourished the coach whip again and again, the braided leather with the hard, metal tip slicing Beau's new morning coat straight on through to his skin, setting his back on fire. "Putting on airs above your station? That's what coddling your type leads to, damn it. Society in shambles! The very breath you take is an abomination to all that is decent. I should have you bound and tossed in the Thames like the worthless dog you are!"

At last the assault with the whip ended, followed briefly by some well-placed kicks from the footmen, and Beau heard the slam of a door. He tentatively got to his feet, his body a mass of pain, his heart and soul in tatters, just like his fine coat. One of the footmen spat at him before they both shouted at him to go away, their coarse oaths drawing the attention of any passersby who hadn't already stopped to stare at the spectacle.

Still crouching like a whipped dog as he supported his broken arm, Beau turned to look back at the mansion, only to have the door open slightly and the face of Lady Chelsea peek out at him, her eyes awash in tears.

"I'm so, so sorry, Mr. Blackthorn," she said, sniffling, tears running down her cheeks. "Madelyn is vain and heartless, and Thomas is just an ass. They can neither of them help themselves, I suppose. I don't think you a joke. I...I think you're entirely worthy, if a little silly in your head. But perhaps you should go away now. Very far away."

And then she closed the door, and Beau was left to stare down his own groom, who had been waiting with the new curricle that had also been purchased to impress Lady Madelyn. He'd planned to take her for a drive, once he'd spoken to her father, and perhaps steal another kiss—and more—as they rode out to Richmond Park.

"Thank you, no, and thank you so much for springing

to my aid with all the loyalty of a potted plant," Beau said stiffly, gritting his teeth against the nausea that threatened as the groom stepped forward to lend him support. "Return that damned thing to my stables. I'll walk back to Grosvenor Square."

And that's just what Beau did. He walked all the long blocks to his father's mansion. Staggered at times but always righted himself, kept his chin high, his spine straight, looking each passerby in the eye. Let them see, let them all see what they'd done to him while calling themselves gentlemen and ladies, thinking themselves somehow better than he, more civilized. Let them laugh now if they could. And let them remember, so that the next time they saw Oliver Le Beau Blackthorn or crossed his path, they'd know well enough to beware.

With each step, as those he encountered quickly crossed the street to avoid the torn and bloody sight of him, while none of them, acquaintance or supposed friend, raised a hand to help him, that same Oliver Le Beau Blackthorn left more of his youth behind him, until he was left with only one thought, one remaining truth.

His money, his looks, his charm, the friendships he'd believed he'd forged at school and here in London, the acceptance he'd thought he'd found? At the end of the day, they meant nothing.

He'd been a fool, he knew that now. Young and prideful and stupid. The laughingstock Lady Madelyn had called him.

The oldest son of the Marquess of Blackthorn, at two

and twenty years of age, had at last seem himself as the world saw him. Not as a man, not as a friend, not as a mate. They saw him as he was. Illegitimate. Born on the wrong side of the blanket, son of a marquess and a common actress. An educated and well-heeled bastard, yes, but a bastard all the same.

He walked on, his heart hardening, his mind holding on to one thought, the only thought that kept him from giving in to his pain, pitching forward once more into the gutter.

He would do as the brat advised. He would go away. Far away.

But he would return.

Someday.

And when he did, by God, let any man dare to laugh at him again!

CHAPTER ONE

LADY CHELSEA MILLS-BECKMAN, always the epitome of grace and charm, launched the thick marble-backed book of sermons directly at the head of her brother, Thomas, as of the past two years the seventeenth Earl of Brean.

Her aim was woefully off, and the tome missed him completely, which did nothing to improve her mood.

His lordship bent down to retrieve the book, inspecting the spine for any hint of damage before closing it and setting it on his desk. He was a man in his early forties, too well fed, and with a pink complexion that always seemed to border on the *shiny*. He thought himself handsome and brilliant, but was neither. He more closely resembled, Chelsea believed, an expensively dressed pig.

"God's words, Chelsea, delivered through the holy Reverend Francis Flotley himself. 'A woman's role is to obey, and her greatest gift her compliance with the superior wisdom of men. Let her gently be led in her inferior intellect, like the sheep in the field, or else otherwise lose her way and be branded morally bereft, a harlot in heart and soul, and worthy only of the staff.'"

The siblings had been closeted in the study in Portland Place for little more than a quarter-hour on this fine late April morning, and yet this was already the fourth time her brother had quoted from the book of sermons. Which, clearly, had been at least one time too many, as it had prompted the aforementioned action of her ladyship wrenching the book from his hand and sending it winging at him.

"*Herd* us poor, silly, brainless women, lead us gently by the hand as long as we obey, and beat us with the staff if we refuse to behave like sheep. That's what that means. What a pitiful mouthful of claptrap," Chelsea countered, attempting to control her breathing in her agitation. "You're a parrot, Thomas, mouthing words you've learned but haven't taken the time to understand. And did you ever notice, brother mine, that all of this nonsense is always penned by *men?* Is that what's next for me? You're going to *beat* me? As I recall the thing, you were once rather proficient with the whip, and not averse to employing it on someone who could not defend himself."

The earl quickly rose to his feet, open hand raised as if to strike his sister down, but then just as quickly seated himself once more, pasting a truly terrible smile of brotherly indulgence on his pink face.

"Certainly not, Chelsea. But you have just proved the reverend's point," he said, joining his hands in a prayerful attitude. "Women have not the intellect of men, nor do they possess the cerebral restraint necessary to combat rude and obnoxious outbursts. But I will forgive you, for it is just as the reverend has said, again, only delivering God's message as he hears it spoken to him."

"God talks to the man? Well, then, perhaps I should try having a small chat with God myself, and then the next time He *talks* to the reverend He can tell him to stop trying to rub up against my bosom as he pretends to bless me. That may not do much to enlarge my small intellect, but it might just save the reverend from a sharp kick in the shins."

The earl sighed. "Scurrilous accusations will get you nowhere, Chelsea, and only show your willingness to impugn the reverend's character by spouting baseless charges in order to…in order to get your own way."

"Forgot the rest of the words, did you? I mean it, Thomas, you're a *parrot.* You're devout by *rote,* certainly not by inclination."

"We aren't discussing me, we're discussing you."

"Not if I don't want to, and I don't!"

"We've moved beyond what you want, Chelsea. You've had your opportunities. Three Seasons, and you're still unwed, and very near to being on the shelf. Papa was much too indulgent of your fits and starts, and you missed a Season as we mourned his passing, may the merciful Lord rest his soul. Now we are halfway through yet another Season, and you have thus far refused the suits of no fewer than four gentlemen of breeding."

"And one out-and-out fortune hunter who had you entirely hoodwinked," Chelsea reminded him as she paced the carpet in front of the desk, unable to remain still. Her brother had always been stupid. Now he was both stupid and holy, hiding his fears behind this new supposed devotion, and that somehow made it all worse. She believed she'd liked him better when he'd been just stupid.

"Be that as it may, and there is still a question on that head, if you will not choose a husband, it is left to me to select one for you, as I helped do for your sister. You should be immensely flattered that he has taken an interest, most especially as he has firsthand knowledge of your...your proclivity for obtrusive behavior. I can think of no one finer than Reverend Flotley."

"You open your mouth yet again, Thomas, but it's still Francis Flotley's words that come out of it. I can think of no one worse. I'd rather wed a street sweep than put myself in the power of that religious mountebank. I reach my majority in a few weeks, Thomas, and you cannot order me to marry that...that oily creature. Oh, stop frowning. A mountebank, since you obviously aren't of a superior enough intellect to know, is a person who deceives other people for profit. Sometimes it is by selling false cures, and for the reverend, it is selling false salvation. You really think he has a direct conduit to God? I hear Bedlam is full of those who think God speaks to them. You could ask any one of them to intercede for you without paying them a bent penny, and I can go my own way."

"And where would that be, Chelsea?" Her brother was maintaining his composure, something he had struggled long and hard to do ever since he'd nearly died during a bout with the mumps two years earlier, passed to him by one of Madelyn's wet-nosed brood of brats— It having taken Madelyn a run through a pair of female offspring before she'd succeeded in producing a male heir for her husband, who'd then at long last agreed to leave her alone, so she was free to regain her figure, buy out Bond Street every second fortnight and sleep with any man who wasn't her husband.

At any rate, and Madelyn's disease-spreading offspring to one side, Thomas was devoutly religious now, having promised God all sorts of sacrifices in exchange for rising up from what could have been his deathbed, and it had been the Reverend Francis Flotley who had successfully delivered, and continued to deliver, the earl's messages to God in his name.

Since their father's untimely death and Thomas's own near brush with that final answer to the trial of living, the earl no longer drank strong spirits. He did not gamble. He'd given his mistress her *congé* and was now, for the first time in their marriage, faithful to his wife—who, Chelsea knew, was none too happy about that turn of events. He wore expensive yet simple black suits with no ornamentation. He did not lose his temper. He read the evening prayers in the drawing room each night at ten and retired at eleven.

And he continued to pour copious amounts of money into the purse of Reverend Flotley, who, Chelsea believed, had decided marrying the earl's younger sister to be a guarantee that the supply of funds would then never be cut off, even if his lordship were ever to suffer a crisis of faith…or meet another lady of negotiable moral standards he might want to set up in a discreet lodging somewhere.

"Where would I be? Are you threatening to toss me into the streets, Thomas?"

He sighed. "I did not wish for it to come to this, but I have sole control over your funds from Mama until you are married. You have a roof over your head because of my generosity. You have bread on your plate and clothes on your back because I am a giving and forgiving man. But more to the point, Francis and I see your immortal soul in danger, Chelsea, thanks to your headstrong and modern ways. I'm afraid you leave me no choice but to make this decision for you. The banns will be called for the first time this Sunday at Brean, and you and the reverend will be wed there at the end of this month."

Chelsea was caught between panic and anger. Anger won. "The devil we will! You think you almost died, and your answer to that is to sacrifice *me?* I thought it was only your cheeks that got fat—not your entire head. I won't do it, Thomas. I won't. I'd rather reside beneath London Bridge."

The earl opened the book of sermons and lowered his gaze to the page, signaling that the interview was concluded. But he could not conceal that his hands were shaking, and Chelsea knew she had nearly succeeded in rousing his temper past the point the Reverend Flotley had deemed good for her brother's soul. "Not London

Bridge at least. We leave for Brean in the morning, where you will be made safe until the ceremony."

Chelsea felt her stomach clench into a knot. He was planning to make her a prisoner until the wedding. "Made safe? Locked up, that's what you mean, don't you? You can't do that, Thomas. Thomas! Look at me! I'm your sister, not your possession. You can't do that."

He turned the page, ignoring her.

She whirled about on her heel and fled the room, her mind alive with bees and possibilities…and filled with one thought in particular, a memory that had been conjured up thanks to Thomas.

When she reached the main foyer she told the footman to order her mare brought round and then raced up the sweep of staircase to change into her riding habit before her brother came to his senses and realized that a prisoner tomorrow, warned of that pending imprisonment, should also be a prisoner today.

"So, I'VE BEEN LYING here thinking, and I've come up with a question for you. Are you ready? Hell and damnation, man, are you even awake?"

There was a muffled and faintly piteous groan from somewhere in the near vicinity, and Beau turned his head on the couch cushion—not without experiencing a modicum of cranial discomfort—to see his youngest brother lying on the facing couch, facedown and still fully dressed in his evening clothes. Although one of his black evening shoes seemed to have gone missing.

"A moan is sufficient, thank you. Now, here it is, so

pay attention if you please—how drunk is it to be drunk as a lord?" Beau Blackthorn asked Robin Goodfellow Blackthorn, affectionately known to his siblings and many friends as Puck.

"Sterling question, Beau, sterling. Not sure, though," Puck, yet another victim of their dear actress mother's intense admiration for William Shakespeare, replied, lifting his head and squinting through the long, dark blond hair that fell across his face as he commenced staring intently at a brass figurine depicting a scantily clad goddess with six—no, eight—oddly extended and bent arms. At least he probably hoped that was it, because if there were, in reality, only two arms, then he was as drunk as any lord had been in the history of lords. "Twice as drunk as a…a what's it called? Three wheels, place to pile things. Dirt, stones. Turnips. Wait, wait, I'll figure it out. Oh, right. A wheelbarrow? That's it, drunk as a wheelbarrow."

Beau stared at the half-empty wine bottle he held upright against his chest as he lay sprawled on the matching couch in the drawing room, realizing that he no longer possessed any urge to relieve it of the remainder of its contents. Not if he was still drunk enough to be asking his irreverent and weak-brained brother for answers to anything. Besides, his stomach was beginning to protest, threatening to throw back what had already been deposited in it.

"Still the half-wit, aren't you, Puck? Wheelbarrows don't drink. Stands to reason. They don't have mouths. Remember old Sutcliffe? He once said he was drunk as

David's sow. Don't know any Davids, do you? One with a sow, remember, that's the important part. Not enough to know a David. Has to be a sow in there somewhere."

"David Carney is married to a sow," Puck said, grinning. "Says so all the time. I've seen her, and he's right. Are we still drunk, do you think? Shouldn't be, not seeing as it's light outside those bloody windows over there, and the mantel clock just struck twelve while you were talking sows. Or that might have been eleven. I may have lost count. Or perhaps we're dead?"

"The way my head is beginning to pound, that might be best, but I don't think so. Now, back to the point. I'm drunk, you're drunk. We're drunk as bastards, surely. But are we as drunk as lords? Can bastards be as drunk as lords?"

"You going to start prattling on again about bastards and lords? Thought we'd done with that by the time we'd cracked the third bottle. Bastards, I have found, can't be *anything* as lords," Puck said, cautiously levering himself upward far enough to swivel about and sit facing his brother. He pushed his hands straight back through his nearly shoulder-length hair, so that he could tuck it behind his ears. "See my ribbon anywhere? It'll all just keep falling in my eyes otherwise."

"I could ring for somebody to fetch Sidney. The man owns a scissors, which is more than I can say for your valet."

"Blasphemy! The ladies would never forgive me. My hair is a necessary part of my considerable charms, don't you know. If I am to be Puck, then I shall be Puck. Mischievous. A sprite, a magical woodland creature."

"And none too bright."

"Ha! So you say. But still, much better-looking and virile, and definitely more amusing. Every maiden's dream, although I've not much time for maidens. They demand so much wooing, and once you've finally got them into bed they don't know what they're doing. By and large, a dreadful waste of time."

Beau had also sat up and placed the wine bottle on the floor, next to the table positioned between the pair of couches, so that he could better rub at his aching head. "Is that it? Are you done now? Because there are times I think you'll never truly grow up. I left and you were a child, and I came back to find you older, yet no wiser."

Puck merely shrugged, clearly not taking offense at his brother's words, as a less confrontational fellow would be difficult to locate within the confines of England. "You long for acceptance where there is no acceptance. Brother Jack would spit in the eye of anyone who dared to call him respectable. And I? I applaud myself for my complete indifference to it all. I have more money than any ten men with rich appetites would ever need, thanks to our guilt-ridden father. I have been educated and dressed up and taught to be mannerly, and there is nothing left for me to aspire to than to be happy with my lot. Which, brother mine, I am. Besides, you and Jack are deadly serious enough for all of us. Some one of us should have some fun. You look like hell, by the way. I must remember to give up strong spirits before I reach your age."

At last, Beau smiled. "You're only four years my junior, and at thirty I'm far from tottering about with one foot hovering over a grave." But then he stabbed his fingers through his own thick shock of sun-streaked blond hair. "Although, at the moment, I might consider it. I don't remember the last time I felt like this. You're a bad influence, little brother. One might even say noxious. When do you return to France?"

"Hustling me back out the door only a few days after I've come through it, and after only a single night's celebration of my return to the bosom of my wretched family? Papa keeps this great pile for all of us, you know. Why, I might just decide to take up permanent residence in London. Wouldn't that be fine? Just the two of us, rattling around here together, driving the neighbors batty to know that there are now two Blackthorn bastards in residence rather than just the one. Never be all three, considering Black Jack won't come within ten miles of the place."

Beau attempted to straighten his badly wilted cravat. "Oh, he's been here. Haughty, grumpy, scowling and bloody sarcastic. Don't wish him back, if you don't mind. Neither of us would like it."

"He would have made a fine Marquess, aside from the fact that you'd be first in line. And if our dearest mother had deigned to marry our doting papa. There is still that one other niggling small detail."

"Jack wouldn't take legitimacy if someone were to hand it to him on a platter. He likes being an outlaw."

Puck raised one finely arched eyebrow. "You mean that figuratively, don't you? *Outlaw?*"

"God, I hope so. Sometimes, though, I wonder. He lives damn well for a man who refuses our father's largesse. I'd reject it, as well, if it weren't for the fact that I do my best to earn my keep, running all of the Blackthorn estates while you fiddle and Jack scowls."

"Yes, I admit it. I much prefer to gad about, spending every groat I get and enjoying myself to the top of my bent, and feel totally unrepentant about any of it."

"You'll grow up one of these days. We all do, one way or another." Beau got to his feet, deciding he could not stand himself one moment longer if he didn't immediately hunt out Sidney and demand a hot tub to rid him of the stink of a night of dedicated drinking with Puck.

"He's lucky with the cards? The dice?" Puck persisted, also getting to his feet, triumphantly holding up the black riband he then employed to tie back his hair.

"I don't know. I don't ask. Jack was never one for inviting intimacies. Now come along, baby brother. We need a bath and a bed, the both of us."

"You might. I'm thinking lovely thoughts about a mess of eggs and some of those fine sausages we had yesterday morning."

Beau's stomach rolled over. "I remember when I could do that, drink all night and wake clearheaded and ravenous in the morning. You're right, Puck. Thirty is old."

"Now you're just trying to frighten me. Ho, what's that? Was that the knocker? Am I about to meet one of your London friends?"

"Acquaintances, Puck. I have no need of friends."

"Now that is truly sad," his brother said, shaking his head. "You had friends, surely, during the war?"

"That was different," Beau said, his headache pounding even harder than before. "Soldiers are real. Society is not."

"The French are much more generous in their outlook. To them, I am very nearly a pet. A highly amusing pet, *naturellement*. My bastard birth rather titillates them, I think. And, of course, I am oh, so very charming. Ah, another knock, followed closely by a commotion." Puck headed for the foyer. "This becomes interesting. I'd think it was a dun calling to demand payment, but you're entirely too deep in the pocket for that. Let's go see, shall we?"

Beau opened his mouth to protest, but quickly gave that up and simply followed his brother into the foyer. There they saw a woman, her face obscured by the brim of her fashionably absurd riding hat, quietly but fiercely arguing with Wadsworth.

"Wadsworth?" he said questioningly, so that his Major Domo—once an actual sergeant in His Majesty's Army—turned about smartly, nearly saluting his employer before he could stop himself.

"Sir!" he all but bellowed as he tried to position his

fairly large body between that of the female and his employer. "There is someone here who demands to be seen. I am just now sending her on the right-about—that is to say, I have informed her that you are not at home."

"Yes, well I suppose we needs must give that up as a bad job, mustn't we, now that I've shown myself. Or do you think she'll agree to go away now?"

"She most certainly will not," the woman said from somewhere behind Wadsworth. And then a kid-riding-glove-encased hand was laid on Wadsworth's elbow and the man who had once single-handedly subdued a half dozen Frenchmen during a skirmish by means of only his physical appearance and commanding voice—and the bloodied sword he'd held in front of him menacingly—was rudely shoved aside.

The woman's gaze took in the two men now before her, sliding from one to the other. "Oliver Blackthorn? Which one of you is he? And the other must be Mr. Robin Goodfellow Blackthorn, as I hear the third brother is dark to your light, unless that's simply a romantic statement and not fact. Such an unfortunate name, Robin Goodfellow. Did your mother not much like you? Oh, wait, you are Oliver, aren't you?" she said, pointing a rather accusing finger at Beau. "I believe I recognize the scowl, even after all these years. We must talk."

"Gad, what a beauty, if insulting," Puck said quietly. "Tell her she's wrong, that I'm you. Unless she's here to inform you that the bastard has fathered a bastard, in which case I'll be in the breakfast room, filling *my* belly."

Beau wasn't really listening. He was too busy racking his brain to remember where he'd ever seen eyes so strange a mix of gray and blue, so flashing with fire, intelligence and belligerence, all at the same time.

"You remember me, don't you?" the young woman said—again, nearly an accusation. "You should, and the mumps to one side, you're a large part of the reason I'm in such dire straits today. But that's all right, because now you're going to *fix* it."

"She said mumps, didn't she? Yes, I'm sure she did. I've been abroad for a few years, brother mine. Are they now in the habit of dressing up the Bedlamites and letting them run free on sunny days?"

"Go away, Puck," Beau said, stepping forward a pace, putting a calm face on his inward agitation. "Lady Chelsea Mills-Beckman?" he inquired, positive he was correct, although it had been more than seven long and eventful years since last he'd seen her. But why was she here? And where was her maid? Maybe Puck was right, and if not quite a fugitive from Bethlehem Hospital, she was at least next door to a Bedlamite; riding out alone in the city, calling on him, of all people. "To what do I owe the pleasure?"

"Ah, so you do remember me. And there's nothing all that pleasurable about it for either of us, I assure you. Now, unless you are in the habit of entertaining your servants with aired laundry best discussed only in private, I suggest we adjourn to the drawing room. *Not you,*" she added, pointing one gloved finger at Puck, who had already half turned to reenter the drawing room.

"Oh, yes, definitely. You heard the lady. It's you she wants, brother mine, not me. I'm off, and may some merciful deity of your choosing protect you in my craven absence."

"Wadsworth," Beau said, still looking at Lady Chelsea, "the tea tray and some refreshments in ten minutes, if you please."

Lady Chelsea stood her ground. "Wadsworth, a decanter of Mr. Blackthorn's best wine and two glasses, now, and truth be told, at the moment I really don't much care whether you please or not. Mr. Blackthorn, follow me."

She then swept into the drawing room, leaving Wadsworth and Beau to look at each other, shrug and supposedly do as they'd been told. That was the thing with angry women. Experience had taught Beau that it was often just easier to go along with them until such time as you could either locate a figurative weapon or come up with a good escape route.

And Beau did long for escape, craven as that might seem. The moment he'd recognized Lady Chelsea the memory of the last time he'd seen her had come slamming into his mind, rendering him sober and none too happy to be thinking so clearly.

His reunion with Puck had given him the chance to relax the guard he'd so carefully built up around himself. They'd laughed, definitely drunk too much and

Beau had realized how long it had been since he'd allowed himself to be young and silly.

Only with his brother could he joke about their bastard births, make light of the stigma they both would carry for all of their lives. Puck seemed to be dealing with his lot extremely well, although he had attacked the problem from an entirely different direction.

Where Beau thought to gain respect, if not acceptance, Puck had charmed his way into French Society.

Jack? Jack didn't bear thinking about, as he seemed to be a law unto himself.

But no matter the path Beau had chosen, he knew he'd come a long way from the idiot boy he'd been seven long years ago. He'd put the past behind him—except for what he believed to be the one last piece of unfinished business that had brought him to London—and he would rather the door to that part of his life remain firmly shut.

Shut, and with Lady Chelsea firmly on the other side. She with her childish teasing and then her sympathetic tears. If anything could have taken him to his knees that day, and kept him there, it would have been the sight of her tears.

"Sir?"

Beau turned to look at Wadsworth, snapping himself back into the moment. "Yes?"

"Are we going to do what she says, sir?" The man screwed up his face for a moment, and then shook his head. "Got the air of a general about her, don't she, sir?"

"That she does, Wadsworth," Beau said, at last turning toward the drawing room. "That she certainly does...."

CHAPTER TWO

HE HADN'T REALLY CHANGED in seven years. Except that he definitely had. He seemed taller, appealingly thicker in muscle, she supposed. He still carried his arrogance with him, but that had been joined now by considerably more self-assurance. His cheeks seemed leaner, his jaw more defined. He'd been only a year older then than she was now, and had obviously lived an interesting life in the interim.

He'd impressed her then, silly as he'd been in his embarrassing calf-love for Madelyn, uncomfortable as he'd looked in his ridiculously over-tailored clothes, gullible as he'd been when she'd teased him. Vulnerable as he had been, lying in the street as Thomas had brought the whip down over his body, again and again.

She'd had nightmares about that terrible day ever since. She assumed Mr. Blackthorn had, as well.

But the years had made him a man. Going to war had made him a man. What had happened that fateful day in Portland Place had made him a man. Then, he had amused her. Now, just looking at him made her stomach rather queasy. He was so large, so very male. Not a silly boy anymore at all.

Perhaps she had acted rashly, coming here. No, she definitely had acted rashly, considering only her own plight while blithely believing he would grab at her idea with both hands, knowing immediately that she was helping him, as well.

But there was nothing else for it. She had done what she'd done. She was here, an unmarried woman in a bachelor household, and probably observed by at least two or three astonished members of the *ton* as she'd stood at the door and banged on the knocker. Oh, and her groom and horse were still just outside, on the street.

She couldn't have been more open in her approach if she had ridden into Grosvenor Square shouting and ringing a bell.

Now she had to make Mr. Blackthorn—or Oliver, as she'd always thought of him—understand that there was no going back, for either of them. She may be frightened, suddenly unsure of herself—such a rare occurrence in her experience that she wasn't quite sure how to handle it—but she would not allow him to see her fear.

"You look as if you've been dragged through a hedgerow backward," she told him as she stood in the middle of the sumptuously furnished drawing room, pulling off her kid gloves, praying he wouldn't notice that her hands were shaking. "And you smell none too fresh. Is this your usual state? Because if it is, my mind won't change, but you will definitely have to."

He reached for a jacket that was hanging over the back of a chair and then seemed to think better of it, remaining in front of her clad only in his buckskins and shirtsleeves. "Much as it pains me to disagree with you, Lady Chelsea, I don't have to do anything I don't want to do. Bastardy has its benefits as well as its drawbacks."

She rolled her eyes, suddenly more comfortable. He might not appear vulnerable, but clearly he still carried the burden of his birth around with him; it must be a great weight he would choose to put down if he had the chance. "Are you still going on about that? You are, aren't you. That's why you've been slowly ruining my brother."

Beau frowned just as if he didn't understand her, which made her angry. She knew he wasn't stupid.

"Don't try to deny it, Mr. Blackthorn. You've sent person after person to insinuate himself with Thomas this past year, guide him down all the wrong paths, divesting him of our family's fortune just as if you had been personally dipping your hand into his pockets. Granted, my brother is an idiot, but I, sir, I am not."

"Nor are you much of a lady, traveling about London without your maid, and barging uninvited into a bachelor establishment," Beau said, walking over to one of the couches positioned beneath an immense chandelier that, if it fell, could figuratively flatten a small village. "Then again, I am not a gentleman, and I am curious. Stand, sit, it makes me no nevermind, but I've had a miserable night and now it appears that the morning will be no better, so I am going to sit."

Chelsea looked at the bane of her existence, who was

also her only possibility of rescue, and considered what she saw. He was blond, even more so wherever the sun hit his thick crop of rather mussed hair, so she hadn't at first noticed that he had at least a one-day growth of beard on his tanned cheeks. He looked rather dashing that way, not that she would tarry long on the path to *that* sort of thought. He also looked—as did this entire area of the large room, for that matter—as if the previous night had been passed in drinking heavily and sleeping little.

Good. He probably had a crushing headache. That would make him more vulnerable.

"Yes, do that, sit down before you fall down, and allow me to continue. In this past year, which happens to coincide with Thomas reentering Society after our year of mourning that also gained him the title, and paired with your return to London now that the war is finally over, we have been visited upon by a verifiable plague of financial ill-fortune, one to rival the atrocities of the Seven Plagues of Egypt."

Beau held up one hand, stopping her for a few moments, and then let it drop into his lap. "All right. I've run that mouthful past my brain a second time, and I think I've got it now. Your brother, the war, my return after an absence of seven years—and something about plagues. Are locusts involved? I really don't care for bugs. But never mind my sensibilities, which it is already obvious you do not. You may continue."

"I fully intend to. You know the *locusts* to which I refer. Mr. Jonathan Milwick and his marvelous invention that, with only a small input of my brother's money, could revolutionize the manufacture of snuff. The so-charming Italian, Fanini, I believe, whose discovery of diamonds in southern Wales would make Thomas rich as Golden Ball."

Beau closed his eyes and rubbed at his temples. "I have no idea what you're prattling on about."

"Still, I will continue to prattle. The ten thousand pounds Thomas was convinced would triple in three weeks' time in the Exchange, thanks to the advice of one Henrick Glutton, who would share his largesse with Thomas once his ship, filled with grapes to be made into fabulously expensive wine, arrived up the Thames. I went with Thomas to the wharf when the ship arrived. Have you ever *smelled* rotten grapes, Mr. Blackthorn?"

"Glut*ten*," he said rather miserably.

"Ah! So you admit it!"

"I admit nothing. But nobody can possibly be named *Glutton*. I was merely suggesting an alternative. Excuse me a moment, I just remembered something I need." Then he reached down beside him to pick up a bottle that had somehow come to be sitting on the priceless carpet, and took several long swallows straight from it, as if he were some low, mannerless creature in a tavern. He then held on to the bottle with both hands and looked up at her, smiling in a way that made her long to box his ears. "You were saying?"

"I was saying—well, I hadn't said it yet, but I was going to—I don't blame you for any of it. Thomas deserves all that you've done, and more. But with this last, you've overstepped the mark, because now you've involved *me* in your revenge, and that I will not allow. Still, I am here to help you."

The bottle stopped halfway to his mouth. At last she seemed to have his full attention. "I'm sorry, I don't follow. You're going to *help* me? Help me what, madam?"

Chelsea held her tongue until Wadsworth had marched in, deposited a silver tray holding two glasses and a decanter of wine on the table and marched out again.

"I haven't made a friend there, have I?" she commented, watching the man go. And then she shrugged, dismissing the thought, and finally seated herself on the facing couch and accepted the glass of wine Beau handed her. "You know that my brother became horribly ill only a few weeks after our father died. It was believed he'd soon join Papa in the mausoleum at Brean."

"I'd heard rumors to that effect, yes," Beau said carefully, shunning the decanter to take another long drink from the bottle. "Am I to be accused of that, as well? The illness, perhaps even your father's demise? Clearly I have powers I have not yet recognized in myself."

"Papa succumbed to a chest ailment after being caught in the rain while out hunting, so I doubt his death could be laid at your door. It was Madelyn's brood, come to Brean for the interment and bringing their pestilence with them, who nearly killed Thomas just as he was glorying in his acquisition of the title. You had a victory there, didn't you? With Madelyn, I mean. Thomas's vile behavior that day had repercussions on my idiot sister, and she had to be married off quickly in order not to have all the *ton* staring at her belly and counting on their fingers. Do you remember what Thomas screeched at you that day? Something about you taking advantage of her innocence? Poor Madelyn, hastily bracketed to a lowly baron when she had so set her sights on a duke, but she couldn't convince Papa. That you and she hadn't—you know. And poor baron, as he's had to live with her ever since. You had a lucky escape, Mr. Blackthorn, whether you are aware of it or not."

His blue eyes narrowed, showing her that she had at last touched a nerve. "You term what happened that day a lucky escape? Your memories of the event must differ much from mine."

"You're still angry."

Beau leaned against the back of the couch and crossed his legs. "Anger is a pointless emotion."

"And revenge is a dish best served cold. Thomas humiliated you for all the world to see, whipped you like a jackal he refused to dirty his hands on. The woman you thought you loved with all your heart turned out not to possess a heart of her own. Between them, my siblings brought home to you that you are what you are, and that Society had only been amusing itself at your expense, while it would never really accept you. I would have wanted them dead, all of them."

"Thank you for that pithy summation. I may have forgotten some of it."

"You've forgotten none of it, Mr. Blackthorn, or else I would not be saddled with Francis Flotley. I, who remain blameless in the whole debacle, a mere child at the time of the incident. Do you think that's fair? Because I don't. And now you're going to make it right."

"You're here to help me, and yet I'm supposed to make something right for you." Beau looked at her, looked at the bottle in his hand and then looked at her again. "Much as it pains me to ask this, what in blazes are you talking about? And who the bloody hell is Francis Flotley?"

Chelsea's hands drew up into fists. She wasn't nervous anymore. It was difficult for one to be nervous when one was beginning to feel homicidal. "You admit to Henrick Glutton and the others? We can't move on, Mr. Blackthorn, until you are willing to be honest with me."

"Glut*ten*," he said again, sighing. "And the others. Yes, all right, since you clearly won't go away until I do, I admit to them. Shame, shame on me, I am crass and petty. But, to clarify, I'm not out to totally ruin the man, but only make him uncomfortable, perhaps even miserable. Ruining him entirely would be too quick. As it is, I can keep this up for years."

"Why?"

"I should think the answer to be obvious. Because it amuses me, madam," Beau said flatly. "Rather like pulling the wings from flies, although comparing your brother to a fly is an insult to the insect. I'm unpleasantly surprised, however, that you connected me with your brother's run of ill luck, although I should probably not be, remembering you as you were. A pernicious brat, but possessing higher than average intelligence."

It was taking precious time, but at least they were finally getting somewhere. "So you admit to Francis Flotley."

"If you'll just leave me alone with my pounding head, I'll admit to causing the Great Fire. But I will not admit to Francis Flotley, whoever the hell he is."

Chelsea sat back in her seat. She had been so certain, but Beau clearly did not recognize the name.

"Francis Flotley," she repeated, as if repetition would refresh his memory. "The Reverend Francis Flotley, Thomas's personal spiritual adviser. The man who interceded with God for him in order to save him from the mumps in exchange for his promise to mend his ways. You used Thomas's vulnerability to insinuate the man into our household, to defang the cat, as it were, make him believe that he had to give up drink, and loose women, and his rough and tumble ways, in order to save his immortal soul. Curb his vile temper, turn the other cheek—all of that drivel. A man who would whip another man in the street, reduced to nightly prayers and soda water, doing penance for his crime against you, even if he doesn't realize that he is, lacking only sackcloth and ashes. How that must please you."

"Ah. The Reverend Francis Flotley. Yes, I will admit that I am aware of a cleric's presence in your household," Mr. Blackthorn said, sitting forward once more. "But no, sorry. I had nothing to do with that. Wish I had, though, having once been at the wrong end of what you call your brother's vile temper. It sounds a brilliant revenge."

Chelsea sat slumped on the couch, like a doll suddenly bereft of all its cotton stuffing. "Oh," she said quietly, seeing her last and only hope fading into nothing. "I'd been so sure. So brilliantly Machiavellian, you understand. I have given you too much credit. Forgive me. I'll go now."

She got to her feet and picked up her gloves, putting them on slowly, giving him time to sift through everything she'd told him. Surely he wouldn't let her leave. He couldn't. He had to at least be curious as to what she'd meant about having her own life ruined, and that she'd come here to help him. Even if she hadn't been correct about the Reverend Flotley, perhaps her plan could still work.

But Beau stayed where he was, not even rising because she had stood up, and very much ignoring her, as if she'd already gone. Perhaps he wasn't the man she'd built him into in her head. Perhaps he was just as bad as her brother in his own way.

Still, knowing she had no other options, she dared to continue hoping, even as she walked toward the foyer, slowly counting in her head. *One. Two. Three. Four. Oh, for pity's sake, I'm here to hand you the perfect revenge, you jackass! Does it really matter that you didn't send Flotley to us? Five. Six…*

"Wait a moment."

Chelsea closed her eyes for a second, swallowed her

fear once more and then turned around. "Yes? Has the penny finally dropped, Mr. Blackthorn? I'll excuse you, considering your drunken state, but you really shouldn't have taken much past three. If I'd gotten to nine, I'd have needed to reassess my opinion of you."

Beau got to his feet, waving a hand in front of him as if erasing whatever she'd said as not worthy of a response. "Why did you come here? Alone? Not just to crow over me that you know what game I've been playing with your brother. And more importantly, why do I get the feeling that you're not here to help me as much as you're here to help yourself? Wait—don't answer yet. Sit, drink your wine, and I'll go stick my head in a basin of cold water and clean up some of my mess, in the hope it clears my head."

"Yes, all right," Chelsea answered, once again taking up both her seat and the wineglass. She didn't really drink wine; she'd ordered it for him, believing he'd need it after he'd heard what she had to say. "But we should be leaving here within the hour, and even that will probably be cutting it too fine for comfort."

"Leaving? We? As in, the two of us? Oh, really. And to travel where, may I ask?"

"You're wasting time, Mr. Blackthorn. My brother is far from an intellectual, but he isn't completely stupid, either. He'll soon be out and about, looking for me, his newfound docile nature stretched to the breaking point. Oh, and to that end, although it is reminiscent of barring the barn door after the cow has escaped, I suggest you have my mount and groom removed from in front of the building."

"I'll order that," the other Mr. Blackthorn volunteered, halting just inside the doorway, a thick slice of bacon in his hand. "Shall we have the fellow bound and gagged, Lady Chelsea, or simply sat down somewhere and told to stay put? Beau, brother mine, clearly you've been holding out on me. I had no idea you led such an interesting life."

Beau grumbled something Chelsea was too far away to hear—which was probably a good thing—and headed for the stairs, bounding up them two at a time.

"Good, he's gone. Now we two can get to know each other better, as it appears you and my brother are up to some sort of mischief. Or is it just you? He is looking rather harassed. It's his age, you understand. Can't hold his drink anymore, either. It's a curse, old age. I have just now, over a plate of coddled eggs, vowed never to succumb to it."

"My mount, Mr. Blackthorn," Chelsea told him, smiling in spite of herself, for Mr. Robin Goodfellow Blackthorn had the most engaging smile and way about him. "And after you've gone off to do that, please order your brother's horse saddled and have his man pack a small bag for him. A traveling coach would be much too slow and easily spotted for our needs for now, I believe. We may also, now that I have a moment to reflect on the thing, needs must keep to alleyways until we're clear of London."

The man opened his mouth, clearly to ask her what

she meant, but she merely pointed behind him, to the foyer. "This is life or death, Mr. Blackthorn, so there is no time for me to stand here and applaud your silliness. Go."

He went.

Chelsea took a sip of the wine.

It didn't help; she was still shaking.

CHAPTER THREE

MUCH TO THE CHAGRIN of his valet, Beau refused to take the time to sit and be shaved, opting for a quick wash at the basin, a brief encounter with his tooth powder and a rushed combing of his hair as Sidney helped him into a clean white shirt before handing him fresh linen and buckskins and then throwing up his hands in disgust and quitting the dressing room.

Beau was still having difficulty believing that Lady Chelsea Mills-Beckman, sister of his nemesis, was downstairs, sipping wine in his drawing room. Sans chaperone, clad in a rather startlingly red riding habit and clearly expecting him to go somewhere with her.

Lady Chelsea Mills-Beckman. Knowing things she shouldn't know. Cheeky and impertinent as she'd been as a girl...and hinting of helping him revenge himself on her brother.

While helping herself. He shouldn't forget that. Women with ulterior motives were the norm rather than the oddity, he'd learned, and as this woman was also intelligent, he would have to be doubly on alert.

"Well, that could be considered by the less discerning as a bit of an improvement, I suppose," Puck said, entering the dressing room to lean one shoulder against the high chest of drawers as he visually assessed his brother. "I have reconnoitered your visitor, grilling her mercilessly for details. She informs me whatever is going on is a matter of life or death. Worse, she seems astonishingly immune to my charms, which would have me descending into a pit of despair were it not that I'm secretly delighted that she has targeted you rather than me for whatever it is she's planning. Not that I'm not here to help."

Beau snatched up a neck cloth and hastily tied it around his throat. "Your enthusiasm for throwing yourself down in the path to protect me nearly unmans me," he grumbled, realizing he'd just tied a knot in the neck cloth—rather like a noose.

"You're welcome. Disregarding female enthusiasm for melodrama, do you think she's right? The brother is a nasty piece of work, as I recall. Are you sure you wish to become embroiled in whatever she's prattling on about?"

"She's in my house, Puck."

"Our house, not to quibble about such a small point. But, as I am also here, I believe I should be apprised of whatever the devil it is I've somehow become embroiled in myself, if only by association. She's ordered me to hide her horse and groom, and then to advise Sidney to pack a bag for you, as you will be leaving within the hour. Which, naturally, begs the question—where are we going?"

Beau shrugged into a hacking jacket and took one

last, quick look at his reflection in the mirror above the dressing table. "*We* are not going anywhere," he told his brother. "Whatever the mess, I brought it on myself by being idiot enough to think I was a cat, toying with a mouse. I should have let it go, Puck, years ago. But, for once, it's my idiocy, not yours. You're not involved."

"What? You'd leave me here to face the wrath of the brother? I think not. If I'm not to go with you, I'll inform Gaston to pack me up and I'll be back off to Paris. The weather is better, for one thing, and the food at least edible. I damn near cracked a tooth on that bacon our cook dared serve me. We should sack him."

Beau turned on his brother. "You do this just to annoy me, don't you?"

Puck pushed himself away from the dresser. "Yes, but I'll stop now. You're much too easy to rile, you and Jack both. Takes the joy right out of a fellow. I was listening from the terrace, you know, and heard most of what she said. You've really been quietly ruining the earl? I'd say that was brilliant, except that Lady Chelsea found you out, so you couldn't be overly credited for subtlety. Comparing you to Machiavelli? Hardly. And now your pigeons seem to have come home to roost."

"We can't know that. Not unless the damned woman left her brother a note before she ran off. Because she did run off, Puck, that much is obvious. It's what women do. Without a thought to anyone else perhaps not agreeing to become an actor in their small melodrama."

"Yes, you're right," Puck agreed as he followed Beau down the hall to a small room he used as his private study. "She would have been better off applying to Mama. She dearly adores a melodrama. But when I left her to come to town, she was about to begin a tour of the Lake District with her troupe. I hadn't the heart to tell her she's getting a little long in the tooth to play Juliet, but as long as Papa finances the troupe, she has her pick of roles and no one gainsays her. Are you listening to me? What are you doing messing around in that cabinet?"

Beau turned back to his brother, the wooden case that held a pair of dueling pistols in his hands. He then opened a long wooden box kept on a sideboard and pulled out both the sword and belt he'd taken to war with him and a short, lethal-looking knife kept safe inside its sheath. "See that these are taken downstairs, if you please. I probably won't need the sword, but I know I'll want the knife."

Puck frowned as the weapons were thrust at him. "Really? Would you be wanting me to hunt up a piece of field artillery as well while I'm at it? You really think the brother will come here, don't you?"

"I was unprepared once, Puck. That won't happen again. Now, take yourself off and do what you said you were going to do—get yourself prepared to return to Paris. This may all come to nothing, but the girl knows things she shouldn't have guessed, and I'm going to believe her until she says something that changes my mind. Damn, what a morning—if I'd known this last night I wouldn't have crawled so far into the bottle with you."

"Yes, of course, blame me. It was a terrible thing, how I held your nose pinched shut and poured three bottles of wine down your gullet as we celebrated your birthday."

"In case you're about to add that the woman downstairs is some sort of birthday present from the gods, let me warn you—don't." Beau left his brother where he stood and headed downstairs to where Lady Chelsea was now pacing the Aubusson carpet, slapping her gloves against her palm.

She was, upon reflection—something, according to her, he didn't have time for—a startlingly beautiful woman. He remembered that, as a child, she'd shown a promise of beauty, but that he'd believed she'd never hold a candle to her sister. Time had proved him wrong.

He'd seen Madelyn a time or two on his visits to London since his return from the war, driving in the park in an open carriage. The years had not been kind to her. She'd developed lines around her mouth, which seemed pinched now rather than pouting, and the nearly white-blond hair aged her rather than flattered her. She looked like what she was—a haughty, clearly unhappy woman.

He'd learned she had taken lovers over the years, sometimes without employing enough discretion, and her reputation, as well as her standing in Society, had suffered. For that, she blamed her brother, and the two of them had not spoken since their father's death. She also probably blamed Beau, as well, for her fall began only after what he thought of now as The Incident.

But Beau had taken little satisfaction from any of Madelyn's problems. To him, justice had been served up very neatly to Lady Madelyn for what she had done.

It was Thomas Mills-Beckman who had yet to feel justice come down on his neck. Hence the cat, toying with the mouse's purse strings.

And now, pacing his drawing room, full of cryptic statements and offers to help him administer that justice, was this intriguing and maddening young woman, fallen into his hands either like a ripe plum or as the agent of disaster, clearly wanting to get some of her own back on her brother and eager to use Beau to help her.

"My brother tells me you assured him that we are embroiled in something very serious. Life or death, I believe he said—or perhaps that was you saying it? I'll admit I've begun to lose track."

She stopped pacing and looked at him, her blond head tipped to one side as she ran her clear blue-gray gaze up and down his body as if he were a horse she was considering purchasing. "You look somewhat better. Are you sober now?"

"I believe I'm heading in that general direction, yes. At least enough so that I want to make it clear to you yet again—I do not know this Reverend Flotley. I did not arrange to have him introduced to your brother, so if the rest doesn't bother you—the smell of spoiled grapes notwithstanding—perhaps you wish to rethink whatever it is you believe you can do for me and go away. Quickly."

"I can't. I think we both know it's already too late for

that," she said and then sighed. "We really don't have time for this, but I have truly burned my bridges just by coming here so openly, and yours, as well, which I'm sure I don't have to point out to you. I'm sorry for that, at least a little bit, but I had no other choice open to me. I left my brother a note explaining every—"

Beau slammed his fist into his palm. "I knew it! Why do women always feel they have to explain themselves?"

She straightened her slim shoulders. "I was not *explaining* myself, you daft man. I couldn't allow my maid to take the brunt of Thomas's anger, not when she helped me tie up some of my belongings and met me at the corner so that I could strap them onto my saddle without anyone being the wiser that I was leaving."

"Oh, yes, of course. I can see the wisdom of that. He won't turn her out without a reference now, not when you'd clearly cowed her into doing what you'd asked."

"Oh," Chelsea said quietly. "I hadn't thought of that. But I didn't tell him where I was heading. I'm not stupid."

"Wonderful. The girl assures me she's not stupid. Tell me, Mistress Genius, did you happen to confide your destination to your maid? Because, were I said maid, staring the loss of my position in the teeth, I do believe I'd try to save myself by being of assistance to my employer."

Chelsea glared at him. "I could truly begin to dislike you."

"I'll take that as a yes," Beau said, looking longingly at the wine decanter. "How long before he misses you and comes racing hotfoot over here, brandishing a pistol and demanding I present myself?"

Chelsea glanced assessingly at the mantel clock. "We should probably be going."

"Yes. Going. And where would it be that we should probably be going to, madam? Oh, and one more small thing. *Why?* Why me? Why am I going to be helped by you, and how am I going to assist you? My mind is still a little fuzzy on those two points."

She looked toward the clock once more. "We don't have time for this now."

Beau crossed his arms over his chest, prepared to stand his ground for the next fortnight. That she should wish to flee her brother's household was commendable. That she should involve him in her escape? Not quite as laudatory. "Make time."

"Only if you come with me now," she told him, heading for the foyer and then unerringly turning toward the rear of the house. "Your brother has ordered your horse saddled, and both mounts await us in the stables. If we keep away from the main thoroughfares, I'm sure we can be clear of London before Thomas can pick up our scent and kill you."

"Oh, this gets better and better," Beau said as Puck, never to be left out of anything even remotely exciting, joined them as they passed through the green baize door that led to the servant area of the mansion. "One minute I'm fairly happily contemplating my life through the bottom of a bottle in celebration of my birthday and my brother's return from France, and the next I'm running from someone else's irate brother, who may already be on his way over here to save his sister from the clutches of a man *who hadn't even remembered her existence a mere hour ago.*"

Chelsea stopped just at the doorway to the kitchens and turned to face him. "Shut. Up. I've been trying to tell you since I arrived, but you keep interrupting me. Now we have to leave, unless you really are stupid enough to want to face Thomas while you're still so obviously intoxicated. And obnoxious, as well, although I have begun to doubt that will change much even once you're sober again."

"I take it all back, brother mine," Puck said, snorting. "I think I'm beginning to like her."

Chelsea pressed her palms to her cheeks, seemed to perhaps be counting under her breath for a few moments, and then dropped her hands to her sides and let out a breath.

"One, my brother did you a great, unforgivable harm seven years ago. Two, he is by nature a very stupid man—and easily led, as you seem already to have ascertained on your own, hence the spoiled grapes. Three, just after our father died, Thomas became very ill and thought he was going to die before he could enjoy the fruits of our father's labors now that he was earl. Four, he truly believes that Francis Flotley came into his life as a gift from God, the same God Thomas had made all manner of promises to if only the good Lord would allow him to rise from his sickbed. Five, Francis Flotley delivered Thomas's promises to God, personally—yes, I know that's insane, so you can stop making those odious faces at me—and now Thomas is not only still stupid and easily led, but he thinks he is on some holy path, and in charge of *my* soul, which he is not! Seven—"

"I think you skipped six," Puck corrected helpfully. "Sorry," he added quickly, when Chelsea glared at him.

"Six," she said heavily, "because I have chosen not to marry any man Thomas could like, he has decided to take me to Brean first thing tomorrow morning, lock me up and then marry me to Francis Flotley as soon as the banns can be read. In order to save my inferior female soul."

"Seven," Beau interrupted, holding up his hand, "as you were clever enough to ferret out that I am responsible for your brother's financial plagues of locusts— don't ask, Puck, just listen—you assumed, incorrectly, I might add, the reverend to also be one of my inventions. So that, eight, it is now my fault that you are to be bracketed to the man. Ergo, I am responsible for saving you from this fate, which I, nine, will somehow do by escorting you out of London with your brother in hot pursuit and out for my blood. For which, ten, you will offer me some sort of favor in return. To which, one, but not to worry because my list is quite short, I say no. Thank you for the honor, putting my head on the chopping block the way you have, but no."

"I may never drink again," Puck said quietly. "I mean, I actually think I understand this. But what could Lady Chelsea offer you that would help you? And to help you, it would follow that whatever she'd offer would somehow revenge you against her brother in a way that makes up for the audacity you had as to come to his house and, bastard that you are, besmirch the family escutcheon by asking for his sister's hand in—uh-oh. Beau? Do you even *know* the route to Scotland?"

Beau looked at Chelsea—the bane of his existence at fourteen, a ripe plum fallen out of the sky seven years later. The perfect revenge against Thomas Mills-Beckman and all of London Society, wrapped up like a lovely gift and dropped into his lap.

No. He couldn't do it. Could he? He'd prided himself on being a gentleman in a world that, for the most part, had branded him as something all but inhuman. Yes, he was taking his revenge against Brean, but that was different; it was only money.

To elope with the man's sister, bed the man's sister? That was not only despicable, it would be akin to signing his own death warrant if they were caught before the deed was done, the girl was deflowered and her reputation already so ruined that killing Beau could only make a bad situation worse.

Brean would be disgraced, the entire family would be disgraced.

Madelyn? She'd said that he would "never be one of us." It had never occurred to him that he could turn that particular table, make her one of him, that she could be made to know what it was like to be secretly laughed at, looked down upon, kept to the fringes of Society. Beau had become a student of Society since The Incident, and he knew what would happen. Her sister's ruin would be Madelyn's final ruin, as well, even after all these years.

But that would be petty revenge, beneath him. He could never forgive her, but that was because he hadn't been able to forgive his own youth, his own blind assumptions about the way the world worked. He could have friends, even a few real friends, among the *ton*. But rich as he might be, well-mannered as he might be, educated and affable as he might be, the Marquess of Blackthorn's bastard son could never marry any of their sisters.

"Beau? You're staring, and I have to tell you, it's a little repellant," Puck said, stirring his brother from his thoughts. "What are you going to do?"

Beau shook himself back to the moment and looked at Lady Chelsea, who returned his look as she nervously bit at her bottom lip.

"No," he said, shaking his head. "I can't do it. I'm sorry, but one of us has to think of the consequences. You'd be shunned by Society, disowned by your family. Perhaps this all seems romantic to you, perhaps you see it as some sort of adventure, the sort best reserved for the pages of a novel, but—"

"His mouth is always wet," Chelsea said quietly. "He says a female on her knees is a woman who knows her place. He preaches that women are inferior in their minds and must be led, guided, or else be considered harlots who must be shown the staff."

Puck pulled at his brother's **arm,** leading him a short distance away to whisper, "**Which** one, brother mine?

The staff of obedience, or his own personal rod? Wet mouth, spouting religious nonsense, a girl as luscious as this one—I think we both know the answer. Not a pretty picture, and I would sleep nights, thank you. Damn it, Beau, we can't let it happen, not now that we know. We can't let her go back to her brother and this Flatley fellow."

"Flotley," Beau corrected distractedly, feeling Fate slipping its strong fingers around his throat, and squeezing.

"Doesn't matter. Man's a rotter, plain and simple. If you don't marry her, I will. There are worse things than marriage to a rich, handsome and eminently affable bastard. That would be me, you understand. You're just rich and passably handsome."

Beau looked across the hallway at Chelsea and saw a single huge tear run down her cheek. The girl in tears, his brother threatening to sacrifice himself, the girl's brother probably on his way to Grosvenor Square even now, armed to the teeth and with half his serving staff with him. If the girl were gone, Brean couldn't try anything, but with the girl here, he could probably claim she'd been kidnapped, shoot both Puck and him and not be charged. After all, everyone knew their shared history; Brean would be believed.

But if Beau managed to put a hole in the earl? That would mean the gallows for him and probably for Puck, as well.

And the always-wet mouth for Lady Chelsea.

So why was he still standing here? There was only

one decision, only one route to travel, and that led straight to Gretna Green and marriage over the anvil.

"Damn it all to hell," he said, grabbing Chelsea's elbow and turning her toward the kitchens once more. "Puck, get yourself out of London. Leave now, with us. Take the yacht, and let your baggage follow you to Paris. Brean is most probably about to lose his new-found religion, and I don't want you anywhere in the vicinity when it happens. Give me five minutes to instruct Wadsworth, and we're off."

"Then…then you'll do it? You'll marry me."

"Or die in the attempt, yes. You've left me no choice."

Her smile nearly knocked him off his feet. "Yes," she said sweetly, all trace of tears now gone. "I know. Escape is only a temporary solution. But marriage rids me of Thomas and will, even though you did not send Francis Flotley to us, probably go a long way toward pleasing you—as our marriage will make him positively *livid*. See? It's all working out."

"So, it's settled? I had supposed she might object. I prayed over that, entreating our good Lord to intervene, lead her feet down the correct path."

The Earl of Brean looked up from the papers from his estate steward he'd been reading for the past hour or more without much hope of understanding them— something about yields per acre and a request to leave four of the fields fallow next season, which he most certainly would not allow, not if that had an impact on his wallet in any way. He'd had some bad investments of late. He waved the black-clad reverend to a chair.

"She did protest with her usual heat. But she'll come around," he told the man with some confidence. After all, Chelsea was not raised to be prepared to live beneath London Bridge. Besides, she had no other recourse. When in doubt, always remember who held the reins, and the reins were in his hands.

"Your sister is willful, Thomas. I have prayed on this, as well, and the only solution is to take her most firmly in hand. I shall begin with her books. Too much education is not for women. Their intellect is too frail to fully understand complex ideas. I have, in fact, taken the liberty of preparing a list of the more laudatory works fit for her more limited sensibilities. Books on proper deportment, the efficient running of households. And a fine variety of sermons, of course."

"Good, er, good," the earl said, perhaps thinking of the book of sermons that had so lately come winging at his head. "My father let her run wild, you know. Thought it amusing that she wanted to learn Greek."

"Heathens," the Reverend Francis Flotley said flatly. "With unnatural sexual practices."

Thomas perked up his ears. For the past few years, his sole knowledge of unnatural sexual practices was that he'd bedded only his stick of a wife, and although others might not think that unnatural, it still was damn boring. Prayer was fine, he knew that, but when the woman beneath you prayed aloud, asking *Oh, God, when will he be done?* No, there were times even prayer hadn't been able to rid his mind of memories of his last mistress, Eloise, and her willingness to do anything he asked. She'd cost him, but what were a few baubles when she'd helped dress him in her silk stockings and garters that one night—that had been quite the giggle. "Really? And what were they? Perversions, I suppose?"

Flotley ignored the question. "I have no fears that she will accept her lot, in time. Once we are wed. A woman must cleave only to her husband."

"If muttering a few vows in church was all it took, Francis, Madelyn wouldn't be tipping back on her heels all over Mayfair. It is my greatest fear that Chelsea will be just like her."

"Yes, I know well your fears. Her husband is weak. I am not. Do you doubt me, Thomas? Have I not shown you the way?"

The earl seemed to think about this for a moment. "She throws things."

"Not once under my roof, I assure you. Speaking of which, Thomas, you had promised me the deed once Chelsea and I were affianced."

The earl may have found religion, but that didn't mean he'd entirely given himself over to parting with his money unless he saw a good chance of receiving something in return. "When you two are married, Francis. On that day, I will turn the deed to Rosemount Manor over to you, as promised."

"And the dowry? I do not ask for myself, as you well know."

"The Flotley Haven For Soiled Doves. Yes, I remember. You are a good man, Francis."

The reverend nodded solemnly. "I will have them on their knees, repenting of their sins so that their souls may be saved."

The earl thought of a few other reasons the soiled doves he'd encountered over the years had been on their knees, but that was an evil thought and he needed to banish it. Francis was so pure, and he was still such a wretched sinner. "As you rescued mine, Francis. Yes?" he then said, turning his head toward the doorway, where the butler hovered, looking as if he'd rather be anywhere but where he currently stood.

"I am so sorry as to bother you, my lord, but it seems that Lady Chelsea has…disappeared."

"What? In a puff of smoke? Don't be daft, man."

"No, my lord. That is to say she…it would appear that she has run off. She left a note."

"What!" The earl leaped to his feet, his hands drawn up in fists. "Damn that girl! When I get hold of her I'll—"

"Thomas? Sit down, Thomas," the reverend said quietly but with an air of command. "Anger aids no man, and nor does violence. We will see this note, and we will find her. We will pray together for her safe return to the bosom of her family, and the Lord will guide us to her. But it is as I said, Thomas. She is female and therefore, willful. I promise you, this will be the last of the rebellion you will see from her. I will lead her steps to the Almighty, and with me to guide her, her husband

and master to show her the errors of her sex, she will learn well the pathways she must trod."

"That's all well and good, Francis," Brean said with some hint of intelligence. "But first we have to catch her."

CHAPTER FOUR

AFTER SNEAKING OUT of London like thieves—Puck had seemed delighted to make that comparison—they rode southwest, the three of them, because Scotland lay to the north. It wasn't a brilliant plan, but hopefully it would suffice for the moment. It wouldn't do to tell his brother and Chelsea that he was making up his steps even as they were taking them, but in truth, other than getting himself shed of London and his brother, he really hadn't thought of what step would come after that.

There had to exist some way of getting rid of Chelsea, as well.

Sadly, inspiration seemed to have deserted him.

They'd left Wadsworth behind to take the knocker from the door, signaling that the master was not in residence, and given instructions to inform any visitor rude enough to demand entry that he and a young lady were accompanying Mr. Robin Blackthorn to France, by way of Dover.

Indeed, Beau's traveling coach had set off, heading southeast, for Dover Road, the coachman told not to spare the horses, as if the devil himself was after them. The earl and his entourage would surely overtake the empty coach by the time it reached Rochester, but by then Beau and his small company would have arrived on the outskirts of Guildford, a lovely forty or more miles of countryside between the two points.

He considered it a brilliant diversion.

He hadn't considered Chelsea's horsemanship, or if she even knew one end of a horse from the other. He'd only rather rudely thrown her up onto the sidesaddle and told her to hang on and not complain or else he might be tempted to leave her to her fate.

Which, he had to admit several hours later, she had not done.

The same, alas, could not be said for Puck.

"I still don't see the point of keeping the family yacht at Brighton," he was saying now, for at least the third time. "Who goes to Brighton, anyway, except fat Prinny and his fat ladies tottering about that monstrosity of his, probably bouncing off one another. Minarets? What possessed the man, do you think? I mean—*minarets?* What's wrong with good old-fashioned English turrets, I ask you? Ah, there it is, another fingerpost pointing the way to Hove. Since you probably won't wish to go any farther south before turning north, I imagine we part company here."

"Thank heaven for small mercies," Beau said as the three of them pulled up their mounts at the crossroads and looked at the fingerpost. Brighton lay to the south, Blackdown Hills and one of their father's lesser estates to the west; a good stopping point for the night, and some serious thinking. "Although, of course, we'll miss you terribly."

"I won't," Chelsea said, half standing in the side-saddle and none too discreetly rubbing at her derriere. "It's not a proper elopement if one brings one's brother along. Especially one who sings."

"Ah, my dear soon-to-be-sister, I am known for my fine voice."

"Not to me, you're not. I imagine people are just being kind if they compliment you on it," Chelsea said, settling herself once more, but not quite able to hide a wince of pain as she did so. She turned her head to look at Beau. "You haven't changed your mind, have you? He can find the Channel by himself, without us accompanying him?"

"I'm not sure," Beau answered, as he'd been considering an alternate plan these past two hours, ever since their hurried meal at an out-of-the-way inn, when he'd noticed Chelsea's reluctance to remount her horse. "You've a good seat, Chelsea, but I don't know that you'll enjoy riding all the way to Scotland. I've been thinking we might leave Puck to his own devices once we reach Brighton, and take the yacht."

"What? All along the Channel, 'round Cornwall, out into the sea and *up?* It would take forever," Puck pointed out. "I can see you wanting to get to know your bride, Beau, but confined together like that on a small boat? I'd give you odds that by the time you reach Scotland you will have murdered each other."

"He has a point," Chelsea said, nodding. "I'm not

certain I like the idea. I'll be fine as soon as you locate a coach for us." She looked at him with some intensity. "You *are* planning to hire a coach, aren't you, now that we're safely away from London?"

"I'd *planned* to spend the day reclining on a comfortable couch, nursing this damned headache that still won't quit. Instead, within the space of a heartbeat, you, madam, have turned my entire life, my orderly existence, upside down. But to answer your question, no, I have not considered hiring a coach."

"Then I suggest you consider it now," Chelsea said, rolling her eyes at what she clearly believed was a horrible overreaction to her brilliant plan. "Honestly. I had only a few minutes to come up with my plan, so, of course, it wasn't complete in all areas. But you've had entire *hours* now. I should think you might be able to pass beyond the idea of us riding all the way to Scotland on horseback, and I don't think spending the next several weeks bobbing up and down on the water during spring storms could possibly be considered a laudable plan in any case."

"Yes, Beau, for shame," Puck said, gleefully joining his voice to Chelsea's. And then he frowned and put a hand to his ear. "This is the main road to Brighton, correct? We didn't take some lesser highway, because we didn't have to worry about pursuit? Because that doesn't sound like a coach barreling toward us. We've heard plenty of those."

Beau, who had not been precisely jolly from the moment he'd first set eyes—and ears—on Lady Chelsea

Mills-Beckman, opened his mouth to say something cutting about his brother damn well knowing what road they were traveling. The words died halfway to his tongue, however, and he quickly leaned over, grabbed the bridle of Chelsea's horse and turned both mounts into the trees, Puck urging his own horse off the road on the other side.

"What on earth do you think you're—"

She got no further, because he'd unceremoniously dragged her out of the sidesaddle, holding on to her as he kicked his feet free of the stirrups and rolled the two of them onto the ground.

"You had to wear red," he gritted out just as he rolled on top of her, covering as much of her riding habit as he could with his body even while reaching up one hand to grab on to the bridles of both horses, to keep them in place. "Lie still, damn it."

He could feel the rumble now, and by the way Chelsea's magnificently expressive eyes widened, he was sure that she, lying on her back in the weeds, could feel it even more.

Horses, at least a dozen, were approaching rapidly. There had been other travelers along the way, but this was different. This was like the advance of a small troop of soldiers. If he sniffed the air, he could almost smell the stink of pursuit; he imagined a cavalry charging down a hill and into the fray of battle.

Beau lifted his head slightly, peering through the long grass and underbrush, hoping he would not see any hint of his brother on the far side of the road. He didn't. What he did see, about ten seconds later, were a dozen horsemen, four of them wearing the Brean livery, pounding past them, not sparing their horses.

"How?" he asked, not really addressing Chelsea, who still lay beneath him, her complexion gone rather pink. "How did he know?"

"I think I can answer that, and I apologize for not thinking of it sooner," she said, pushing at his shoulders. "Thomas loathes you, most especially so since he has been losing money while you, so clearly his inferior, are also so clearly odiously wealthy. I've heard him go on for hours about you with Reverend Flotley, as you are the one sin Thomas can't seem to expunge with prayer. How he detests you. Your father's money. All those unentailed estates the marquess plans to gift you and your brothers with upon his demise. The Grosvenor Square mansion. The hunting box in Scotland, the townhouse in Paris. The box at Covent Garden."

"The yacht berthed at Brighton," Beau supplied dully, shaking his head, cursing himself for his stupidity. "He's probably got men riding to each of my father's properties. Damn."

"Yes, well," Chelsea continued, still pressing against his shoulders. "Now that that's explained…?"

Beau looked down into her face once more, belatedly becoming aware—very aware—of her body beneath his. "I was attempting to cover up your red habit," he explained, still not moving. "Are you all right? Am I crushing you? You seemed uncomfortable."

"I'm fine. I've…I've simply never been this…close to a man before."

"Is that so?" he said, smiling…and still not moving.

"Oh, don't look so smug. I didn't say I *liked* it. Now get off me!"

"Ah, getting to know each other better, I see," Puck said from somewhere above them. "Good for you."

Beau rolled himself away from Chelsea and got to his feet, helping her up, as well. "You can't go to Brighton," he told his brother unnecessarily. "And I can't take Chelsea to Blackdown, damn it."

Puck sat himself down on a tree stump, taking off his curly brimmed beaver and slapping at it with one of his riding gloves to rid it of road dust. "You know, Beau, I've always looked up to you and Jack. The elders, the ones I'd turn to for assistance and advice. I probably shouldn't have done that. You're no smarter than I am, and Jack, probably considerably less. May I make a suggestion?"

"No," Beau barked just as Chelsea said, "Yes, please."

"Making my vote the tiebreaker," Puck pointed out happily, "and I vote that I make the suggestion. Let's head back to Grosvenor Square. It will be nightfall by the time we get there, so no one will see us if we keep to the same dank alleyways we employed for our exit. A good meal, soft beds, Wadsworth and his fellow former soldiers keeping guard. Yes, it's brilliant."

"It is, you know," Chelsea said, tugging on Beau's arm. "Thomas has everyone out hunting us, with himself leading one of the groups, I'm sure. No one would think to look for us back where we started. Besides, then perhaps I can sneak back into the house and gather more clothing. The servants all dislike Thomas, but they seem to like me. They'll help, I'm certain of that. Because I checked when we stopped at that inn a while ago, and all Beatrice seemed to pack for me was some clean under—well, she didn't pack much at all, not even my tooth powder. And I do want to apologize if Beatrice was punished in any way."

"I should have allowed you to figuratively throw yourself on the sword, Puck, and sent you two off to Gretna Green while I stayed behind to fend off Brean. You suit each other so well, the both of you missing several slates off your roofs. Go back to London? Sneak into the house you've just escaped in order to pack your tooth powder?" He rubbed at his forehead. "I'm never going to be rid of this headache, am I?"

"Don't be such a stick," Puck told him. "My part of the plan is brilliant."

"It is, you know," Chelsea said, smiling at Puck. "After all, who looks for something twice in the same place, when the something you were looking for wasn't there when you looked the first time. I mean, it would be rather pointless, wouldn't it?"

"Beau? Did you hear that? Beau? It's getting on toward five, and we really should be on more familiar roads before dark. Because you're right when you say I can't continue on to Brighton, and you certainly would be all kinds of a fool if you took Chelsea to Blackdown. Where else is there you'd have us go?"

"I'd answer that," Beau bit out, feeling rather abused, "but supposedly there is a lady present. All right, let's go."

"I STILL DON'T SEE why *I* must be involved," Madelyn said as she stripped off her gloves and tossed them in the general direction of her long-suffering maid. "For pity's sake, Thomas, just go get her, you and your conscience over there, hulking like some great black crow. You have to know where she's gone. And I, God help me, know why. Marry her to *that?* It wasn't enough for you to have destroyed *my* life?"

"I think you did that rather effectively on your own, Madelyn," Thomas said, although he retreated to the mantelpiece before he said it.

Lady Madelyn sat herself down in the drawing room of the mansion in Portland Place, slapping at her maid's hands as that woman attempted to relieve her of her short, fur-trimmed pelisse. "Will you just *go away? I* decide whether or not I wish to be shed of my clothing, and I do not."

"For which you have my eternal gratitude, dear sister," the earl told her. "Now, if we could only keep you from shedding it as do trees their leaves each fall, and with all and sundry, I might consider my prayers answered."

"Prayers? I liked you better when you were godless, *dear brother,* not that I ever liked you much at all. It wasn't as if you were actually going to *die,* you know. None of my brats did, now did they? This man here has sold you a bill of goods. Or should I say that's the other way round, hmm? How much lighter *are* your pockets since the black crow here pecked his way into your life promising salvation?"

The Reverend Flotley bowed to the earl. "I should retire, my lord. This is clearly a family matter, and I should not wish to intrude, as I am not family."

"No, but you're as near as such, and when we get Chelsea back from that arrogant, encroaching bastard, you will be."

Madelyn had taken a small mirror from her reticule and at that moment was examining her reflection, clearly pleased with the look of her new bonnet with the dark blue ribbon as it contrasted so well with her white-blond hair while highlighting her blue eyes. "Yes, yes, Thomas, and who is this encroaching bastard? Some half-pay officer with a winning smile and empty pockets, I'd suppose. That would be just like my silly sister. You *play* with the ineligible if they take your fancy, but you don't *marry* them. Do I know him?"

The earl pushed away from the mantelpiece. The Lord punished, the Lord prodded…and the Lord sometimes rewarded. Thomas could have included the name in his note, but he'd wanted to see Madelyn's reaction when she heard the news. He'd do penance for that small sin later, but he would enjoy the sin. "The bastard is Beau Blackthorn. Our sister, it would seem, has allied herself with our old enemy."

The mirror dropped to the marble floor and shattered as Madelyn sprang to her feet. "That *bitch!* And yet you stand here, doing *nothing?*"

"Far from nothing. I've sent out riders everywhere I could think of, thinking they couldn't have gotten far, but all have yet to report back to me. Now I intend to go straight to the marquess myself and demand that he either turn Chelsea over if she is there, or tell me where his bastard son has taken her."

"There's no question where he's *taken* her, Thomas. They're for Gretna Green, obviously. How could she *do* this to us? We'll be a laughingstock!"

Reverend Flotley, who had stayed after all, advanced on her, holding out his hands as if to soothe her. "Now, now, ma'am, we must remain calm. We have right on our side, and right will prevail."

"If right were to prevail, you pious buffoon, I would be a duchess." She then shot him a look that had him reconsidering any notion of taking her hands and asking that they pray together and stepped back a pace. "But you're right, Thomas. Like any low animal, Blackthorn will most probably run first for his den, thinking himself safe there, and only from there continue to Scotland. What I wonder again is, why are you lingering *here?*"

"I was hoping for an easy capture and a swift return," he told her as his pink cheeks went florid. "But we must get to her now, before this goes too far. For that, Madelyn, I need you. Once we have her she will need female companionship, in case we are seen. Now that you understand the gravity of our situation, will you agree to accompany us?"

"Us? The black crow goes, as well? In *my* coach?"

"In my coach, and we should leave within the hour. Francis is Chelsea's affianced husband, Madelyn," the earl reminded her. "We'll find her, take her, bring you back here to London immediately and then travel directly to Brean, where they will be married. If I have to tie her down to get it done. But we'll have to spend one night on the road, at least. One small trunk, Madelyn, and within the hour—I mean that. We have no time for more."

Madelyn seemed to consider this for a few moments and then agreed. On one condition. "But no praying. I do not want to hear *any* praying!"

"I will converse with my Lord in silence, ma'am," Flotley said. "And pray for your immortal soul."

"Pray for Blackthorn's immortal soul, Reverend," Madelyn told him. "You think you know my brother, you think he is a man of God now? Then more fool, you. I've known him longer and I know him better. Thomas? You're going to kill Beau Blackthorn, aren't you? Shoot him down like the bastard cur he is. You have every right, as he absconded with your sister, *kidnapped* her. I will swear to it. *Thomas!* Answer me!"

The earl looked to his spiritual adviser, the florid cheeks now advanced to an unlovely shade of puce. "Francis says I must turn the other cheek, forgive not the sin, but the sinner."

"Francis is an *ass,* and you, Thomas, have turned

yourself into a sniveling coward hiding behind religion," Madelyn said, already heading for the foyer. "Very well, just get me to him. *I'll* do what you aren't *man* enough to do, what you should have done seven years ago!"

She slammed out the door, her maid trotting to keep up.

The earl picked up a figurine and smashed it against the marble of the fireplace. Then he turned about to face Flotley, his fingers drawn up into tight, white-knuckled fists, his breathing so quick he could feel his heart straining to burst.

"By God and all that is sacred, Francis, I'm the worst of sinners. And may God strike me down, because I want that man dead! I *ache* for it. I will whip him, no matter how you made me confess sorrow for what I did when he dared to ask for Madelyn. I wanted to whip him then, and I want to whip him now. I—I—I want to rip out his liver and put it on a spit! And I *will* do it, in front of his own father if I must. Do you *hear* me? I'm a sinner. I'm a damn and damned *sinner!* That's what I was, that's what I am, no matter how you say God wants me to be better than I am, no matter how many promises I made Him. *And I don't care anymore!*"

All remained quiet in the drawing room for some minutes, as the earl collapsed into a chair and lowered his head into his hands. Did he feel remorse for his out-burst? Guilt for his violent desires? Or relief, because after two long, God-fearing years, he had once more embraced the Devil, whom he felt much more of an affinity for, at least.

"For it is written, 'Vengeance is mine, sayeth the Lord,'" Flotley finally reminded him quietly. But then, perhaps seeing that his personal disciple might be experiencing a crisis of his newfound faith that could end with his spiritual adviser tossed out into the street—to land on his empty pockets—he added, "But I do believe there are a few Old Testament writings that may apply here. I will find them for you."

CHAPTER FIVE

CHELSEA LAID HER HEAD back against the small pillow the maid had placed behind her and allowed the wonderfully warm water to soothe her aching muscles, not a few of them located in an area of her body never named in polite company.

Beau's Grosvenor Square mansion was wonderfully modern. None of the bathing tubs at Brean or in Portland Place were this large, or anchored in one spot, as this one was. In its own private room, no less, and not carried into her bedchamber and placed before the fire, with a small army of servants forced to haul in buckets and buckets of hot water, sloshing some of it on the floor and generally making a mess of things.

This tub even had pipes located at one end of it and turning levers, and when you turned them, water gushed out of the pipes and into the tub. This had so amazed Chelsea that she'd turned them again and again, so that now the tub was in danger of overflowing.

Not that she cared; it was too heavenly, being submerged up to her chin in the lovely water, and with the mounds and mounds of scented bubbles tickling her nose.

It was difficult to believe that only hours ago she had been faced with the idea of being wed to Francis Flotley. Kidnapped, spirited off, locked up and made into some twisted bit of Thomas's promises to his Maker.

But in only those few hours, she had saved herself, frustrated Thomas, met two fools and was, at least marginally, now the affianced bride of one of them.

She would think that she and Mr. Robin Goodfellow Blackthorn appreciated each other more, but it was Mr. Oliver Le Beau Blackthorn who most deserved the honor of, well, of pushing Thomas's face in the muck, she supposed it could be said.

It mattered not who she married—wet-mouthed men and anyone Thomas approved of excluded. Marriage was a social dance, and nobody really cared whether the people involved actually liked each other. Marriage was an exchange of dowry for title, or the other way around, a duty to procreate in order to keep one's lands and fortunes out of the hands of disliked relatives. Emotion had nothing to do with the thing.

She knew this because she was a student of history. Ask Josephine if her Bonaparte had truly loved her, when he'd cast her off for a younger womb. The royals had it the worst, bartered away for the sake of a few acres of land or a military alliance, or simply because the prince or king had decreed it, and when those men tired of their wives, the chopping off of heads had many times been the accepted method of being rid of said wives.

At least she would be spared that!

She could only hope the man realized how grateful he should be to her for thinking of him and this particular revenge in the first place.

But she very much doubted that he did.

"Men can be so annoyingly obtuse," she muttered, holding up a palm full of bubbles and blowing at them.

"My lady? Was there something you wanted?"

Chelsea smiled at the maid, who had been adding another log to the fireplace that was also situated in this lovely bathing chamber. "No, thank you, Prudence. I was only reminding myself that women are supremely superior to men in intellect and understanding. Haven't you always found that to be true?"

"If that means that my brother Henry is thick as a plank, then yes, my lady, that's true. He once tried to milk a cow from behind, our Henry did, which is why he's only got the two teeth and why we brought ourselves to London to find work when Mr. Beau offered, as far from cows as we could get. Poor Henry, they aren't even his front teeth. I'll leave you to your bath, my lady," Prudence said and then curtsied and quit the room, hopefully never noticing that Chelsea's shoulders were shaking with suppressed mirth.

Maybe she was tired. Perhaps the strain of the day had been more than she'd realized. The argument with Thomas, the moments of horrible panic, the mad dash to Grosvenor Square. Convincing Oliver Le Beau Blackthorn that he was a lucky man, except, of course, if he dragged his heels enough that Thomas and his gaggle of brawny footmen and grooms showed up and strangled him, at which point he would have been an unlucky and very dead man. Three hours on a horse, riding pell-mell away from London. Three more hours in the saddle, riding back again.

No matter what the reason, Chelsea was suddenly giggling at the thought of poor Henry and his two teeth. Laughing. Chortling so hard she sniffed some bubbles up her nose and then laughing even more.

"And here I assured Puck that you weren't a fugitive from Bedlam. Or is it that the bubbles tickle? Interesting thought, that second possibility. Precisely where would they tickle?"

Chelsea sucked in a breath midgiggle and turned her head to see Beau standing not five feet away from the tub. The quick action, when combined with the slipperiness of the tub bottom, caused her to slide helplessly beneath the surface of the water. Throwing up her arms and wildly grabbing for purchase on the rim of the tub, she resurfaced gasping, choking, blinking soap out of her eyes and caught between an urge to kill the man and a heartfelt desire to sink below the bubbles once more.

"Monster! Take yourself off, Mr. Blackthorn. I'm in my bath."

"Actually, you're in *my* bath," Beau pointed out, which is when she noticed that he was clad in a burgundy banyan, his bare chest visible, along with his bare legs and feet.

She'd seen Thomas dressed—or undressed—in much the same way a time or two, when he'd been convalescing from his bout with the mumps. Thomas had looked silly, all skinny white legs and paunch. Beau looked nothing like Thomas. His legs were tanned—she'd have to ask him how he'd managed that particular feat—and his calves bulged with muscle. There was a dusting of golden-blond hair on his chest, and his waist, marked by the tied sash, was remarkable in that fact that it was so small, his belly so very flat.

She didn't know if any of this should affect her in any way, but it did. She just wasn't sure quite *how*. She looked away quickly.

"I ordered you put in my father's wife's chamber, which adjoins his. As neither my father nor his wife has been to town in a decade, I've taken over his chamber, mostly because of this tub. Or did you think we have one of these contraptions in every chamber? Are you planning to spend the entire evening in there?"

She hadn't thought at all, which she wasn't going to tell him. Prudence had led, and she had followed, half asleep on her feet and longing for a lengthy soak. "I'll be in here as long as you're out there, if that answers your question. Go away!"

Instead of doing as she'd asked—ordered—the miserable man pulled a chair away from the wall and sat himself down, just as if he planned to take up residence.

"No. I think, as the saying goes, I have you just where I want you, Chelsea."

"Well, you're not where I want you," she said, surreptitiously fishing around the bottom of the tub with one hand, attempting to locate the washing sponge that had sunk to the bottom. Except that, when she moved, bubbles popped. When she breathed, bubbles popped. Unless she remained very, very still, bubbles popped.

She would have cried, except that would have given him satisfaction. She would have pled, except he was probably expecting that, as well. If it killed her, utterly destroyed her, she would not let him know how mortified she was, how frightened she was, how vulnerable she felt at this moment.

He had thrown down the gauntlet, that's what he'd done. Insufferable lout. She would confound him by refusing to pick it up. Just as if she was entirely accustomed to having a man in the room as she bathed.

Or better, as if she could not care at all that he was here because, even though they were going to marry, she was totally indifferent to him. He was openly a means to an end, nothing more. That should give him pause!

"I did not give you permission to address me so informally, Mr. Blackthorn."

"You didn't invite me into your bath, either. And yet, here I am. I didn't invite you into my home, my life and my business. And yet, here you are. My headache is gone, by the way. I might actually be beginning to enjoy myself, difficult as that is for me to believe. Water getting cold? You can simply sit forward and depress the lever on the left, unless you've used up all the available hot water, which you probably have. It isn't magic, Chelsea, there are mechanics involved. There are detailed explanations and drawings somewhere in the house. As I recall the thing, you enjoy reading. I can find them for you if you like."

Chelsea was so far submerged in the bath that water and bubbles were sloshing in her ears, making it difficult for her to understand him, which was probably a good thing, because the way he was smiling—no, grinning—she was certain he wasn't saying anything very nice. Especially that business about sitting forward to call up more hot water. As if she could do any such thing. And if part of what she'd missed was an offer by him to do it for her, well, she would have ignored that anyway.

"Let me know when you're finished being an ass," she told him, the tickling bubbles forcing her into the unladylike gesture of sticking a finger in her ear and wiggling it to stop the itch. "I don't frighten easily, you know. If you had attempted any such idiocy with another female, she would have swooned straightaway and drowned. I, however, am made of sterner stuff, *Oliver.*"

She turned her head slightly, just in time to see him wince.

"Beau, please. Or even Mr. Blackthorn. No one calls me Oliver."

"I will call you a lot worse if you don't leave this room," she warned. "Oliver."

"You were an insufferable brat at fourteen. Now you're rather amusing. And, as I believe I've already mentioned, I seem to have you where I want you at the moment."

"In your tub?" Chelsea glanced down at the bubbles, blowing out her breath in exasperation. *Pop. Pop. Pop.* She took in a breath, but slowly, so as not to move her chest up and down too much. "You are no gentleman, Oliver."

"Yes, I think we established that rather forcefully seven years ago. If I were, I'd be your brother-in-law now, wouldn't I? But we need to talk, and since you aren't in a position to run away if you don't like the direction our conversation will be traveling, I repeat, I have you where I want you. Which is rather novel for our short and unpleasant acquaintance, you'll admit."

"You want me to go away, don't you? I'm back in London, and now you want to be rid of me, having decided that Thomas is too much for you, that he'll find you and kill you. You're going to take me back to Portland Place and my horrible fate."

"Actually, I was going to suggest that you retire early, as I would like to be once more outside of London before the sun rises tomorrow. However, if you're intent on sermons and the always-wet mouth, yes, I can have you taken home. Nobody can say for absolute certainty that you were here at all."

She looked at him, expecting to see proof that he was lying to her. "Really? You're not going to renege on your promise?"

"Promise? I may have been fairly deep in my cups earlier today, Chelsea, but I'm certain I'd remember something so binding as a promise. But no, I won't take you back to Portland Place. However, please don't read too much into that, as I wouldn't send a dog to Portland Place. Well, perhaps I would, were it rabid. But that lovely thought to one side, I'm here to offer you a third alternative."

Chelsea bit her bottom lip, as the water was growing cooler, and soon she'd not be able to hide the fact that her teeth were showing a tendency to chatter. "You'll agree to take me to a nunnery?" she asked him, all but sneering the words.

"Would you go?"

She rolled her eyes at him. "Do I seem to you the sort of person who would do well in a nunnery?"

He smiled, the smile reaching all the way to his rather marvelous blue eyes. "You could found your own order, I would think. The Holy Sisters of the Ridiculous Assumption. No, Chelsea, I would not inflict your brother's plans on you, nor would I inflict you on some poor females who don't deserve to have their faith tested by dropping you in their midst. I was thinking more of simply remaining here in London, purchasing a Special License—I have the necessary funds—and presenting our marriage as accomplished fact by the time your brother returns from hunting half of England for us."

"You could do that?" She narrowed her eyes at him. "But that would mean appealing to the archbishop of Canterbury, wouldn't it? Even if you paid twice what is usual, would he countenance a marriage between a... well, you know."

"A lady and a bastard," Beau supplied flatly. "That is potentially troublesome. And therein lies the risk, I'm afraid. If we are denied, we could still be in residence here when your brother returns."

"The alternative being flight to Gretna Green, with Thomas and his minions in hot pursuit. I will admit to being terrified today when we saw his men on the road. No, if I have a choice, and I think you're saying that I do, I would rather leave for Scotland as soon as possible. Is that all? Because I really must insist that you go away now. Trapping me here in my bath—*your* bath—is no longer amusing."

He got to his feet and replaced the chair against the wall. "It could be," he said, able now to see over the high rim of the deep tub and raising one eyebrow at what he saw. "At least in another few minutes it could be. But at least now you are thoroughly compromised. In fact, I could join you, as being hung for a sheep seems more sensible than dying only for a lamb."

"I liked you better young and nervous," Chelsea told him, crossing her arms over her breasts beneath the water, too fearful to actually look and see what he might be seeing.

"Young and nervous and stupid, you mean. You also probably liked me better half drunk and dull with the headache. For myself, I liked you better when—no, I can't say I remember liking you in the least. However, since there is no going back, not for either of us, we'll simply have to make the best of things, won't we?"

"I do not consider having you accost me in the tub as making the best of things."

He raised that same maddening eyebrow once more.

"Ah, I thought that bubble would never pop. A suitable reward for a patient man. Very pretty, Chelsea. Very pretty, indeed. Why, that might even make it possible for me to overlook a veritable multitude of your failings."

Chelsea gasped and quickly submerged. When she surfaced once more, pushing her long hair out of her eyes, he was gone.

She wasn't quite sure exactly what had just happened. Fatigue had probably dulled her wits. But one thing was certain. If they had been challenging each other to see which was the stronger, she knew that the first round of the battle had gone to him.

"But one battle is not a war," she reminded herself, picking up the sponge and continuing with her bath.

"Ah, THERE YOU ARE," Puck said, taking up his seat on the facing chair in front of the fire, across from where his brother sat sprawled, resting most of his weight on the base of his spine as he held a snifter of brandy in his fist. "I would have thought you'd be swearing off strong spirits for a space."

"If I'm to be married to that piece of work, I may have to purchase my own vineyard," Beau grumbled into the silken collar of his banyan. "But this is all my fault, I suppose. Whatever in hell's name was I thinking, playing with Brean like a cat toys with a mouse? And, worse, how did she find me out? It's as if I personally handed her the ammunition she would use to shoot me."

Puck made a great business out of blinking rapidly as he peered at his brother. "Oh, it is you over there. Dark in here, you know, so I could have made a mistake. For a moment there, I thought you were Mama. A tad melodramatic, brother mine, just a shade over the top, but uncomfortably close to dreadfully heavy overacting. You'd think the world was about to come to an unlovely end. Can't you look upon this as a grand adventure? I would."

"And that matters to me? You're an idiot. What do I care what you think?"

Puck laughed. "I may always be the youngest of us, brother mine, but I've somehow managed to grow up since last we saw each other, just before you took yourself off to war to bury your misery over your humiliation at the hands of this same Brean, not to mention the beating he inflicted on you. By God, you were a mess! I believe you've acted with considerable restraint. I doubt I would have been satisfied with merely enjoying his financial discomfort. So is it that you haven't the heart for a true revenge, or is Lady Chelsea so completely unappealing to you?"

Beau looked at his brother, searching for an answer that wouldn't betray the very real misgivings he'd been having ever since he'd unexpectedly found himself lying on top of Chelsea, watching the betraying blush steal into her cheeks even as she declared that she didn't like having him in such close proximity.

Their encounter a few hours ago in the bathing chamber, and its effect on him, he would not mention at all, even if Puck were to hold his feet to fiery coals, demanding details.

"No, she'll do," he said at last. "I spoke with her earlier tonight, made myself very clear on a few points. At least now we both understand who is in charge of this small adventure." *And it's not me.*

"Laid down a few rules, did you? Well, good for you."

Beau shifted rather uncomfortably in the chair. If one more bubble had burst he probably would have promised her the moon. God, but she excited him. "Yes, thank you. When are you setting out?"

"At first light. I've hunted you down to say my farewells. Your messenger will have reached Brighton by now with your instructions for the captain to move the yacht to Hove. I'll catch him up there, and be on my way, sorry as I am to go. I'd planned to remain here in London for at least two months, you know. I haven't even caught sight of Jack, and Mama expected me to linger until she's done playing the grand actress and returned home. Are you certain I have to leave?"

"We've already discussed this. It will be safer for you if you are nowhere in the vicinity. Brean is familiar with all of our holdings, and he'll have sent some of his hirelings to each of them, even as he personally is probably already on his way north after discovering that we hadn't run for Dover. I just pray we don't stumble over him from behind somewhere along the way."

Puck slapped his palms against his thighs and got

to his feet. "Very well, then, but I'll be back for the christening."

Beau nearly dropped his glass. "What?"

"You do have to bed her, you know, or else Brean will demand an annulment, and when it comes to proof, there's nothing more convincing than a babe in arms. And he'd be able to have the marriage set aside, too, since he's the earl and you're the—do you know, Beau, even in French, the word bastard doesn't precisely roll off the tongue. Ah, but having an earl's daughter as sister-in-law? I rather like the idea.

"Be kind to her, brother mine. We may not rise because of this alliance, but she is going to fall, mightily. I wonder if she's truly realized how far."

CHAPTER SIX

CHELSEA ALL BUT STAGGERED into the breakfast room the following morning at the ungodly hour of five o'clock, having been pointed in that direction by the uncomfortably formal Wadsworth. There she discovered Beau, sitting at the head of the table dressed to travel and looking, if possible, worse than she felt. He was engrossed in a letter held open in front of him and didn't seem pleased with its contents.

"No, no, please don't rise on my account," she told him, not really at her best before the sun was up, at least, so her sympathy hadn't been evoked by his frowning face. "After all, we can't really get much more *informal* than we were last evening."

He looked up at her rather owlishly, as if surprised she was still in residence. "What?"

She picked up a plate from the sideboard, waving away the footman who'd stepped out of the shadows to assist her, and began loading it with coddled eggs and a lovely thick pink slice of ham—lovely if she didn't think about Thomas and his complexion.

She added an apple and two slices of bread to her plate. If she was going to be on the road with this man, who yesterday proved he seemed never to think a woman may have to stop for a while every now and then for personal reasons she shouldn't have to mention, then she'd better load her belly as much as possible.

"Is something wrong?" she asked as she allowed the footman to pull back her chair for her, and sat down. "You're scowling more than usual."

Beau folded the single sheet and set it beside his plate, where other items that must have arrived in the post were already stacked.

"It's, ah, I was reading over yesterday's post, which arrived after we'd taken off on our short journey to nowhere."

"Not nowhere. We rode in a lovely circle. Upon reflection, we could all three of us have simply hidden in the attics until Thomas went away again."

Beau didn't smile. He didn't scowl. He just sat there, tapping two fingers on the folded letter.

"Oh, for pity's sake. Obviously something is wrong, and I can't abide secrets. I'll ferret it out of you one way or another, you know—I'm quite accomplished at ferreting, the proof being that I know you were behind the spoiled grapes and the rest of it—so you might as well simply tell me. Oh, and for your future reference, I can't abide tapping, either."

He looked down at his hand and seemed to command his fingers to cease their movement. "If I had shown you the door yesterday, did you have an alternate solution to your dilemma? Perhaps trading release from any plan to bracket you to the wet mouth in exchange for handing your brother my head on a platter, telling him about—"

"Telling him that I'd learned how you have been *amusing* yourself with him? If it had been my only way to escape Francis Flotley, yes, I might have. I'm not quite as nice as some might wish, me included, but I am a Mills-Beckman, and that is probably excuse enough. Except that I know Thomas, and I would have only postponed the inevitable, and then you'd be dead or in some prison, or transported to Botany Bay, and where would that leave me? Entirely without options is the answer to that. And so here we are."

"Yes," Beau said, looking at her strangely. "Here we are. Aren't I the lucky one? Difficult to believe that a bastard could be blackmailed into marriage with a lady of quality. One would think that, if anything, it would be the other way around. I should probably be flattered. For the record, Chelsea—I'm not."

Chelsea shifted her gaze away from him, not wishing him to see how nervous she was. Because she wasn't fragile; she needed him to know that. She was a very determined woman, and he could walk in on her bath ten times a day; it wouldn't make her afraid of him or his ridiculous show of power, his none-too-subtle demonstration that she was, in fact, entirely at his mercy.

She hadn't really thought much beyond escaping Portland Place before her brother came marching up to her bedchamber with a key to lock her in. As she'd learned to her sudden confusion and astonishment while lying on the ground, her now affianced husband's body disturbingly close to her, there was more to this elopement business than thwarting Thomas. There would be other consequences.

"This can all be traced back to Madelyn, you know. If she hadn't thought to amuse herself with you all those years ago. If her silly children hadn't brought their puffy cheeked pestilence to Brean, nearly killing their uncle, so that Thomas engaged Francis Flotley as his supposed spiritual adviser.

"Or we could blame you. I know you were young, and that Madelyn was beautiful—and probably offered you liberties that made you believe your suit would be favored—but honestly, Oliver, how could any man be so naive? I tried to warn you, but you were so love-mad. And that ridiculous waistcoat, and that jacket that made it impossible for you to take a deep breath, let alone defend yourself. In any event, you aren't blameless in any of it, are you?"

He didn't say anything for long, uncomfortable moments, and eventually she stole a look at him from beneath her lashes, wondering if she'd gone too far. Then she decided that she hadn't. She hadn't sneaked in to trap him in his tub while his bubbles popped, had she? No, she had not. Therefore, as they were far from even, she could verbally torment him all the way to Gretna Green and still not feel entirely vindicated.

"I liked that waistcoat. I thought it was inspired. In retrospect, yes, the jacket was too precisely tailored. I couldn't raise my arms past my shoulders. Although, to be fair, I hadn't come to Portland Place expecting to have to physically defend myself."

Chelsea propped one elbow on the table and dropped her chin into her palm. "What, precisely, did you like about that waistcoat? The material, which could have blinded someone if the sun hit it just right? Those terrible horizontal stripes? You looked like a faded bumblebee. And then I got you to toss the bouquet into the garden…." She covered her smile with her hand. "Oh, I'm sorry, but you'll have to admit it, telling you Madelyn loathed them was truly inspired. You looked positively horror-struck. It all ended terribly, but for a while it was rather amusing. We have a history, Oliver, whether either of us likes it or not."

"Yes, I suppose we do. Whether or not we have a future is still very up in the air, however. And I'm afraid I'm going to have to expose you to even more possible danger on our way to Gretna Green, but it can't be avoided. We will be stopping at Blackthorn. My father's wife has died."

Shocked, Chelsea shot a look toward the folded letter and then raised her eyes to Beau's face. "Oh, I'm so…" She paused, not knowing what to say. Did you offer condolences to the son of a mistress whose lover's wife had just expired? "I mean, that's very sad."

"Yes, it is. Abigail was a good person. My mother will be devastated when she finds out. My father has already sent a rider to find her, bring her home, and I've done the same with Puck, to turn him back from leaving for Paris. God only knows about Jack, as I doubt anyone would even know where to look for him. Still, he always seems to know everything, so I won't be surprised if he turns up."

"I see," Chelsea said, looking down at her plate, not *seeing* at all. Did the man realize what he was saying? His mother, the marquess's mistress, would be upset that the man's wife has died? *Odd* did not begin to explain that statement, or the notion that the Blackthorn bastards would be gathering for the funeral of their father's wife. "They...your mother and the marchioness, that is. They were friends?"

Beau laughed, and Chelsea realized he didn't laugh enough, and when he did, it was at the strangest things. "I suppose I should explain."

She put down her fork, since she wasn't going to eat anyway. Her appetite had completely deserted her. "Yes, I suppose you should."

He got to his feet. "We'll be taking my traveling coach, just back from its aborted trip to Dover. I've already sent both our horses off ahead of us. If we can be on our way in the next five minutes, I would be most appreciative...and will tell you the story on our journey."

"So there is a story? I imagine there would be," Chelsea said as she, too, pushed back from the table. "But for the life of me, I have no inkling of the plot."

"Don't berate yourself, not many would."

TEN MINUTES LATER, with a thick mist providing convenient cover, and the interior of the traveling coach dark, thanks to the leather shades that had been pulled up to hide its occupants, the silence of predawn Mayfair was unexpectedly broken by a feminine voice raised in shock.

"She's *what?*"

"How encouraging to know that you understand that this is meant to be a clandestine departure," Beau drawled from the facing seat.

Chelsea closed her eyes and pinched at the bridge of her nose with thumb and forefinger. And counted to ten, all the way to ten, because it was clear the man wasn't going to speak again without prompting.

She took a deep, hopefully calming breath, and attempted to recapture her composure. It wasn't the easiest thing she'd ever done. "All right, I'm better now. But you will admit that I had every reason to be shocked. Your father's wife was your mother's *sister?* Your father's wife is your *aunt?*" She sat back against the squabs. "No, I'm sorry. I still can't quite take it in."

"That's probably because you have never met my family. It all seems quite logical to us."

"Logical," Chelsea repeated, shaking her head. She certainly didn't wish to marry Francis Flotley, but was she seriously considering wedding a man who would see such a bizarre situation as *logical?* The nunnery, just until Thomas regained his senses, was beginning to look like a viable alternative to either situation. "I don't quite see how such an arrangement could be logical. Or very comfortable for those involved. One the wife, the other the mistress, the progeny running tame on the estate—you did do that, I imagine. That's a level of civilization I don't think I could ever aspire to, myself."

The coachman tapped three times on the roof and then immediately sprang the horses, indicating that they were now out of the confines of London. But it all happened rather quickly, and Beau, who had been slouching in his seat like some recalcitrant schoolboy, was suddenly catapulted across the space between them, all but landing in her lap. He saved himself by firmly planting his arms on either side of her, his forward progress stopping only as they were all but nose-to-nose in the dark.

"Sorry," he said, not moving. "I'm not usually this clumsy."

Chelsea attempted to speak without breathing. "Is that so? Tell me, how clumsy are you…usually?"

"My reputation would have it that I am not clumsy at all. Indeed, in many areas, I'm considered quite… accomplished."

Chelsea rolled her eyes at this blatant nonsense, even as her heart rate jumped dramatically. "I imagine I'm supposed to be impressed all hollow now, being told that my soon-to-be husband is…well, whatever it was that you were hinting. *Clumsily,* I might add."

He pushed a bit away and sat himself down beside her on the front-facing squabs. "No wonder your brother turned to religion. A sister like you could send anyone into a sad decline and hunting desperately for salvation." He unlatched the leather shade next to him, letting in the first light of day, and then turned to look at her. "You aren't at all impressed?"

"I saw the waistcoat, remember? The years may have changed your outside, thank goodness, but I know who you are. People don't really change that much. They just learn to hide themselves better. That's why I know that Thomas's new outside is only hiding the same uninspired inside. He wears his devotion like a cloak, to conceal and to be easily removed."

"I'll have to remember that."

"If you plan on surviving until we're safely married, yes, I would say you should. And Francis Flotley is just like my brother, only worse. At least Thomas believes he's doing God's work. The Reverend is pious for money."

Beau took her chin in his hand and turned her head to look at her. Rather strangely, she thought. "You're not a child anymore, are you? In fact, I'm beginning to worry that you're wiser than I." He let go of her chin. "But then I remember that you actually think you're being brilliant, bracketing yourself to a bastard, and I relax again."

Until he looks at me that way, unless he touches me. Chelsea coughed into her glove, a ruse meant to make him think she was doing nothing more than that, when in truth, she was trying very hard not to admit that she had been having second thoughts.

She hadn't realized how *manly* he would be; she'd still kept him in her mind as the raw youth he'd been. Silly, sympathetic, not at all worldly.

Easily manipulated.

The man sitting beside her, especially now that he was not suffering from the misery caused by strong drink, was anything but easily handled, led, directed.

Worse, he actually seemed to be *attracted* to her. Perhaps that came more easily to men, this being attracted thing. Show a man a skirt and an at least passably pleasant countenance, and he could easily convince himself that he found that woman attractive.

It wasn't that way with females. At least it wasn't that way for her.

She certainly wasn't new to the marriage mart, the annual spring hunt for a suitable husband and father for her children. She'd weighed and discarded wealthy gentlemen, titled gentlemen, both wealthy and handsome gentlemen. None of them had affected her in the slightest, until she had at last concluded that this business about flutters in her stomach and daydreams about sweet stolen kisses in the moonlight were fine for the pages of a marble-backed novel, but had no equal in the real world.

But then this man, this truly ineligible man, had scowled at her, made fun of her, barely even *tolerated* her…and suddenly she was interested, intrigued and eager even for his insults.

Perhaps she was one of those terribly shallow persons who wanted only what they could not or should not have. That was a lowering thought…

Chelsea mentally shook herself back to the moment— as she really didn't wish to pursue the thought she was having—and steered the conversation back to the bizarre revelation that the marchioness had been Beau's aunt. She'd avoid thinking about the other relationship that followed, that the marchioness had been sister to the marquess's mistress.

"Shall we return to the subject of your recently deceased aunt? We seem to be constantly sidetracked, which tells me perhaps this isn't as *logical* as you would like me to believe."

He took her hand in his, companionably—or at least that was what she told herself. "Let's see, where shall I begin? Ah, I have it. Once upon a time—"

"If you refuse to be serious…" She attempted to tug her hand free, with no success.

"I am being serious," he protested. "Or as serious as any of us gets, I suppose. All right, stop frowning. Once upon a—sorry. Over thirty years ago my mother, Adelaide by name, by the way, was the unhappy daughter of the local squire. She had one father, one mother and one sibling, the aforementioned Abigail. They all lived together quite unhappily in a tumbledown manor house about five miles distant from Blackthorn. One day, a handsome young man rode up the lane on his snow-white charger and—you're squeezing my hand rather hard, Chelsea."

"Be happy I'm not banging you about the head and shoulders with my reticule. I said I wanted to hear the story. Not a fairy tale."

"I'm telling it the way it was told to me, by my mother, and innumerable times, so that I've committed most of it to memory. Almost romantic, rather than seedy and strange. May I continue?"

Chelsea struggled to control herself. The man was enjoying himself entirely too much and all at her expense. "Please."

"Thank you. Now, where was I?"

"The snow-white charger."

"Ah, yes. The *limping* snow-white charger, which is why the handsome young man had stopped at all, hoping for some assistance with his injured mount. He got as far as the small stables when he encountered a lovely young thing, ethereally beautiful. Waiflike, delicate, almost as if she belonged in the heavens or some other celestial sphere. In a word, she was exactly like something out of a fairy tale. She came running toward him, not because of the sight of his handsome self, but because the fair maiden was dismayed to see the injured steed."

Chelsea nodded. "Your mother."

"My aunt. Close on Abigail's heels, however, was my mother, yes. And where the younger sister was a delicate sprite of a thing, the older sister was clearly the one who saw the danger, pulling her sibling back just in time from being stomped on, as the startled white charger had reared up at the sound of said younger sister's cries of dismay."

He turned to smile at Chelsea. "I think what my mother had been trying to say, without actually using the words, was that Abigail ran at the horse screeching like a banshee."

"Probably," she agreed, fascinated in spite of herself. "Then what happened?"

Beau crossed one long leg over the other and rested his hand on one strong buckskin-clad thigh, and as he was still clasping it, Chelsea's hand, as well.

"As I said, the horse reared. The handsome yet hapless young man, dumbstruck—by the combined beauty of the two young ladies, of course—toppled off the white charger and lay, stunned, at their feet. One, my mother, immediately grabbed at the white charger's bridle and kept the handsome young man safe, and the other, by deduction Abigail, promptly fainted across his prone body."

"Oh, my goodness," Chelsea said, trying not to smile. "I know I'm asking you to deviate from the story, but did the horse survive?"

"It did. As did my father, my aunt and my mother. Relatively speaking. I'll spare you the details of the romance, but the upshot was that my father and mother fell in love, my father asked for her hand in marriage, and she turned him down flat."

Chelsea's eyes widened in astonishment. "So he shrugged his shoulders, told himself one was as good as the other and married your aunt?"

"Hardly. My father was devastated, for he truly loved his Adelaide. But Adelaide truly wished to be an actress, traveling the countryside with a troupe, one day performing at Covent Garden. She was, and is, quite dedicated to what she calls her craft. She knew that a man who would one day rise to the title of Marquess of Blackthorn could not possibly be wed to a common actress, but that didn't mean she didn't love her dearest Cyril with all of her being—that's nearly a direct quote, by the way."

The coach hit a hole in the road, and Beau instinctively reached over with his free arm at chest level to hold Chelsea in her seat. *Her* instinctive response was to slap her free hand against her chest before realizing that, yes, the man's palm was all but cupping her breast...and she was *helping* him by holding it there.

"Now, that's interesting," Beau drawled maddeningly, clearly amused. And not moving his hand, even as she dropped hers in her lap.

"Take it off," she said quietly, knowing she both looked and sounded the fool.

"Oh, yes, definitely. Would that be my hand, or your jacket?"

"I will count to—"

"Not again," he said, withdrawing his hand. She struggled not to touch herself again, to ease the tingling burn his touch had caused. "You know that was an accident."

"For three seconds, it was an accident," she corrected primly, at last succeeding in withdrawing her other hand from his grip. "After that, it was deliberate. You're no gentleman, Oliver Blackthorn."

"Once again, you point out the obvious. I would also point out that I don't care to be called Oliver, but that's probably why you're doing it, so I won't. But I do apologize." He was silent for the space of three heartbeats.

"At least I suppose I should. We are going to be married, remember."

"There's many a slip between the cup and the lip, Oliver. We may find a way out of this yet." As soon as the words were out of her mouth, she wished them back. "I mean, yes, of course. We're going to be married. But I don't think we should…that we should *anticipate* our vows."

"In case you change your mind," Beau said quietly.

"In case circumstances change," she put forth, hoping she sounded reasonable. "Thomas might realize that he was wrong to demand I marry Francis Flotley and be racing even now to Gretna Green, to apologize. You… um. You may not have to sacrifice yourself. I mean, this was all my idea, and I am coming to realize that I have put a terrible imposition on your, um, your…"

"Good nature?" Beau supplied, which made her want to slap his grinning face for him. "Then again, if Thomas were to, as you say, catch us up before we reach Gretna Green and jump over the anvil or whatever the devil it is we have to do, and shoot me straight through my heart, it might put a crimp in his plan to sneak you back to London with nobody the wiser if you were to present him with the bastard's bastard nine months later."

Chelsea's cheeks went hot, as did other parts of her she would only think about later when she was alone. "I cannot believe we are having this conversation."

"I can't believe I'm on my way to Scotland to wed my enemy's sister, which probably makes us even if either one of us is keeping a tally. Again, I apologize. I hadn't realized I've been skulking about England for the past day and night, and risking my life, by the way, although I'm confident you feel that is only a secondary consideration."

"Oh, stop it," Chelsea demanded, not needing him to point out all the flaws in her plan. They'd been presenting them to her almost hourly since she'd first stepped foot in the mansion in Grosvenor Square. "If you're that concerned, simply have the coachman turn the coach and take me back to Portland Place. I will say I took the public coach yesterday and then thought better of it once I ran out of pin money. Thomas will accept that explanation as he believes what he wants to believe. Marriage to Francis Flotley surely can't be any worse than marriage to a *martyr*. Although I will say, you are not exactly an uncomplaining martyr, are you?"

Beau was silent for so long that Chelsea had all but concluded that he was going to do exactly that—return her to her brother's house. Tears stung her eyes, but she blinked them away. She shouldn't have gotten so starchy, all because he'd innocently touched her...not so innocently continued to touch her. After all, he was making a very large sacrifice for her. Even if she was, in a way, rather blackmailing him into it. And at least his mouth wasn't always wet...

"So, although they were in love, and knew they could never really be apart for long," Beau said at last, just as if the uncomfortable interlude hadn't taken place, "they both realized that marriage was out of the question. At the same time, Cyril knew he could not have an easy moment if Adelaide were to be running about England with no real protection save a gaggle of actors who wore tights and simpered and would probably squeal and run away if any danger came near them. In the end, a compromise was struck. Cyril would finance Adelaide's adventure upon the stage, and Cyril would wed Abigail, who would otherwise never marry."

Chelsea had thought she didn't care anymore about the man, the wife and the mistress. But she was wrong. "Why would Abigail never marry? You said she was beautiful."

"Yes, she was. Very beautiful, although quite fragile in her health. And good, and sweet, and kind. And always a child. Some call people like Abigail simple, but that's either mean or misleading, I'm not sure which. Adelaide only stayed home because of Abigail, as their parents were rather old, and her father had no real patience with Abigail. My mother needed to see her sister settled, and that also meant she needed her married, out from under the control of their father, who often threatened to put Abigail *away* somewhere when she made small mistakes. And some larger ones I'm afraid, such as accidentally starting the house on fire. Three times."

"Your mother is right. That is a fairy tale. One with a very sad ending, considering that you and your brothers are bastards because of what she and your father did together. That is, what they planned together," she added quickly, when Beau laughed. "For the good of her sister, which although quite commendable in some ways, could be looked upon as—oh, stop that! You know what I mean."

Beau sobered, nodding his head. "Yes, I understand what you mean. But that was our life, and as it was the only life we knew, it made sense to us. My father never went to London again, never wanting to take the chance of missing one of Adelaide's stops at the estate. He never stepped foot inside the Grosvenor Square mansion after he met Adelaide, save for a single time, about ten years ago, when he took Abigail there, seeking medical advice. Abigail, of course, couldn't possibly be exposed to Society. She was much too fragile."

"You did say that her health was a concern. Is that how she died? Did she become ill?"

"According to my father's note, she slipped away quietly in her sleep. Thank God. But back to the fairy tale. My father set my mother up in a cottage on the estate—Mother insisted on a real cottage, complete with a thatched roof and goats in the yard—and my brothers and I grew up running the entire estate, and as Abigail's beloved nephews. Actually, we were very often in charge of her, because she adored playing games and dancing on the lawns, things like that. She was like a sister to us, I guess you'd say. A happy, beloved, wondrously beautiful and pure little sister who may have grown older, but never grew up."

"And now she's gone. I'm truly sorry for your loss, Oliver, I'm sorry I was so difficult about it, and I'm sorry most of all that I won't ever get to meet Abigail."

Everything else could wait its turn. Thomas, Francis

Flotley, the elopement and its consequences. None of that was important right now. They were going to Beau's family home to help say a final farewell to his sister.

Chelsea slipped her hand back into his and rested her head against his shoulder. Hoping to in some way comfort him in his real grief.

The coach traveled on toward Blackthorn.

CHAPTER SEVEN

BEAU WOKE AS THE COACH turned from the road onto a private drive; he knew the feel of it, the singular sound the wheels made on the smooth surface. He didn't have to lower the shade, peer out into the darkness for his first sight of lighted windows somewhere ahead. His soul sensed it; he was almost home.

Back where he belonged.

His body relaxed, the façade he was forced to wear in London no longer necessary. Here, in this special small part of the world, nobody cared which side of the blanket his mother had been lying on when she'd conceived her three sons. Here, even now, as he'd just reached the ripe old age of thirty, he was still Master Beau, and Puck was Master Puck. Strangely, the servants several years ago had taken to calling Jack Mr. Blackthorn. Jack, the middle child, the one his brothers had dubbed Black Jack.

Beau wondered if Jack knew about Abigail. The man disappeared for months at a time, doing what only he knew. But he always seemed to turn up when he was needed, and sometimes when everyone only wished he would go away again.

Puck would be the worst, as he'd always been Abigail's favorite. He'd dance with her, and compose silly songs that made her laugh, and read to her when she was ill and confined to her bedchamber. They none of the three of them thought of Abigail as their father's wife. Mama was his true mate, any fool could see that.

But Mama was gone more often than not, still chasing the glorious dream she'd had since she'd been a child, never making it to London and Covent Garden, but only really happy when she was trodding the boards. She'd be ecstatic whenever she returned to Blackthorn, full of hugs and tears and kisses for everyone, regaling them with tales of her successes, the grand applause she garnered as she took her bows.

But as he'd told Chelsea, she never stayed at the mansion, preferring her own small cottage, where she would play at gardener, at cook, vowing that there was nothing like the simple life of an "ordinary person" to refresh her soul and replenish her weary body.

Puck had remarked that it was always like Christmas morning when Mama was in residence at the cottage. Their papa smiled all the time, everyone laughed, often, and her three "babies" wanted nothing more than to shower her with affection she very clearly returned.

Her young children loved her, the marquess worshipped her.

But she was not without her faults.

A few weeks would pass, even an entire glorious summer one year, and then they'd all recognize the signs, the restlessness, and she'd be off again, leaving her admirers with hugs and tears and kisses…but always leaving them, just the same.

And, increasingly, as they grew, her children had become less enchanted with her. It was difficult to love what they couldn't trust to be a constant in their lives, and knowing that they came in a poor second to their mother's love of the stage had all three of them guarding their hearts when she was present.

Beau understood that his father loved her. But he'd be damned if his wife would take him so much for granted. Happy to see him, happy to leave him. Leave their children.

But that was the point, wasn't it? His father and mother weren't married. The angelic oblivious Abigail had been his father's wife, if only in name. Beau didn't know the order of importance on his mother's list of what made her happy, but he knew that *freedom* figured higher than almost anything or anyone else.

I'll have none of that, he told himself as Chelsea, who'd fallen asleep shortly after they'd gotten back on the road after a mediocre dinner at a backwoods wayside inn, lay heavily against his shoulder. *My wife will be my wife, in every way. There will be no half measures, and no bastards to pay the price for their mother's selfishness.*

Beau gave himself a small shake, not realizing how much he'd resented his mother for choosing her freedom over her own sons. Not until now, when he faced marriage himself. Thank God he'd had no sisters. What was tolerable for him and Puck and Jack would have been a living hell for a bastard daughter.

He would ask much of Chelsea, not because she would owe him anything, but because marriage was important. Ask any bastard and he'd tell you that.

What would Chelsea ask of him? Clearly she wasn't as certain of her grand plan as she'd been yesterday, but there was no going back now. She'd realize that soon enough. The action of a moment, that's all coming to Grosvenor Square had been for her, a wild and rather juvenile response to her brother's demand she marry a man of his choosing.

But it is the actions of a moment that often have the most permanent of consequences. Beau knew he had been damned from the second she'd set foot in the mansion. In her brother's eyes, especially now that more than an entire day and night had passed with Chelsea in Beau's company, the action of that moment would forever be seen by both the earl and the world as the ruination of one Lady Chelsea Mills-Beckman—and the total humiliation of her brother, which Beau knew himself to be mean-spirited enough to see as the silver lining in the threatening clouds hanging over him as he struggled to get Chelsea to Gretna Green before said brother shot him, or worse.

At least there was one good thing—if he survived long enough to be wed at all—he and Chelsea were not in love.

Because love made a person stupid and prone to doing stupid things. He'd done that once, fallen victim to cupid's dart in rather spectacular fashion and with spectacularly disastrous results. He wouldn't do it again.

The coach began to slow, indicating that they were nearing the end of the mile-long drive that led up to Blackthorn. It had to be close on to ten o'clock, but he knew all the lights would be blazing behind the windows, his father confident that his sons would come rushing home the moment they'd received his announcement of his wife's passing.

Puck, riding on horseback and able to cut across country, was probably already in residence. Jack could be on the moon for all anyone knew, but he'd show up somehow, just like a bad penny.

"Chelsea," Beau said, close against her ear, ignoring the sweet perfume of her unbound blond hair. She'd taken it down earlier, complaining that the pins were giving her the headache, and he'd carefully ignored how she'd looked with the masses of loose curls tumbling down over her shoulders.

He'd been ignoring her eyes from the start. He'd ignored the rather exotic slant to them above her tiptilted nose, reminiscent of a fairy sprite if he wanted to get romantical about them, which he most assuredly did not. They were not gray, not blue, but rather like a startlingly clear pond on a sunny winter's day. He'd ignored the way she'd sometimes look at him in question, sometimes in what might almost be admiration, at other times in agitation—he rather liked the way her eyes flashed then. And how they'd welled with tears when he'd told her about Abigail.

He'd spent the past few hours pointedly ignoring the way her body fitted so easily against his side, the sound of her soft, even breathing as she slept.

He'd concentrated on the trouble she'd brought him, rather than on her smile, her scolds, her insults, her bravery.

He remembered who she was, the sister of his enemy, the sister of his first and only love, and how wicked was the former, how fickle the latter.

No matter what, Lady Chelsea Mills-Beckman was, at long last, his perfect revenge.

"Chelsea," he repeated. His hand was on her shoulder, because he'd had to hold her in place as the coach moved as quickly as possible along the moonlit road, Beau warning them that they did not want to be caught out in the open by the earl's men. So now he gave her a gentle shake. "Come on, wake up."

"Don't want to," she murmured sleepily.

"Ah, isn't that a pity."

"Yes, it is," she said, burrowing in closer to him, clearly not awake enough yet to realize what she was doing. Unless she did, but he didn't want to think about that; he didn't think she should trust him quite so much. Besides, he preferred her to be what he wanted her to be, and what he wanted her to be was...was...damn. He didn't know.

He tried another tack. "You've already disproven the notion that it is only those with a clear conscience who sleep soundly. Unless it truly doesn't bother you that you've so badly compromised an innocent man."

That did it.

"Innocent?" Chelsea levered herself away from him, pushing her hair back from her face. "Well, now I'm awake, most certainly. Innocent. I doubt you've been innocent, Oliver, since you were in leading strings. Oh, drat this hair! Now it's stuck on one of your buttons. Ouch! Hold still."

She had so much hair, tons of it, but it was fine, like that of a child, and prone to forming ringlets along its blond lush length. He knew, because he'd found himself idly stroking her hair as they rode on through the dusk, only realizing what he was doing when his fingers seemed to become tangled in those living curls, just like a hapless insect that has flown, unnoticing, into the spider's web.

"Here, let me help you," he said as she fumbled with one of the buttons on his coat, her head bent beneath his chin as she struggled to see in the dark. His hands touched hers, and she looked up into his face, those winter pond eyes flashing.

"Stop. You'll only make it worse."

"Oh, I don't know," Beau said, some imp of mischief setting his tongue to moving before his brain could fully engage on what it was he was saying. "It would appear the hapless insect has somehow managed to turn the tables on the spider."

"What? Are you drunk again? You only had the one mug of ale at the inn. I know, because I watched. While I've been sleeping, have you been drinking from some bottle I missed, one you hid inside the coach? I won't be married to a sot, you know, no matter how hand—"

"Yes?" he questioned when she abruptly shut her mouth. Yes, he really did like her eyes best when she was…agitated. "No matter how what? You think I'm handsome? Is that it? I appeal to you?"

She tried to lower her head, pulling on her hair as if she could untangle it from the button by brute force. "Handy. No matter how handy. As in, Oliver, you came in very *handy* when I needed you to rescue me from Francis Flotley."

"He of the always-wet mouth. Yes, I remember. You had Puck all but ready to sacrifice himself when he heard that. But that's because Puck is a romantic. I'm the practical one. Now hold still. I paid a good penny for these buttons, you know."

He leaned back against the squabs and pressed his chin into his chest as he looked down the length of his nose to the offending button. This also put him within a few inches of Chelsea's face, because now it seemed that even more of her hair was imprisoned around the button. "How in blazes did you manage that? Sit still, I'm going to have to take off my coat."

"You can't take off your coat, you imbecile. I'm *attached* to it."

That was true. She was. And he didn't have the heart to tell her that she was supporting herself by putting her right hand directly on his… "Do you have a better suggestion?"

She must have wearied of looking at him, because

she turned her head downward, away from him, which brought not only her hand but her face in closer proximity to the last place she probably wished to be at the moment, or any moment, he supposed.

Her close proximity wasn't bothering *him* all that much, he realized, although it could soon prove embarrassing, as she was a rather beautiful woman, and he wasn't three days dead.

The coach stopped. The door to the coach opened. Light from the flambeaux on either side of the front doors of Blackthorn spilled inside the coach.

There was a short, uncomfortable silence, followed by Puck's voice saying, maddeningly, "Ah, I see you two are getting to know each other better. Well, good on you, brother."

Chelsea yelped, jerked her head upward (which forced her hand sharply downward, causing Beau to see pretty bright lights winking inside the coach for a few seconds), and then yelped again, much more loudly, as her hair finally pulled free, leaving several golden strands behind, still wrapped around the button as she tumbled unceremoniously onto the floor of the coach.

"You didn't see that, Puck," Beau warned as he helped a now grumbling Chelsea back onto the seat.

"I didn't? Are you quite sure? Because I could have sworn I did. None of it?"

"None of it," Beau agreed as Chelsea struggled to pull back her hair and then rubbed at what must have been a newly tender area of her scalp.

"It will be our little secret?"

"There's no *little secret,* you great giant looby," Chelsea protested, now straightening her riding habit, which probably didn't help change Puck's mind about what he'd just seen. "My hair got caught on Oliver's button and we were trying to release it, that's all."

Puck held up his hands. "Oh, no, please don't explain. I'd rather simply treasure the moment. It is, in fact, burned into the back of my eyeballs."

"Are you done?" Beau asked him, caught between laughter and some odd urge to punch his brother straight in his grinning mouth.

Puck sighed. "Yes, I suppose so. But I must tell you, I've seen a whole other side of you just now, brother mine. Until now, I saw you as old and, dare I say it, faintly starchy? I don't think so!"

"Your brother has gotten entirely the wrong impression. You need to explain," Chelsea demanded as Beau kicked down the steps and emerged from the coach, and then turned to hold out his hand to her to assist her to the drive.

"Oh, I don't think so," he said, echoing Puck as she laid her left hand on his forearm and they headed up the wide marble steps to the door being held open by one of the Blackthorn footmen, her blond hair a shining cloud of gold around her face and shoulders in the light from the flambeaux. She certainly looked as if they'd been doing what Puck had been so mischievous as to pretend he believed they'd been doing. "I think I'd rather also simply treasure the moment."

Chelsea stopped dead on the second step from the

top, turned and delivered a sharp and rather painful kick to his ankle with her pointed riding boot. "And I will treasure this one," she said as Puck collapsed in laughter against the shoulder of the openmouthed and goggling footman.

To SAY THAT SHE'D entered a house of mourning under rather odd circumstances did not begin to tell the tale of Lady Chelsea Mills-Beckman's introduction to this strange family she had stumbled into on impulse.

It was, in fact, the furthest thing from a house of mourning that she had ever seen.

There were flowers everywhere. Bowls, vases, nearly overflowing with colorful blooms. Several potted palms with white ribbons streaming from them as if they were fully topped Maypoles lined the enormous entrance hall. None of the mirrors was draped in sheets, and no black crepe hung anywhere. Every chandelier was lit.

The bedchamber she was immediately led to had been similarly decorated, the fragrance of flowers everywhere, and the maid assigned to her even had a flower tucked into the brim of her mobcap.

Although it wasn't possible to avoid the fact that the young girl had red-rimmed eyes, as if she'd been crying more than just a little bit.

"Edith?" Chelsea asked as she waited for the tub to be prepared in the usual way—a long line of footmen carrying bucket after water bucket of heated water from the kitchens and pouring them into the enamel tub, with a lovely floral design painted all over its exterior, rather amateurishly, unfortunately. "The footmen all have flowers in their buttonholes. In fact, there are flowers everywhere. May I ask why?"

Edith sniffled, pulling a handkerchief from her apron pocket and loudly blowing her nose. "It's for Miss Abigail, ma'am. She did so love flowers. Painted that there tub herself, she did, when his lordship said he was sorry, but he'd very much like it if she didn't paint the piano. Anymore," she added quietly, and then her bottom lip began to tremble and she broke into sobs.

Chelsea didn't know what to say, nor what to do. Clearly the maid was overset. The footmen had all been stone-faced and sad-looking as they'd filled the tub, and the Major Domo she'd been rushed past by Beau had first shaken hands with him and then grabbed him in a tight hug, saying, "She's gone, Master Beau. Our sunshine has left us for another place."

Chelsea had squirmed uncomfortably as she'd stood there, unused to such open displays of emotion. She didn't belong here, she knew. She wasn't a part of the family, she hadn't known the marchioness, and she could be more easily inserted under the heading of Problem than of Mourner.

And she didn't understand these people. Yes, she'd been warned that the marchioness had been different, rather special, but she'd had no idea that the woman had been so loved. Chelsea had very little experience with that emotion, considering that her love for her cat, Twiddles, had been her main source of affection growing up at Brean. Her parents had ignored her, her brother had at times forgotten her name and Madelyn had actively loathed her. Even the servants were far from the fuzzy sort of kindly people she'd read about in novels, coming and going so quickly that it had been impossible to get to know any of them.

She'd had her books. Thank God for her books, and her imagination.

But no book could have prepared her for this, and her imagination certainly had never stretched so far.

"Edith," she ventured once the maid had gotten her sobs under control, "I'm perfectly capable of bathing myself. If you'd just unpack my night things and place them on the bed, I'm sure I can muddle through, and you can…well, maybe you should lie down?"

The maid's eyes widened in horror. "And leave madam to fend for herself? I would never, ma'am! His lordship prides himself on his hospitality, not that we see much of it, what with him not being the sort to give grand parties and such. Oh, he tried sure enough, years ago. My mam told me how it was, she being a maid like me back then, when Miss Abigail first come. But they came to laugh, my mam said, and then when Master Beau and his brothers started to grow up there was some nasty talk. Master Beau, he blackened a few eyes, my mam said, and then everyone left us alone. Oh, and now here I am, prattling on. I'm that sorry, ma'am. We all loved her so much."

Halfway through this lengthy speech, Chelsea had led Edith to the chaise lounge and sat her down, and was now sitting beside her and patting her hand, something the maid didn't seem to think was out of the ordinary. How odd. Or perhaps not. The marchioness, according to Beau, had been a child in a woman's body. She wouldn't have understood the hierarchy of master and servant; she would have had *friends*. How lovely. Perhaps it was the rest of the world that was odd. After all, why dress in black, and cover the mirrors, and speak only in whispers, and hide your sadness if you were sad?

And why not decorate the house and even yourselves with flowers, if the person you were mourning loved flowers? It seemed a finer tribute than sitting around like lumps, clad in heavy, depressing black, with opened but unread prayer books in your laps, and meanly whispering to your sister that she would not get any of Mama's jewelry because she wasn't the oldest.

Tears and stories and flowers. What a lovely way to be remembered.

"Edith, I hesitate to say this, but my bath water may soon be too cool if I don't take advantage of it now, and if there's only one thing I wish more than crawling into that bed over there, it is a bath, and to wash this mass of hair."

"And very pretty hair it is, madam," Edith said, sniffling one last time and then slapping her hands on her knees and getting to her feet, suddenly all efficiency. "It will take us some time to dry it by the fire, so we'd best get started. Don't know why we're dawdling, so whenever you're ready we'll get to work."

Chelsea hid her smile as she also got to her feet.

"What a marvelous idea, Edith. And while we're busy, you can tell me more about Miss Abigail, and all of the people here at Blackthorn. Could you do that?"

"Oh, my, yes," the maid said as Chelsea handed over the jacket of her riding habit. "Talking is about the best thing I do, my mam says."

"Isn't that wonderful? Because listening is about the best thing I do, and everyone says it. Let's begin with Master Beau…"

CHAPTER EIGHT

BEAU WAS WAITING at the bottom of the wide, sweeping staircase the next morning when Chelsea walked down the steps. He'd stationed himself there a good thirty minutes earlier, after he'd watched Edith enter the bedchamber, that same ruby-red riding habit he'd seen for the past two days draped over the maid's arm, the material now brushed clean and pressed.

As he lingered in the entrance hall, avoiding the footmen's quizzical looks and pretending a nonchalance he didn't feel, he wondered what they were to do about Chelsea's wardrobe. The lack of one, actually.

The bag she'd carried with her when she'd arrived in Grosvenor Square had hardly been large, so he believed it safe to assume her maid had packed up only the essentials, which probably did not include a gown, or pelisse, or even shoes other than those pointy boots she'd employed to such good effect last evening. He had the bruise on his ankle to prove that.

So now he didn't just have an unexpected fiancée, he also had a fiancée with a pitifully minuscule trousseau. One might even say she had pretty much come to him in the clothes she stood up in and nothing more.

Sidney had arrived early this morning with three trunks carrying Beau's own extensive wardrobe, not that those trunks or his valet could travel with him to Scotland, considering the pace they'd have to keep, the secondary roadways they'd be forced to travel and the inferior inns they'd rest in along the way.

But where Beau and Chelsea went on horseback, Sidney would follow with the traveling coach and those three trunks. Once the deed was done, Beau would be damned if he'd ride all the way back to London in anything less than comfort.

Three large trunks. One small, hastily packed bag containing God only knew what. That one dark red riding habit, day after day after day.

No. It wasn't possible. Nor fair. Nor even practical. But what else was there to do?

"Then again, who tarries to do a little shopping while engineering an elopement, with an irate brother hotfoot on your trail?" he asked himself quietly.

"Master Beau? There's something you'd be wanting?"

"No, John, thank you," he said to the footman. "I was just looking for my conscience." He looked up the expanse of staircase and realized that Chelsea would know he was loitering down here, waiting for her. He was about to head for the drawing room when she suddenly appeared along the balcony. "Ah, and there it is now."

John looked up the staircase, shrugged and went back to doing whatever it is footmen do when sitting in an entrance hall in a grand mansion on a grand estate, waiting for no one to arrive.

"Good morning, Chelsea," Beau said, holding out his hand to her as she neared the bottom of the staircase. "Don't you look…familiar." But then he noticed the white flower pinned to her jacket, and his notion of teasing her died an abrupt death. The bloom matched the one stuck in his buttonhole.

"Is his lordship downstairs as yet?" she asked, ignoring his hand and turning unerringly in the direction of the morning room—probably coached by Edith, but still, she had the look of one who knew where she was going at all times and did it with grand panache. "I would like to offer my condolences on his loss, as well as thank him for his hospitality."

Left with the options of either trailing after her like some puppy or shouting his answer to her departing back, Beau chose to follow her as he replied. "My father is over at the cottage, awaiting my mother's arrival. But Puck is in the morning room, or was the last time I saw him, slopping down eggs. *Now* where are you going?" he asked as she turned down a hallway in the opposite direction of the morning room.

Because he doubted very much she was lost. Lady Chelsea Mills-Beckman seemed to know what she was doing at all times, or at least thought she did at the moment she was doing it. It was one or the other, and he was never quite sure which.

"Edith told me there's a portrait of the late marchioness in the music room. I want to see it."

"And why did she tell you that?"

"I should have thought that would be fairly obvious. Because I asked her if there might be a portrait somewhere, that's why." Chelsea stopped and turned to face him. "I asked Edith quite a few things. We talked until nearly midnight, as a matter of fact. I know all about you now. Do you mind?"

"Does it matter if I do?" he asked her as she set off once again, turning left at the next hallway, and then right, into the music room. He'd had hunting dogs with a less perfect sense of direction.

He'd been avoiding the music room all morning, wanting to visit with the portrait, to try to feel Abigail's presence in the house, yet knowing that he'd only feel a keener sorrow if he did. The flowers helped, as did bringing those absurd potted palms she'd decorated herself in from the conservatory and lining them up in the entrance hall like some sort of honor guard. But Abigail was gone, and he'd never see her smile again, hear her innocent laughter, be able to marvel at the world as seen through her eyes. For she'd been unique, special and irreplaceable.

"Oh, my," Chelsea said beside him, stopping just inside the doorway, looking at the large portrait that hung over the massive white marble fireplace. She advanced slowly, her gaze on the portrait. "Oh, my goodness. She looks like an angel."

Beau smiled. "That could be the effect of the wings she insisted on, although she called them fairy wings," he pointed out mildly. "I remember when that was painted. My father had to pay the artist twice what he would have, because Abigail would only pose for a few minutes before deciding she'd rather be somewhere else. Puck bribed her with sugarplums if she'd sit still until he'd counted to five hundred, but that rarely worked. Especially since Puck was only seven or so, and seemed to get lost somewhere around four hundred and ten. I'd forgotten that."

Chelsea leaned the side of her head against his upper arm, sliding her hand around his waist. "Such an ethereally beautiful woman. Delicate, perhaps even fragile. And yet with the happy, open mind of a child. Your mother was right, Oliver. To have Abigail put away in some madhouse would be to invite disaster on her. Still…couldn't she have married your father and brought Abigail here with her?"

Beau slid his arm around Chelsea's shoulder and absently rubbed at her upper arm as the two of them stood there, unable to look away from Abigail's image. It seemed almost alive, as if she could at any moment fly out of the portrait.

"You're forgetting my mother's ambition," he said, feeling a knot forming in his gut, for there were some things that still could touch him, hurt him, even as he tried to convince himself that they didn't matter. "I was born in Ireland, you know, because she was performing there that summer. My father didn't even know she was carrying me. She didn't tell him because then he would have forced her to stay, forced the marriage on her. By the time she returned, his marriage to Abigail was an accomplished fact."

"And you and your brothers born after you were declared bastards. You could have been your father's heir. This estate, the mansion in Mayfair and all the rest. Even Madelyn, although if I were you I'd still say I'd had a lucky escape there. Still, your mother robbed you of all of this. Will you ever forgive her?"

"What is there to forgive?" Beau looked down into Chelsea's upturned face, surprised to see his own hurt reflected in her eyes, possibly even some anger. But not pity, which was as marvelous as it was lucky for both of them. He would not be pitied. "My life is my life. What I can't change I choose to ignore. I could have been raised in a hovel, wondering where my next crust of bread was to come from. Instead, I was raised here, on my father's estate. Educated above my station, many would say, clothed, fed, given every advantage possible to give."

"Yes, but all of it here, within sight of all that can't be yours, that should be yours. I would go out of my mind, I know it. But, then, I am probably selfish."

She lowered her arm and made to move away from him. But Beau rather liked her where she was, so he slipped his hand down to her waist and turned her to face him.

"You do know, Chelsea, that you're giving up all that you do have, all you were born to, throwing it all away on marriage to a bastard. I never had Society's approval, not really. But you did. They will consider your slap in their collective face as worse than the circumstances surrounding my birth. You ask if I've forgiven my mother. Do you wonder if our children will forgive either one of us?"

"Children?" She said the word as if he'd been speaking some foreign language she didn't understand— or wished she didn't understand. "I...I hadn't really thought that far. I mean, how they would feel. Neither fish nor fowl, some would say they'd be, wouldn't they?"

He touched the tip of her nose with his index finger. "You've thought no further than this, have you? Perhaps having to stop here is Fate sending you another chance to rethink your plan. We could make up some faradiddle about you being called away to the country for a funeral, which is almost true, if we squint sideways at the thing. Your brother would be wise to agree to such a story."

She looked daggers at him. If he wasn't mortally wounded, it was only out of sheer luck. "From the moment I met you, Oliver, you've been trying to get rid of me. When you're not looking at me as if you'd perhaps like to kiss me. Is that because I remind you of Madelyn?"

"Please don't hold that ancient mistake against me, if you don't mind," he said tersely. "And you don't look the least like her."

"Oh, I do so. She's blond, I'm blond. We've both got the Brean chin. And our eyes are—"

"Nothing alike," Beau said, rather vehemently, he realized. "Hers are beautiful, yes. But cold, lifeless."

Chelsea looked up at him from beneath her lashes, suddenly shy—he hadn't realized she could even *look* shy. "And mine?"

He knew he was in trouble now. Saying things he shouldn't say. Thinking things he shouldn't think. "Yours…yours are like nothing I've ever seen. One moment gray, the next blue, or even slightly green. They're…they're like transparent, sparkling jewels. Fascinating. And they show your every emotion."

"Oh," she said quietly, dipping her head to hide her eyes from him. "I didn't know that. I mean, I thank you for saying that. I wasn't pushing you for a compliment, you know. That would be shallow and silly. But it is nice to know that…well, that you noticed. That you see me not just as Madelyn's sister, that is, or as your revenge on Thomas. Not that you shouldn't wish revenge on all of us, just as you probably would like revenge on the entire world for—"

He lifted her chin and put his mouth to hers, shutting off her nervous prattling. He'd regret his action later, he was sure, but at the moment it seemed to be not only expedient, but expected behavior.

What he hadn't expected was his response to feeling her untutored mouth under his. He'd avoided innocence for all of his life, perhaps because he didn't think he deserved it, perhaps because he'd had no interest in innocence. He'd never questioned why.

Another woman would have drawn away. Another

woman would have melted against him, yet another would have gone further than that, rubbing her soft body provocatively against his strength, his arousal.

Practiced women. Knowing what they wanted, what he expected in return.

But not Chelsea. She simply stood there, her hands at her sides, her head tilted up to him, those so-revealing eyes closed so that he couldn't see into her head, her soul.

So he drew her in, closed the physical gap between their bodies, thinking to engage her more, and ended by finding himself engaged in a way that shook him to his core. He wanted her.

He wanted her innocence. He wanted to be her first. He wanted to be the one who awakened her. He'd thought he was above such things, but he wasn't. In two short days the damned girl had moved beyond nuisance or means to an end. Beyond revenge.

He simply wanted her.

"My God, man, there are thirty bedchambers in this pile, at the least. The coach, now the music room? What next? The stables? Give a man some warning, if you please. I've a sensitive nature."

Beau broke off the kiss and stepped in front of Chelsea, a move that was definitely a case of too little, too late, if he thought he was protecting her reputation. "Twenty-six rooms, the hell you do and why are you here?"

"I'd say I'm here to torment you, but stating the obvious is so boring, especially since I've been doing it all of my life. Good morning, Chelsea."

"Puck," she answered shortly, stepping out from behind Beau. "As one youngest sibling to another, I feel I should compliment your ability to be annoying to your elders. However, you are not half so amusing as you suppose yourself. After all, we must all grow up at some point."

Puck shrugged his shoulders eloquently, in the French style, Beau supposed. He'd probably studied the move, practiced it in front of a mirror until he'd gotten it perfect.

"I think you've just been put in your place, little brother. I'm gratified I could be here to witness it."

"Well, as long as you're feeling gratified, I suppose it was worth it. But I've come to tell you that Mama has returned to the cottage, and is in fact even now at the ice house."

"At the—oh," Chelsea broke off, turning to look up at the portrait, and then at him and Puck. "Have…have you been? I shouldn't if I were you. My mother and father both were laid out in the drawing room at Brean. But, then, it had been wintertime both times. There isn't much dignity in death, either way. My biggest memory of Mama's service is watching to see if she might suddenly sit up. I was only ten," she added in explanation. "Oh, I'm sorry. I shouldn't be talking like this, should I?"

"No, it's all right," Puck told her. "Isn't it, Beau?"

"I should have smothered you in your cot when I had

the chance," Beau told him calmly, but then looked at Chelsea. She was biting her bottom lip, clearly upset. "You don't like thinking about dead bodies?"

"I don't think I *enjoy* seeing dead bodies, no. I feel so sorry for the dead person, being put on show like that. Do you know my greatest memory of my papa's laying out? That I'd never realized how much hair he had in his ears and nostrils. Isn't that terrible? I swore then and there that when I die I will be put immediately in a box and the box be nailed shut, with nobody standing over me as I lay there dead and on some ghoulish sort of display, with everyone saying how *wonderful* I look. How could I possibly look wonderful? I'd be *dead*."

"Well, that settles it for me, Beau. I'm not looking. You?"

Beau shook his head, insanely thinking how much he'd like to kiss Chelsea again. She was such an odd, frank-speaking creature, with more sides to her than a...well, a thing with many sides.

"I believe I'd also much rather remember Abigail as she was the last time I saw her. Will the service be this afternoon then, Puck? I told Papa that Chelsea and I must be on our way, but if it's not to be until tomorrow, I suppose we can take that chance. After all, the earl has already been and gone yesterday."

"Thomas was here?" Chelsea's eyes had gone very wide and somewhat frightened. "Oh, no. And with the poor marquess's wife just died. And I'm sure my brother was bullying and obnoxious as only he knows how to be. I will have to apologize at once. Was it very terrible?"

Beau took her hand without consciously thinking about what he was doing, and the three made their way to the morning room. "It wasn't pleasant, no," he told her. "My father denied knowing anything, of course, because he didn't know anything, and eventually they went on their way."

"They? Oh, you mean my brother's servants."

He held back her chair for her as Puck offered to fill her plate from the silver dishes on the sideboard. "There were five riders with him, yes," he said, easing into what he had to tell her. And he had to tell her. "There was also the Reverend Francis Flotley, who refused to depart until he'd said a prayer over Abigail's *corporeal remains,* which the marquess flatly denied permission for him to do. Papa didn't think the man seemed truly holy."

"The marquess is a very discerning man, and Francis Flotley is a pig," Chelsea said, reaching for her fork. "I shouldn't have an appetite after hearing all of this, but my stomach doesn't seem to share my scruples. It must be getting used to its new, altered circumstances."

"Then I suggest you eat quickly," Beau told her as he accepted a cup of coffee from one of the footmen and sat down across the table from her. "Because it seems that Madelyn also is traveling in company with your brother."

The fork dropped noisily onto the fine china dish. "Madelyn? Good God, no. Why?"

"I can answer that one," Puck volunteered as he snatched up a piece of toast. "If the earl is going to rescue you, Chelsea, he has to do it quietly, and you have to be seen in female company. Ergo, the sister was the logical choice. The lovely bits about this are, as I'm sure you'd have quickly grasped on your own, that a female in the group means a coach and, with a coach, a slower progress toward the border. Plus, the earl was nice enough to inform Papa that they were on their way to Scotland, to rescue you. And to have Beau's guts for garters, I believe he said."

"But Madelyn hates traveling. She always feels certain she's forgotten something she'll absolutely perish without, so she brings almost everything with her. She detests inn food, so she never travels without her cook and full hampers. She sleeps only on her own scented sheets. She has the bladder of a flea, our father always said, and if she rides for more than two hours at a time she's very likely to become messily sick to her stomach. I can't believe she'd agree to ride all the way to Scotland."

"That sounds promising, Beau," Puck said. "It sounds as if the sister will slow the earl's progress very neatly."

Beau nodded his agreement. "Traveling lightly, on horseback, we should be able to overtake and pass them, even with this delay."

"Delay? *Delay?* Is that how you see my sister's death, Beau? As a *delay?* 'How sharper than a serpent's tooth it is to have a thankless child!'"

Beau and Puck both sprang to their feet and went to

full military attention, just as if the Iron Duke himself had deigned to enter the officers' mess.

SO THIS IS THE WOMAN who chose her freedom over the man she purports to love, over the futures of her own sons. She doesn't look evil.

Chelsea sat quietly in her chair in the drawing room, part of her still longing for the breakfast she had missed, but most of her too captivated by the woman now holding court with her men. Her admirers.

Adelaide was everything her sister had been in looks; she and Abigail had looked astonishingly, almost eerily alike. But Adelaide was definitely not wearing wings.

Her slim frame was draped in unremitting black, including the veil she'd gracefully lifted back off her face as Beau introduced her to Chelsea. Her huge blue eyes had assessed Chelsea coolly even as her mouth had formed kind words of welcome.

Chelsea had immediately known she was being weighed, measured and most definitely catalogued. Was this unexpected female friend or foe? Useful to her, or useless? Controllable, or did she need to be put in her place? Was she an admirer or her competition? It was almost as if Chelsea could hear small wheels turning in the woman's head.

Chelsea decided she didn't much care for Adelaide Claridge.

It would appear, however, that her lover and her sons believed she set out the stars at night.

The marquess sat beside her, holding one slim hand

in both of his, tears brimming in his eyes as she talked about her darling Abigail. Beau stood at the mantel, watching his mother as if transfixed, and Puck was actually seated at her feet, like some obedient puppy.

The queen and her court. No, her audience.

Chelsea squirmed in her seat.

But at least everyone was ignoring her, which she appreciated, as it gave her time to look at them all, watch them all, perhaps put them in nice, neat pigeonholes in her mind.

Puck and Beau, with their thick manes of blond hair, both most resembled their mother in coloring. But they had taken their looks from their dark-haired father. Beautiful mother, handsome, well-set-up father—no wonder both sons had turned out to be so physically attractive.

Although Chelsea believed that, while Puck was certainly every young debutante's dream—a sentiment with which he'd undoubtedly concur—it was definitely Beau who had gotten the best of both of their parents. And his personality, it would seem, definitely more from his mother, although she thought he might not like to believe that. There was a bit of the ruthless in Beau.

Because the marquess, kind and welcoming as he had been to Chelsea during this sad time, appeared to have all the backbone of a sponge now that his lover was on the scene.

Everything was *Yes, dearest* and *No, my sweet,* and *Whatever you think best, Adelaide.*

As the woman left off her recollections of her sister

and began regaling her audience about her recent triumphs on the stage in Tewkesbury and Chepstow, Chelsea clearly saw two things: Adelaide's delight and her lover's despair. If the man had entertained any thoughts of Adelaide giving up the stage now that her sister was gone, he'd had those hopes dashed within ten seconds of the woman opening her mouth.

Chelsea couldn't watch any more of this.

"Excuse me," she said when Adelaide paused for breath, or for effect, or whatever, getting to her feet. "You've all been very kind, but I believe I should give you some privacy now as a family."

Adelaide put out her hand, leaving Chelsea no choice but to take it. "What a sad introduction, I'm afraid. You and I will speak later, I hope. We have much to talk about, now that you're to be my daughter. Right after I tease my naughty son for having very lovely taste in having scooped you up and run off with you, although I will say he's being unaccustomedly romantic."

"Mother, please," Beau said quietly.

She dropped Chelsea's hand and turned to the marquess with a delighted squeal. "Good God, Cyril, we could soon be grandparents. I'm much too young to be a grandparent. Chelsea, my sweet, please tell me you're not already increasing."

Chelsea felt her cheeks catching fire even as she kept her smile steady. She debated whether or not she should curtsey to the woman—after all, Chelsea clearly outranked the actress—but then decided that the woman was probably one of those creatures who kept score.

Which, Chelsea knew, meant that she was already trailing badly in the contest.

"Mama, I believe that will be enough," Beau said quietly, pushing himself away from the mantelpiece. "I also believe you never got your breakfast, Chelsea. Let's see if we can remedy that. We'll see everyone in the chapel at two."

She nodded her agreement, deciding not to thank him because she was confident he was as anxious to be shed of the drawing room as she was, but only took his offered arm and allowed him to guide her back into the entrance hall.

"Oliver, I—"

"Shh, not a word, not yet," he told her, leaving her to stand by herself as he walked across the hall and gave a few quick orders to the footman. Only then did he motion for her to follow him.

Once they were standing outside the massive doors they'd entered through the previous evening, he turned to her, his expression bleak. "I used to adore her, you know. Puck recognizes what she is, and chooses to pretend he hasn't noticed. And Jack? Well, Jack hasn't seen or spoken to her in years."

"But you're the oldest. Son of the man, if not the next marquess. You feel you have to do what, Oliver? Set some sort of example?"

They walked along the drive before cutting across the lawns, clearly heading somewhere, not simply ambling. "My father loves her. I have to respect that. It would hurt him to know that I don't think she's the paragon he has had on that pedestal for so many years. Damn. How did you know?"

"I didn't know," Chelsea admitted as their destination became apparent. They were heading toward the stables. "I merely watched, and then I guessed. Does she know, do you think?"

"God, I hope not. After all, what good would it be for her to know? We can't change any of it. She actually told me I was lucky to be a bastard, that all three of us are lucky, as we'll never have to wonder if the women we love chose us for ourselves, or for our wealth and titles. She said this as I was still licking the wounds inflicted by your brother, by the way. I think she thought to comfort me."

"Well, that's simply stupid," Chelsea said, angry all over again. "Do you want to know what I think, Oliver?"

"I imagine I'm going to hear it no matter how I answer, so, please, enlighten me."

Chelsea felt herself blushing again. "I can't help it. I say what I think, sometimes even before I think."

"'Do you not know I am a woman?'" Beau quoted. "'When I think, I must speak.' Sorry. I grew up listening to my mother rehearse lines, helping her by taking different parts. She always says Shakespeare has an answer for everything."

"Does he have one for selfishness?" Chelsea took in a breath and let it out in a rush. "Oh, now I apologize. I have no right to say anything. But it seems to me," she went on quickly, before he could agree with her, "that your mother twists everything, and everyone, so that it and they suit what she wants. I only wonder how she manages to keep your father so enthralled, even after all these years."

"She'd probably tell you if you applied to her, but you women have all the advantages anyway, so I'd rather you didn't."

"Oh, but I didn't mean…I mean, I wasn't going to *use* what she—that is…you're quite annoying, Oliver, do you know that?"

"I believe that's been mentioned a time or two over the years, yes, and much more often in these past few days. Would you like to hear more about your brother's visit to Blackthorn?"

Chelsea considered the question for a moment and then shook her head. "I think I'll content myself with the knowledge that all three of them will be stuck together in the traveling coach all the way to Scotland, and hope that they murder each other. But may I ask you something else?"

"If I say no, will you be satisfied?"

"I don't think so, no. What I want to ask—what I'm asking—is why you carry the name Blackthorn. Your father's family name is Woodeword, and your mother was introduced to me as Adelaide Claridge. Blackthorn is a place, a title. Yet you and your brothers bear it as your surname."

They had reached the stable yard, to see that a fine curricle had been brought out and a team put into the shafts. "Let me help you up onto the seat," Beau said.

"We're going to the village. It sits on Blackthorn land, so we won't be exposing ourselves all that much."

"There's no longer any food in the kitchens?" Chelsea asked him, sure her stomach would soon begin to grumble in protest if she didn't feed it.

Beau laughed and went around the back of the curricle, soon joining her on the seat and taking up the reins. "We can stop at the inn first if you're that hungry, but I'm hoping we can find you some clothing. Unless you have some great attachment to that riding habit and wish to live in it for the next two weeks?"

"Oh." She hung on to the edge of the plank seat as they set off out of the stable yard. "That's...very thoughtful of you. Do you really think there will be anything suitable in the village?"

"I doubt you'd wish to wear any of what we find to Almacks, not that you'll be invited there again, but we should be able to manage something. And it was because nobody told her she couldn't."

"Excuse me?"

"You asked why we carry the name Blackthorn. Mama gave it to all of us."

"Because nobody told her she couldn't," Chelsea repeated, shaking her head. "Well, of course. I doubt anyone tells her what she can or cannot do, or that she'd listen if anyone tried. You know, Oliver, between the bastardy and all that comes with it, not to mention what you've lost thanks to it, and your, I'm sure, lovely yet clearly selfish mother, not to mention your well-meaning but just as clearly muddled father, I'm surprised you turned out as well as you did. Upon re-flection, and remembering my suitors over these past years, and dismissing the horrible Francis Flotley all together, I could do much worse than to marry you."

He looked at her for a moment, rather startled she supposed, and then threw back his head and laughed.

She really did like his laugh.

MADELYN SAT in the forward-facing seat, alongside her brother, and stared at a spot somewhat to the left and approximately three inches higher than Francis Flot-ley's left ear. "I cannot believe you have done this to me, Thomas. You *said* we'd have Chelsea by now, and be on our way back to London. You know I cannot travel all the way to Scotland like this. Only one maid, no more than three changes of clothing. Without my own sheets. Good God, man, you expect me to sleep on someone else's sheets?"

"From what I've heard, Madelyn, this will not be a new experience for you. And this from a woman who had come home weeping after her wedding night, saying that no woman should endure such indignities."

Madelyn's maid, seated next to the reverend, by cir-cumstances forced to share the coach with her mistress, closed her eyes and pretended to be asleep. And deaf.

"With that ham-handed boor you bracketed me to, yes. It was *your wife,* by the way, who explained to me that husbands are rarely proficient with their own spouses, but with other men's spouses they're really rather much better." Madelyn turned to him and smiled.

"Now you sit there, Thomas, and attempt to deduce how she knows *that*. Or even better, pray that your son and heir, if you ever manage to produce one, is cursed with that hook you call a nose, or those horrible ears."

"My lord, don't," Reverend Flotley cautioned quietly, and after a moment the earl lowered his hand back onto his lap. "Women have always bred violence in men. They are the cause of all the world's ills. We've spoken of this at length, my lord. It is my lady's husband who is lax. She needs to be schooled, learn her place."

"Learn my *place*! Why, you impudent *nothing*! And you *listen* to him, Thomas? You've been listening to him for two long years? You gave up drink and gaming. You don't frequent the theater or the races anymore, and wear nothing but that dreadful black. You've forsworn mounting a mistress—oh, yes, I know that, too. All this because you promised God? Did God *ask* you for this promise? Or did he ask that wet-mouthed man over there to deliver the message outlining this particular path to salvation? You never once wondered why, if God thought the message so important, He didn't deliver it directly? And now this…this *creature* has the nerve to sit there and call *me* the cause of all the world's ills? Thomas, you've lost your mind."

"My lord?" the reverend prompted when the earl didn't answer his sister. "Remember the many ways a woman may tempt you into sin."

Madelyn threw back her head and laughed. "*Tempt* him? My God, man, my brother and his ilk *invented* sin. Women had nothing to do with it."

"That will be enough, Madelyn," Thomas said at last, clearly clinging to his temper with the last of his strength. This was a test of his new faith, his new path. He would face it and overcome it. Somehow. "I will pray for you."

"Oh, yes, you do that. You pray for me, Thomas. You pray we catch up with Chelsea tomorrow. And you pray there is a decent inn about to appear in the next few minutes, one with tolerable food and clean beds. Because if I have to spend another *hour* in this damnable coach today, I will spend *all night* inventing new hells for you to visit."

CHAPTER NINE

THEY RODE IN SILENCE for the first two hours, the pall of the simple chapel service fading slowly as they kept to meandering back roads Beau had ridden all of his life, just in case Thomas had left one of his men behind to watch the main entrance to the estate.

Beau wondered if perhaps he was being overly cautious. With a well-sprung coach, fresh teams in the shafts along the way, stopping only to rest and eat and keeping to the established route, he and Chelsea could be standing in front of a blacksmith in Gretna Green in a matter of days. Hell, they might even catch up to and pass the earl and his sister along the way. That would actually be amusing.

Or Beau could be dead, and Chelsea dragged to Brean and her wet-mouthed minister—and that wasn't quite as jolly a thought. He wasn't a coward, would stand up to Thomas Mills-Beckman if he should present himself, but Chelsea was another matter. If her brother didn't value her, someone had to, and it would seem that, for good or ill, Beau was her choice of protector.

Three-hundred-and-twenty miles from the center of London to Gretna Green. He'd read that as he was plotting their journey. Less from Blackthorn, but not by much. He wasn't sure they'd travel any faster by horseback, but they would definitely travel safer. The idea of possibly having to leave Chelsea's mare and his own Pegasus behind at some point bothered him, but Puck knew the route, and after a quick return to London to purchase some proper clothes for Chelsea, he would be following along after them to "tidy up," as his brother had called it.

Puck and two well-loaded traveling coaches would be traveling the Great North Road, and all that any pursuers would find inside the first coach would be the maddeningly silly and purposely obtuse Puck—his brother was rather looking forward to being stopped, actually—and in the second Beau's and Chelsea's trunks, Sidney and Edith, embarrassingly delighted to be included in the adventure.

"You're being very quiet," Beau said now, not unaware that he hadn't exactly been jabbering like a magpie, either. "Are you thinking about ways to murder me for insisting we ride all the way to Scotland?"

She flashed him a smile that both shocked and surprised him. "Oh, no, not at all. I've never been anywhere, you know. Well, to London, but that's all. Everything here in the country is so fresh and beautiful. I don't think I'd mind if it took us weeks to get where we're going. Will it take us weeks?"

"At this pace? Months. But we'll soon be on better roads, I promise. And your brother is a full day ahead of us, probably driving his horses into the ground, which is very considerate of him. We won't have to be constantly looking over our shoulders, worrying that he's catching up to us. I'd say the plan is brilliant, except that this wasn't the plan at all. And we got a much later start than I'd hoped. We'll soon have to stop somewhere for dinner, and maybe for the night, as well."

"It was a lovely service," Chelsea told him. "Everyone shared such wonderful stories about the marchioness. But what was everyone so upset about when we first entered the chapel? Your mother seemed nearly fit to burst, as my maid would say, before your father whispered something to her and she seemed better."

He probably promised her something if she didn't make a scene, perhaps new costumes for the troupe, Beau thought, knowing he was being unkind. His mother had a right to be upset. He supposed.

"You saw the single red rose on top of the casket?"

Chelsea nodded. "Yes, I did. There were so many flowers, but that one was tied with a black ribbon. It was the only black I saw, save for your mother's gown. You all were upset about a rose?"

"Not the flower. What it meant. That rose was from Jack. He was there. Probably in the middle of the night, knowing him."

Chelsea jerked on the mare's reins in her surprise and had to quickly get the horse back under control…which she did firmly and competently, proving that she was a capable rider, something Beau had already concluded on their first mad dash out of London.

"Are you saying your other brother came to the

estate, was even inside the family chapel, and didn't show himself, say good day to everyone, or give his condolences to his father, but then just snuck away again?"

"Yes, I'd say that fairly well sums it up. I'd also say my brother is an ass, but we all handle our circumstances in our own way. I think I have come to grips with my lot in life, mostly thanks to spending several years fighting on the continent, and I'm fairly content now living a quiet life, taking care of my father's estates, occasionally visiting London."

"Tormenting my brother," Chelsea added.

"I didn't say I don't amuse myself from time to time," Beau reminded her as she rolled her eyes. "In any event, Puck feeds on his bastard status, I swear it. The moment Napoleon was back in his cage, Puck and his quarterly allowance were off to Paris where, to hear him tell it, he is the darling of Parisian Society. It's only by chance that he's here in England now, and he'll be heading back overseas soon. He makes a great business out of being a wastrel, silly and useless, but I happen to know he's also quietly working for our government."

"Oh, good. I really do like him, and I'd hate to think he's just another well-dressed grasshopper, fiddling through life. But what does he do for the government? The war is over for good now, isn't it, with Bonaparte recaptured?"

"There will always be Bonapartists, I'm afraid. They managed to free him once, remember, and no one thought that would happen. But I agree. At some point Puck is going to have to come home and stay home. Our father handed over the deed to one of the unentailed estates to him just before Puck visited me in Grosvenor Square. He's very upset about it."

"Why is that?"

The roadway changed from dirt track to crushed and compacted stone. They could increase their pace now, and make it to the village he'd chosen for their first night before it became fully dark. Tomorrow they'd ride more, talk less, but he couldn't seem to rouse himself into any sense of urgency at the moment, knowing the earl was already barreling along the Great North Road.

"I'm not sure. It was also my birthday, and we spent much more time drinking to the day than we did talking about our lives. Puck also told me that Papa wanted me to come to Blackthorn before I set out to inspect any of the other estates, which was my plan before his summons—and before a certain young lady rushed into my drawing room, upbraided me on several counts and then proposed marriage."

Chelsea shrugged her slim shoulders, clearly unashamed at his teasing. "If that's the way you wish to see the thing, I won't argue with you. Except to remind you that without the rotting grapes I never would have even thought about you, let alone *proposed* to you. So you're not entirely innocent in this, Oliver."

"And I will take my punishment like a man," he teased her, watching her eyes as she sorted through that statement. Then he sobered. "I did take my father aside earlier and ask him what it was he wanted to tell me."

"And now you're going to tell me? Because, you

know, I won't give you a moment's peace until you do.
I abhor secrets."

"Is that so? In that case, abhor this—he didn't tell me.
What he did say was that he'd always promised himself that when I turned thirty—that birthday of mine,
remember—he would tell me something that would
change my life, although I was not to tell my mother
I knew, or to hate him too much. However, now that
Abigail is gone everything is even more important, yet
also changed somehow, especially since you and I are
entering into a marriage of convenience—my mother
is very against it, you know, and not only because she's
too young to be a grandmother. In any event, now he
thinks he might not tell me for another year, because the
time isn't right and he still has to convince my mother.
How's that for maddening?"

"Delicious? Infuriating? And you merely said that
was fine with you, you were in no great whacking rush
to know what it is that he's been waiting thirty long
years to tell you? God, Oliver, maybe you are a dull
stick, just like Puck keeps saying. Again, rotted grapes
being the exception, I suppose. I mean—aren't you even
curious?"

He was. And he wasn't.

"Does it matter? Abigail has died, my mother is in
residence at least for the next several weeks, I suppose,
and then life will go back to where it was. Oh, and in
case the mice in that head of yours are galloping ahead
to next year when we're out of mourning, and you're
thinking perhaps Adelaide will finally agree to marry

her Cyril, let me remind you of something. It is not permissible in England for a man to marry his dead wife's sister."

"No! Are you saying to me that someone actually made up a *law* about that possibility? What sort of person even thinks about such things, let alone takes the time and energy to interfere with other people's lives by actually making a *law* about it?"

Beau gave a short laugh. "Probably the same brilliant minds that wrote the Marriage Act all those years ago, and made Gretna Green and other Scottish border towns the scene of more English marriages than half the churches in London. The road ahead looks empty, Chelsea. Let's pick up the pace for a bit, shall we?"

CHELSEA EASED into the chipped and rather battered tub in her room under the eaves, thankful that another long day was over. She ached all over, even in places she hadn't previously been aware she possessed.

Each day, they'd risen early, downed a quick breakfast and ridden until midday. And then they'd ridden again, sometimes cutting across country, sometimes daring to travel for several miles along the Great North Road itself, until she'd not reacted quickly enough and had nearly been run down by one of the mail coaches barreling along as if the hounds of hell were after it.

Beau had been so sweet when he'd yelled at her.

She'd found little to suit her in any of the village shops along the way, and nothing at all in the way of a riding habit, so that the day they reached Scotland and outfoxed Thomas with their marriage would be the day she would hand her increasingly grubby riding habit over to someone with orders it be burned in the kitchen grate.

"You wanted to see the countryside," she reminded herself—grumbled to herself was more like it—now as she picked up the thin, rough washing cloth that did not hold a candle to the lovely large sea sponge she'd left behind in Portland Place. There were no piles of scented bubbles, either, and the water had barely topped tepid even before she'd climbed into the tub. "And now that you have, you may never want to see it again, at least not from horseback."

She didn't even know the name of this village, which looked very much like the last village, and the one before that, and the one before that.

The journey wasn't turning out to be quite so romantic, in fact, as it had seemed in theory. Much of the food was inedible, the sheets damp and today they'd been caught in a sudden downpour that had left her with her teeth chattering by the time Beau could consult his map and make this unplanned stop at the Rusty Gate or the Mist Over The Middens, or whatever this fairly decrepit wayside inn was called.

And he'd been so *jolly* about it! There must be something about seeing a woman with her hat sodden, the jaunty feather in it drooping over her eyes, that delighted something in men. And if he'd called her a *good sport* one more time while they'd searched for the inn as rainwater seemed to unerringly find its way down the back of her collar, she had thought she might have been forced to throttle him.

Men were such boys. He probably had been purposely prolonging his search for the inn, more on the lookout for a few muddy puddles he could wade in instead.

Still, there was one thing she liked very much about their unorthodox journey. She liked getting to know Beau away from London, away from his strange parents, away from what many would call the trappings of civilization.

For one thing, he had a fine voice. She still wasn't quite sure about some of the words he'd used in one of the songs he'd sung for her—she was rather sure he'd altered them somewhat to protect her sensibilities, or something—but they'd spent a pleasant hour or more during one of their cross-country interludes singing together.

And when he'd sung "Greensleeves" for her, so quietly, so sorrowfully, she'd actually had to blink back tears, not that she let him see how he had affected her.

Sometimes they'd ridden in silence, but it was never a strained silence. It was a comfortable silence, as if they had known each other for a long time, and didn't feel the need to make conversation just for the sake of courtesy.

Of course, they could have been having one very interesting conversation, that of when he was going to stop looking at her in that way he had and *do* something about it. But that wasn't the sort of question she should ask. Probably.

He'd allowed her an entire mug of locally brewed ale at one of the inns, and she'd slept more soundly that night than any night in her recent memory and woke only when he banged his fist against the door the next morning and informed her it was time all slugabeds were up and moving again.

And at each inn, he insisted on a tub of hot water for her bath, no matter how late their arrival.

Bastard, she had decided, was only a word for *the parents were not married,* and not a description of the man himself. She'd heard Thomas more than once say things like, "That bastard was using fuzzed cards, I vow it," or "What a bastardly thing to do." But that was as wrong as calling Thomas a *gentleman* simply because his parents had said their vows before witnesses. In either case, the child was no more than the product of the union; the child had been in no position to dictate terms.

"I like him," Chelsea informed the large yellowish lump of soap as she rubbed it between her hands in a vain attempt to raise some lather. "It was enough at first that I could use him to thwart Thomas, and that I didn't actively dislike him, as I do Francis Flotley—but this is better. And I think he likes me, too, or at least seems to tolerate me well enough. Besides, when it gets right down to it, his strange family is no better or worse than my own strange family. Why, we're possibly the sanest of either bunch, if that means anything. We could both do worse. Or perhaps a lot better, if he'd stop being such a gentleman."

A knock on the door startled her, and she dropped the soap, causing a small splash that, naturally, caught her exactly in the eye, so that she was blinking and squinting as she looked toward the door and called out, "Yes? Who's there?"

"It is I, Mrs. Claridge, your husband," Beau said with what she thought was unnecessary volume from the other side of the thin door.

Still rubbing at her stinging eye, Chelsea turned her head toward the door as if she might be able to see through it to the idiot on the other side. "What did you say?"

"Don't bother to get up if you're already in bed, sweetest. I have a key."

"What! No, don't you—oh, God," she said as the door opened, and Beau walked in, closing it behind him as she grabbed the thin toweling sheet the chambermaid had left, pulled it over her and sank down into the water. "Honestly, Oliver, not again…"

He'd stopped just inside the door, had turned to one side and seemed to be at least pretending to avert his eyes. But the room was small, and he was tall, and the tub was fairly low. And there were no bubbles. If she put aside the towel, maybe then he'd turn around and—no, she couldn't look too eager. This being a lady business did have its drawbacks.

"I will count to five, Oliver. No, three. No more than three. And you will be on the other side of that door."

"I can't believe you're still in there. You take longer at your bath than any six women I know."

Ah, he was embarrassed. Well, she supposed at least one of them should be.

"Oh? You've made a small vocation out of interrupting women in their baths? Don't you think that's rather odd, Oliver? Oh, yes, and once again—get out!"

"I'm sorry, but I've nowhere else to go. Where's the chambermaid?" he asked, still standing where he was, just as if his boots had somehow become rooted to the floor.

"Out purchasing me a pistol so I might shoot you," Chelsea told him, doing her best not to laugh. What a silly game they were playing. But perhaps it wasn't a game, for he really did look uncomfortable. But then he seemed to collect himself. "Oliver, what are you doing? Oliver! Don't you dare take off your coat!"

"I'm not going to sleep in this. It's bad enough I have to stand up in it all day," he told her, shrugging out of the hacking jacket and tossing it on the bed. "I could only arrange the one tub, Chelsea, and that cost me a guinea, so if you think you're done, I'd like to wash away this dirt before ice chips form in there. Oh, and only this one room. Therefore, until we depart in the morning, you are Mrs. Claridge. I'm protecting your reputation, you understand. You should probably thank me."

"*What* are you talking about? Have you been drinking your dinner?" She'd seen his traveling bag in the room, but had only thought the porter had brought it here by mistake. But he was planning to sleep here? Her naked body seemed to clench in on itself as she remembered the only night rail she'd brought with her, the one she and Edith had been forced to select from Abigail's wardrobe. Sweet Abigail had had a penchant for silk. And ruffles. And not much else. He'd probably take one look at it and run screaming from the room.

Beau put his hand on the door latch, still half turned away from her. "It's a small inn, Chelsea, and they've only got the one single room. Everyone else is sleeping in the attics, lined up like cord wood, cheek by jowl, snoring and spitting, and hoping to rob each other blind during the night. I've seen them in the taproom, and I have to tell you, some of them are fairly…ripe. You wouldn't wish that on me, now would you?"

"If I said I did, would that make me a horrible person? There's only the one bed, you know."

"I'll sleep on the floor."

He was going to give up this easily? Shame on him! "This floor? Then I suggest you don't bother about the bath, and worry more about the bugs. If it weren't still raining, I'd say we strike out again in the dark, and hope for something better. A damp cave, perhaps? With bats in it."

"Chelsea, you're wasting time. Very well, I'm going to the stables to check on our mounts, but I'll be back in ten minutes. You've been warned."

"I've been *warned*," she said singsong as the door shut behind him. "The man has *warned* me. Aren't I the fortunate one?"

And then she realized that what she was was the *naked* one, and she hopped up and out of the tub so quickly she forgot about the sopping wet toweling and tripped over it, nearly crashing to the floor.

There was no other toweling sheet. She'd used the only one to cover herself.

"Of course," she said, looking about her for something with which to dry herself and finding nothing. She had to do something. Quickly. She was not going to look like some half-drowned cat when he returned!

Her wet hair dripping down her back and into her eyes, she all but tore Beau's traveling bag open and grabbed a perfectly folded white shirt she'd concluded she needed more than he did and dried herself with it as best she could.

It only seemed fair, as this whole thing was clearly his fault.

The chambermaid—more probably called the *serving wench,* as chambermaids at least pretended they cared about their charges—had not laid out her night rail, nor had she hung the sodden riding habit up next to the fire, rendering that more thorough concealment useless at the moment.

She dug the terrible night rail out of her own bag and pulled it on over her head so that it dropped onto her shoulders...and then promptly slid off her shoulders and settled around her waist. Abigail had looked the forest sprite in her portrait, but clearly she had grown considerably more *substantial* over the years since the painting had been commissioned.

As she had the previous nights, Chelsea fished the drapery cord she'd taken from her bedchamber at Blackthorn and tied it twice around her waist to hold the night rail at least marginally in place, and then turned her attention to the bed.

The coverlet looked at least reasonably clean, but even if it was alive with bugs, it was her only hope of at least looking decent, as opposed to ridiculous, when Beau returned.

Elopements, according to the novels she'd read, in which elopements always seemed to figure highly, were not quite as romantical as their authors suggested. There were logistics to be considered, and none of them were very pleasant. A mad dash across the moors, an irate father in hot pursuit, was never mentioned in the same breath as long hours on horseback, inferior inns or drenching rainstorms.

And the main participants, of course, had always been madly in love, so if there had been impediments, they probably hadn't noticed them.

But still, Beau was doing the best he could, given the short time he'd had to plan this elopement, and it wasn't his fault that the two of them weren't in love. Why, they hadn't even seen each other in seven years, and she'd been a brat then, and he'd been an idiot.

Chelsea giggled at that thought in spite of herself. But by the time the key turned in the lock once more, she still managed to be seated on the hearth rug, tied into her night rail, the coverlet wrapped around her and her brushes in her hands, ready to dry her hair by the fire.

She told herself she might look at least slightly romantical.

And Beau seemed to agree with that assessment—at first.

"Lovely," he said, locking the door behind him. "The firelight dancing in your hair, the coverlet puddled around you as you pose by the fire. A very pretty scene, Chelsea. I commend you on your ability to organize yourself so quickly when faced with—is that my shirt on the floor? What happened to it? Bloody hell, woman, that's my only clean shirt!"

So much for romantical.

"It's one more than I have left," she told him, dispassionately looking to the shirt that now lay damp and crumpled on the floor, ridiculously angered that he'd not finished his compliment. "Unfortunately, it is a better shirt than it is a towel, but it's all we've got." She chanced looking up at him, for she hadn't heard any signs that he might be even at this moment undressing himself. "Why, Oliver, where *is* that smile you were wearing the first time you came into this room?"

"I look forward to meeting your Reverend Flotley, if only to tell him what a lucky escape he's had, and to perhaps ask him to pray for me," Beau grumbled.

Chelsea couldn't help herself. She giggled.

"Oh, wonderful. The woman is amused." Beau sat down on the edge of the bed, taking a deep breath even as he ran a hand through his thick crop of hair. Between the hat he'd worn all day and the rain, any thought of gentlemanly styling had long since departed, and he looked mussed, and young…and more than slightly appealing.

"No, I'm not. Not really," Chelsea told him honestly. "I know we're to be married, and that even if you had earlier harbored any thought to renege on your promise made back in London, I am now so compromised that you really have no choice left but either to marry me or condemn yourself to being even more disreputable than Society has labeled you. However, Oliver, putting all of that together, and not leaving out that, yes, I was the one who did the proposing of this plan, I have to tell you—oh, blast, now I've tied my tongue in a knot! What was it I was going to say?"

"I think you were about to remind me that you are a gently bred female and, while many anticipate their wedding vows, you have limits to the rules you will bend, you are appalled at our current situation which is not at all what you'd thought it would be, and you would be greatly comforted if I'd be a gentleman and take myself off to sleep in the stables."

Chelsea considered this statement and then nodded her agreement. Clearly he was not going to take advantage of their situation. The dolt. "Yes, I would say that about sums it all up. Thank you."

Beau got up from the bed and began unbuttoning his waistcoat. "I'm not sleeping in the stables, Chelsea."

Her heart soared. Her stomach, on the other hand, unexpectedly began to feel slightly queasy. Perhaps he wasn't a dolt. Still, she could not look too eager. "Oh, but—"

"Close your eyes, turn your head or offer to wash my back. Those are your choices."

She turned her head. But only to hide her smile.

CHAPTER TEN

SHE WASN'T A CHILD. He didn't think she was extremely innocent, although he knew instinctively that she was a virgin. You don't grow up the daughter of an earl without knowing the value of virginity on the open market.

But he knew she knew what the world was about, or at least thought she did, in theory. As she'd reminded him from time to time—she read books. When she'd corrected him on a small matter of Greek mythology, he'd decided she'd read whole libraries.

She knew she was beautiful, desirable. Nobody with eyes like hers, hair like hers, a slim yet luscious body like hers could be unaware of her beauty even if she'd grown up in a house without mirrors.

And she'd been flirting with him. Occasionally. Possibly. Unless he was reading too much into what he saw, hoping that would assuage his conscience as he mentally pictured slowly ridding her of that damnable riding habit.

They'd been on the road for three days, three nights. Apart only to sleep, getting to know each other in a way many people would never know someone if they knew that someone for a lifetime.

They'd shared meat pies he'd purchased at an inn on the outskirts of Grantham, and he'd held her head as she'd been sick at the stomach an hour later, vowing never to eat meat pies again in her lifetime, if she lived to be one hundred, which she probably wouldn't do, as she was certainly going to die at any moment.

She hadn't wanted pity. She'd been angry. With the meat pie and possibly with herself for having shown weakness, or some such womanly nonsense. But she'd not turned on him, blamed him in any way. Which, of course, made him feel even worse, especially as his own stomach, used to much worse during his time serving under Wellington, had tolerated the meal quite well.

And then she'd rinsed her mouth with a mouthful from the flask of wine he'd handed her, spat out the excellent vintage as if it was water, delicately patted her lips with a handkerchief, asked him to help her back onto the sidesaddle and never mentioned the incident again.

That took pluck. A man had to admire pluck, if not her abuse of good wine.

He admired a lot about Lady Chelsea Mills-Beckman. And he had been spending some of his quiet moments forming decidedly detailed ideas for how to show that admiration. With his mouth, his hands, his...

She had yet to complain about anything. Had never asked him to stop early, or insisted on knowing how far it was before the next resting place. He'd seen the blister at the base of her thumb while they were eating lunch just today, and knew it had come from holding the reins for long hours, but when he'd asked her about it she told him she hadn't even noticed it.

She was a terrible liar. He'd learned that, too.

She delighted in the countryside, each new vista that opened before them, bright with soft English sun, green as only England could be. He was seeing his country through new eyes, thanks to her. Although he knew he would never see what all the fuss was about with sheep. Chelsea had been very taken with the sight of a field filled with the things and had made him stop and let her watch them as a barefoot youth and a small black-and-white dog herded them toward their pen.

Three days, with this their third night. Together. Her smiles. Those flashing eyes that showed her every thought, her every mood. Watching her ride ahead of him at times, her spine straight, her rounded bottom outlined by the stretch of the habit of her skirt.

There wasn't much a person could hide when traveling by horseback for nearly ten hours a day, isolated, dependent on each other, with no chaperone or anyone else to ease any tension, smooth any sharp conversational edges.

Which meant she had to know that he wanted her.

Which, Beau also knew, made him a bastard in more ways than he was used to thinking of himself.

Now, as he unbuttoned his shirt, he watched Chelsea, her back turned to him as she sat on the hearth, pulling her brushes through her hair. Even damp, it seemed to want to curl around her wrist; a living thing, glorious and bewitching, reaching more than halfway down her back. Wild, free. Hair a man could lose himself in.

Did she know she was driving him insane? If he was a betting man, and at times he had been, he would say that she did. Did she know what she was daring? On that head, he wasn't so sure.

Beau spied the bootjack and used it to remove his boots, and then sat on the single rough wooden chair and removed his hose, noting that there were a few small burrs on one of them because they'd quickly left the road when they'd heard a coach approaching around a bend, and he'd chosen badly, ending them in a thicket of some sort of prickly bushes. A few more encounters like that, and he'd arrive in Scotland with his hose in tatters.

And a dirty shirt. He shook his head as he looked at his last clean shirt, now damp and wrinkled as it lay on the floor. She'd hung her riding habit on the fender to dry it, but hadn't picked up his shirt. He guessed that fell under the heading of *so there* as far as Chelsea was concerned. *Insist on bathing in this room, insist upon sleeping in this room and expect no help from me.*

He didn't blame her. There had been another chamber he could have used, but it was on another floor, and he knew this was not the sort of inn where he could rest easy a full floor away from her.

If it hadn't been for the rain, they'd be just outside of Gateshead by now, where he'd planned for them to rest for a day before pushing off to the border. Instead, they had been forced to stop here, and if this inn wasn't a haven for highwaymen, smugglers and assorted felons, he would be mightily surprised.

His story to the innkeeper had, he'd thought, been quick-witted and bordering on brilliant. They were the Claridges, staying with a party at the country estate of "his lordship"—after all, there had to be a lordship somewhere in the vicinity. They'd been out for a ride, got caught in the rain and sent their groom back to the estate to inform his lordship that they'd return in the morning, as Mrs. Claridge refused to travel a step farther in such inclement weather.

In other words: slit our throats and rob us and "his lordship" will have you hanged forthwith.

Still, he'd wake Chelsea at least an hour before dawn and have the two of them out of here before the sun rose, just to be safe. And he'd sleep with his knife under his pillow and his pistols on the table beside the bed.

Beau looked at the tub. What was he waiting for? The water wasn't getting any warmer. Hell of a time for a belated attack of modesty.

He looked toward Chelsea again, still with her back to him, to see that she was now finger-combing her hair, holding out the long tresses toward the meager fire as she did so. Suddenly he found it difficult to swallow. The silence in the small room was deafening.

He was a man. She was a woman. They were alone together. She was barely dressed. He was nearly undressed.

If ever there was a recipe for disaster, this was it. Still, not exactly a disaster. They were going to be married, after all. They'd only be anticipating their vows by a few days. What was the harm in that, after all they'd already been through?

God, I'm a fool.

He opened the buttons on his buckskins and slipped them off, then quickly lifted one foot over the edge of the tub, as if he was the maiden in the room.

And stepped on something. The soap. Before the short, pithy curse was halfway out of his mouth, he was on his back in the small tub, his head under water, his legs stuck in the air.

"Oliver!"

"No!" he all but shouted as he managed to right himself. "I'm all right." Wiping water out of his eyes, he shot her a look, to see that she was on her feet, and staring at him, her eyes wide. He pulled his knees up to his chest. "Really. I'm fine."

"Did you slip? It sounded as if you hit your head. Are you sure you're all right?"

"Now that you mention it," he said, raising one hand to the back of his head and wincing as he felt the small lump that was probably going to grow considerably larger. He looked at his knees, sticking up out of the water. Bare knees weren't half as scandalous as the alternative would have been if he'd landed in the tub face-first. "No, I'm fine. I stepped on the soap, that's all. Go...go back to what you were doing."

"I was attempting to dry my hair," she told him, still staring at him, "until some great lummox sent bath water splashing everywhere, just as if a huge rock had been plopped into a pond. Look what you've done. We may as well be out in the rain."

"Chelsea, please, turn your back," he said as she moved closer to pick up his now sodden shirt, look at it and then drop it again. He probably should be grateful she didn't attempt to strangle him with the sleeves. "We're not married. This is entirely improper. Even if we were married, I would consider this improper."

"Improper? Oh, piffle, Oliver. If you cared a whit about proper and improper, you wouldn't be here, would you? I'm seeing you at a disadvantage—not that I really saw, you know...anything. Well, your knees. And your chest. And, just for a moment, really, your—"

"For the love of God, woman."

"That's what's bothering you, you know," she suggested, her eyes shining. "The impropriety. But it was not improper for you to enter the room while I was in my bath? *Twice?* It isn't very comfortable, is it, being put at such a disadvantage? And all while that water gets colder and colder. Are you sure your head is all right? Really, it was a very loud bang. You're not going to pass out on me or anything? You could drown in there."

"I'll live."

She nodded her head. "Well, if you're sure. You have a lot of hair on your chest, don't you?"

"Chelsea, I swear to you, if you don't be quiet and turn your back now, when I get out of here..."

"Oh, all right," she said, finally turning her back to him. "But it's very nice, I suppose. Blond, just like on your head. Does it ever itch? It looks soft, but I suppose you'd know best."

Still rather nonplussed, Beau reached for the soap that had caused him to come to grief and began quickly lathering his body. "You're doing this on purpose, aren't you? You have absolutely no sense of shame."

"Oh, for pity's sake, Oliver. We've been on our own for three days. I have to apply to you to stop whenever I feel the need to excuse myself and go into the bushes if we're not near an inn. I cast up my accounts in a roadside ditch while you watched and muttered ridiculous platitudes. How much maidenly shame could any of that possibly leave me?"

"I suppose I can concede that you've got a point there." He reached over the side of the tub and picked up the wet shirt, knowing it wasn't going to do him much good, and got out of the tub. Moments later he was struggling to force his still wet legs into his buckskins, for he usually slept in the buff and had not brought any nightclothes with him. "All right, I'm decent, or as decent as I care to be at the moment."

She turned around yet again, not doing a very good job of hiding her smile.

"Someday we will look back at all of this and laugh," she said. "At least I know I will. I will gather our grandchildren around me and tell them of the day their venerable grandfather did battle with soap, and lost. I can say venerable, I'm sure. After all you are so much older than I, the mere slip of a girl you snatched up and romantically carried off to—"

That did it. He had borne all he was going to bear without getting some of his own back!

In five quick strides he was in front of her, his hands on her shoulders. He captured her open, laughing mouth with his own, grinding his lips against hers in a combination of frustration and a nearly uncontrollable desire to sit himself down on the floor and then roll about, laughing like a loon.

But the unexpected amusement vanished as quickly as it had come when Chelsea slid her arms around his bare back and held on tight.

He'd thought the tension he'd been feeling for at least a day and a half had been his alone, but clearly he'd been wrong. She'd been feeling it, too. Like a watch spring, wound tighter and tighter, they'd been aware of each other, of the future, of what this mad dash to Scotland meant. Marriage. A shared bed. His hands on her. Her introduction to a part of life she might have heard about, read about, but was now going to experience for herself.

He cupped her face in his hands and continued to kiss her, teasing her with his tongue, drinking her in, breathing her sigh as she melted against him, the coverlet sliding to the floor as she ran her hands over his bare back, setting his skin on fire.

"Finally," she breathed as he lowered his hands, skimming them down over her shoulders, easily dislodging the material that covered them, so that she was suddenly bare to the waist.

And clearly unashamed. He could hardly hide his surprise.

But he managed it. He'd have cursed himself for a thousand kinds of fool if he hadn't.

His mouth still locked with hers—otherwise she might say something else, and he didn't dare chance any interruptions at this critical point—Beau cupped her bare breasts, amazed at their perfection. He might not be able to see them—he'd correct that lapse later—but his hands told his rattled brain they were the two most beautiful breasts in the history of the world.

And her nipples, as he grazed them with the pads of his thumbs, were the most responsive bits of flesh in the entire universe, turning instantly into tight, hard buds that clearly appreciated the attention he was giving them.

"Oh…good," Chelsea murmured against his mouth, holding herself very still as he stroked, stroked, stroked. "They always feel…strange when I look at you. I guess they wanted this. Yes, please do that some more…"

Maybe he should let her talk. Beau knew words could serve as an aphrodisiac. He'd read that somewhere. But until this moment he hadn't realized that his brain could turn his body rock hard and ready simply by opening its ears.

And why the devil was he trying to think anyway? In the lexicon listing Gifts From The Gods, he'd just been written down as having been handed the top prize.

He scooped Chelsea up in his arms and carried her to the bed, laying her down gently but quickly, before whatever aberration had struck her melted away and she remembered they were in a sordid country inn, not yet wed and had only been in each other's company for a few days. Strange, glorious days.

With only the small light from the fire to break the darkness and Chelsea's arms pulling him back to her each time he attempted to move away, undo his buttons, remove her night rail, he was becoming increasingly frustrated as he attempted to undo the tie at her waist.

He was bumbling like some raw youth. He might not lump himself in a class with the famous Casanova, but damn it all to hell, he was competent! He hadn't bumbled in fifteen years.

Finally, as Chelsea nipped at his earlobe—where had she learned that!—Beau gave up, sat up and looked down at the last barrier to seeing this woman half-naked in the firelight.

"A *knot?* You tied this damnable thing in a *knot?* What *is* this?"

"A drapery cord," she told him, running her fingertips down his bare chest, setting off small fireworks in his groin. "I borrowed one of your aunt's night rails. It's the only way to keep it up. Oh, for pity's sake, Oliver, don't look at me like that. Just untie it."

He pushed determinedly away from her and sat up. Even using both hands, he couldn't seem to get the braided silk cord undone. That might be because his hands were none too steady—he'd have to think about that at another time, as well. Because he damn well wasn't going to tell Chelsea to stop running one curious finger along the inside of his waistband; he wasn't that much of an idiot. Besides, he was having trouble concentrating on the knot when the sight of the night rail ruched up and partially exposing Chelsea's bare thighs was diverting his attention.

"Honestly, Oliver, you'd think it was the Gordian Knot," she said as he continued to fumble. "Anyone would suppose that you were the virgin in the room."

"Stay there," he ordered, getting up from the bed.

"Where else would I go?" she asked as he stubbed his toe against the bootjack while searching his jacket for his knife. "Oh, for pity's sake, Oliver. You're not going to *cut* it off me, are you? What will I use to hold up the night rail?"

"Don't worry about it, because you're not going to be wearing nightclothes again in my lifetime," he told her as he neatly sliced through the silken cord before tossing the knife onto the floor.

Chelsea laughed as he moved to cover her with his body, figuring he needed to build her passion once more after leaving her. He should have worried instead that he might not be able to keep up with her, for she was already wriggling free of the night rail as if she undressed in front of men every day.

"You...you are a virgin," he half said, half questioned as he joined her again on the bed, unable to rip his gaze from the sight of her perfect breasts, her flat stomach, the seductive flare of her hips...and lower.

"And destined to remain one, I'm beginning to think," she told him, tugging at the buttons on his buckskins. "What have I done or said in these last days that would lead you to think I am at all shy or missish?

Really, Oliver, if you are to be condemned as a seducer of innocents and I'm going to be ruined for all time, don't you think we should at least enjoy it? I know my sister-in-law vows it is the most terrible of God's inventions, but my maid told me that's because Thomas probably doesn't do it right, and she herself can't think of anything she likes better, except perhaps marzipan."

He gently slapped her hands away from his buttons. "You mean this, don't you? You've cast aside shame, modesty, all of that—and you're seducing me? You're not frightened? Nervous? God, woman, at least a little apprehensive?"

"Oliver," she said, speaking slowly, as if to a backward child. "I am a practical woman. Until a few short days ago I was going to spend my life with a mean-eyed bastard by nature, with a wet mouth, grabbing, pinching hands and a mind probably crawling with maggots. But I like you for some reason, and your mouth is rather wonderful, and you're a bastard only by birth, having behaved as very nearly a knight in shining armor over these past days.

"Losing my virginity was a foregone conclusion. It has been waiting these past days, always wondering *when* it would happen that might make me, as you said, nervous, as I could tell whenever you looked at me you were wondering the same thing. And it needs to be done, Oliver, before Thomas catches up with us."

This time when he took her hand, he kept it, settling in beside her, face-to-face on the thin pillow. "It needs to be done," he repeated. "Don't I think we should enjoy it. Better than everything save marzipan, if done right. Oh, and *very nearly* heroic. Suddenly I'm feeling about as amorous as that tub over there."

"Really?"

He smiled, moved her hand back down to his buttons. "No, not really. But I probably should be. Luckily for you, men aren't made that way. We hardly ever ignore a beautiful woman lying naked in bed with us. So, if you're quite sure you're ready...?"

"Quite sure," she said, her voice only trembling a little, at last showing her nerves. "I've thought about it and thought about it. Thomas, the run to the border, everything. It's the only way, really."

"We do this, and there's no going back, Chelsea. Until now, even now, I could probably work something out with your brother, arrange to have you transferred into his custody somewhere. It isn't as if anyone has been running through London handing out broadsides alerting everyone that we've run off to Gretna Green. You could go back to London with no one the wiser, and perhaps he'll agree that you don't have to marry this Flotley fellow. But we do this? We do this, Chelsea, and there's no more going back."

"One, Thomas won't change his mind—he's fairly dotty over Francis Flotley and is convinced my soul needs saving, which it may well do, but I'll save it myself, thank you. Two, I would have put you in Thomas's sights again and you wouldn't have gotten your revenge out of the thing. And three, my hair is still rather damp and I'm starting to feel the chill. So if you're going to keep talking, and not *do* anything, then I think you should just tell me, rather than to try to wriggle your way out of...of *doing* this because I don't really attract you."

Beau put his hand on her stomach and began walking his fingers up to her breasts. "Where, in anything that I've said or done this evening, Chelsea, have I shown any indication that you don't *attract* me?"

"Well...I don't know. I suppose I was just saying that because I couldn't think of a good number three. Oh...I really do like that," she breathed as he lightly pinched her nipple between finger and thumb. "Should I really like that?" She swallowed visibly, her breath catching in her throat. "Yes, again. It makes me feel all...all I don't know what. My sister-in-law was always a goose..."

Any worries Beau might have had that his manhood had turned in for the night fled his mind as Chelsea began moving against the lumpy mattress, her body seemingly unable to keep still as he maneuvered his own body lower so that he could take her other nipple in his mouth, where he teased it with the tip of his tongue.

The damn woman all but began to purr. He'd expected a reluctant virgin, not a virgin reluctant to remain one. If she'd been experienced, he'd know what to do next, how to proceed. But she wasn't, and he didn't; he'd never bedded a virgin.

But then she raised her hips again, nature taking the reins from both of them in that ancient invitation neither of them could ignore, and he slid his hand back down over her belly and insinuated it between her thighs.

And found his own small private heaven on earth.

She was just reluctant enough, just interested and aroused enough. She held her legs tight together long enough for him to feel a surge of protectiveness, and then let him in, let him touch her, and he knew he was now feeling some primeval glory at having roused her to the point where the unthinkable became not only logical but desired.

She was going to be his. She was his. His for the taking. He would teach her, show her, pleasure her, tear away the fragile veil of her girlhood and introduce her to the pleasures of a woman, the pleasures he would give her. Him, and him alone.

She was so tight, so amateurishly eager, moving against his rubbing, stroking fingers as her hips rose and fell, as her breathing became quicker, more shallow. Her eyelids were squeezed tightly closed as if she was concentrating, learning each new pleasure, feeling as much as she could feel. And wanting more. She drew up her legs and pressed her heels against the mattress, her thighs wide and open and yearning.

For him.

She was ready. She wouldn't become more ready without toppling over the edge all alone. If she was going to fall, take that plunge, she wasn't going to do it alone. She would know that they fell together.

He had to do it now. Her pleasure would be his pleasure, and much as he longed to linger, learn her, watch her as passion overtook her, something told him he had to take her now, while the newness of what she was feeling overshadowed everything else.

Somehow, he managed to rid himself of his buckskins and levered himself up and onto her, hovering over her, suddenly unsure of himself yet again.

But he who hesitates is probably damned to fall back, regroup and start all over again...so he plunged into her, all at once, his breath catching as he met and conquered the resistance her body offered.

He didn't apologize for the pain but caught her small cry with his mouth, sealing them together everywhere, his bent arms on either side of her, holding himself away from her even as she reached up and clawed at his sides in an attempt to pull him down to her.

He pushed himself deep, ground their bodies together so that he knew he was touching her everywhere, that the small, hard bud of her desire would feel his every stroke. And then he began to move. Deep, deep inside her. Slowly at first, still trying to keep most of his weight off her, the bastard taking her virginity trying to play at the gentleman...and losing badly.

The ancient ropes holding the spindly four-poster together creaked and strained as Beau drove into her, again and again and again. Faster. Harder. Deeper. Until he felt her body nearly melt beneath his, then turn taut, grow still, as if waiting on the precipice for something it knew was finally within its grasp.

And then it happened. Dear God, it happened. Chelsea cried out, in wonderment—he was certain it was wonderment—and her body began to buck against his, clench around him, over and over and over, until his own release shattered any thought he'd ever had that he was master of his own body.

It was done. He had deflowered a virgin.

"I never want to do that again," he said, mostly for his own benefit, as he lay on top of Chelsea, trying to recapture his breath and possibly his sanity.

She didn't respond for a moment but finally asked quietly, "Excuse me?"

Beau immediately realized his mistake. "No, no," he said quickly, carefully rolling off her and then pulling her close against his side. "That's not what I meant. I meant, I never want to be anyone else's first—that is, I don't want to be the one to take anyone else's—oh, God. I remember a time when I thought myself at least halfway intelligent, and at times even passably articulate. Did I hurt you? That's what I meant, what I was trying to say."

She put her palm against his chest, her fingers splayed as she moved them through the mat of hair she'd commented on earlier. "Well, yes, I think you did. Hurt me, I mean. But not very much. I really don't remember. You have to marry me now, Oliver. I've well and truly seduced you."

He looked down at the top of her head, the mass of loose ringlets that bound him to her tighter than any stout rope. Was she about to cry? Such a thing wouldn't be unexpected, not in the circumstances. She'd been all bravado, even eager, just a few minutes ago. They'd both been.

But, now that it was over, now that they'd done what both of them knew needed to be done, he was caught between pleasure and his conscience, and she was— well, he didn't know what she was thinking. Probably that she wished he'd simply go away for a while and give her time to figure it out. After all, that had been a very large step she'd just taken. She couldn't go back, but that might only beg the question of where she would now be going.

Beau tried to recapture some of the way they'd been before this new intimacy, which might have, in reality, broadened any distance between them.

"Yes, you did, didn't you? It will be something to tell our grandchildren. I'll tell them all about their sweet gray-haired old grandmother sitting over there, her feet up on a stool, squinting over her knitting, and how she was once a wanton woman who chased me about until she caught me, dragged me into her bed and had her wicked way with me. Ouch!" he ended as she managed to take hold of a few short hairs on his chest and give them a sharp tug.

"We do get along well, don't we?" She sounded nervous. Why, after all of this, was she nervous? "My parents rather detested each other, which is completely expected in arranged marriages. But we shouldn't be too much trouble to each other."

"Says the woman who has me on the run to Gretna Green with her brother in hot pursuit, plotting my demise. Not that I mind," he added quickly, also quickly removing her hand from his chest. "Now come on, let's get you settled and sleeping, while I prepare for the rest of the night."

Seeming to have suffered a moment's modesty, belated as it was, Chelsea sat up, dragging the threadbare sheet over her body. "What are you going to be doing the rest of the night?"

"Why, that should be obvious. I'm going to stand guard over my lady while we must remain in this thieves' den, as would any knight in armor. Or, in my case, damp shirt. I want to leave here in a few hours, so it would hardly be worth my while to sleep. Do you... blast, how do I say this? Do you want to wash again?"

She nodded, avoiding his eyes. "Would you mind not watching?"

"No," he said quietly, wondering if she still hurt, if she'd bled at all. She probably had. She was probably also sore, now that she had time to notice. "No, I don't mind at all."

He busied himself dressing, pulling on his boots, and when he finally turned around again Chelsea was tucked into the bed, even the coverlet replaced. She was lying on her right side, with her back to him.

He pulled the wobbly wooden chair over so that it was facing the door, knowing he was taking up his vigil a little late, one of his pistols on his lap, the other on the floor beside him, his knife slipped into the top of his right boot.

A log broke in the fireplace, making the only noise in the room for the past quarter hour.

It was, he realized, the first awkward silence he and Chelsea had had between them.

He didn't think it would be the last.

CHAPTER ELEVEN

"YOU'RE LOST, aren't you?"

Chelsea sat primly and rather self-righteously on a fallen log, watching as Beau consulted his hand-drawn map for at least the fourth time. He'd look at it, look at their surroundings and frowningly consult the map again. Pace about the high, rolling meadow where they'd decided to rest the horses, and then look at the map once more. Possibly he thought it would change.

If he'd lifted his fine, aristocratic nose to sniff the air like a hound, she wouldn't have been the least surprised.

They'd had a pleasant morning, all things considered, and Chelsea considered the fact that she could even glance in his direction, let alone hold a conversation with him to be an achievement worthy of some sort of award for courage.

They had been, for wont of any other word to explain what had happened, *intimate* last night. Now, today, they were strangers, about as far apart as two people could be without one of them leaving the country. The world certainly was a funny place.

It hadn't precisely been a pleasant morning, especially

as they'd started out in the gray light of dawn, heading back, or so Beau had told her, to the Great North Road and Gateshead.

Which, he also had informed her, was approximately fifty miles below the Scottish border.

Which, she had then informed him, sounded as far away as the moon.

Which, alas, had probably been a nasty thing to say, because he'd gotten this sort of *pinched* look around his mouth, asked her if she felt uncomfortable in the saddle, and when she had begun to ask him why he'd ask that and then realized why he'd asked that, and lifted her chin and told him coldly that she was fully recovered, thank you very much, well, then they hadn't spoken again until now.

She had learned something else about this man she was going to marry. He was a worrier. That usually went hand-in-hand with having a conscience. He was a man who *cared,* who considered the consequences— sometimes after the fact, granted, but it was nice to know he hadn't just taken when she'd offered. What she'd all but thrown at his head, actually. Perhaps she was the one who should be endeavoring to develop a conscience. He was making her look rather shallow in comparison, for her conscience didn't seem to be bothering her at all this morning, except to occasionally inquire as to why it wasn't bothering her.

She supposed she should have complimented him last night. Said thank you, or something. Did a woman say thank you to the man who had just deflowered her—and wasn't *that* a silly term for the thing. She had nothing to compare last night to, but she was fairly certain that it had gone rather well. He'd seemed…satisfied.

For her part, she'd been shocked, surprised, confused, eager, hesitant, anxious and so many other things all at the same time that she wasn't quite sure what she felt. Except she'd like to try it again, so that she could sort out what exactly she'd felt most. For now, she'd think about it as *a good beginning*.

It also had been difficult. Afterward. She'd felt suddenly modest, which was the outside of stupid after what they'd just done. And she'd felt this insane urge to cuddle against him, spend the night sleeping in his arms. And that, she was certain, was not the way it was done. Her parents had kept their own separate apartments both at Brean and in London, as did Thomas and his wife, and Madelyn said she'd keep her own domicile entirely, if she could.

Only the lower classes slept in the same room, let alone the same bed, and that was simply because their dreary little dwellings did not lend themselves to separate bedchambers. Madelyn said that was why they should pity the poor.

Madelyn was a stupid cow. That wasn't a nice thing to think about one's own sister, but there it was. If Beau had one failing, it was in believing himself in love with her so many years ago. Chelsea sometimes thought she should tell him that he would be so much happier with her…at least once Thomas realized he couldn't actually shoot him or something.

But now they were lost, she was sure of it. And the woman who wouldn't point out the obvious to a man who is struggling to deny it, she was fairly certain, had yet to be born.

Beau finally stopped his pacing and sat down beside her on the log. "You know, my mother once said that you're not ever lost if you're happy where you are."

Chelsea's heart did this little skipping thing in her chest. "What a lovely sentiment. The question, Oliver, is—are you happy where you are?"

He turned his head to look at her, probably the first time he'd looked directly at her all morning. "Well, let's see. I could be clapped up in irons in a nameless dungeon somewhere. I wouldn't be happy there. Or captive on a galley sailing some far-off sea, rowing all day, my only scenery the back of the poor sot in front of me. I wouldn't be happy there, either."

He was so adorable when he was evading her questions. "You could be sitting in the tooth-drawers chair in a stall outside Covent Garden," Chelsea said, giving an involuntary shiver. "I know I wouldn't be happy there. Or you could be sitting on a hardback chair for nearly two hours, listening to one of Francis Flotley's sermons. I see those two as equally painful, by the way, for both thoughts make my teeth ache. But the question remains, Oliver—are you happy where you are? Right now."

He picked up her gloved hand and raised it to his mouth, kissing the skin between glove and cuff. "I am happy with my company," he told her with a small smile, and then he shook his head. "I can't believe we're lost. We should have met up with the Great North Road again by now, I'm sure of it. Instead, I have the terrible suspicion that we've been traveling in circles and will soon be back where we started."

Chelsea lightly rubbed the skin he had just kissed, rubbing the kiss in, not out, although she didn't know why she would do either. She'd had her hand kissed before, dozens of times. Often by supposed experts. But none of them had ever affected her in the least. Now her skin tingled, as did the rest of her. And his kiss had been an offhand gesture; he hadn't even been trying!

Perhaps there was some switch inside females. It just sat there in its secret place, biding its time until something like last night happened, and then it was switched on, like a mechanical toy. Off for girlhood, on for womanhood. Once on, it couldn't be turned off again, and she would spend the remainder of her life being kissed on the wrist and having her newly switched-on body whispering in her ear: *There's more, you know. Much more.*

And Beau had found that secret switch, turned it on and here she was, going round and round and round. Yes, she probably really should thank him...

"I'm very good with maps," she told him, knowing her mind had gone as far as it could go without her making a complete fool of herself. "Let me see yours." He hesitated, one eyebrow raised in that way men have of saying without words, *Oh, so now you're smarter than I am?*

Honestly, men were so thick sometimes. "Come on, Oliver, hand it over. I can't do any worse than you have."

He reached into his pocket and grudgingly handed the map over to her. "I'll have to explain it to you," he said as she unfolded it, her own eyebrows climbing high as she looked at the mass of lines and scribbles that might as easily have been drawn by a chicken with a length of charcoal tied to its little foot.

"No, no, I think I can understand it," she said, hoping she wasn't holding the dratted thing upside down. "Look, here's London. There's Blackthorn, yes?" She put a fingertip to the paper and traced the line leading North. "Ah, yes, and there's the Great North Road. And all the other towns and cities we passed by but I never saw. Highgate, Hatfield, Steven—goodness, Oliver, but your penmanship is atrocious—all right, Stevenage. Litchworth, Peterborough."

She lapsed into simply moving her lips as she counted up, up, up the winding depiction of the Great North Road and, she supposed, other lesser roadways. "Ah, and there's Gateshead. That's our next almost destination, isn't it? Another tiny inn somewhere outside Gateshead? And then there's Newcastle upon Tyne, Brunswick-upon-Tweed, and then—"

"Berwick."

"Pardon me?" she asked, looking up at him.

"That's Berwick-upon-Tweed," he told her. "You said Brunswick."

She squinted at the paper and then shrugged. "It was a guess, either way. I was trying to remember the names as you'd told them to me a few times. I can't really make out more than every other word you've scribbled here."

"Your pardon, ma'am. I was in a bit of a hurry at the time I drew it. Something about an irate brother momentarily breaking down my front door to shoot me or worse, and a young lady whose existence I'd barely remembered impatiently demanding I elope with her. Penmanship was not my main concern."

Chelsea nodded. "And you were three parts drunk," she added, since he seemed to have forgotten that part. "All that considered, I think you managed very well. Now, point to where you think we are, or at least where you thought we were when it began to rain."

He slipped one arm around her shoulder, and together they contemplated the crude map. "Here," he said at last. "At least I think so. I want to get to an inn outside Gateshead. You don't have to worry about anything more north than that, as Gretna Green lies much more to the west. See? The line going that way," he added, pointing to yet another wiggly, wavy line. "Custom does have it that many eloping couples rest in Gateshead, I'm told, before turning west and moving on to Scotland in one great rush."

"Well, that's above everything silly, isn't it? If everyone knows that, then everyone can just rush to Gateshead, set up camp and snatch up any runaways as they're idiotically enjoying a leisurely dinner in one of the hotels."

Beau laughed. "I hadn't thought of it that way, but I did think of something else, if your brother hasn't gotten this far yet. Being a bastard isn't always fun, but behaving like one from time to time does have its pleasures. Tell me again, how much trouble can your sister be?"

Chelsea thought about this for a few moments.

At last she thought she had a reasonable answer. "How much trouble do you suppose Hannibal had getting all of those elephants up and over the Alps?"

"A considerable amount, I'd imagine."

"Yes, I would, too. But if we were to compare Thomas's chore with Madelyn these past few days with Hannibal's, as to which of them had the most difficulty, I would say we'd have to rewrite all the history books to read that Hannibal and his pachyderms enjoyed a leisurely journey over a few low, rolling hills."

Beau laughed. "That sounds promising."

"Yes. Even with the fact that they were on the road a full day before we were, I would say that we are now probably ahead of them, heartless taskmaster that you are, or were, until you got us lost. Sorry. What are you planning to do once you're in Gateshead? Burn down all the hotels and inns?"

"Nothing that drastic, no." He stood up and held his hand out to her. She folded the map and handed it to him, then got to her feet. "Come on. We'll forget about the map for now. At least I know that we're heading north."

"Oh? And how do you know that? You can't be charting our way by the stars because it's daytime."

They walked back to where he'd tied up the horses. "I don't know how I know," he told her, shoving the map back into his pocket. "I just know that north is that way. I can feel it."

She looked where he was pointing. What was he feeling that she wasn't? "Really? How do you know that isn't west? It's gray and overcast, and we can't see the sun. So it could be west, yes? Or northwest, I suppose. Or southeast. How can you simply sniff the air and then point and be so odiously certain you're pointing north?"

"You're doing this on purpose, aren't you?"

"Probably. I have no idea which direction is north. But I will tell you that it's maddening to me that men seem to know which way is north, and which way is west—and are always overweeningly *proud* about that accomplishment, by the way—and yet still you all more than likely will manage to get us poor women lost."

"Are you referring to all men, or to your father and brother?"

"My father, brother *and* you," she corrected sweetly. She didn't care what they talked about. They were talking again. Teasing and joking and even arguing again. She'd take that above his concerned silence and be very happy with all of it. "Oh, and a certain male admirer who promised me a ride in Richmond Park up on his new curricle, but couldn't seem to find his way out of Mayfair. For a while, I despaired of ever seeing Portland Place again, as a matter of fact."

Beau smiled as he reached for her. "Come here," he said, putting his hands on her waist. "With some women, a man might think they were talking just to hear the sound of their own voices. But with you, I think it's so you can hear the sound of my voice. Am I right?"

She lowered her gaze to his boot tops. "You've been a veritable Sphinx for the past two hours," she said quietly. "At first I thought you were angry with me, but then I decided you were angry with yourself." She lifted her head and looked fully into his eyes. "Which you shouldn't be. Because I'm fine, Oliver. I really, really am."

He began lightly rubbing her back. "You don't complain about the hours in the saddle. You don't complain about the food, the damp beds or the weather. You just keep smiling and enjoying yourself and making the best out of every moment in a way that makes me variously doubt your sanity and envy you the way you look at the world. However, there are times I think you'd tell me you were fine if you had six arrows sticking out of your back."

She shook her head. "Oh, no. I'd be complaining most loudly if I had six arrows sticking out of my back." Then she grinned. "But not for long, I would imagine."

She was still smiling when he kissed her, and it was the most natural thing in the world to put her arms around him and kiss him back.

It was rather like coming home after a long time away, being in his arms again. Had it only been a few hours since they'd fallen into bed and he'd made love to her? It seemed like forever.

He ran his hands over her body as if on a journey of discovery, and she felt her body coming alive, hungry to feel that same rapture he'd introduced her to, this time without the fear of the unknown standing between them. Because now she knew. Now she wanted, instantly, and when she pushed her lower body against his it was clear he wanted her, too.

"Yoohoo! I say, you up there on the hill! Deuced sorry to interrupt and all of that. But— *Yoohoo!*"

Chelsea watched as Beau aimed what could only be described as a homicidal glare in the direction of the intruding voice.

"Yes, that's it, you! Sorry to be a bother! I say, good sir, could you lend some assistance to a fellow traveler?"

"I could shoot him, put him out of his misery," Beau suggested as they looked at the tall, thin young exquisite as he attempted to climb up the bank and into the rolling meadow in what appeared to be red-heeled evening shoes fit only for the dance floor. "What in bloody hell is he doing out here, dressed like that?"

Chelsea had been half turned away, buttoning the jacket of her riding habit, as Beau seemed to be an expert in undoing buttons while she was unaware of anything but his touch. She spared a mere half second wondering where he had gained his expertise but dismissed that thought as unworthy of her. After all, he was seven years her senior. He was bound to have bedded other women. Possibly scores of them. Not that he'd ever do it again, or there would be six arrows sticking out of *his* back. Goodness. It would appear that she was one of those dreadful jealous sorts. She hadn't known that.

But she'd have to examine that new knowledge later, for the man was still advancing toward them as rapidly as his mincing walk could manage.

Now she got her first really good look at their, quote, fellow traveler, and she understood Beau's question. The young man was dressed for a ball; satin knee breeches, clocked hose, those dreadful shoes and more lace at his throat and wrists than that which adorned her great-grandmother Enid's hideous heirloom tablecloth. He was so painfully young, and trying much too hard to appear sophisticated.

A further inspection revealed that there was what looked to be a high perch phaeton on the roadway below them. There appeared to be a young woman hanging on to the precarious seat for dear life because one of the wheels of the equipage was sunk deep in the mud thanks to a combination, Chelsea decided, of muddy roads from yesterday's rain and some cow-handed driving.

"There's a woman down there," she told Beau, pointing in the direction of the phaeton. "A young woman by the looks of her. Oliver! Do you suppose they're an eloping couple? Oh, they must be. Just like us. Do you know what that means, if it is?"

"Yes. It means, if that wheel is as stuck as I think it is, that I am about to become very angry."

"No, silly. Well, yes, you probably are going to do that, because I think we're honor-bound to help them. But what it really means is that we must be on the correct road, after all."

"Unless little mister dandy is as lost as we are," Beau pointed out dully. "And if I've no better sense of direction than that hair-for-wit looby heading for us, I may feel obliged to slit my own throat. Come on, let's mount up and meet him halfway. Otherwise, he'll break one of those damned heels and I'll end up carrying the twit."

Chelsea carefully, and probably wisely, hid her smile by turning her head and then felt herself being half lifted and half tossed up onto her sidesaddle before Beau mounted his horse and they walked them down the grassy hill to where the young gentleman had stopped and was now attempting to pick some small burrs off his stockings.

"Who the hell are you and what in blazes are you doing with that young woman?" Beau said without preamble.

"Oliver!" Chelsea exclaimed, not as shocked as she probably could have been by his bad manners. After all, anyone who thought to drive a high perch phaeton all the way to Scotland with a young lady sitting up beside him wasn't really deserving of courtesy. She wasn't sure what Beau deserved, having his runaway bride making the same journey on horseback, with only a small satchel of increasingly tired undergarments with her. But now probably was not the time to point that out to him.

"Kind sir," the young man said, taking off his chapeau—it had a feather in it!—and sweeping Beau and Chelsea an elegant leg—or at least as elegant as it could be, considering he was slipping on the wet grass. "Dear lady. Please allow me to present my sorry self to you both for your explanation and edification."

"I believe I can safely state that I won't be edified in the least," Beau said. "But do go on. I departed London early this season, before I could attend a farce."

The young man, who couldn't possibly even have reached his majority, blushed becomingly, which rather tugged at Chelsea's heartstrings. Why, she would imagine he had only just begun to shave.

"Sir," he said, standing up very straight now, as if in the presence of his schoolmaster. "I am Jona—that is to say, John…Smith. Of Leicestershire. The fair lady is under my protection."

"Your protection. That should be sufficient to terrify the creature," Beau said, looking toward the phaeton. "And her name is—no, wait. Let me save you the trouble. Her name is Mary. Shall we call her Mary Brown?"

"You mock me, sir," Mr. Smith accused, his fair cheeks growing ever more colorful. "Think what you wish of me, but the lady is sacrosanct. You will not malign her or else I shall demand satisfaction from you."

"Good God, man, I would never do that. Pity her, long to shake some sense into her, yes. But I will not malign her, as she probably believes herself in love with you, you arrogant young puppy. Have you really driven all the way from London in those clothes?"

This also probably was not the optimum moment to remind Beau of his own "arrogant young puppy" days, Chelsea decided. Or his own rather ill-judged sartorial choices back then. Although she felt fairly certain he

must have been having at least some small nigglings of
remembrance, which was probably all that was saving
young Mr. John Smith from a truly blistering scold by
the now older and wiser Oliver Le Beau Blackthorn.

"London? Why, I should say not! We fled a dashed
dull masquerade ball at my…that is to say, at a home
in…several miles distant from here." If at all possible,
he seemed to draw his slight frame up even higher, as if
he'd gone up on tiptoe. "I shan't hide what we're about,
as we know our minds. We are in love, just as you say,
and we are flying to Gretna Green ahead of our disapproving parents. You will not stop us!"

"Stop you? And why would I do that? Chelsea, why
don't you go see to Miss Brown while Mr. Smith and
I get to know each other a little better. With any luck,
she may be having second thoughts."

Chelsea brought her mare close beside his mount.
"Don't scold him," she whispered. "They're in love."

"They don't know what love is," Beau shot back.

"No, but neither do I. Do you?"

He turned his head to glare at her and probably to
say something extremely cutting, but then he stopped,
shook his head slightly and smiled. "You'd drive a man
to strong drink."

"I thought not. Thank you, Oliver," she said, happy
again, and then urged her mount forward, toward the
phaeton.

THE EARL OF BREAN paced the packed dirt of the inn
yard as the coach horses stamped in their traces, eager

to be on their way. He muttered under his breath, occasionally stopping to lift his head and peer toward the street, hopeful he would see his sister approaching with her maid.

He longed to see Madelyn now, but once this was over, he hoped never to lay eyes on her again in this lifetime. Francis was right. Women, all women, were one occasion of sin after the other.

It was as if they were traveling to Scotland while dragging an anchor behind the coach. She rose late, breakfasted leisurely in her room, found trumped-up excuses to stop in every village along the way and had indulged herself in a near fit of hysteria when he'd dared to suggest they continue on after dusk thanks to a full moon, swearing that highwaymen would accost them.

And she shopped. Wherever they stopped, Madelyn shopped. The coach boot was nearly overflowing now, and yet she was at it again. Ribbons, bolts of fabric, yards of lace, parasols. A round of cheese, cutlery, plates, a basket of fruit. Soaps, candles, bed linens—and two large trunks to store her purchases. A damned wooden rocking horse sporting real horse hair and painted all over in white with blue polka dots, meant as a birthday present to her son—and Thomas was surprised she even remembered the brat's name— was now strapped to the coach roof.

The woman would buy mud, if some enterprising shopkeeper were crafty enough to put it in a jar and charge for it.

In fact, the only thing she didn't purchase on any of

her stops was books. When the reverend offered to loan her one of his own books of sermons she informed him that she considered reading a waste of time—and reading anything the reverend wrote bordering on a criminal waste of time.

Thomas knew what she was doing. She'd invented those several hells she'd threatened him with, and she had done so with an evil genius he would have to admire if he were not the recipient of her craftiness.

She had set out to drive him round the bend because he'd insisted she accompany them all the way to Scotland, and with every day that passed, Thomas knew himself to be getting closer to the final turn.

She'd even had the nerve to explain that it mattered little if they arrived in Gretna Green in time to stop the marriage or only encountered Chelsea and Blackthorn once the deed was done. Blackthorn was a dead man either way, and an immediate marriage to Reverend Flotley would easily explain away any brat their sister might pop out nine months later.

Madelyn should have been born a man. She probably could have ruled kingdoms. Or goaded them into revolt.

In any event, Thomas had begun including her husband in his nightly prayers. Last night, he had prayed that the man somehow manage to grow a spine and take to beating her.

"There she is now, Thomas," Flotley said from his seat inside the coach. "Ah, she has bandboxes. Perhaps she bought you a gift. She must remember that today marks the anniversary of your birth."

"If she did, she bought it with my blunt."

"Perhaps if you stopped giving her money?" Flotley suggested. He'd been treading more carefully these past days, as the earl was becoming increasingly volatile, one moment praying, the next eyeing each inn's tap-room as if he'd very much like to enter it.

"She's bad enough as she is, Francis, and would only find new ways to torment me. Say a prayer, will you, that we reach Leeds before the sun drops below the ho-rizon. We should have been all the way to Gateshead by now, the coachman tells me. You won't be marrying a virgin at this rate, Francis. I'm sorry." The man didn't answer him. Thomas looked toward the coach window. "Francis?"

"She will be purged of her sin," the reverend said, the late morning sun in his eyes, so that they seemed to glitter.

"Yes," the earl said, looking away from that sudden and disturbing gleam. "Yes, of course. I...I think I forgot something inside. Please see that my sister's packages are secured and that she and her maid are settled in the coach. I won't be above a minute."

He was seeing new and rather disturbing sides to his spiritual mentor. Perhaps he could lay the blame at Madelyn's door. She had no use for the reverend or his teachings and had made that painfully clear almost hourly for the past few days. The further Thomas got from what he'd believed might be his deathbed, the more *some* of what she said made sense, what Chelsea had been saying made sense. These past two years had been the longest of his life, and he hadn't enjoyed them overmuch. Thinking about what he'd do to Beau Blackthorn didn't feel like sin. It felt good. He felt alive again.

He stepped inside the inn and entered the taproom.

After all, if God hadn't wanted man to drink ale, he wouldn't have created hops and barley...

CHAPTER TWELVE

HIS NAME WAS Jonathan Harwell, and he was the only son and heir of one Baron Robert Harwell, a tough old bird who'd buried two wives before getting lucky with a fortunately fertile third, a woman not quite half his age. Having borne him his heir, the third Lady Harwell absconded three years later with the head groom and most of the family jewelry and silver, and was now, according to rumor, living very comfortably on some island off the southern coast of America.

"Mary" was Emily Leticia Somerset, youngest and definitely dowerless daughter of the local squire, a lusty buffoon of a man who wore his riding boots to dinner, slept with his favorite hunting dogs sharing the bed with him and who was very definitely far beneath the lofty level of expectation the baron had for a mate for his son.

This and more, Beau reluctantly learned over the course of the next two hours.

Jonathan was nineteen, but just barely, as the ball they'd fled had been held in honor of his birthday, the high perch phaeton one of his birthday gifts, as a matter of fact, which might explain why he'd run it into a ditch, as he'd never before tooled the ribbons on anything more daring than his father's old curricle. Emily swore she was of a similar age, but Beau didn't believe she was a day over seventeen.

The Harwell heir's other present from his doting papa was a yearlong trip to the Continent, and he would be leaving England in the next week. Jonathan and Emily hadn't been pleased at the news and had immediately fled. They'd been on the road since midnight of the previous evening, their only clothing that which they stood up in, and had six pounds four pence between them.

They were confident that they would not have been missed until sometime this morning, so they had a lovely head start and were not really concerned about pursuit. Or clean underclothes, it would seem.

But they were in love. Determined to marry. Even though the baron and the squire were undoubtedly at this moment armed to the teeth, soused to the gills and riding hotfoot to put a stop to the nuptials.

Oliver Le Beau Blackthorn, sitting alone in the darkest corner of the small taproom at the wayside inn he'd been forced to stop at—or else, Chelsea had promised, she would not cease telling him he should until he either did or his ears fell off—stared into his mug of home-brewed beer and almost believed he could hear the squire's hounds baying as they picked up the scent of fleeing daughter.

If Puck were here, and thank the good Lord he was not, he'd be laughing so hard at his brother's new predicament that Beau felt sure he would have had to stuff his cravat down his throat.

"Well, I had no trouble tracking you down, did I? They're fine now," Chelsea said as she slipped into the chair across the table from him, looking entirely too self-satisfied for her own good, not that she probably cared. "Emily's had a bath and a good cry, and she's sound asleep. Jonathan is standing watch."

"Oh, good, I can relax now. The twit is standing watch. In my opinion, if Wellington had only had another twenty like him, we'd all be speaking French now," Beau grumbled and lifted the mug to his mouth, taking several long swallows that would probably do him as much good as the other two mugs he'd downed in the past two hours—which was none. "I've been sitting here, looking back over my life, contemplating my deeds and misdeeds and wondering precisely what it was I did to make the fates believe I deserve any of this."

"I'll ignore that, mostly because I have an answer for you that I'm convinced you wouldn't much care to hear," Chelsea said, shifting slightly in her seat. "I've paid one of the barmaids to brush the mud off your clothing as soon as it dries, and one of the ostlers has promised he knows all about cleaning boots and will tend to them tonight, so you don't have to worry about that."

"I've already mentally consigned my clothing and my boots to the rubbish. But I thank you for the effort. I'll be even more grateful if you were to remove from your mind any memory of the damned wheel becoming unstuck all at once, and my unfortunate fall into the puddle. Which, as I am learning the unfairness of the world all over again, meant that Jonathan, sitting up on the seat, is still ridiculously overdressed but pristine, and I am sitting here in a pair of trousers that itch unbearably and a shirt no respectable rag-and-bone man would attempt to sell in the bowels of Piccadilly. Where did you say you found these clothes?"

Chelsea lowered her chin and spoke softly.

"Excuse me? I'm afraid I didn't quite catch that."

"I said, I borrowed them from the innkeeper's wife. For ten pence. She wants them back."

"Oh, no, really? But I had so hoped to keep them." Beau leaned back against the chair, stretching his legs out beneath the table. "God. To think that only a few short days ago I was that happiest of men, a still fairly young, reasonably well-set-up, deep in the pocket and entirely unencumbered male. Now I've got an angry brother pursuing me, a pair of irate fathers hunting us, an almost wife and two nursery brats."

Chelsea laughed, clearly delighted. "Hardly children, Oliver. They're going to be married. And you forgot Madelyn and Francis Flotley."

"And the bloody hounds," he said and then sat up, reaching across the scarred tabletop to take her hand in his. "I'm sorry. I should be seeing the humor in this adventure, the way you do. Puck's right, I'm becoming old and stodgy."

"No," Chelsea said, resting her chin in her hand, "you're responsible. It's probably because you're the oldest brother. Thomas certainly keeps reminding me that he's the oldest and therefore responsible for me. And we can't just leave them to their own devices, Oliver, now can we?"

Beau realized that if he answered honestly, Chelsea would look at him as if he'd just announced he enjoyed pulling wings from butterflies. "No. No, of course not. For one, I don't think they possess any. We...we have a Christian duty. Something like that. We definitely can't leave them to their own, nonexistent devices. Why, they might take it into their heads to stand outside in a rain-storm with their mouths open, and drown."

"They're not sheep, Oliver," Chelsea said sternly. She leaned forward, both elbows now on the table, her eyes shining, her expression bordering on the beatific. "I have formulated a plan."

Beau, who had been in the process of washing down his most recent words with the last of the ale, was hard-pressed not to spray the air with the sudsy mouthful, although he didn't come off unscathed—it was fully a minute before he could stop coughing.

Through it all, even as he fished his handkerchief out of the roughly sewn pocket of his borrowed trousers, Chelsea looked at him through slitted eyelids. "You aren't all that amusing sometimes, Oliver."

He wiped at his eyes one last time and returned the handkerchief to his pocket. "I was choking. Many an affianced bride would have jumped up and pounded me hard on the back, you know."

"I thought about it," Chelsea said, folding her hands

on the tabletop, "but I didn't have a weapon. Do you want to hear my plan or not?"

"Do I figure in this plan in any way?" he asked, irrationally longing to kiss her.

"Well, yes, as a matter of fact, you do."

"In that case, I plan to listen very closely. Go on."

"Thank you. It's really very simple, and quite obvious. We take Jonathan and Emily with us to Gretna Green, to be sure they get there safely."

"Oh, God..."

"I'll ignore that, as well. They can neither of them travel as they are, of course, or riding up on that ridiculous perch phaeton—which Jonathan clearly does not know how to drive. So you will ride into Gateshead, Oliver, just as you planned, but after ascertaining that Thomas and Madelyn are not already there or have come and gone, you will hire a closed coach and the best team you can find, purchase some clothing for all of us if Puck has not yet caught up with us, as you said he would wait for us in Gateshead, and then return here. Also, I'd truly adore some *real* soap, if you can find any, please. At any rate, we've already outrun Thomas, or so you believe, and if we hide the phaeton somewhere here in the village, the pursuing parents will spend their time looking for it, never thinking the eloping pair is now an eloping quartet."

She sat back on her chair, looking much too satisfied. "Oh, and the same goes for Thomas and Madelyn. They also will not be inquiring about *two* couples traveling to Scotland."

"All right. It's better than I'd hoped for," Beau said, knowing he wasn't going to convince her to abandon the young couple.

She cocked her head to one side and looked at him inquiringly. "And what had you thought I was going to say?"

"Truthfully? I thought you might want to hand over our horses to them in exchange for the phaeton. I hadn't, by the way, thought at all of outfitting either of them. Are you certain you'll be all right here while I'm gone?"

"Jonathan's here," Chelsea said, just as if that meant something.

"Oh, good. How that soothes my mind."

"Now you're being facetious," Chelsea told him, following him out of the taproom. "Can't you simply pretend he is Puck and treat him accordingly?"

Beau turned in the small entryway and smiled at her. "You mean submerge his head in the horse trough until he came to his senses and took the girl home? Yes, I thought of it."

Chelsea stepped closer to him and took hold of his shirtfront, going up on tiptoe to whisper in his ear. "They've anticipated their vows, Oliver."

"They've *what?* Damn it to hell, Chelsea, where is he? I'm going to break that idiot's scrawny neck for him."

"No! Oliver, you can't do that. Emily spoke to me in confidence."

Wasn't that just like a woman. "Then why did you tell me?"

"I didn't want to, but I wasn't sure you'd be...amenable to helping them. It was, I believe it's called, my ace in the hole?"

Beau rubbed at his aching head. "Is the girl pregnant?"

"I don't know. I didn't ask how *often* they'd done their anticipating, for pity's sake! But clearly you can see that they must be married immediately. From the sounds of it, neither father is the sort who would take such news calmly."

"You know, Chelsea, you've just thoroughly put me in the middle of two families I do not know, protecting two people I'd never met until a few hours ago and liable to get my nose broken for my efforts. Wasn't having Thomas out for my liver enough for you? Perhaps while I'm gone you can take a stroll around the village, see if there are any waifs or stray dogs you might want me to put under my protection."

"I don't think so, no," she said, lifting her chin. It was still early days in their acquaintance, but he already knew this was not a good sign. "I'll be much too busy getting us settled for the night. Ordering a substantial dinner, and then arranging a room for you and Jonathan. Emily, naturally, will stay the night with me. It may be a little late for such things, but clearly those two need chaperones."

Beau wasn't often at a loss for words, but since the only ones he could find lining up to leave his mouth were not those fit for female ears, he had to satisfy himself by slamming the inn door on his way to the stable yard.

Ten minutes later he was on the road to Gateshead, wearing his still muddy boots, the ostler's wide-brimmed hat with the rip in its brim pulled down hard over his hair and ears, and riding one of the sorry nags kept at the inn for renting out to the desperate, which he considered to be a realistic definition of what he was at the moment.

But he could not afford to be recognized, neither he nor his horse, and since he doubted his own mother would give him a second glance in these execrable clothes if she were to pass him by on the street, he felt fairly safe as he headed for the first coaching inn the ostler had described to him.

Two hours later he was back at the inn, several paper-wrapped packages tied to the saddle, and feeling rather smug, actually.

Chelsea may have had a plan, but he could also plan, and he liked his much better.

And it was Chelsea who had given it to him, not that he'd tell her that. She certainly had given him the motivation he needed to come up with that plan. That much he might tell her at some point, preferably after they'd made love again.

Share his bed with the twit? Not in this lifetime, not when Chelsea was in the same inn, a wall away from him.

Damn but the town had been crowded with eloping couples, as well as those in the pursuit of errant sons and daughters. A person could hardly step more than ten paces in any direction without meeting up with either a stupidly grinning couple or an irate father with wild eyes and a pistol stuck in his ample waistband.

He felt fairly certain he'd spotted Emily's father, unless more than one pursuing parent traveled with a yapping pack of brown-and-white hounds, and had made sure to stay out of sight as he'd been joined on the flagway outside a small hotel by a man who'd looked depressingly like Jonathan, if the boy had another fifty or more years and five stone tacked onto him.

But no one had fit the description Beau had given to each of the innkeepers: portly, pink-faced gentleman with no lips, accompanied by a minister and a beautiful woman with nearly white-blond hair, huge melting blue eyes and the temperament of a snake. He also had described the crested coach he'd seen Thomas riding in about Mayfair, down to its yellow spoked wheels. He'd refrained from mentioning Flotley's always-wet mouth.

Beau dismounted, untied the packages and gave the horse a pat on its head before heading for the inn to find Chelsea and tell her what he'd done.

Not that he needed her approval. Craved her approval. He had made a decision, and that was that; she had no choice but to go along with him.

He hoped.

Because he'd had this niggling thought in the back of his mind from the moment he'd walked into his entrance hall and seen her for the first time in seven years.

That he'd been usurped as the, well, as the captain of his own ship, in charge of his own fate.

It might be that he'd been taken in by the thought of the perfect revenge on Thomas Mills-Beckman.

It might also be that he'd felt honor-bound to protect a clearly distraught young woman from a fate such as the Reverend Francis Flotley.

But, mostly, he was fairly certain, it was the way she called him Oliver. He would have cheerfully murdered anyone else who would dare such a thing, and yet each time she said his name something strange and unique happened inside of him.

She was bossy and unpredictable, a mix of intelligence and naiveté. Resilient, vulnerable, funny and determined. Curious, long-suffering, brave to the point of fearless.

She didn't know what love was, she'd told him as much. She'd dared him to say the same. He'd thought he had an answer for her, the one that had taken up residence in his brain as he'd been recovering from the whipping her brother had delivered to him that day, the same one his mother had quoted for him as a warning as she'd tended to his wounds, begging him not to die from his fever and his injuries: "Men have died from time to time, and worms have eaten them, but not for love."

He had vowed then, as he lay on his belly for a fortnight because he could not lie on his abused back, that he would not die for love, not then, not ever...because he would never love again.

But he did very much like the way Chelsea said *Oliver*.

CHAPTER THIRTEEN

As she wandered rather aimlessly through the rabbit warren maze of rooms that was The Baited Bear Inn, doing her best to avoid other people as she awaited Beau's return, Chelsea berated herself for being such an absolute fool.

She should have pressed Emily immediately on what she'd said, this business about she and Jonathan anticipating their vows. Even Madelyn hadn't been mean enough to tell her younger, motherless sister that kissing a man more than three times would give you babies. But that's what Emily believed, thanks to her older sisters, who all should be very ashamed of themselves, because it was partly because of them that their sister was on her way to Gretna Green in the first place.

Jonathan truly believed himself to be in love and had no interest in seeing the Continent. Emily, on the other hand, only had been flattered to have gained the attention of the baron's son when her older sisters had not and was now frightened spitless that she was about to become a mother while Jonathan was romancing pretty *mamzelles* in Paris.

Of course, now that Chelsea had corrected Emily's

misconception—Misconception! Ha!—Emily had locked herself in her room—hers and Chelsea's room—and refused to come out, or even to speak with Jonathan through the door. The innkeeper and his wife were both looking at Chelsea strangely and would soon be asking for answers, probably fearing an abduction was in progress.

What a fine mess.

Well, there was nothing else for it, she would have to tell Beau everything the very moment he returned from Gateshead. Then she'd have to tell him that she'd decided Emily and Jonathan must not continue on to Gretna Green with them, now that they knew the truth, but be turned over to their worried parents as soon as possible. Yet this very day, if they could.

She promised herself not to watch as the dratted man then danced a jig, or else she might be tempted to do him an injury.

Poor man. All things considered, she had certainly complicated his life.

It had all seemed so simple when she was formulating her plan in her bedchamber in Portland Place. Find the man, offer him his perfect revenge, ride to Scotland, marry and frustrate Thomas. She'd put much more thought into frustrating Thomas than she had the rest of it, most pointedly Beau, and what it would mean to be his wife.

But he was a good man. He was a gentleman and a gentle man, not to mention an extraordinarily patient one. She still believed she could have done a lot worse.

He, on the other hand, probably could have done considerably better, for now he was to be doubly an outcast, having absconded with the sister of an earl.

She wondered if he minded that part of it all that much. After all, he'd been accepted on at least the fringes of Society, thanks to his natural father's name, his considerable wealth and even his service with Wellington. He might never be invited to Almacks or be allowed within ten feet of his friends' sisters, but he'd long ago recovered from the hideous public humiliation Thomas had visited on him.

At least Chelsea thought so, for she'd seen his name in the daily newspapers on many occasions, as part of a party of gentlemen that traveled to Newmarket for the races or attended a boxing match at some country inn. She'd seen him from a distance as he'd ridden his horse through Hyde Park, and he'd certainly not been shunned.

So perhaps, once the gossip had taken its course, he would continue to be accepted by those who were his friends. It was she who would be given the cut direct when and if she dared to show her face in Bond Street or at some recital or the theater.

She still wasn't quite sure how she felt about that but was fairly certain it fell under the category of cutting off one's own nose to spite one's face—hurting herself in order to hurt Thomas. But she'd made her bed, and now she would lie in it.

"Quite literally," she said aloud, realizing she was blushing. There were a multitude of small, unimportant losses she could consider, but her experience of last night clearly made up for them. She couldn't do more than begin to imagine what losing her virginity would have been like with Francis Flotley, what it would be like to have his mouth on hers, his hands exploring her most intimate places, and just that small bit of imagining had threatened to make her nauseous.

With Beau, it had been…so many things. All of them unexpected, all of them fairly wonderful. She was so very grateful to him, for his gentleness, his kindness, his understanding and patience. Especially when she considered that she had been the aggressor.

She was not like Jonathan or Emily. She had little patience with the idea of being in love, unable to consider life apart from one another, always thinking about the other person, behaving stupidly, sighing deep sighs and all of that drivel. It was enough that she and Beau seemed reasonably compatible, and that alone was much more than most Society marriages could boast of, from her observation.

And then Chelsea, alone in an upstairs hallway, smiled. She really did like him, though. Very much.

"Your pardon, madam."

Chelsea roused her mind from its wanderings and looked rather blankly at the gentleman now standing in front of her, holding a large traveling bag. She was surprised to see that such a fashionably dressed man would be staying in such an out-of-the-way inn.

She nodded mutely and stepped aside, then watched as he entered the room next to the one assigned to Beau and Jonathan. She could hear voices through the thin walls, both of them masculine. Fellow travelers, she supposed, perhaps on the hunt for yet another eloping couple. They certainly were becoming more thick on the ground the closer they came to Scotland.

And then she gave the incident no further thought as she heard the door at the base of the stairs slam shut and hastened to see if Beau had returned.

He had.

"Oliver, you're back," she called out as she carefully descended the steep, narrow flight, pleased beyond measure to see him standing there, smiling up at her. Her heart gave a small flutter, and she had to hold herself back or else she would have sought his embrace or some such silly thing. She hadn't known she could be so pleased to see someone she had last seen only a few short hours ago. And didn't he look fine? The man would probably look wonderful clad in flour sacks. "I see you're carrying packages. Please tell me you found some soap that doesn't smell of lye."

"I did," he told her, holding up the string-tied packages. "Do I merit a reward?"

She tipped her head to one side and contemplated his smile. He looked awfully pleased with himself. "I suppose so. Put those packages in your chamber, where your clothing awaits you, clean and well-pressed—well, pressed, at least—and we'll walk outside. I have some very good news for you."

"News? Hmm, it seems I'll have to readjust my vision of a reward. I was rather hoping for a kiss."

"Oh, you were, were you?" she said as he brushed past her, bounding up the stairs two at a time, suddenly looking as young as Jonathan. But that was the most telling difference in the two eloping couples: Jonathan was a mere boy. Beau was a *man,* from the top of his blond head to the tip of his muddy boots. And she, as of last night, was no longer a girl, but a woman. "Hoping for a kiss? So was I," she added under her breath.

By the time he had changed and come back downstairs, Chelsea was standing outside in the late afternoon sun, thrilled to be sprung from the confines of the inn, which smelled of many things, but mostly of cabbage, which she detested.

"What the devil is going on upstairs?" he asked immediately, offering her his arm and heading them toward a path that led into the trees and probably to a spinney or some such thing. "The chit is crying, the twit is on his knees outside her door, begging, and another guest, damnably encroaching woman, stopped me to say that she thinks the constable should be called. I fobbed her off, saying it was a lover's quarrel and none of her concern. Am I right? Are our lovebirds having a spat? Please say yes. I believe I saw their fathers while I was in town. I could have them here in an hour if you just give me the word."

Chelsea stopped on the path. "You saw them? Really? Are you quite certain?"

Beau looked at her quizzically. "I can't say so with complete assurance, but the one had a pack of hounds on his heels and the other looked amazingly like our

Romeo, which, by the way, should have been enough to give our Juliet pause before she agreed to this adventure."

Chelsea told him then, slapping his arm only once when he laughed a little too long during part of the telling. "If you're correct, Beau, we could have them out of here by nightfall. I mean, not that I mind sharing my chamber with…that is, now that we know these two should be anything but wed, we could reunite them with their parents, assure them that nothing untoward happened because we were with them at all times. They'll thank us. Jonathan and Emily, I mean. Although probably not right now."

"They can thank us or curse us," Beau told her, turning to face her, his hands on her upper arms. "Go back to that first part, if you please, the part where you wouldn't be sharing your chamber with a hysterical Juliet. That's the part that interests me most, and figures most in my plan."

"Oliver," Chelsea said accusingly, lowering her chin, but then looked up at him through her lashes even as she felt her cheeks flaming. "Is that why you're so hot to be shed of them?"

"It's better the second time," he told her softly, rubbing her arms. "I mean, I've heard it said."

Chelsea had to concentrate on standing very still, for her body was reacting quite strangely, growing warm and tight between her thighs, her breasts tingling and aware. "You…you don't have to, you know. I'm already sufficiently ruined."

He took her hand and led her deeper into the trees, out of sight of the inn. "I loathe that expression. Ruined. Do you feel ruined, Chelsea?"

She shook her head, finding it difficult to find her voice. "No."

He stopped again, looked back in the direction of the inn and then gently maneuvered her backward until she felt the trunk of one of the large old trees at her back. "Then what do you feel?" he asked her, his voice soft, his expression anything but, as his eyes seemed to be searching her face for some sort of reaction to his question.

Her heart was suddenly pounding so hard she was amazed he couldn't hear it beating. What was he doing? What did he want to hear her say? Why wasn't she joking, pushing him away, telling him to stop teasing her with inappropriate questions? Why was her mouth suddenly so dry, her breathing so quick and shallow? "I...I don't know. I mean, it's difficult to...to put into words."

Beau leaned in close, his mouth just beside her ear, and whispered one word. Just one. "Try."

She closed her eyes, concentrated on what her body was trying to tell her. Felt a new shock of awareness as Beau moved closer, took advantage of the divided skirt of her riding habit and cupped her, pressing his hand against her, his strong fingers pushing upward with gentle yet firm pressure.

She should have been shocked.

She wasn't.

She should tell him to stop.

Had to remind herself that she should tell him to stop.

"Don't…" she said breathlessly as he nibbled on her earlobe, ran the tip of his tongue in small circles inside the lobe, softly blew on her now moist skin.

"Tell me," he whispered, just his voice sending delicious shivers down her spine. "I want to hear. What do you feel?"

"You…can't be serious. Not. Here. Not like—Oliver. Oliver? Oh…"

She couldn't help herself. She leaned back against the tree and spread her legs wider, inviting what she'd so unsuccessfully protested they couldn't do. Thank God the man didn't give up easily, at the first hurdle.

But had he no knowledge of logistics? They were outside, where they could be discovered at any moment. He was delighting her, yes, but she knew there could be so much more. Needed to be so much more.

"We're wearing too many clothes," she told him, not caring if she'd just damned herself as not only willing but eager.

He laughed softly against her ear. "I was just thinking the same thing. Come on," he said, abruptly taking her hand and leading her deeper into the trees, farther away from the path.

She laughed as he pulled her along, turning his head back to grin at her like a carefree, naughty boy. She didn't know how far they'd come when he finally stopped in the middle of a small, sunlit clearing and pulled her hard against his chest as he swooped down to capture her mouth.

Laughing, gasping for breath, holding each other, they dropped first to their knees, and then lay down fully in the soft, fragrant grasses, tumbling over and over as their hands became busy, greedy, as their mouths sought and tasted and bit and explored.

"Don't…don't rip it," Chelsea managed as he pushed down her chemise after opening the buttons of her riding habit. "I only have the one."

"I'll buy you a dozen," he promised as at last he was able to cup her bare breasts. "Two dozen—hundreds. Just so I can rip them off. Oh, God, Chelsea, you're so perfect…"

He kissed her again and again. Her eyes, her nose, her mouth…and then turned his attention to her breasts, stealing her breath as he roused her, causing small explosions deep in her belly that warned of delights still to come.

He kissed her belly, even as his hands worked to rid her of her riding skirt, even as she raised her hips to assist him, even as she struggled with the maddening buttons of his buckskins.

Laugher died, words evaporated into the air, until there was just their mingled breathing. Quick, shallow, fraught with tension, frustration, small advances, minor successes that at last became long sighs of release as the last scraps of clothing that had impeded their growing passion were dispensed with, cast aside.

Chelsea lay on her back, looking up at him as he

levered himself over her, his hand busy between her legs, his expression so intense she could only wonder what he was thinking. He was doing things to her she would not have been able to imagine even a single day earlier, and she was not only allowing him but encouraging him.

She watched his eyes, how they seemed to darken as he slid one finger inside her, lightly brushed the pad of his thumb across the small, tight bud that seemed to pulse with a life of its own.

She hadn't known, had never known. Would never have known, she was certain, if not for him. He was showing her who she was, what she was meant for, born for.

She'd known the basic premise of the thing; she wasn't some innocent fool. The man pushed himself inside the woman, planted the seed and the woman nurtured it until the child was born. But that was mechanics. This was…this was *everything*.

She raised her hips to him, her gaze intent on his reactions, her own response intensified because he seemed pleased with her.

The sunlight slanted down through the trees, shining on his blond head, warming both their bodies. The grasses were soft, fragrant as the weight of their bodies released the sweet scent of the small purple flowers that grew between the grasses.

She saw it all. She saw none of it. Because there was really only Beau.

And what he was doing to her.

With her.

The heat inside her grew and then redoubled. His fingers moved in ways that satisfied, yet kept her yearning for more. She knew there was more; her body was crying out for more. More.

She closed her eyes, giving herself up to sensation. "So good...so good..."

"Do you want me now, sweetings?" he asked her softly, slipping two fingers up and into her, advancing and retreating, hinting at what was to come if she said yes.

There was no shame. No shame. She could tell him anything, he could do anything. In the darkness of a bedchamber. Here, in the sunlight. Anywhere. She would take all that he could give, give all that he asked of her. "I do. Yes. Please..."

"Not yet. There's more I can give you...more I want to give. Will you let me? Do you trust me?"

She opened her eyes, looked up into his face. Saw the passion there, and perhaps something more. She didn't know what he wanted, but it didn't matter. Not when he looked at her that way, as if she were somehow precious to him. As if what they were doing, feeling, was completely separate from what they, either of them, had imagined even a few short minutes ago. More than just their bodies, the pleasure of the act. Some nebulous thing that had sprung up, unexpected.

Something much more glorious than mere pleasure. And yet, somehow frightening. If she said yes, would she be simply giving him her body, or would she be giving something she could never take back?

She searched his eyes. She lifted a hand to touch his cheek.

She nodded her head.

He kissed her then, a long, slow, sweet kiss that brought quick tears to her eyes. She held him, felt the warmth of the sun on his bare back, rubbing her palms up and down the sleek length of him, shocked to feel the hard ridges of old scars. *Thomas,* she thought, a white hot anger slicing straight into her heart.

Chelsea pulled Beau closer, almost as if she could take his ancient pain from him, erase the humiliation, all the hurt, inside and out, he'd had to deal with for so many years. Her vehemence shocked her, but she believed what she thought with all of her heart: *If Thomas dares to touch him again, I will kill him with my bare hands.*

Beau continued to kiss her, take her mind away from all thought as he moved his mouth along her body, stopping here and there, to linger, to touch, to taste. She welcomed each new intimacy, marveled in the feeling that he was worshipping her body…and perhaps her, as well.

Something wonderful was happening. New and strange, and yet utterly reasonable. Of course he would kiss her there…and there. Touch her there.

She melted beneath him, became pliant, quite nearly boneless, allowing him to shape her, mold her, lift her.

Put his mouth on her.

She held her breath for the longest time, not realizing what she was doing until her lungs cried out for air. Feeling...feeling. All but weeping with wonderment.

"Oliver."

He took her over the edge...

"Much as I appreciate a day without that coach, Thomas, and although the shops look promising, why won't you tell me why we are staying another day in Leeds?"

"Madelyn, I did tell you. We have had a problem with the coach. That's all you need to know." If he told her more, she'd laugh, he knew she'd laugh. Damn Beau Blackthorn, he had to have been behind this!

"Oh, really? Then I suppose I shouldn't ask where you're taking yourself off for then?"

The earl looked at his sister, feeling a kindness for her he didn't know he possessed. She was beyond salvation, yet for the most part seemed to be happy in her own way. The same, he supposed, could be said for Chelsea. They really weren't all that terrible. His parents could have had two more sons, and he'd now be paying out his blunt to educate them, send them on Grand Tours, save them from the moneylenders when they gambled too deep. He would know that they'd be rejoicing that his wife had yet to provide him with an heir, while hoping he might conveniently break his neck while taking a fence with his horse, clearing the way for the second son. He'd spent enough years watching his father, eager to wear that dead man's boots.

So, all in all, that they were girls wasn't that terrible in itself. He didn't *hate* them. He didn't hate *all* women, as Francis seemed to do. A pious hatred, often backed by scripture, but hatred all the same. The man was beginning to make him nervous.

Thomas hated Beau Blackthorn and had for a very long time. He hated him because he had just lain there that day, silently taking the whipping Thomas had handed out to him, not begging nor pleading, and then gotten up and walked away. *Walked away!* Walked with his head held high along the streets of Mayfair, causing more than one man—including Thomas's own father—to say that one had to wonder who was the gentleman; the one wielding the horsewhip while assisted by two footmen, or the one who had borne the brunt of the assault.

Francis said it was a sin to hate Blackthorn. Thomas wondered about that. But at times it seemed that his unwillingness to say he was sorry for what he'd done that day...and the rest...was keeping him from the salvation he had been seeking. But if that was true, why had God only sent Francis to tell him so? As Madelyn had pointed out, if it was that important, why hadn't the good Lord come to him directly?

And why the rest of it? No women, no drink, no amusements? Didn't the Lord want him happy? Look at Madelyn. A sinner, yes. But, in her own way, happy.

I didn't want to die. I'd just come into the earldom, and I didn't want to die. God should understand promises made under such duress. I was sick, I wasn't thinking clearly. If I hadn't met Francis, what would my life be like now? What would all our lives be like now? Did I force Chelsea into this elopement with Blackthorn? Is this all my fault? Is this God's judgment?

"Thomas! Stop staring at me like that. You look uncomfortably like a fish. It was a simple question—where will you be all day?"

"Does it matter?" he asked, reaching into his pocket and pulling out a purse. "How much do you want?"

"Why, Thomas, you make it so easy. Are you sickening for something? Never mind." She reached out and took the entire purse and then quickly made for the front door of the inn, her maid scurrying after her, attempting to open a parasol.

Thomas turned and entered the taproom. Ale had been a good beginning, but the innkeeper had promised he had a few fine bottles of burgundy his lordship might enjoy…

CHAPTER FOURTEEN

BEAU SAT in the taproom of The Baited Bear with the young Romeo, having arranged with the innkeeper to keep the boy well supplied with home-brewed beer.

Jonathan had been a reluctant drinking partner at first, insisting that he would stand outside Emily's bed-chamber door until his bones dried up and turned to ashes unless she agreed to speak with him. She was his love, his life. He was nothing without her.

But he was beginning to show signs of changing his mind.

"So there are the customary streetwalkers, you're saying, to be avoided at all costs, and then the courte-sans—above my touch, those, yes? It is the *lorettes* I am to be safest with, since they're clean, but not so de-manding? How much would you say it would cost to set up one of these ladies for a week or two?"

Beau shrugged his shoulders as if the question was of no importance. "It's Paris, Jonathan. Nothing is cheap, but everything is for sale. Now, in Brussels there's a bit more government involvement, so you need to be care-ful there, and in Berlin? Ah, Berlin. And even better— Italy. Schooling is one thing, my new friend, but there's many a London gentleman who owes the women of the Continent for their most useful education. But you don't need to hear all of this. After all, you'll be here, with your Emily, all safe and married."

"Hmm?" Jonathan seemed to shake himself out of some private reverie. "Oh! Oh, yes, I'm going. I mean, no, no I'm not going. Dashed dull things, Grand Tours. Fine enough in m'father's day, but I've no time for it. O'course my friend Bertie, he says he's going, too, but he's still a boy, you know, green as grass, and he'd probably need to know about such things. So perhaps you should tell me more about—Italy, you said? Bertie talked about Greece. All these statues without heads or arms. Seems silly, and dashed dull. But if you've been, then you'd know. What are the women like in Greece? They do have arms, right?"

"We can talk more about that later. For now, Jonathan, you've a young lady upstairs," Beau said, sensing that the boy's head would soon be making a close acquaintance with the tabletop, so he'd better strike while he could. "What are we to do about the fair Emily?"

"Doesn't want me," the boy said, instantly maudlin, reaching again for his mug. But maudlin didn't last. "Made that plain enough, didn't she? You know," he went on, pointing a rather unsteady finger in Beau's direction, "I may have been a little hasty there. Seemed a fine notion at the time. Runnin' off, racing for the border, papas in hot pursuit. Dashed roman...romanan- ant...dashed jolly good fun."

"Alas, some ideas are more appealing in theory than

in practice. Women are like that, more often than not," Beau agreed. "Damn, man, I hate seeing a fellow gentleman pushed against the wall by a conniving female. Man to man, women can turn a man inside out and then ask *why* we're inside out—they can't help themselves, I suppose. Perhaps I can help you."

Jonathan's chin, which was in the process of searching out the tabletop, lifted. "You could? You could get me shed of her? I mean, not that I want to be, you know. Shed of her. I think. Cries all the time. Makes nasty remarks about how I handle the ribbons—as if she knows better? But now here I am, stuck with her. Got to do the honor-ara...honororit...got to do the right thing."

"Yes, you dug yourself quite the hole, old boy. Still, you've been with Mrs. Claridge and myself the whole time—or near enough so as not to matter. We both will vouch for the fact that you and Emily were never alone."

Jonathan was now looking so eager for rescue it was almost embarrassing to watch. "You'd do that? That would go a long way with the squire. Hunts, you know. Never shoots anything, not once that I ever heard of, but he could get lucky. I'm a lot larger than a hare."

And with a slightly larger brain. But only slightly, Beau thought. He pulled his watch from his pocket and made a business out of opening it, consulting it. "Why, it's no more than seven o'clock. What a full day we've had, hmm? Did I tell you, Jonathan—I may have seen your respective sires while I was in Gateshead earlier. How about this? How about I go to them, explain everything and bring them back here? Emily could be on her way home, which it would seem would make her happy, and you could be on your way to Paris, and the *lorettes*. With the war at last over, the Continent is crawling with fine young gentlemen like yourself. Ah, the memories, they will last you a lifetime. I envy you the adventure."

"I do, too," Jonathan said solemnly. "M'father's a good man," he then went on more brightly. "He knows what's best for me. Yes, I'll do it. I owe it to him to go. Don't I?"

"Absolutely," Beau said, getting to his feet. "You owe it to somebody." Then he left the now slumbering Lothario at the table and headed off to find Chelsea, to give her the good news.

He found her in his assigned bedchamber, curled up on the window seat, politely gnawing on a chicken leg. It was all he could do not to take her in his arms and carry her over to the bed. Worse, he could tell she knew that. He was fast losing control of any part of his life. She looked toward him hopefully.

"He's agreed," he said shortly, reaching for his hat.

"He has? Oh, Oliver, how wonderful. How did you manage it?"

This could be tricky. He wasn't sure she'd appreciate his tactics. "I described some of the glories he would see on the Grand Tour."

"Well, of course. That was good thinking. The churches in Paris, the Colosseum in Rome, the remnants of the ancient Greek civilization. It's one thing to visit our museums, or look at drawings in books, but to see such things in their natural settings? Who could resist such grand enticements? Will he be traveling to Egypt, do you suppose?"

Beau kept his expression neutral but not without effort. "I don't know. Happily, the glories I did describe seemed to suffice. Um…will you be all right until I return?"

She rolled her eyes. "I won't go wandering off, I promise. I would have stayed in here this afternoon, if you had but left the key with Jonathan. But how was I to know Emily wouldn't allow me in my own chamber?"

"I understand your dilemma, but I don't like that you were moving about the inn all day, unaccompanied." He had become very protective of her, he realized.

"And met next to nobody," she assured him. "It's a funny little inn, isn't it? So cut up, with so many twists and turns inside it? And I do believe that either the innkeeper was lying to you, Oliver, or all of our fellow travelers have slept the day away save for that nosy woman who wanted to call in the constable to help Emily, but she and her three daughters already departed. I'll be fine." Then she smiled. "But you could hurry back."

He hadn't the heart to tell her he'd decided that the nosy woman was a madam, and her daughters the prostitutes in her charge, or that they'd left now because they'd serviced the needs of the inn guests and were on to their next stop. It was clearly time to ferret out a higher class of inns.

"Minx," he said, dropping a kiss on her forehead and

feeling rather content. Almost self-satisfied. He was a lucky man. "For all I know, Puck may have arrived in my absence. I left messages for a *Monsieur* Robin Goodfellow at every establishment in the town."

"Your brother? So you really think he could have caught up with us by now?" Chelsea uncurled herself from the window seat and stood up, her expression delightfully eager. "With our trunks? With *clean clothing?*"

"Thanks to the rain and our extra night on the road, yes, it's possible. Now, aren't you going to ask more about your siblings? By rights, they should have been and gone, possibly even already awaiting us at the border. Perhaps something unfortunate happened to them."

"Nothing really unfortunate ever happens to Thomas." But then she smiled and added, "Unfortunately. Although I doubt he is very happy with Madelyn's company. And you can't be sure they would stop for a night in Gateshead, can you?"

"No," Beau admitted. "It's just that most do. As I told you, resting before the last mad dash. Hiring fresh teams. After all, there are only a few more logical stops between Gateshead and the border. Your brother is going to have some trouble there, by the way, especially if Puck is going to be able to get ahead of him. I took care of Gateshead."

"You took care of what? What is Puck going to do?"

Beau smiled in spite of himself. It had been a costly idea, but he still considered it to border on the brilliant.

"I told you I had a plan. While I was checking in at all the hotels and inns, I also stopped at every coaching stable and hired all their teams for the next three days' time. Puck will do likewise from Gateshead on west as he travels to Gretna Green. There will be many a pursuing parent who will find himself stymied until his own team can be rested and he can move on. We may have put a halt to one runaway marriage, Chelsea, but we are probably aiding a dozen more."

Chelsea's mouth opened and closed several times before a rather evil light began to dance in her wonderfully spectacular eyes. "Why, Oliver, that's quite mean. You're brilliant!"

"I rather thought so, yes. I believe you may be marrying a man with a devious mind."

She shrugged her shoulders dismissingly. "Then we are very suited on that front, I suppose. Shouldn't you be leaving? I told Emily you were going to fetch her papa to her and she's turned back into a watering pot, although she assures me that now her tears are happy tears. Whatever they are, I'm afraid I have little patience with them. That's another reason I'm sure to stay right here until you return with the anxious papas."

"At which point you will join us and assure them that Emily has been properly chaperoned at all times?"

She gave an audible sniff. "That would be protesting too much, Oliver, and only invite questions as to who *we* are. No. I've given it quite a lot of thought, and I believe I have found a better way. I have a plan."

Beau scratched at a spot behind his left ear. "And am I going to like it?"

Now she smiled, and he realized that he had once again lost control of the situation. He was doing that a lot with Chelsea. Soon she'd have him entirely tamed, sitting at her feet, purring in the hope of a pat on the head, a treat. How low he had sunk in just a few short days; even his own brothers would probably not recognize him. Surprisingly, this did not seem to bother him.

"That doesn't signify, Oliver, as you don't have to like it. I do."

Well and duly chastised, and not minding that so much, either, Beau gave her a jaunty salute and left the room, sticking his head back in two seconds later to point out that she had yet to lock the door.

She stuck out her tongue at him.

He went off to the stables, wondering how long it might take to wipe the smile from his face.

Chelsea was very much aware that Beau was standing close beside her as they faced the baron and the squire in the nearly empty taproom—the small inn did not stretch to private dining parlors. He had her back, that's what his presence told her, even though he did not know what she had planned. There wasn't a moment that passed that she didn't like him more and more.

What they'd done last night, what they'd done just today—that was separate. That was…fortunate. It was more important to her that she liked him, and that he seemed to like her. After all, they could be married for decades, and people did have to converse with each other from time to time, even if for the most part they maintained separate lives.

If he were coarse in his language, or chewed his food with his mouth open—as her brother was prone to do—she could not abide being in the same room with him for above a minute, no matter how lovely their moments in bed. If he looked at her as if the sight of her gave him dark, lascivious thoughts, or was devoid of humor—both of which described Francis Flotley—she might one day be forced to do as Jonathan's mother had done and take a flit.

But she and Beau rubbed along so well together. It was almost uncanny. She would have thought, had thought, that all they would really have in common was a mutual dislike for Thomas.

Beau put his hand on her back and gave her waist a small pinch, as if he'd noticed that her mind had been wandering as the squire, his face florid and quite unlovely, had been claiming that he wanted "satisfaction from that reprobate upstart who'd ruined his daughter."

Yes, she supposed she'd let the man rant long enough. Now it was her turn.

"You demand?" she said, pulling herself up to her full height. She was, after all, the daughter of an earl, even if these two fools weren't to know that. They only had to know that she knew how to intimidate; she'd learned at the feet of masters of that particular art. She'd seen her mother reduce the Brean Major Domo to tears with only a look and a few choice words. "You *demand?*

And who are you to dare to presume any such thing, sirrah!"

The squire screwed up his apple-red face and leaned his head forward, as if he could not quite believe what his ears had just delivered to his brain. "How...how *dare* I? Me?"

"Yes, you," Chelsea told him flatly. "You, who allowed your motherless child to be teased and bullied by her sisters, and did nothing. You, who allowed them license to *lie* to her, make her believe that a few curious kisses meant she could even now be carrying that boy's child. Have you no idea what goes on beneath your own roof? You're not a fit parent, sir. You're not fit to keep those fine hounds over there. You are, in fact, a disgrace."

Beside him, the baron sniggered. Clearly, just as Chelsea had thought, there was little love lost between these two men; one not wanting his son to marry beneath him, the other seeing his expectations for an advantageous marriage being crushed in the dust. Why, the squire was probably only coming along on this journey in order to be assured his daughter had made it over the threshold. All the rest was simply bluster.

Chelsea immediately turned to the baron, secretly rejoicing that the man seemed to shrink slightly as she leveled her stare at him. "And *you*. Oh, I've heard all about you, sir. Shame on you!"

"Me?" The baron looked so guilty the hangman would have had no second thoughts about dropping the noose over his neck...even though Chelsea had no idea what the fellow could be guilty of. She had decided that all men have something for which they should feel guilty, and she relaxed when the baron proved her right.

"You owe those two desperately unhappy children an apology, both of you. That they would dare such a disastrous marriage only proves how miserable you have managed to make them both. And yet, although blameless, there they are upstairs, cowering in fear, terrified of what you will do to them. They aren't marrying for love. No, no—they are marrying to escape untenable situations. And whose fault is that? I think we know the answer. The two of you storming in here like wild beasts? And so I say again, shame on you! Unfeeling monsters, the pair of you."

The squire broke first. "What? My little Emmy— afraid of me? Never say something so cruel, madam! I have been both mother and father to that girl from the day she was born."

The baron, not to be judged the inferior parent, pounded his fist against his chest. "That's my boy upstairs, my heir. I would cut out my own eyes before I'd harm a hair on his head, God's truth, madam!"

"I doubt you'd have to go that far," Beau said, stepping in front of Chelsea. "I think we're satisfied now. Although an apology to Mrs. Claridge here might be in order, if there is still any question that your children have been safe as houses with us. My wife, as you see, is a formidable woman, and of the highest character. She is very much set against elopements. Tawdry things, she calls them. Don't you, dearest?"

She was very good. She didn't laugh. Or surreptitiously kick him.

She was, however, forced to bite the insides of her cheeks as she extended her hand, allowing both men the honor of bending over it in turn. Then she held her breath until Beau directed them to the two upstairs chambers where their children waited for them, fearing the worst, before she sat herself down all at once and laughed until tears came to her eyes.

Beau leaned himself against the tabletop, chuckling softly. "And that, *my good woman,* was as good as a play. 'I've heard all about you, sir.' What the devil did that mean?"

She took the handkerchief he'd offered and dabbed at her moist eyes. "I haven't the faintest notion. But you will admit it worked."

He laughed again. "I'll have to remember that, and never apologize until you tell me what I'm apologizing for. I might even be innocent."

"Were you ever innocent, Oliver?" she asked him as he held out his hand and helped her to her feet.

"I seriously doubt it, no." He lifted her hand and turned it, kissing her palm. "You were brilliant. They came in here angry and demanding and left thoroughly chastened, their tails between their legs, and off on their way to apologize to their errant children. A lesser man might think you a witch."

"Oh? And you are not a lesser man? What kind of man are you, then?"

"Any sort of man you want to term me, as long as the

twit departs and you are my bed partner for this night and every night until we reach Gretna Green," he told her, causing a blush to steal into her cheeks. The man would appear to be insatiable.

Wasn't that nice.

Chelsea put her hand to her mouth and feigned a yawn. "But it is nearly ten, Oliver. I believe I may be sleepy."

"You wouldn't dare," he said, reaching for her, his grin adorably wicked.

They were interrupted by the sound of many feet trampling down the stairs outside the taproom. Beau took her hand and led her to the doorway, to watch as first the baron and his moaning, worse-for-drink, green-complexioned son departed the inn with alacrity, followed hard by a finally dry-eyed Emily and her red-faced papa…with a half-dozen brown-and-white, tongue-lolling hounds tumbling down the stairs behind them.

Beau slipped his arm around her waist. "I shall treasure that sight until my dying day," he said fervently.

She leaned her head against his shoulder. "Perhaps we can have it preserved in oils and hung above the mantel. *The Elopement, Undone, With Hounds*."

"And Puck missed it. He'll be crushed when I tell him. He'd suggested we just leave the two of them on the side of the road—heartless, my brother is, it would appear. But I'm certain the things I brought back with me are in our rooms by now, along with the tubs I ordered for both of us. And did I tell you that Puck made a flying visit to Bond Street before heading north, and selected a few pieces for you? He assures me he is extraordinarily adept at choosing feminine garments, having kept sufficient mistresses in Paris this past year to have become expert."

Chelsea instantly straightened, giving a small cry of genuine delight. "Puck is in Gateshead? And you waited until now to tell me?"

"Puck will arrive here with the coach tomorrow morning, but we'll be gone by then, as I think we need to stay with our original plan and go all the way to Scotland on horseback. The last thing we want is to run into your siblings this close to our goal. Puck will pick up anything we can't bundle and carry with us, so choose what you like best, and leave the rest. And yes, I probably should have told you straightaway. However, in my defense, as you're still glaring at me, I'd just spent the better part of an hour attempting to keep those two great oafs from killing each other. One for the marriage, the other against. But you knew that, as well, didn't you?"

"I thought it a reasonable assumption, yes. Even in our marriage, one could say that one of us gains more by the union than the other."

His eyes clouded for a second. "Me. All the benefits come to me."

She looked at him, her smile starting small but then growing, even as her heart swelled inside her. "Why, Oliver, thank you. That wasn't going to be my answer at all."

And then, while she was watching his jaw drop, she

turned, picked up her hated red skirts and raced upstairs to her chamber, her bath, her soap and her lovely new clothes. With everything else that was going on, she believed herself terribly shallow, to be so nearly over-joyed with the prospect of new clothing. But she wasn't ashamed at all. She only hoped nothing she found was red.

CHAPTER FIFTEEN

IT WAS A SHAMEFUL thing, but she nearly fell asleep in the tub. She hadn't realized how long the day had been, and how much drama and emotion had been laced through it, from the early-morning departure from the inn, to the discovery of Jonathan and Emily along the road, to the heart-shakingly intense interlude with Beau in the woods, to the confrontation with the squire and the baron.

She'd lived more today, she believed, than in any ten years she would experience in her lifetime.

Inspecting the contents of the small portmanteau served to revive her quite a bit, and she sighed regretfully as she replaced the lovely silk shift and dressing gown, blushing only a little at the thought Puck had chosen it for her, and instead dressed in her new midnight-blue riding habit for the walk down the hallway to Beau's chamber.

Emily had made a mess of the bed in this chamber, variously napping on or crying in it all the day long, so it seemed more than reasonable that Chelsea go to Beau, rather than the other way round. Tomorrow evening she would wear the dressing gown for him because that, she'd promised herself, would fit in her small traveling bag if she had to shove it in with her foot!

She tied back her still damp hair with a black riband, stepped into the hallway, locked the door and pocketed the key before turning down the twisting corridor in the direction of Beau's chamber.

And then she stepped quickly into a dark corner as she heard voices and approaching footsteps.

"Who do we ask for at The Crown?"

"The Spaniard. You remember me telling you his name. Don Pedro Messina. He speaks for the French."

"To speak is one thing. To do is another. You said he swore he'd have the money tonight? And why so damned late?"

"Because you didn't arrive until this afternoon, remember? I didn't know when you'd get here, so I said tonight. Did you find it yet? Damned thing to leave behind. Go back and check in the room."

Chelsea recognized the first man's voice; he was the same man she'd encountered earlier in this very hallway. It would seem they had some late-night business to attend to. The man whose voice she recognized did not seem overjoyed at the prospect.

She peeked out of her hiding spot to see that the men had stopped in the hallway, the man she recognized patting at his pockets, as if trying to ascertain whether or not he had something he needed.

He did. He pulled out the narrow object. Chelsea heard the click of some sort of button, and a sharp blade appeared in the man's hands.

She quickly shrank back into the shadows.

"Nasty thing, that sticker. And I told you, the Spaniard swore he had the money, as long as he got to meet you," the second man said. "But who knows? Haven't you learned yet about these damned Frogs? They do as they do."

"If they want our help, they'd damned well better do as they do *toot-sweet*."

"Our help? Christ on a crutch, man, it's not like we're going to *help* them."

"They don't know that. What do we care about what they want? We meet with him in his room at The Crown like we said, we take the money, thank him kindly and then we slit his throat and walk out of the place innocent as you please, just like we did with the others. I just want it done. What's that? Did you hear something? Over there—have a look."

Chelsea knew she had two options open to her, neither of them appealing. She could stay where she was and surely be discovered, or she could step out of the shadows and face them head-on.

She chose the latter.

"Mon Dieu!" she exclaimed, clapping her hands to her chest as she feigned surprise, and then immediately let loose with a torrent of French, telling them she was very afraid, telling them she feared her maid had disappeared, just when she needed help with her buttons, and had either of these fine gentlemen seen her?

"It's only some dumb female. I thought the whores had all gone. What's she gibbering about?"

"I don't know," the man Chelsea had encountered earlier said, looking at her intently, the knife no longer in sight. "Do you speak English?" he asked her slowly, as if that might help her to understand.

Chelsea very nearly shook her head before she realized what that motion would betray. Instead, she repeated what she had just said, this time employing a few more *Mon Dieus* and a fervent *par tous les saints* even as she tossed in some dramatic hand gestures to hammer home her point. And then she fell back on the most powerful weapon in any woman's arsenal: she began to cry.

"Crazy female," the other man said in disgust, giving his companion's arm a quick, nudging punch. "Come on, Jonas."

"I don't know," the man called Jonas said slowly, still looking at Chelsea as if trying to decide if she was genuine. "She could have understood us. Maybe we should take her along. Pretty piece, at least. Looks cleaner than the others."

What! Didn't the man have *business* to do, murdering to do? Men were so obtuse. She could scream, she supposed, but that would bring Beau on the run, probably unarmed, which she knew these two men were not. She had to handle this on her own. How did a woman get rid of a man?

That's simple enough. Beg him to stay, a voice in Chelsea's head explained with amazing clarity.

She grabbed Jonas's arm, looked up at him implor-

ingly and repeated her lie for the third time, tugging at
him as if she desperately required his help.

"Can't stand that yammering. Bugger off, bitch,"
Jonas said, shaking her free, the movement of his arm
sending her crashing against the wall, knocking all the
air from her lungs. "God, I hate the French. Running
around England just like they won the war. I'd slit this
one's throat for free, just to shut her up. Let's go have
that drink you promised me and be on our way."

Chelsea remained where she was, needing the wall
for support as she willed her knees not to crumple beneath her, and struggled to regain her breath. And then
she took off running around the turn in the hallway,
heading for Beau's chamber.

She banged on the door with some force and then immediately depressed the latch, hoping he hadn't locked
it. He hadn't.

"Get up!" she demanded, seeing him lying fully
dressed on the bed, his long legs crossed, looking entirely at his ease. "Someone is going to be murdered."

The dratted man didn't react. "Yes, I can see that.
My brother, most likely. Much as you look charming,
my dear, I don't believe I'm comfortable with Puck's
assessing eye. That riding habit fits you entirely too
well."

She proudly looked down at herself for a moment,
only a moment, and silently agreed that the outfit flattered her; even the length of the hem was right. But
then she recovered. "Not now, Oliver," she said with
some heat. "I just overheard two men in the hallway,

and they're planning to kill someone tonight. In Gateshead, I think."

"Is that so? I shouldn't worry about it." Beau levered himself up and off the mattress. "It has been my experience that people do that all the time. Especially when they have access to a taproom. Plan to kill, talk about killing. They rarely do it."

"Don't you dismiss me, Oliver Le Beau Blackthorn! I am not in the habit of overreacting. I heard them, and they mean it. They're going to rob him and then slit his throat. I even saw the bloody knife."

"You saw the bloody what?"

"Well, all right, it wasn't bloody when I saw it, but it will be. I only said that for emphasis. And something else, Oliver. Did you know that those women who were here today are whores?"

He suddenly looked a little sheepish. "I knew it might be a possibility."

"Honestly, I must live with shutters over my eyes. Not that any of that signifies anything. We should be able to find the man and warn him if we leave now, and I can tell you everything on the way to Gateshead." She jammed her fists onto her hips, truly out of patience with him. "Unless you'd rather continue to just stand there like some hair-for-wit village idiot and gawk at me."

"Just when I was lying here, waxing nearly poetic about the way we two seem to rub along so well together. I was deciding it was your appreciation of my better qualities that I admired most." He took her arm and steered her to the window seat, and then sat down beside her. "The village idiot awaits, madam. Speak."

She had a momentary urge to wring his neck, but suppressed it. "You need to hear more, don't you? In fairness, I suppose I would, as well."

He listened with half an ear at first, she could sense it, too busy playing with the fingers of her right hand to be truly paying attention. Allow a man to bed you, it would seem, and their minds become somehow fixated, unwilling or unable to concentrate on anything else. But then he seemed to become more alert.

"Say that again."

"What? The Crown? You visited all of the hotels and inns, you told me so. Is there a Crown?"

He nodded, getting to his feet and crossing the room to pick up his jacket. Something had changed, the very air in the room had become charged. He suddenly seemed bigger, more muscled. Almost dangerous. "The Crown and Feathers, and The Crown and Harp. Two of them. Tell me the name again. I want to believe I misheard you."

Chelsea stood up. Something was wrong, something more than some sudden resolve to put a spoke in the wheels of the two prospective murderers. "Jonas? No, wait, you mean the other one, don't you? The Spaniard. Don Pedro Messina." She frowned. "You know, Oliver, there's something vaguely familiar about that name."

He was bustling about the chamber, not aimlessly, but with grim purpose, pulling his brace of pistols out of his saddlebag, checking them and then quickly replacing them, hefting the bag up and over his shoulder. The knife and its sheath, lying on the bureau, were just as quickly secreted inside his right boot top.

"Shakespeare's *As You Like It*," Beau told her shortly. "Don Pedro, the legitimate heir, as opposed to Don John, the bastard son and villain of the piece. The setting Spain, Messina to be precise about the thing. It's too close to be anyone else. Damn him, it's exactly the sort of dramatic nonsense he'd find amusing. All of England to choose from, and he shows up here."

"Oliver, I'm certain you know just what you're talking about, and to whom you are referring—but I don't."

He stabbed his fingers through his hair. "No, of course you don't." He picked up his hat, his riding gloves. "Our mother named us all after characters in Shakespeare's plays. Oliver Le Beau, Robin Goodfellow. Don John, the bastard brother of Don Pedro in *Much Ado About Nothing,* even though we call him Jack."

"But if it's as you said, Don John is the villain. Why would your mother name your brother for a villain?"

"You'd have to ask her. Some would say she'd had a premonition. Christ, Chelsea, he's working for the French?" He slammed the hat down on his head and approached her, taking hold of her upper arms. "With any luck, one drink downstairs will turn to two or three, to build courage. That should give me time to round up Puck and find Jack. I think this will make the first time in five years that all three of us have been in the same place at the same time. You'd think we'd planned a damned party. Stay here, lock the door behind me."

She put her hands on his, holding him where he was. "Oliver," she said carefully, as if speaking to a faintly dim child. "Take a moment to think. I know the names of the two possible inns. I have a horse and money of my own in my reticule. I can ask the direction to Gateshead or even hire someone to guide me. Plus, I have been here all day, and this inn is not so lovely as you might think. I do believe I'd have to follow you."

"And I can pull the sash off that curtain over there and tie you to the bedpost," he pointed out and then sighed. "All right. As far as Puck's room at the White Swan, but no farther. I've had misgivings about this inn from the start. Too many people in it sleep all day and rise only at night, but there seemed to be no budging that silly girl once she'd locked herself in the room. We're probably surrounded by itinerant highwaymen and thieves, not that I was going to point that out to you. Or the whores. So you come along, but you do as I say. Agreed?"

She pulled the key to her own room from her pocket. "Agreed. Let me fetch my new hat and gloves, and I will meet you in the stable yard. There's a full moon, and you know I can ride well enough." She went up on tiptoe and kissed his cheek. "Your brother will be fine, Oliver."

"Not when I get through with him, he won't," he told her and headed out of the room.

HE'D ALREADY traveled this roadway twice today and knew it to be in fairly good repair. With his recent familiarity, along with the full moon, he felt confident the journey would take no more than a half hour, even with Chelsea riding with him.

And if one of the supposed highwaymen from the inn accosted them, well, he already was in the mood to do violence to somebody, so that would be all right.

He'd checked the taproom before they'd departed and gotten a fairly good look at the two prospective murderers, sure of who they were thanks to the descriptions Chelsea had provided. Happily, the taproom, fairly well deserted all day, was now filled with the inn's tenants, all of them male, all of them dressed in dark clothing, all of them wearing the alert, wary expressions of men ready to fight or flee if they so much as sniffed danger. They probably would be heading out around midnight, to wreak havoc on any coach they might encounter.

In his more reasonable moments, he knew this was a good thing, as he felt he could do without punching a prospective thief tonight; he'd save all his wrath for Jack.

Beau had planned to rouse Chelsea after they'd made love and slept a few hours, then depart this inn the same way they had done the last one; before dawn, and very quietly. He'd told himself he was being an old woman, seeing danger where there was none. He should have listened to himself better and left along with the baron and the squire, pushing on until he could find another small village and a less threatening atmosphere.

But he'd wanted Chelsea in his bed. He wanted her never out of his bed; he might as well admit that to himself. Admit it and move on. Get back to some semblance of sanity somehow. She wasn't what he'd wanted, because he'd wanted nothing from any female, expected nothing from any female.

She was the perfect revenge. That ripe plum, fallen unexpectedly into his hands. That's all she was supposed to be to him.

Now, almost to his horror, she was becoming, very simply, his *all*.

How did that happen? When did that happen?

And what the hell was he going to do about it? In the space of a few short days, his entire world had been turned upside down, his life now seemingly divided into two parts: before Chelsea, since Chelsea.

He never wanted to know what life would be like if it could ever be described as *after* Chelsea.

He had to tell her. He had to swallow down all his assertions, his protestations, his determination to be his own man, and admit that he was no longer that man. He was a man whose heart was held in the palm of one small hand.

That shouldn't seem so terrible, but it did. He'd been too long with the belief that love was not for him; he didn't want it, he wouldn't recognize it if it came up to him and rapped its knuckles against his forehead.

And yet…and yet here it, or something very near to it, was. First knocking on the door, but now inside and unpacking, settling in, taking up residence in his heart.

Chelsea liked him, she'd awakened wonderfully well to their physical union, even if she had made a calculated decision to lose her virginity to him so that her brother could not annul the marriage. She was a woman of spirit and determination. But none of that meant that she might love him.

Her practicality was startling, as was her ability to negotiate, get the best deal she thought she could get. And she seemed content with her lot, unflinchingly living up to her end of the bargain.

But how would she feel if he told her the devil with her brother, with revenge, the reverend Flotley and the whole damn world? Tell her that he believed himself to be falling in love with her, which certainly had been no part of their bargain and that he wanted their marriage to be much more than the mutual convenience they'd both seen it as a few days ago. He'd long ago forgiven her for dragging him into her scheme and was even beginning, at times, to think of it as his own. This is what having feelings for a woman did to a man.

But did he tell her? Did he dare risk it?

He'd had a one-sided love and wore the scars to prove it. He wasn't actively seeking another.

"Wait," Chelsea called to him as they crested one last hill, and the town of Gateshead lay below them. They sat side by side on their mounts, looking down at the lights and buildings; nothing too impressive, compared to London, but worthy of a moment's pause while Chelsea admired it. "Have you had sufficient time to come up with a plan?"

"Over and above saving my brother so that I can kill him? No."

"That's what I thought." Chelsea carefully controlled her mare, which seemed eager to move on, probably thinking the accommodations in the larger town would come with a higher quality of stable. "Which is why I have. Come up with a plan, that is."

He signaled that they should proceed once more, this time at a walk. "Really? How very helpful of you. Does this plan, just by chance, of course, include you in any way?"

"Well…"

"No. Chelsea, you promised."

"I beg your pardon, Oliver, but I most certainly did not. I would remember if I'd promised. I think I merely agreed."

"There's a difference?" As they rode, his gaze swept this way and that; he was trying to remember, of the half-dozen inns he'd visited earlier, the location of the two possible Crowns the murderers—he'd have to stop thinking of them that way—would be heading for to meet with his brother.

"Oh, yes, definitely. An agreement only holds if the person who has done the agreeing finds it possible to do what he or she agreed to do, after which time—if it is not possible—it becomes null and void. A promise is forever. It's…it's like a vow."

"Like a marriage vow. That's forever, which more and more is beginning to look like a very long time."

"Yes, Oliver. That's forever—and once again you

aren't all that amusing. But I will explain anyway. Agreeing to stay in Puck's rooms at the hotel was *agreeable* to me as long as, agreeing to it, that agreement got me here. However, now that we're here, I find it *disagreeable* to me to have been the one who told you what I heard and then be shunted off to hide, like some child, while you effect a rescue."

"Making the agreement null and void," Beau repeated, sorting through everything she'd said. Female logic. Nothing could frighten a man more. "It's a strong argument you've got there, Chelsea, but the answer is still no."

They were already into the outskirts of the town, the lack of others on the street making their presence more obvious. Gateshead certainly wasn't London; in Mayfair, the streets would be jammed side to side with coaches and partygoers. Here, the residents would appear to retire early to their beds. They needed to get off the street; the two men would recognize Chelsea if they saw her, and that couldn't be a good thing to have happen.

"You think I'd be in the way, don't you?"

"On the contrary. I *know* you'd be in the way. There's a reason women don't go to war, you know."

"Yes. It's called the inflated hubris of men. Have you never read about the Amazons? Well, there were also the Sirens, and some others of that ilk, but we won't discuss them now. Besides, I wouldn't actually *do* anything. Anything much. I know you must have been cudgeling your brain for some way to get yourself inside your brother's room while the murderers are there. You're probably thinking about breaking down the door, aren't you? That's entirely unnecessary."

"Is that right? And how would you do it?" How did she know that had been worrying him? If he tried to kick open the door, there could be a knife in Jack's back before he and Puck could level their pistols at the men.

"Simply. I'd do it simply. I'd knock on your brother's door, once we locate him and the two murderers have gone inside. Men open the door to ladies, especially ladies offering…well, I'll offer something. And then, even before the door is opened, I will quickly and prudently take myself off to go hide somewhere safe and let you and Puck take over the rest, all the bashing together of heads and remonstrations with your brother. Simple, yes? Why break down a door when someone is willing to open it for you? Men just make things more difficult sometimes."

Beau was quiet for a few moments, mulling the plan, because it was a good plan. And immediately saw her mistake. "I can pay a barmaid at The Crown to knock on the door," he pointed out, thinking he'd just trumped her ace.

"You'd do that? You'd *steal* my plan and not let me be a part of it? Oliver, that's beneath a gentleman."

He pointed to the right, and she followed him into the stable yard adjoining the White Swan, allowing him to help her dismount. "You forget. I'm a bastard, Chelsea," he said quietly as he held her in front of him for a moment. "Nothing is beneath me."

"Oliver…" she said, her lovely eyes darkening, looking somehow bruised. "I'd just worry the whole time you and Puck were gone. After all, I came to you with the information. Now you and Puck will be in danger, and if anything happens to either of you, it will be on my head for having told you in the first place. I would spend the remainder of my life—with Francis Flotley, remember—wondering if things would have been different if only I'd been able to accompany you. Don't do that to me."

"I'm an idiot," he said, giving up. After all, she was right. If it weren't for her, he wouldn't even know Jack was in Gateshead and in danger. There was also the very real prospect that she might follow after them anyway. Or maybe it was the thought of Francis Flotley touching her. No matter what the reason, he knew he was beaten. "If Puck agrees, you can go with us. But a knock on the door, Chelsea, and that's it. You understand?"

"That's a promise," she said and then took his hand and began pulling him toward the front door of the hotel. "I know you can't see it the same way, Oliver, but I feel as if I'm on a grand adventure, and this is just another part of it. I feel so alive, nothing at all like the boring and *prayerful* life Thomas has forced me into these past years. Oh, and won't Puck be surprised to see me, and I really must thank him for my lovely new riding habit," she said, sounding annoyingly jolly. Of course she was happy; she'd gotten what she wanted, and now all was right in her world again.

While his world kept turning upside down, inside out, and at this particular moment, damn near sideways.

Women. A man could shoot and box and fence and ride with the best of them. He could walk, and run, and talk and reason. He could climb mountains, ford rivers, conquer armies, build empires.

But put a woman in his life, and all his skill, his prowess and definitely his intelligence, deserted him. God may have taken a rib from Adam to give to Eve but, one way or another, Eve had been bashing Adam over the head with it ever since.

CHAPTER SIXTEEN

CHELSEA WAS SHAKING so hard on the inside, trying to appear as calm and composed as possible on the outside, that for a few moments she'd believed she might actually become physically ill.

She knew she was being, in the words of Francis Flotley, an *abomination*. She had tricked and cajoled and browbeaten and anything else she could think of to do, to get herself included in the rescue of Beau's brother.

She'd had to. The thought of Beau going off without her, getting himself hurt or worse, was simply too much for her. Not that she could say as much, for he'd then only point out that men protected the ladies, not the other way round. As if women were helpless, squeamish, hysterical and bound to faint at the sight of a single droplet of blood. And as if women could contentedly stay home and mind their embroidery without a fear that anything bad could happen.

Men could be so thick.

So let him think she was demanding, interfering, even downright sneaky. As long as she got to go along and make certain he didn't attempt to do anything heroically stupid.

"Oh, look," she said, tugging at Beau's sleeve as they entered the small lobby of the unimpressive hotel—unless a person had just spent several days at vastly inferior wayside inns, in which case the lobby now seemed to rival that of the Poultney in London. "There's Puck. Over there. Doesn't he look handsome."

Puck must have heard her, because he turned his head away from the man who'd been speaking to him and then deserted the fellow entirely, walking toward them, his arms wide—almost as if trying to block the other man's view—exclaiming, "Mrs. Claridge! Mr. Claridge! How exquisitely delightful to see you both."

He took Chelsea's hands in his and surprised her by kissing the air beside her right ear and then her left... where he lingered long enough to say, "Let's get out of here. Follow Beau. That man already informed me that he knows him."

Chelsea moved quickly, realizing that Beau already was ahead of her, his head purposely averted until they were back on the street.

"Bloody hell, Beau," Puck said as they hastened along the flagway, "why not just stand on a chair and announce yourself? Where's that dreadful costume you had on earlier? You looked like death on a stick, but at least nobody would give you a second glance."

"Never mind that. What's Carstairs doing in Gateshead?"

Puck sighed and shook his head. "Did you really think I cared enough to ask? Really, Beau, what does it matter what he's doing here? I imagine the man's a

bore anywhere he travels. The question is, what are
you doing here? I thought the idea was to keep Chelsea
hidden. If you're going to keep changing the rules, you
really should let a brother know. By the way, where are
we going?"

"To The Crown, to rescue your brother Jack," Chelsea answered, all but skipping to keep up with the two
men, as Beau looked as if someone had just wired his
jawbone together. "There are two, so we need to find
the right one. Your brother is there and he's going to be
murdered."

Chelsea had to hand it to Puck, she supposed. The
man didn't so much as blink before saying, "Well, isn't
that just like Black Jack? Loves his excitement, doesn't
he? Beau? Have you explained to my new sister that
Black Jack is never murdered? If anything, I'd imagine
it would be the other way round. Perhaps we're to rescue
someone from him? There's a Crown just at the end of
the next street," he added, and the two men picked up
their pace even more.

Chelsea was fast getting out of breath. "Don't you
want to know *why?*" she asked Puck. "Why he is going
to be murdered, that is?"

"No, I don't believe so, thank you," Puck answered.
"Beau? It would appear I'm at a disadvantage, as I had
dressed for a late supper, not a brawl. Do you perhaps
have a spare weapon somewhere on your person?"

Beau pushed back the riding cloak he'd donned to
conceal them, reached into his waistband and pulled

out one of the two pistols he'd tucked there, silently handing it over to his brother.

Puck slipped the pistol into his waistband. "Well, that really ruins the line of my waistcoat, doesn't it? You had nothing smaller to hand? Pity."

What was the matter with these two men? One had gone silent as the Sphinx, and the other seemed more concerned with his appearance than he did any danger. "I don't care if you don't want to know, I'm going to tell you anyway. He's fallen in with the French, Puck."

"Jack? Really? Whatever for?"

"We haven't got all the particulars," Chelsea told him as she saw the inn sign just ahead of them. "But it is my opinion that he has hired some very bad men to assist in freeing Bonaparte."

"No, that can't be it. Already been done, remember. Why do it again? Seems a man could find something more interesting to do."

"All right," Chelsea agreed. "But what then?"

"But what then? Let me see. There's quite a lot, actually. Not everyone in France is happy with the new government, and there are still a lot of scores, I guess you could say, to be settled. Therefore, a coup of some sort would be my first guess. Nothing like a good overthrowing of the government every few years. Marching in the streets for lost causes, building barricades, wearing colors, singing patriotic songs, hanging the odd fellow or three from lampposts. The French love that. And I do think we English have helped them along a time or two over the years, pointing out to them how unhappy and oppressed they are with themselves, and that they don't need to be angry with us. *Vive la France, maison des idiots.*"

"Be quiet," Beau said, taking Chelsea's elbow and leading her toward the door to the inn. "Let me do the talking."

"A bit out of sorts this evening, isn't he? Sadly, all three of us are prone to having our moods at times. Comes with being Blackthorns, I suppose. I do hope he's been treating you well. For all his great age, I begin to doubt he's had much experience with females. Let me amend that—with well-bred females," Puck whispered into Chelsea's ear as they hung back in the entrance hall and Beau approached the fat innkeeper at his station.

"Are you ever serious?" she whispered back, her stomach still doing its best to upset her.

"Rarely. I don't remember the last time any such thing was required of me. Let's see. There was the evening the Comte returned early from—no, I handled that with amazing aplomb. So no, I don't remember. Ah, here comes Beau, looking at least marginally pleased, thank God."

"First time's the charm. He's here," he told them quietly. "And, as far as the landlord knows, he's in his room, alone. That's saved us some time we didn't have to spare. Now let's get out of here."

Puck opened his mouth, probably to ask a question, but he would have had to ask it of Beau's back, for the man had already turned for the door, leaving Puck and Chelsea no option but to follow.

Once outside, he strode quickly to the end of the building and turned into the shadows, again leaving them no choice but to follow. Chelsea would have pointed out his rudeness to him, but she felt fairly certain he wouldn't see the humor in any jest at the moment. He positively oozed anger from every pore.

Finally, Beau spoke, tersely telling Puck what was happening, the plan Chelsea had devised. They would wait here, concealed in the darkness, until the two men entered The Crown and Harp. They'd then wait another full minute before they'd go inside, upstairs, and Chelsea knocked on the door, requesting entry.

"I'm going to be the maidservant, offering clean towels," she told Puck, not without a hint of pride, for it had been her idea. "Then, as the door begins to open, I'll step away and you and Beau can burst in and heroically extricate your brother from his imminent danger. Save him, that is."

"Sounds like great fun. I've always wanted to be heroic," Puck said. "But here's a thought. What if he doesn't want clean towels? Perhaps you might wish to offer something few men ever turn down."

Chelsea nodded. "Yes, I did consider that. Do you know, there were soiled doves at the inn we're staying at tonight. I think they'd stopped by to... um, to entertain the travelers."

"Really? I always pick the wrong accommodations."

"Puck," Beau said threateningly.

"No, no, I'm serious. I mean really, Beau. Excuse me, good sir," he said in a remarkably female voice, "but I thought, whilst you were busy betraying your country, you might wish to take a moment to have a bit of a wash and brush up." He shook his head. "No, sorry, I know you were forced to plan in haste, but I don't think that will work. Besides, we know Jack is alone, that we've beaten the bad men here. Why don't we just nip on in there and warn him? Seems straightforward enough. In fact, except to prod at my brains for a better solution, you really didn't need me at all. I'd ordered a fat pork chop, you know, and was really looking forward to it."

Chelsea put a hand against Beau's chest, as he'd taken a single step toward his brother, murder in his eyes. "But he's right, Oliver. Why don't we just go upstairs and warn your brother?"

"Because, you pair of happy nincompoops, there is still the chance, albeit slim, that Jack is working for the Crown, not against it."

Chelsea was completely at sea for the space of a few seconds, trying to imagine Jack Blackthorn working for the inn. "Oh, you mean the government," she said before she could stop herself. "I knew that."

"No you didn't," Puck teased quietly. "Not to put too fine a point on it, Beau, but the idea of our brother working for anyone, friend or foe, doesn't seem plausible. Mama told me in confidence that he still continues to refuse an allowance, and that she's extremely worried that he has turned to something nefarious."

"Cards. I think he's a gambler," Beau told them both, keeping one eye on the inn yard. "But maybe he's more. God, I've always hoped he was more. In any event,

I don't want to give these two would-be murderers a chance to lope off somewhere, not if Jack has set up some sort of trap for them."

"That's very sweet, Oliver," Chelsea said kindly, giving his chest a quick pat before lowering her hand. "We would all like to think our relations better than they almost always are. I once harbored the hope that Thomas would grow a brain and Madelyn a conscience, but it went for nothing."

Beau gave a sharp crack of laughter before quickly recovering. "I'm standing in a puddle in a dark alleyway with an idiot worried about his belly and a woman who thinks I'm a sad, pathetic case, waiting for two murderers to meet with my other brother, hopefully not a traitor, and I'm wondering what I ever did to be here."

Chelsea glared at him. "It must have been terrible, whatever it was. You're not very grateful, you know. We're standing here with you. And I don't even know your brother. It really is a lot to ask of us. Isn't it, Puck?"

"*Ask* of you? You *begged*— Puck, damn it, stop that."

Puck was leaning against the brick wall of the inn, clutching his stomach and silently laughing. But then he stood straight once more, pointing toward the inn yard. "Are these your murderers?"

Chelsea stepped forward a pace and peeked around the corner of the building just before Beau grabbed her at the waist, picking her up bodily and hauling her back into the darkness. "Oliver, put me down. And yes. That's them. I suppose we have to go with my terrible plan as Puck termed it. You said a minute. We should count. One, two—"

"Don't you simply love her, *Oliver?* Lord knows I do. You must be having a grand old time with this elopement, while all I get to do is follow after you in that damned coach, sweeping up."

Chelsea bent her head and smiled at her boots, not wanting to let Beau see how funny she thought this whole thing had become. She could positively feel the agitation coming off him in waves. He was so dear…

"All right, let's get this finished," he said, taking Chelsea's hand and leading her back around to the front of the inn. "Now remember, you knock, ask if they require towels, and then immediately take yourself off to the end of the corridor. I mean it, Chelsea. Do you have that?"

"I could scarcely forget my own plan. And we are being serious, aren't we, Puck? It's just that it's also an adventure. Of sorts," she ended weakly, as Beau really did look rather oppressed.

Once inside, they headed immediately toward the stairs, only to be stopped by the innkeeper.

"Here now, where do you lot think you're going? You can't just nip in here and take yourselves upstairs. You got to pay, sign the book."

Beau stopped. Swiveled his head to his left. Glared at the man.

"Oh, yes, m'lord, quite right," the innkeeper said hastily, pulling the ledger back across the counter. "You can just do that later, can't you, sir?" And then he turned on his heels and quickly waddled away toward the taproom.

"Bully," Chelsea whispered as they mounted the stairs. "Much as I'm loath to have you look at me that way, I'm still going to ask—do we know where we're going?"

"Three-B," he told her, turning to mount another, more narrow staircase, Puck following behind, as he'd stopped to snatch up an apple from the bowl on the counter.

"Missed my dinner, remember?" he said as they arrived on the third floor and Beau saw him with the now half-eaten apple, which had him glaring again. "Don't worry. You can pay the man on our way out."

Chelsea had heard it said that emotions can manifest themselves in strange ways sometimes. Fear, even grief, can suddenly make a person erupt in hysterical laughter, for instance, and great happiness can reduce another person to tears. Why, she even remembered a quote from the essayist Charles Lamb, where he explained that awful things often made him laugh, and that he'd once badly misbehaved at a funeral. She'd often wondered what he'd meant, but now she thought she knew. It was either laugh or cry.

She dearly hoped they were not about to take part in a funeral. But Chelsea believed Mr. Lamb had her full sympathy, because, terrible as this moment could be, and the next moment even more so, watching Puck eat his apple struck her as so funny that it was all she could do not to plunk herself straight down on the floor and laugh until her belly hurt.

Somehow she composed herself and followed Beau down the corridor until they stopped just outside the room with *3B* chalked on the door, along with a few words she pretended she did not recognize.

Beau nodded his head one time, and she lifted her hand, made a fist and then hesitated. Now she would show him what she could do. She hadn't lived her entire life surrounded by servants of all ilk and station without learning a few things.

She knocked three times on the door.

"Fresh towels fer yer washin' up, mate," she sang out, and then turned to grin at Beau in triumph.

He pinched the bridge of his nose and closed his eyes for a moment, looking pained.

"I don't require any, thank you," came a voice from the other side of the door.

Jack? Puck mouthed, shrugging.

Beau nodded. Chelsea was amazed. The brothers saw each other so seldom that Puck couldn't even be certain he recognized his brother's voice? She sighed inwardly. If only she could say the same about Thomas.

Beau took hold of her elbow as if to pull her away, but Chelsea wasn't about to give up at the first hurdle. She knocked again.

"I ain't askin', m'lord, I'm tellin'. It ain't worth m'skin ta go downstairs to that great lump and have him twistin' m'ear off 'cause I ain't done m'job. The man says ter fetch Three-B towels, I fetch Three-B towels. They ain't much, but they're clean. Now open up!"

Puck, the apple stuck in his jaws, silently applauded her performance, so that she politely curtsied to him, and then she caught her breath as he abruptly grabbed her arm and sent her spinning off down the corridor as footsteps could be heard approaching the door.

She pressed her back against the wall, watching wide-eyed as the two men, pistols suddenly in their hands and cocked, waited for the sound of the latch depressing and then burst into the room after Beau had given the door a mighty kick, sending it cannoning straight into somebody on the other side.

There was a loud *thunk,* an even louder curse, followed by several more curses, much shouting and then silence.

She covered her ears in case one of the pistols still might be discharged or somebody said that word again, squeezed her eyes nearly shut as she wasn't sure she really wanted to see what she really, really wanted to see, and headed for the room.

What she saw when she entered was a much nicer chamber than any of those she'd slept in the past few days, the two men she'd encountered in the hallway of her own inn, their hands raised and their faces black with frustrated rage, Beau holding a pistol directed at the two men, Puck leaning at his ease against a table edge, finishing his apple…and the most devastatingly handsome man she'd ever seen.

And quite possibly the most angry.

Jack Blackthorn was tall, even taller than Beau. It was possible to see that all three men were brothers, they had much the same look about the eyes and chins. But there the similarities ended.

Where Beau and Puck were fair, Jack was dark. Dark as night. His hair, his eyes. His skin seemed somehow tougher, bronzed by the sun, weathered by the wind. Where Puck's features curved, seemed somehow mischievously cherubic, just like his name, and Beau wore the look of a man who knew who he was and was reasonably content with that, Don John Blackthorn's features seemed to have been chiseled out of some hard, perfect stone.

When he turned those dark eyes on her, he actually made her shiver.

Black Jack.

The name suited him down to the ground.

"And who's this? Our maidservant, I assume? Say something, darling, so I can be certain."

"I'm not your darling, nor am I a dog, to speak on command," Chelsea told him with some heat.

"Thank you, yes, you're the one. Damn, Beau, is this the young woman you plan to marry? You might want to think twice about that. She's much too good an actress, and we all know where that can lead, don't we? Oh, and put that pistol down, if you please. Those two aren't going to attempt an escape. Especially the poor fellow you conked in the face with the door. I think his nose is broken."

"Shame you don't answer your own door," Beau said

with a quick grin, moving the pistol to his left, to indicate Jonas. "However, I know for a fact that this one's got a knife on him somewhere."

"You mean this nasty little sticker?" Jack said, pulling a familiar-looking piece from his pocket and pushing on it somewhere. Chelsea heard a click, and the blade appeared. "We've only just met for the first time this evening, but I'd been warned what to expect. I had it from him immediately. Clumsy me, bumping up against him as we prepared to sit down and speak of our plans."

"Bloody hell!" Jonas lowered his hands to pat at his pockets. "Bastard. You picked my pocket?"

"Nonsense. I merely relieved you of the means to an end. My end, to be precise. I didn't much relish the thought of having this clever toy stuck in my neck. Now raise your hands again, if you please. As you've already seen, this man here tends toward the volatile, and I wouldn't wish for you to miss your date with the hangman." He then smiled at Beau. "Tell me, when did you first labor under the misapprehension that I'm stupid?"

"I think you were still in your cradle," Beau told him. "So that's it? We raced here to protect you, mostly from yourself, and all we did was get in the way?"

"Yes, I believe that about says it all. But the gesture is much appreciated. Now, if you don't mind, there are two gentlemen about to arrive to assist me in taking these traitors to London. I'd rather you didn't meet, as they prefer anonymity. As do I," he added without inflection.

"When are you leaving? I haven't seen you in two years. You could have stayed for the funeral, you know, instead of sneaking in and out like a thief."

"I could have, Beau, yes. I chose not to."

"Because of Mother."

"Because I don't belong there," Jack answered and pulled out his pocket watch to consult it. "You'd best go."

"She thinks you're a highwayman or some such thing," Beau told him. "But you work for the government."

"I work for no one. I do, however, occasionally amuse myself."

Chelsea shot Beau a look. *Amuse* himself? Oh, yes, they definitely were brothers. Even Puck *amused* himself, probably by pretending he was all fluff and no bottom, but she'd seen how differently he'd behaved once the action had begun.

Jack held out his hand first to Beau and then to Puck. "Cutting quite the dash in Paris, I hear. But as we all know, the real challenge is in being accepted here, in England. Any fool can be a pampered pet in Versailles."

"Bloody wonderful seeing you again, too, Jack," Puck said easily, withdrawing his hand. "Come on, Beau, before we get all sentimental and maudlin. Let's simply say our fond farewells, and I can get back to my pork chop. We aren't needed here."

Chelsea had been standing quietly, growing more uncomfortable by the moment. Her family was obnoxious, but this one was downright strange.

"That's it?" she finally demanded, furious. "You don't see each other for years on end, and five minutes' time is all you have for each other? Don't you even *like* each other? Shame on you. Shame on all three of you."

"Chelsea, please," Beau said, turning to her.

And that's when Jonas made his move. After all, when cooperating with his captors only meant he certainly would hang, he might as well hazard any chance to escape.

"Oliver!"

Beau had his pistol up and ready as he whirled about, neatly bringing its barrel down heavily across Jonas's temple, and the man crumpled to the floor.

"Oh, bravo, brother," Puck said appreciatively. "There's one you won't have to truss up, Jack. See? We've been exceedingly helpful."

"As long as you didn't kill him now that I finally got him to show himself." Jack seemed to relent. "I apologize, to all of you. This night has been months in the planning, and you interrupted my *coup de grâce*. I'm selfish enough to have wanted to put an end to him and the others myself. Their small business enterprise has already taken the lives of three good men. At first we thought they were true political conspirators, but it turned out that they're just common cutthroats, preying on the gullibility of fools. Either way, they had to be eliminated."

Feeling silly even as she did it, Chelsea raised her hand as if she would like to be called on to speak. "I overheard them talking together, earlier, and they were

planning to take your money and then slit your throat."
She pointed to the now slumbering Jonas. "He said he'd
slit your throat, just like *the others*. You can see why
your brothers were concerned."

"Is that true, Beau? Were you *concerned?* Or were
you thinking I'd tossed my lot in with some French conspirators?"

"The possibility did cross my mind. I apologize."
Then Beau rallied. "But if you weren't so damn secre-
tive I wouldn't have thought it. Don Pedro Messina, the
Spaniard. Acting, that's what you were doing."

"Yes, yes. Apples never drop that far from the tree,
do they? I suppose I come by my small talents naturally.
But we all play our parts, don't we? The dutiful son, the
fribble—oh, don't scowl, Puck, I know you work quite
diligently to not be taken seriously. And me, of course,
the black sheep. We're damned predictable, aren't we?
Filling the roles Mother, in her genius, assigned us."

Chelsea blinked back sudden tears. How sad. If Society had branded them bastards, their own mother had
been worse, casting them in roles she'd chosen them to
play. And then all but abandoning them.

"You don't have to be what she thinks you should
be," she heard herself saying before she could stop herself. "You're grown men now, free to do what you want."

Jack bowed in her direction. "Thank you, Lady Chelsea. But you see, I think we rather enjoy our roles. Don't
we, brothers?"

"I think one of us enjoys his too much," Beau said

flatly. "We have to leave, as we're making an early start in the morning."

Jack nodded. "You to the north, me to the south and Puck here blowing with the wind. Be careful. I saw the Brean coach last night as I traveled here from Leeds. I took it upon myself to make a stop at the inn and created some small mischief to hopefully detain them, but he may have simply hired another coach."

Chelsea put a hand to her mouth to suppress a gasp. Suddenly it seemed cold in the room. Cold as the grave.

"Mischief?" Puck looked at his brother. "Not that I'm worried, you understand, but you do have this seeming penchant for consorting with murderers. That said, what sort of mischief?"

"The sort you'd probably enjoy. Cutting partway through the wheel spokes could have caused an accident, although I did consider it. In the end, I made do by borrowing a half dozen of the innkeeper's chickens and locking them up in the coach for the night. But please don't concern yourself about the welfare of the birds, as I made sure the fellow I hired to do the deed put plenty of feed in there with them. On the seats, on the floor… why, Beau, you look positively delighted with me. How nice."

THEY RETURNED to their former hiding place after leaving Jack, Beau wondering why his brother always made him so angry, and why he liked him so much.

"I'm really tired, Oliver," Chelsea said, and then

yawned rather prodigiously, as if to prove her point. "Can't we please go now?"

Beau looked at her in the near darkness. She looked away.

"It's Jack. He doesn't trust him," Puck said, munching on yet another apple. "Jack says he has men coming to help him with his captives, but Beau here isn't so sure, thinking that perhaps Jack just wanted to be rid of us. Isn't that it, brother mine?"

Beau dragged his attention away from Chelsea. Something was wrong. He didn't know what, or why he knew, but he knew. She hadn't laughed at Jack's genius with the chickens. She'd laughed at Puck's stunts. But not Jack's. So what was different now?

Her brother. Jack had brought her brother into the conversation, and the fact that he was still in pursuit. Had she really thought he'd give up and turn back to London? Damn.

"No, it's not true. I'm simply being nosy. I want to see if I know these two men. If there are two men," he added, because Puck hadn't been entirely incorrect. There was even a part of him that wondered if the fate that Jonas and his cohort had planned for Jack was the same fate he'd planned for them. With Jack, you could never be certain what was in his head. "We'll give it another five minutes, Chelsea, and then we'll head back to the hotel. Puck and I will secure and share another room, and you can take his chamber. I wouldn't ask you to ride back to our inn this late at night."

"Oh, well, isn't that nice? Thank you, Puck."

"You're welcome," he said dully. "I'm simply a generous man. And, of course, I look forward to sleeping in the same bed as my brother, who most probably snores."

"He does not," Chelsea said, adding quickly, "I mean, he doesn't seem the sort to snore."

Beau smiled in the darkness. *That ought to serve to shut up Puck for a space.*

They were just about to give up their vigil when two men on horseback, looking ready to travel and followed by a small, nondescript black coach, rode into the inn yard and dismounted. Their faces were in shadow until they reached the door to the inn, but then the light from the flambeaux captured their features as they looked all around the inn yard before disappearing inside.

"Well, damn me for a blind fool. And I said he was a bore?"

"I didn't disagree with you, Puck," Beau said, taking Chelsea's hand as they turned toward the White Swan. "Dickie Carstairs. I wouldn't have believed it if I hadn't seen him with my own eyes. And Baron Henry Sutton. Both highly admired in London Society, as well as two of the last people I would ever think could be involved in something like this. Jack keeps interesting company. All right, let's go."

CHAPTER SEVENTEEN

CHELSEA SAT TUCKED up in the window seat, stripped to her shift with a thin blanket wrapped about her shoulders, and looked out over the town of Gateshead, or as much as she could see of it in the dark.

It had been a long day before she'd overheard the man Jonas. Now that long day seemed like an eternity, and yet she couldn't seem to fall asleep.

Thomas and Madelyn and Francis Flotley were out there somewhere in the dark beyond the window. They hadn't given up the chase.

She couldn't believe it.

What could they do if they did find them, overtake them before she and Beau could reach Gretna Green? It had been days and days. Nights and nights. They'd have to know that by now she had become a ruined woman, sullied, compromised beyond redemption. Why hadn't they simply done the logical thing, given up and turned back to London?

She had so counted on them giving up the chase.

They must think she could still be saved from her willful disobedience. Or needed to be punished for it.

Chelsea winced at the thought. If that were the case,

then she believed she knew how her brother's mind worked. He'd hand her over to Francis Flotley without a thought, condemning her to a lifetime of penance and prayers and…no. She could not even think about the rest. If the thought of a life with Francis Flotley had been untenable before, now it was ten times worse; she'd rather kill herself than allow that man to put his hands on her.

Beau wouldn't let that happen if he could prevent it. He wouldn't simply turn her over to Thomas without a fight. He'd wanted to thwart Thomas at least as much as she had wanted to escape her fate.

But now he worried her. The original idea had been to seek his protection, yes, and give him his revenge in return.

She hadn't thought about the danger to him. A selfish, selfish, unnatural creature, that's what she had been at the time.

But that time had passed.

Now she knew him, knew what sort of man he had become. And now that she was in his care, he would fight for her. She'd seen the calm, efficient way he'd struck down the man Jonas with the barrel of his pistol. He wasn't unnecessarily violent, he hadn't shot the man, but he didn't run from a fight.

Tonight had been frightening. Seeing Beau with a pistol in his hand, that look of grim determination on his face, seeing how he'd responded to the thought of someone he cared about being in danger—no wonder she had taken refuge in Puck's silliness. The reality of what they had been about had been almost too much to bear.

And it would happen again, if Thomas found them.

When Thomas found them, for that was now as inevitable as tomorrow's sunrise. Married or on their way to the blacksmith and his anvil, at some point they all would confront each other.

And if anything...terrible were to happen, it would all be her fault.

Escaping Francis Flotley had been the impulse of a moment. Fleeing on horseback had been exhilarating and even fun—except for the rainstorm, of course. Getting to know Beau continued to be a wonder to her.

And the rest of it.

But seeing him tonight, seeing that pistol in his hand? The game, the adventure, they weren't real. Tonight had been real.

He would protect her. He would defend her.

But who would defend him?

Chelsea's mind persisted in moving in circles. She wiped at her wet cheeks with the backs of her hands and tried to concentrate, because she had to do something if Thomas was still on the hunt.

"Growing up would be one consideration," she told herself, sniffling. "This is not some mad lark, you silly girl. It is a pursuit. There is no Finish line to be crossed in Gretna Green, where Thomas will have to stop, turn around and know himself the loser. There will be consequences."

She hastily wiped her cheeks again when there was

a knock on the door, and she heard Beau outside, quietly asking to come in.

"Just…just a moment," she called out, quickly heading for the washstand and splashing cold water on her face before unlocking and opening the door. "I was… you woke me up."

He walked past her just as she realized that the bed may have been turned down, but although it had gone three the last time she'd heard the mantel clock chime, it was obvious she hadn't been sleeping in it.

He didn't tease her. "I couldn't sleep, either. Puck, on the other hand, sleeps the sleep of the dead, proving he possesses either a quiet conscience, or no scruples whatsoever."

The blanket was slipping, and Chelsea readjusted it across her shoulders, clasping its edges in front of her. "Is that your way of saying that we possess neither?"

"No," Beau said, seating himself on the side of the tester bed. "I think we both have scruples."

"But not a quiet conscience, at least not me." She nodded her head. "How did you know?"

He held out his hands to her, and she went to him, stepped into the open V of his legs and put her hands on his shoulders. He had become so important to her. Did he know that? They had been together for only these few short days, and yet she could no longer imagine life without him. She might even love him. No wonder she was so terrified. She'd never loved before; she didn't know how to react, what to say.

She couldn't tell him. Not if she didn't know how

he'd react to any such declaration. He might even tell her she was wrong, that physical pleasure was something entirely separate from love. And he could be right. Because she didn't know, couldn't know.

But for now, he was here. For now, that was enough.

The blanket slipped to the floor.

He looked at her with sympathy in his eyes. "You thought he'd given up by now, hadn't you? The moment Jack told us he'd seen your brother's coach, you went quiet. You've been thinking he would have turned for home by now, believing we'd outrun him. You thought it was over."

She nodded her head, avoiding his eyes. "He never really liked me. Why should he suddenly care so much?"

Beau stroked her cheek. "Truth? This isn't about you, Chelsea, and it never has been. This is about Thomas, about how what you do reflects on him. And on Madelyn. That I'm the man involved only compounds his potential for disgrace."

"And Madelyn's," Chelsea pointed out quietly. "She could have had you, all those years ago. Instead, I've got you."

"Not many would consider that a grand accomplishment," he said, smiling. "But now you think we're looking at violence, don't you?"

She sighed. All the way down to her toes. "Are we?"

"Not on my part, no. The way I see it, I've already won, and in ways I hadn't even expected. What your brother is willing to accept? That I don't know. How deep does this new devotion to religion run with him?"

"I told you, it has served to make him worse. He used to rant, and scream, and hit things. Now he speaks softly and supposedly reasonably, all while saying the most inane things, and then reminds me that God saved him on his deathbed, and now lives in him, and approves of him and whatever he does. Such a surfeit of claptrap, and all thanks to Francis Flotley. It was becoming unbearable, living with Thomas, watching him become more and more a cat's paw to Francis Flotley. And then to say that I must *marry* the man?"

She sighed once more. "But I should never have involved you. That was selfish."

"Now you're giving yourself too much credit. Chelsea, I do nothing I don't want to do. You came to me with a proposition, and I accepted it. I don't renege on my word once it's given."

Yes, she'd already figured that out on her own. She fingered the folds of his cravat. "I suppose we could leave the country. Only for a little while. Until Thomas is...until he's..."

"Dead of old age?" Beau suggested, smiling at her. "The insult I've offered him is not the sort of thing a man forgets. Let's just get to Scotland, marry, and deal with Thomas and his wrath when it comes. It's too late for anything else."

And there it was. He thought it was too late. Because he'd taken her to his bed, even though it was she who had instigated her own ruin. It wasn't because he hadn't warned her. It wasn't because he had fallen in love with her or any such romantic nonsense. He had begun something, and he would finish it. Jack had called him dutiful, and he was. "Are you certain?"

His smile faded. "Damn it, Chelsea, I was right, wasn't I? You're thinking about going back to him, throwing yourself on his mercy or some such fool thing. Sacrificing yourself like some Penny press heroine. Were you even going to be here if I'd waited until morning to come fetch you?"

"You interrupted my thinking, so I don't know," she said truthfully. "I may have come to that conclusion, eventually. I was considering it. It seems the right thing to do, right up until I think about Francis Flotley, and then I keep losing my courage."

"That's not losing your courage, it's gaining some common sense."

"But I had no right to put you in this position, to put you in danger. If Thomas thinks I can still be saved, which he must or else he would have broken off his pursuit by now, then it won't be over just because we've married. I don't know why I thought it would. But if I were to go to him now, and plead for forgiveness, then there would be no reason for him to…to try to hurt you."

"He's not going to hurt me, Chelsea."

"You say that, but you can't know. Please, Oliver, look at this from my perspective. I did this, not you. If anything were to happen to you, it would be my fault."

"Oh? And I'm innocent in all of this? I could have said no, Chelsea. Admittedly, I may have been slightly in my cups when you arrived in Grosvenor Square with your plan, but I immediately saw the benefits to me. I don't like your brother, it's that simple, and perhaps even that petty. I put no more thought into your welfare in this than you did into mine—you wanted escape and I wanted revenge. I could have told you what to expect before we took this step, but I didn't."

"You make us both sound terrible," she told him. "Perhaps even worse than terrible, because I think we've been rather…enjoying ourselves."

"Enjoying each other," he said, pulling her closer between his legs, to begin lightly nibbling on her earlobe. "Why don't we concentrate on that tonight and let tomorrow take care of itself?"

"You're only saying that to divert me," she told him, tipping her head slightly to give him better access to her.

"Damn, you've found me out. Is it working?"

"It shouldn't. Then again, I suppose I can't be any more ruined than I already am." She closed her eyes as Beau untied the ribbons on her shift and then slid his hands inside the bodice to cup her breasts. She tried once more to concentrate on more important things, but she knew it was a losing battle. After all, what could be more important than this? He'd awakened feelings in her she hadn't known she possessed. If enjoying such pleasures made her a sinner in Thomas's eyes, then so be it. *And no wonder there were so many sinners…*

Beau began stroking her nipples with the pads of his thumbs.

Chelsea was finding it more difficult to care about anything but the sensations he was arousing in her.

What a clever man he was. And if tomorrow had to come, why shouldn't they enjoy tonight?

"Good. No more talk. I'd much rather see you naked," he said, his voice low, faintly husky. As if to prove his point, he pushed the shift from her shoulders and tugged it down until it passed her hips, puddled at her bare feet. "God."

He was looking at her. Just looking at her.

Perhaps she wasn't quite as debauched as she'd supposed. "Oliver...shouldn't we get into bed?" *Under the covers...*

"No. Not yet. Take the pins out of your hair for me, Chelsea. Please."

The fire was still burning brightly. She hadn't doused any of the candles. She could see his face. He could see all of her. She felt an instinctive tightening between her legs, although it was much too late for modesty of any kind.

Besides, she wanted what he wanted. She wanted to forget everything, and she knew he had the means to make her do that.

Slowly, she raised her hands to her hair, tugging out her pins with shaking fingers as he stroked her rib cage, swept his hands up and over her breasts and then back down, to skim her hips.

"Yes, that's it. Let it fall, Chelsea. Look how it spills down your back, teases at your breasts. Like a living thing. You've a woman's body now, sweetings. Awakened. Knowing. But there's so much more to know. A woman's body is full of secrets. So many ways to unlock them."

He slipped one hand between her thighs.

Within moments she had grasped at his shoulders to support herself, to keep from collapsing against him as her knees went weak, as she gave herself up to his touch. Just the fact that he was fully clothed and watching her, watching her so intently, sent a different sort of pleasure through her. Being his to touch, to do with as he pleased…pleasing her.

When her body convulsed around him she cried out with the pleasure, even as a terrible frustration seized her. She wanted the feel of his body against hers. In hers. Wanted it. Needed it. *Would have it.*

She pushed against him with her full weight, toppling him back onto the bed, and sealed her mouth to his, ground her mouth against his, becoming the aggressor, this new, wild, wanting thing inside her guiding her.

He'd joked about her clothing, but it was his shirt that would have been ripped from him if he hadn't helped her slip the buttons out of their moorings. But not fast enough…not fast enough.

To hell with his buckskins…opening the buttons was enough…no time for more. Not in this heat, not in this need.

He sat up, lifted her up and told her to put her legs around his waist, straddle him.

She would do it. Anything. Anything at all. Only hurry. Hurry.

Ahhh....

He was so big, so solid. She could feel him deep inside of her, deeper than logic would tell her possible—if she had time for logic, which she did not. She caught his rhythm as he held on to her hips and urged her to move, sliding her hands beneath his shirt and digging her nails into his bare back. He put his hands between their joined bodies, spreading her, stroking her, making her wild with need, pushing her toward some new precipice she had to reach, must reach, would die if she didn't reach...

"No!" she cried out when at last what she was seeking came to her, but then gave in to the inevitable, collapsing against him as she shuddered, as her body clamped and released, clamped and released, turned liquid, took her beyond anyone's comprehension of pleasure and to a place where there was nothing but him, nothing but her, nothing but this one perfect moment in time as she felt his seed fountain deep inside her.

"I love you, Oliver...I love you."

SHE'D BEEN THINKING about leaving him. Planning to leave him. Sacrifice herself in some cockeyed notion that this would save him.

Despite her performance as a maidservant, she wasn't quite the actress his mother was. A person isn't full of mischief and energy one moment, and then yawning and complaining of terrible fatigue the next. Not when the moment in between had contained the knowledge that Thomas was close and coming closer.

Beau acknowledged to himself that, like any man, he could never consider himself an expert on reading a woman's mind. But he'd concluded correctly that she'd intended to sneak away while they were still here in Gateshead, find her brother, give herself up to Francis Flotley in order to save the man who'd agreed to elope with her to keep her away from her brother, away from Francis Flotley, away from a future that would be, for an intelligent, vital person like Chelsea, nothing less than a living hell.

Yet here she was, asleep in his arms, safe in his arms. He'd held her with him the only way he knew how. With sex.

He wasn't proud of that.

Worse, she'd told him she loved him. In the throes of carnal passion, she'd said the words. And she'd probably believed them to be true.

She was young and vulnerable, and he was experienced. He'd shown her physical pleasure she hadn't known existed, and she had confused that with love. Why else would she even consider sacrificing herself in order to protect him?

He wasn't worthy of that sort of sacrifice. Or any sort of love.

I never should have touched her. I never should have agreed to her plan. I'm the bastard the world calls me. Jack knows that, Puck knows that; we're cut from the same cloth in so many ways. Nothing more has been expected of any of us.

I should have expected more from myself.

Chelsea stirred in her sleep and attempted to snuggle closer to him, but he carefully disengaged himself instead, pulled the covers over her and left the bed. He couldn't think rationally while she lay so trustingly against him.

He dressed quickly and quietly, and then sat himself down on the window seat overlooking the inn yard and the dark streets of Gateshead.

He'd be damned if he'd give her back. Because her sacrifice wouldn't change anything. She'd still end up married to the fanatical Reverend Flotley, and he'd still be the target of her brother's quest for vengeance. What had happened between him and the earl of Brean had begun seven long years ago and would have continued indefinitely if not for Chelsea's proposition. Now it had to end.

Chelsea didn't know how far her brother's hatred for him had extended over the past years, and Beau wasn't going to tell her, as it would only appear self-serving, give him more reason to have taken such advantage of her.

Once recovered from his injuries at Brean's hands, Beau had taken the young Lady Chelsea's advice to go away, go very far away. He had gone into the army because there was nowhere else for a man like him to go to prove himself. Fighting Bonaparte, he'd thought, would level the playing field, for they'd all be concerned with one thing—staying alive. You don't inquire as to the circumstances of a man's birth when you are relying on him to watch your back in battle.

He had eventually found friends there, among the rank and file, along with a few officers, gentlemen. But for those first terrible months he'd been condemned as a coward, the sort who would cut and run at the first sight of the enemy. Twice he'd been brought up on charges, first for theft from another soldier and then for looting. If the fool who had actually placed the items in his rucksack hadn't talked himself into a corner during questioning Beau would have been convicted and summarily executed.

There had been the rumors. The white feather tacked up outside his field tent. He'd had to watch his own back in battle, for some of his enemy wore his same uniform. Yet it was on the battlefield that he finally distinguished himself, and slowly he had been accepted. All he'd had to do was be reckless and ruthless and insane enough to fight twice as hard and take three times as many risks as any other soldier on the line.

He'd enlisted as an ordinary foot soldier and departed the king's service a lieutenant, a feat reserved for gentlemen. Along the way he had gained the respect of his fellow soldiers, and learned that the earl of Brean had been behind the rumors, the accusations, calling in favors from friends and even paying for others to make deadly mischief.

Clearly, if they had not been in London, the earl would have killed Beau that fateful day. At the time, Beau had thought that was because the man loved his sister. But that hadn't been the case at all. He had simply despised Beau for who, and what, he was.

All the while he'd served, Beau had plotted his revenge. He was going to stay alive, return home, and once there, he would destroy Thomas Mills-Beckman, completely and utterly. When the man was down to his last farthing, he would send him a letter explaining what he'd done and enclose a loaded pistol so that Brean wouldn't have to go to the trouble of finding one before he blew his brains out all over his study walls.

Madelyn had been long forgotten. She'd been the fantasy of a young idiot. But Thomas Mills-Beckman had killed something inside Beau that day, his youth, his naiveté some might say, and for that he would pay.

He'd told Chelsea he'd only been amusing himself, that his actions against her brother were mere pranks. He didn't know if she believed him or not, and at the time he hadn't really cared. His bleeding of Brean had been slow and not as satisfactory as he would have liked, and Chelsea had dropped into his hands unexpectedly, but was definitely not unwelcome.

He could try to convince himself that he wasn't a bad man, because he had attempted to talk her out of her plan, but he knew the truth. His protests had been less than halfhearted. Now he saw himself as he really was. Over the years, his plan for revenge had become an obsession, blinding him to right and wrong as he refused to see anything other than Brean's destruction.

Without more than a passing thought to what eloping to Gretna Green with him would mean for her, he'd gone ahead. With the plan, with the grand adventure, with the seduction of the earl's virgin sister.

And he'd been wrong. He'd started something he never should have begun, and now he had to finish it. It would soon be time to pay the piper, take his punishment. Puck had fought him on it when he'd told him what he'd decided, but he'd finally agreed to help. It was the only way to protect Chelsea.

It would be a gamble, and he could lose, but Chelsea would be safe.

Everything hinged on getting to Scotland without encountering Brean…and on not allowing Chelsea to know his plan.

MADELYN DREW her shawl around her shoulders as she quietly made her way down the dark corridor toward her assigned chamber of the inn. It was past three, and she craved her bed. Her own bed, her own new sheets.

But what a happy surprise it had been to discover Viscount Watley had stopped at this same inn. And without his jealous wife in tow, no less.

He'd been on his way north, to sit by the deathbed of his great aunt, the one with the surprisingly fat inheritance earmarked for her favorite nephew, but George had assured Madelyn that the old biddy would linger on for at least another week, not that she cared, since none of that money would ever find its way to her. Although he had offered her a pair of diamond earbobs if she'd allow him to turn her on her knees like a hound bitch. Men must lay awake nights, thinking up such nonsense.

Although it had been rather fun…

"Madelyn."

She turned her head toward the voice, to see her brother approaching, looking rather the worse for drink, his horrible black jacket hanging open over his not inconsiderable belly, his unfashionable black cravat undone. She remembered when he'd been neat, trim, if not any more handsome. Now he looked as if he'd just come from a strangely raucous funeral.

"Thomas?"

He put a finger to his lips. "*Shhh.* Don't want to wake the crow. Here, hold this."

He held out a bottle and, amazed, she took it, clutched it to her breast.

"There you go. Looks natural on you, Maddie," he said, grinning. Then he took her hand and led her toward one of the doors, having some difficulty with the key but eventually gaining entry and pulling her in behind him.

Once inside, he relieved her of the bottle, using it to motion her to the fireplace and the pair of uncomfortable-looking chairs that bracketed it.

"Thomas," she said, pointing out the obvious, "you've been drinking."

"Damn straight I have. I'd be whoring, too, but the barmaid said I was too drunk to keep up my end of the bargain. Clever minx, yes? Keep *up* my end?"

She couldn't believe her eyes or ears. "Thomas, what is going on?"

He lost his smile, lowering his chin toward his chest. "I don't know. Am...am I a bad man, Maddie?"

"Oh, is that all? Yes, of course you are. But no worse

than most, Thomas, really. If God were going to rain down fatal rounds of mumps on every bad man in England, the island would be populated only by women and small boys."

"I made promises. To God, you understand. If he'd let me live."

She rolled her eyes. Clearly her brother intended to be a maudlin drunk this evening. Well, if he began to weep into that horrid cravat, she was leaving! "I just ten minutes ago called on God myself, but we all invoke his name at some point or another, for one reason or another. It was the desperation of a moment for you, Thomas, and soon forgotten, if not for that damned Flotley and his fire and brimstone." She looked at him closely. "But you're beginning to see that now, aren't you?"

"He said I could be saved if I just listened to him and changed my ways. Although you're going to roast in hell. Sorry, Maddie. He told me that it was your sin that prompted mine. With Blackthorn, you understand."

Madelyn half rose from her chair. "Oh, he did, did he? I've half a mind to…no, it's probably too late, and the sight of the crow in his nightshirt might turn my stomach." She subsided into the chair once more. "And how was it *my* sin?"

Thomas took a long drink from the bottle. "He said that if you hadn't encouraged Blackthorn with your womanly wiles, then none of what happened would have happened."

"Really? I put the whip in your hand, did I?"

The earl shrugged. "Women do that. They goad. Chelsea goads me with her impertinence. Women are the root of all evil. Wars. Pestilence."

"And yet I've caught him out looking at me at times these past days as if he'd like nothing better than to *sin* with me. Thomas, you have been taken in by a charlatan, don't you see that? And a disturbingly licentious one at that. He's been leading you by the nose, and probably dipping his hands into your pockets with regularity. You've always been such an idiot."

"But…but my immortal soul…?"

She laughed in real amusement. "The devil with your immortal soul! He'll probably have it eventually in any event now that the veil of stupidity apparently has been ripped from your eyes. Now, can't we simply drop the crow in a ditch and return to London?"

He shook his head and sighed. "No, I can't do that. I need to be sure that would be the right thing to do. I've come to depend on his judgment in some things. Some things he has taught me seem…good. I need to sort them out, I suppose, the wheat from the chaff, as it were. I nearly died, Maddie…I nearly *died*. And I nearly killed someone—thanks to you. We must continue on until we find Chelsea in any case. I won't make her marry Francis, not now, and I need to tell her that before she throws herself away on that bastard."

"My brother, the saint. This alone, I must tell you, has made the discomforts of this trip worthwhile. It's certainly no secret that I've never much cared for you, Thomas, but I dislike you less tonight than I ever have before. We're rather alike, you know. As for Chelsea? She's too pretty by half, and that annoys me, but she'll never hold a patch on me, so I should perhaps be more forgiving. But what if she's already married to him? Will you make her a widow?"

Thomas turned his head to stare into the dying fire. "I don't know. That's part of what I need to sort out. I...I did some bad things, things you don't know. There must be some place between what I was and what Francis has told me I must be. I don't know..."

"I suppose you could simply disown her if you think that's the *middle*," Madelyn said, knowing that her threats to do the deed herself had been all bluster. She was deathly afraid of pistols. "And I suppose you and I are already well on our way to being laughingstocks anyway. But do you know something, Thomas? If you truly mean to at last throw off your sackcloth and ashes, we two could set London on its ear. The Bad Breans? I rather like that, much as you disgust me at times. Pass over that bottle, Thomas. We need to consider this..."

CHAPTER EIGHTEEN

BEAU AND CHELSEA had overslept, which wasn't unreasonable, seeing how busy their previous day had been.

Dawn had come and gone, and now they were sharing a breakfast in the room, waiting for Puck to return from his reconnoitering of the town, just in case Brean had shown up late last night. It was even possible that they'd have to remain hidden here until dark before heading back to their own inn, or simply moving on toward York.

Chelsea had protested the second option, and when he pressed her, muttered something about not leaving her tooth powder behind, of all things, and in the end Beau had agreed to send Puck to gather their few belongings and bring them to the hotel.

That seemed to satisfy her.

He watched her as she ate, her appetite seeming to have returned, as well as the light in her eyes. He'd congratulate himself for both, except that he did not underestimate the effect clean, dry sheets and edible food could have on a person. She'd already spoken about having a tub sent up if they did decide to stay for the remainder of the day, as the soap at this fine establishment was bound to be fragrant, the water wonderfully warm and the toweling thicker than a sheet of paper, softer than a bristle brush.

Edith and Sidney had yet to arrive, as Puck was traveling more quickly than the second coach, but Chelsea hadn't said a word about how wonderful it would be to have the services of a maid for at least one day…which meant that he had to swallow down his own frustration at having to forgo Sidney's clucking attention and his way with a razor.

She was…adaptable. Wonderfully so. She fit herself in with her surroundings rather than fighting them, and never complained. Puck had gone on for the space of five solid minutes this morning about the futility of finding a properly coddled egg in all of England.

Finally, she put down her fork and looked across the small table at him. "Will he challenge you to a duel?"

Beau roused from his musings. She certainly did have a way of getting straight to the point.

"Your brother? Hardly. He's rather averse to fair fights. Having two burly footmen hold a man down while he wields a horsewhip is more in line with your brother's level of courage. That, and other methods we won't discuss. In short, let's not talk about Thomas, if you don't mind. I'll deal with him when I must, but that doesn't mean he should be constantly occupying my thoughts. Or yours. There are other, more pleasurable ways for us to pass the time."

"Oh, no, Oliver. You won't divert me a second

time. We're going to talk. If I have to hold you off at gunpoint."

"Now that would be interesting. All right, what would you care to talk about?"

"Thank you. I would care to talk about Jack, of course, which shouldn't surprise you. And Puck. And your mother. And why you all and your father allow her to be such a tyrant."

"Hardly a tyrant, Chelsea. She is what and who she is, that's all. I came to terms with that long ago. She made certain all three of us are well provided for. Except for Jack, who refuses our father's assistance."

"He said he doesn't belong at Blackthorn," Chelsea said, pushing back from the table and retreating to the window seat, as if she wished to prove her point that they would talk and nothing more. "Why would he say something like that?"

The statement had surprised Beau, as well. "You'd have to ask him. Jack's always been closed as an oyster when it comes to talking about himself, or about any of us. He said more last night than I've heard him say before, and we know that wasn't much."

"He called Puck a fribble. I think he was insulted."

"It would take far more than that to insult Puck. He knows who he is."

"And you know who you are," she said, pulling up her legs onto the cushion and tucking her skirts around her. "Who are you, Oliver?"

"A man unused to answering questions like that, I suppose," he said, admiring the way the sunlight streaming through the window turned her hair into a bright halo around her face. "We won't see her often, you know. If that's what is concerning you."

She looked at him in some shock. "It's that obvious."

"Women rarely like my mother. Then again, she doesn't much care for her own sex. Especially if they're younger and more beautiful."

"I didn't say I don't like her. After all, I barely met her," Chelsea protested, and then she shook her head. "But just think, Oliver. If she hadn't been so selfish, you would be your father's heir."

"And, as would probably have followed, also your brother-in-law."

"Oh." She frowned. "Yes, there is that again, isn't there? Thomas would have thrown himself on your neck, delighted to have Madelyn marry your title and wealth. You did have a lucky escape there in some ways, I suppose."

Beau threw back his head and laughed. "I agree. Especially when, after you'd finished being an interfering brat, I began thinking I'd wed the wrong sister."

Her eyes softened for a moment, but then she lifted that adorable chin. "You won't get me into that bed again, Oliver, not while I still have so much more to ask you."

"Are you quite sure? Puck won't return for at least another hour."

"Perhaps later," she said with a dismissive wave of her hand, and Beau had to bite the inside of his cheek to keep from laughing again. It certainly hadn't taken her long to learn the ways of a woman, or him very long, come to think of it, to become as close to a groveling idiot begging for her favors as any lovestruck youth.

Women had no idea of the power they wielded.

Or perhaps they did.

"Is that agreement, or a promise? I'd like to be straight on that, as you have explained the difference."

"Do all men and women have discussions like this?" she asked him. "Because I find them…disconcerting."

"How do I answer that? Do I tell you that the women I've been with over the years were none of them known for their conversation?"

She rubbed the underside of her nose with the side of her index finger. Probably to hide a smile, because a smile would reveal that she knew just what he meant, and nice girls didn't know that sort of thing. But then she seemed to think again and surprised him with her frankness. "Am I…very good at it?"

He could pretend that she'd asked about her conversation, but that probably would only serve to make her next question more pointed, and he was already feeling uncomfortable enough.

"I would say so, yes. And you could only improve with practice, which is why I mentioned that we do have some—"

"Yes, I thought I was rather good. My methods of seduction were, I mean," she said quietly. "I had to make my ruination complete. You couldn't be allowed to consider handing me back so that Thomas and Madelyn could make up some fiction that I had only been visiting a sickly aunt, or something."

Beau sat himself down beside her on the window seat. "Damn, woman, I feel so *used*," he said, earning him a look that might possibly have melted iron.

"Stop that. I just thought I should tell you that it wasn't so much of a sacrifice as I initially thought it would be. Losing my virginity, I mean. So I'm guessing that you're also very good at it. Not that I am requesting a list of your conquests, because I'm not."

"How you relieve my mind."

"I didn't relieve your mind very much last night, did I? When I told you that I love you. You kissed me, very nicely, but you didn't say anything. But that's all right, really. I shouldn't have told you. I've made things even worse for you now, haven't I? In fact, I've done nothing but complicate your life ever since I walked back into it. Haven't I, Oliver?"

"Chelsea, what is all this about? I thought we'd settled everything last night. You're not going back to Thomas, and I'm not going to renege on my promise."

"Because you hate him, or because I love you?"

Beau opened his mouth to deny her words, but then realized he was probably walking into a trap. If he said he didn't hate Brean, then why was he still here, unless he loved her in return? If he said he did hate the man, then why should she stay? No woman who believes herself in love wants to know that she is nothing but a means to an end.

He took both of her hands in his. "Chelsea," he began

slowly, "men and women enjoy each other. It's all right that you...enjoy what we've done. That I have, as well. That enjoyment doesn't have to have any other name put to it. It just—it just is what it is. A part of life."

She pulled her hands free, turned her face from his. "You think I'm stupid, don't you? Gullible. Fanciful."

He shook his head. "I think you're young, and that I should be lined up against the nearest wall and shot. Chelsea, look at me."

She only turned her head a little, looking at him out of the corners of her eyes. "Now you're going to tell me that we rub along together fairly well, and that we both get what we wanted from this elopement, but that you would rather not have me looking for more than that because you are prepared to give so much, but not any more than that. Why is that, Oliver? What should it matter to you if silly young Chelsea has perhaps mistaken passion for love? Or is it that you don't believe there is any such thing?"

Beau stood up and crossed the room, then turned on his heel and came back to stand in front of her. She had to stop thinking of him as anything more than her revenge on her brother. Not forever, but for now. He had to be able to know she wouldn't do anything stupid when Brean finally confronted them, the sort of reckless thing women do when they believe themselves to be in love—like saying she'd leave with her brother if she thought Beau's life might be in danger.

"I believe there is such a thing as love," he told her, hearing the bitterness in his voice. If he kept the discussion to his family, there was no need to feign that bitterness. "But not as you suppose it, Chelsea. Love is a weapon or a weakness, depending on who has it, who wields it. It serves only to make you controlled or controlling. It turned my father into an ass, an ill-advised calf-love damn near got me killed, and you were about to sacrifice yourself for me because your supposed love for me turned your mind to mush."

"Oh, Oliver," she said, her voice thick with sorrow. "Is that really how you think love works? As a weapon? A weakness? Do you really believe that love makes you either a villain or a victim? That's so sad."

"But I shouldn't worry, because you're going to correct me? Drawing on your vast store of experience, I'm sure."

"Now you're simply being facetious. It's easier to be angry with me, isn't it?"

He nearly said yes but stopped himself in time. "What do you want me to say instead, Chelsea? That I don't believe in love? Because I'd tell you that you're wrong, I believe it exists. I also think it often does more harm than good."

"Because I was considering going to Thomas and asking his forgiveness if he promised not to hurt you? But don't you see? I did this to you, I put you in this untenable position. It's only fair that I try to fix what I did wrong."

"The hell it is! A few days ago you couldn't have cared what happened to me, as long as you got what you wanted."

"Yes, all right, I've admitted that, horrible and self-ish as it sounds. That was then, Oliver. *Before.* But now I—"

"Now you love me. Isn't that wonderful? And to prove it, you'll throw your life away. No, what you've actually done is to prove my point, Chelsea."

She was crying openly now. "You're twisting everything I say!"

"I can only do that because neither one of us has the faintest damn idea what love is. Do we, Chelsea? I took you to bed. I gave you nothing more than any man could have given you. Allow me, please, to know at least that much. We enjoyed each other. That's something much more basic than love. You don't sacrifice yourself for what I gave you, you don't throw your life away—you go find another man to satisfy you."

Chelsea slowly got up from the window seat and walked over to him, her eyes now a cold, blue ice.

"All right, Oliver," she said, her voice calm, eerily calm. "If that's all it is, for me, for you—*satisfy* me. Right now. Just use me as I use you, both of us knowing that there's nothing more to it."

She'd called his bluff. She saw straight through him. God, she was magnificent!

"Chelsea," he said, nearly pleaded. "Don't do this."

"Don't do what? Not so long ago, you suggested we had time before Puck got back. We still have time. I'm sure I still have a lot to learn about the ways a woman can be...*satisfied.* And you're such a brilliant teacher, aren't you? No? Well, then, perhaps I'll just go find someone else. After all, according to you, one man is as good as another. But don't worry, Oliver, I won't make the same mistake twice. I won't give a damn for him any more than you think you give a damn about me."

"That's not what I meant, and you know it."

"Oh? Am I twisting your words now? Then what did you mean, Oliver? Tell me."

She'd tied him in knots. He'd tied himself in knots. "I don't want you to give me your love. Not now, not yet," he admitted quietly. "I don't know what to do with it, and I don't know how to give it in return. We both still have things to learn, Chelsea, and if we're lucky, time to learn them. If I tell you that I'd kill any man who dared to try to touch you, and that I think my life would be over if you left me—would that be enough for you for now?"

She raised her hand to cup his cheek. "Yes, Oliver, I think that would be enough for now. And I promise, I won't leave you. I will completely forget any idea of sacrificing myself in an effort to save you from Thomas's wrath. Perhaps because I love you, or perhaps just so that we don't ever fight like this again."

"And that's a promise, that last little bit, and not just an agreement?"

"Only if you kiss me," she said, just as a key turned in the lock and Puck opened the door only far enough to slip inside and lock it behind him.

"No time for that, kiddies. I came back to announce my success, only to see Brean and his sister and some near skeleton in a ridiculous black frock coat in the lobby, asking questions about you, if anyone remembers having seen you," he said shortly, as Beau and Chelsea stepped back from their embrace. "The earl's throwing coins around as he asks, so it probably won't be long until he has answers. I hope you're feeling particularly brilliant today, brother mine, because we're in the soup now, considering he may have seen me, and I look enough like you to be—ha!—your brother."

Beau took hold of Chelsea's shoulders. "You promised," he reminded her.

"I promised," she answered quietly, her complexion having gone so pale he was afraid she might faint in sheer terror. But he should have known better, as she confirmed with her next words. "I'd given this possibility some thought last night, since you seemed to think we might have to face something like this. I told you, Oliver, each time I thought I could do the noble thing, I'd remember Francis Flotley's wet mouth and fall into a near panic. So I formulated a plan for if we were caught here somehow."

"What did she say?" Puck asked as he handed Beau his jacket. "Beau, I beg you, don't listen to her. The last time she had a plan, I missed my dinner and ended up sleeping with you."

CHAPTER NINETEEN

HE WAS IN A BOX. He needed to keep thinking of it that way. A box. Not a coffin.

But he was in a coffin.

He had nearly become accustomed to the total lack of light—and probably diminishing air—when Chelsea lifted the lid and looked down at him, the unexpected shaft of sunlight coming into the room through a window nearly blinding him. "Are you sure you're all right, Oliver? You look rather pained."

He blinked a few times and then looked up at her. She looked stunning in black. It would be very nearly a pity to cover her golden hair and beautiful features with a thick black veil, but needs must when the devil—or, in this case, Chelsea—drove.

"He's not pained, Chelsea," Puck said affably, also peering down at him now. "He's dead. Passed beyond all earthly woes. And have I told you enough times how brilliant you are? She's brilliant, isn't she, Beau?"

"Don't encourage her," Beau said, looking up into the concerned yet rather jubilant face of the widow Claridge. "As it is, I'll probably be racked with nightmares for the next decade. If we were already married, I would have refused this, you know. I want that on record."

"Duly noted. By the way, Brean and his small entourage are having luncheon downstairs even as we speak," Puck said and then unceremoniously slammed down the lid of the coffin, and Beau was cut off from sight and sound once again.

Chelsea had explained that it was the memory of his aunt's recent demise that had served to also spark memories of the deaths of her parents, which had most probably served as further inspiration. People looked away from death, or at least she knew she did. They turned their backs on death or bowed their heads, which was rather like turning their backs so that they wouldn't have to see, but seemed more polite and pious.

There was no need to tie strips of bedsheet into a crude ladder in order to escape detection by Thomas, and no need for violence. They would leave the White Swan as they had entered it, through the front door. Well, except for Beau, who would be carried out.

All she would need would be for Puck to sneak out and find some widow's weeds for her, so that she might cover her face in a heavy black veil. Oh, and a doctor and an undertaker both willing to be convinced to partake in their little farce.

She'd suggested he take a large, heavy purse with him on his quest.

That, and to help her convince Beau that there was nothing in the least cowardly in what she considered to be her brilliant subterfuge. Beau didn't know why he had fought her so hard on that one point; probably because he would be unable to defend her if Brean saw through their charade. It certainly had nothing to do with her mention of becoming aware of her father's nose and ear hair as he lay in his coffin…but that thought had occurred to him.

Within the hour, Puck had wrought a miracle, and Beau's purse had been lightened by fifty pounds, a small price to pay, according to Chelsea, who'd dismissed the sum with the wave of one hand.

Puck had just come back to the room to happily announce that the entire hotel was most probably soon to be in an uproar, as someone—that someone quite possibly being himself—had put it about in hushed tones that there may be a case of plague in the hotel, that one man had already died. That particular twist had been Puck's own, and he was much too proud of himself, Beau thought.

He felt himself becoming slightly lightheaded, and pushed up the lid of the coffin. "Much as I'm loath to point out even one small flaw in your plan, Mrs. Claridge, I think I might truly be a corpse by the time you get me out of here. Puck, use your knife to poke a few holes in this thing, won't you? It would seem I've become accustomed to breathing."

"Always a complainer," Puck told Chelsea as he withdrew a knife from his boot. "This box cost five pounds, just for the hour, you know, our undertaker being a greedy sort. Now we'll probably have to buy it. Not much call for air holes in coffins, I don't think, and lovely as it is with those soft cushions and all, I doubt you want to keep it."

"Some people have bells attached," Chelsea told them, at which point both men looked at her, waiting for her to expand on that statement. "Don't look at me as if I've said something outlandish. They attach them to the *coffins,* not the corpses, for pity's sake. I read about them in a book."

"I'm going to have to start monitoring your reading choices, I see," Beau said, sitting up in the coffin. "But do go on. Please."

She rolled her eyes, which made him want to kiss her, and then explained. "It's in case they aren't really dead, you understand. The bell is put up on a pole of sorts that is stuck into the ground with a chain or something attached to it and running straight down and into the inside of the coffin. That way, if the person is not dead, and wakes up, he or she merely reaches for the chain and pulls it, alerting everyone to dig them up. Although I did wonder if you would have to pay someone to linger in the graveyard for a day or two, or else who would hear the bell?"

Puck grinned at his brother as he went about desecrating the coffin. "Would you perhaps want to rethink that decade of nightmares, Beau? Make it two rather than one? Ah, and that knock tells me our escort is here. Don't have time to finish the holes, got only the one small one, sorry. You might want to hold your breath. I'll be slipping out the window once I'm certain everything is in place. So until we meet again in heaven—or the undertaker's establishment—rest in peace, brother, or at the very least, in silence," he said as Beau quickly lay back, and then the lid came down and darkness descended once more.

But at least he could breathe marginally better. And even hear. The dark wasn't so bad. As long as he could keep forgetting that there was a heavy wooden lid only a few inches above his nose. He was all but stuffed in this damn box. Didn't they come in *sizes?*

"There's word downstairs that the plague is running rampant in this hotel. I must protest, Mr. Blackthorn. I never said anything of the kind. If the truth were to come out, I'd be ruined."

Ah, the doctor.

"Now, now, nothing to fret about. Have another five pounds."

Very free with my money, aren't you, Puck? You could have had him for two.

"Well, if you insist. Thank you. It will be only a few minutes now," the doctor said. "I'll watch at the window." But it was nearly ten minutes before he announced in some relief, "Mr. Hayes and his hearse await us just outside the hotel."

Hayes, hearse, hotel. Hayes's Hearses. Hmm, hmm. Hayes's Happy Hearses, since the man's pockets had already been fattened by ten pounds. More, when he catches sight of the hole in his coffin. Hmm, hmm, hmm...perhaps one wasn't enough...

"Oliver? Can you hear me?"

She was whispering. Why was she whispering? The

*Whispering Widow. Hayes's Happy Hearty Hearses...
with bells on. Hmm, hmm, hmm—* Hmm? That is, yes.
Yes, I can hear you. Was just...napping." *Happy Hearty
Whispering Widows...*

"Good. The men are coming now to pick you up, so
continue to lie still. I would have opened the lid, but the
doctor's assistant only left us alone just now, to show
the men the way up to the room. And stop humming.
Why are you humming? Never mind, don't answer me.
Here they come."

Beau felt the coffin being lifted and had a sudden
vision of the rather long, steep flight of stairs that led
down to the lobby. It was one thing being carried to bed
on six men's shoulders, but something entirely different
if he ended up being dropped halfway down the stairs.

He had a sudden vision of the coffin sliding down
those stairs the way he and Puck and Jack used to sled
on the hills around Blackthorn when the snow was thick
on the ground, and then skidding to a halt in the middle
of the foyer, perhaps even knocking down Thomas
Mills-Beckman and his sister and Francis Flotley, *bam,*
like so many ninepins.

The urge to laugh became almost overpowering, but
the knowledge that whoever was carrying him believed
they were carrying a corpse stopped him. If he laughed,
they wouldn't just drop him, they'd probably launch him
down those stairs.

Ah, they were down, they'd made it. Now to get
through the lobby and into the hearse.

Hayes's Happy Hearty Hearses Hopping...

Someone was weeping.

Chelsea. She was crying for him. Wasn't that nice...

"Hold there! I will say a prayer over the deceased, for the peaceful repose of his immortal soul."

Beau's eyes shot open in the darkness. *Francis Flotley. It had to be. Damn!*

Beau tried to throw off his strange, happy lethargy, without much success.

"Reverend, come away. I just this moment heard it could be plague."

Brean. Wonderful. All we need now is Madelyn. Puck, Jack, him. Chelsea, Thomas, Madelyn. Family reunions all round. And Flotley can say grace...

"Not plague," Beau heard Chelsea say, her voice altered somehow, and slightly muffled, as if she had a handkerchief pressed to her mouth beneath the heavy veil. "Mumps."

"God's teeth, Reverend, did you hear that? Get away, man. Save yourself!"

Which was why Oliver Le Beau Blackthorn went to his grave without benefit of prayer, or would have if he'd really been dead, which he wasn't, and didn't plan to be for at least another four decades, all of which he would live happily as long as Chelsea was by his side.

Mumps? The girl was a genius! Hayes's Happy Happy Hearty Hear...

Beau hummed the alliterative ditty as he slipped into unconsciousness.

THE WELL-SPRUNG Blackthorn coach tooled smartly, far ahead of Brean, Puck had assured Chelsea, before Beau finally not only opened his eyes with every indication of them remaining open this time, but even asked if there was any reasonable chance they might stop to eat something any time soon.

"And you're quite sure you're all right now, Oliver?" she asked him, still concerned. Her plan had seemed so complete. Except for allowing the poor man enough air. At this rate, their grandchildren would be entertained with stories for all of their childhoods.

When they'd finally been left alone in a horrid little room at the back of Hayes's Funeral Parlor and Puck raised the lid on the coffin, it was to find Beau unconscious, so much so that Puck had been forced to slap him awake—something Puck seemed to have enjoyed rather much once Beau had uttered his first, faint moan. Which had sounded rather like *Hayessssss*.

"I told you, I'm fine. Sleepy, but fine. Although I do now see the flaw in that bell contraption you spoke about. Mr. Hayes, at least, fashions a fine, tight coffin. If you aren't dead when they plant you in the ground, you will be very soon, simply for lack of air."

"Meaning you'd still wake up dead," Puck said from his seat across from them. "Do you think we should tell anyone? In the interests of—would that be science? Somehow I don't think so. Are you recovered enough to ride? Not that your horses aren't doing fine with the groom riding one and dragging the other back there— but if I were a horse, I'd want to do more than lope along in the dust behind a coach. Seems to be ill-treatment, of the horses, not to mention the groom. And not that I'm against having your company, either, but Brean will be looking out for a coach. You said so yourself."

"All this concern, Puck. You really just object to riding backward," Chelsea told him, joining in with his banter, wishing she could shed herself of the horror she'd experienced when they'd removed the lid to the coffin. Puck hadn't fooled her, either, for the look he'd shot her at that moment had only redoubled her fear.

"And the two of you object to being the three of us," Puck responded, giving her a wink. "I'd be insulted, if not for the fact that you're right, I loathe riding backward. I know where I've been. I want to know where I'm going."

"Many would," Beau said silkily. "Are you still planning to return to France once we're done here, to continue your career as a fribble?"

"Being the youngest sibling is never easy, is it, Puck?" Chelsea said sympathetically. "Everyone else seems to believe they're in charge of you. You don't have to answer him."

"That's a comfort, but I believe I actually have an answer. I'll probably return to Blackthorn for a space, as I had promised, and our mother has likewise promised to remain there for the summer, and then head back to Paris until the spring. Jack said something about being accepted in London—it was rather a dare, I think—and I believe I may take him up on it. I'll probably start by visiting his two coconspirators, who we saw last night. I think I might be able to trade my silence for a few introductions, don't you, Beau? I pride myself on being an affable enough fellow, but first I need at least one door opened for me."

"You've got a devious mind, Robin Goodfellow," Beau told him, stretching out his long legs and slapping at his thighs a few times, as if to rouse them from some sort of slumber. "I know, because that's just what I'd do."

"Bastards all," Puck said happily. "I can't imagine how boring it must be to have the world simply handed to you." The coach slowed a bit, encountering a crossroads, and Puck leaned his head out the open side window as the coach turned to the left, to read the fingerposts. "Ah, it would appear we're about to enter some rustic and benighted village. I told Jenkins to find a small inn, off the main roadway. We'll soon have your belly full, and you can be on your way."

Chelsea felt a momentary rush of panic at the thought of leaving Puck. They'd been doing well on their own, she and Beau, but now that they knew Thomas was so close behind them, she had reconsidered the idea of splitting up their small group, finding their own ways to Gretna Green. Giving up the extra pistol, if it came to that.

But she couldn't say this to Beau.

"Oliver, can't we stay with the coach? I'm so weary of inferior inns and horseback."

He reached over and took her hand. "One more night, Chelsea, and then you'll have the coach and the best inns, all the way back to Blackthorn. I promise. Your brother is too close."

"He smelled of peppermint," Chelsea said quietly, reliving those terrifying moments in the lobby of the White Swan. "He always used to smell of peppermint, but not for a long time. I'd almost forgotten. He thought it covered the smell of strong spirits. Do you suppose I've driven him to drink? At any rate, I thought I was going to throw up on his shoes. Madelyn was there, too, you know. She laughed when Thomas turned and ran out of the lobby as if the hounds of hell were after him."

"I wish I could have seen that," Puck said. "Do you think this means they won't spend the customary night in Gateshead before pushing on?"

"I think we have to assume that, yes, thanks to someone's mention of plague and mumps in the area."

"Oh. We hadn't thought of that, Chelsea, had we? Sorry."

"Never mind. As long as we stay well ahead of them. Still, it's yet another reason Chelsea and I need to return to horseback. Brean and his coach will most likely stay to the main roadways, and those roadways will become more clogged with coaches the closer we get to the border. But at least they won't be moving on with a fresh team in the shafts. Remember?"

Chelsea smiled. "I still can't believe you hired every team in the entire city."

"A grand gesture, Beau, but one I'll forgo the rest of the way, considering that I already heard one angry gentleman offering double what the rental was worth so he could put a fresh team to his coach in order to catch up with his mother, of all things. Something about the woman and her butler absconding together. Brean will probably do the same. All you've done with your misguided pocketbook is to make all the stable owners in Gateshead very happy men."

"Oliver! Hadn't you thought of that?"

"Truthfully, no. At the time, it seemed brilliant."

"At the time," Puck said, shuddering slightly at some memory, "I thought a lavender waistcoat flattered me. We all make mistakes, I suppose."

Chelsea nodded. "I didn't consider air holes when we put Beau in the coffin. Lavender, Puck? Really? Did Oliver ever tell you about his waistcoat of several years ago? It had stripes that actually seemed to *glow*. And his jacket was so tight, his shirt points so high, he probably should have had air holes cut into them, as well."

"We all have Brummell to thank for his more moderate approach to fashion," Puck said. "I saw him in Calais, Beau, you know. He's fast becoming one of the local sights. Sad, sad. We visit, we discreetly leave a purse somewhere he can find it, and then we go away again. I've been more careful of my allowance ever since. Debt is a terrible thing."

"Yet you're content to owe your existence to the allowance your father gives you?" Chelsea asked before she could guard her tongue. "Oh, I'm so sorry. That's none of my concern, is it?"

"Don't apologize, Chelsea," Puck said immediately. "I know Beau here oversees all our father's estates, so

he earns his keep, and that Jack refuses to take a groat
from him. I imagine it's more than time for me to follow
their example. In fact, I traded my allowance for one of
Papa's smaller estates, which he said he wanted to give
me in any case. For my sins, I am now a landowner, one
with absolutely no notion of how any of that works."

"It works with you or without you, I've found, as long
as you have good stewards in place, which I have made
sure of these past years," Beau told him. "Go back to
Paris, Puck, finish whatever it is you feel needs doing
there, and return as you said you would, in the spring.
I'll watch over your estate in your absence. It's the least
I can do to thank you."

"But not until you stand up with us as we marry,
Puck, please?" Chelsea begged prettily. "You won't just
stay here, but will still follow us the remainder of the
way, and be there, won't you, and return with us to
Blackthorn?"

She thought she caught a quick exchange of looks
between the brothers as Puck agreed he would be there
and would have asked them to explain it, except that
the coach began to slow before pulling into yet another
small inn yard.

"Time to change out of your so-flattering widow's
weeds, Mrs. Claridge, as your husband has made a
miraculous recovery," Beau said, and the subject was
dropped.

CHAPTER TWENTY

THANK GOD for Chelsea's admitted inability to tell north from south.

They had a quick lunch at the small but reasonably clean inn the coachman found, changed into their riding clothes yet again—the innkeeper's wife was delighted with the gift of the widow's weeds, although her husband hadn't appeared to be similarly jubilant. They then said their farewells to Puck before watching the coach drive off, heading nearly directly west now and toward the old coaching road, promising to meet them over the border in Gretna Green.

And then Beau had helped Chelsea into the saddle and headed their horses north.

His plan was simple: Gretna Green might be the best-known destination for eloping couples and, indeed, had acquired a bit of cachet for those wishing to marry over the anvil. But it was not the only Scottish town to take advantage of the income derived from performing these runaway nuptials.

In fact, Beau had several destinations to choose from—Lamberton, Mordington, Paxton, Coldstream.

He'd chosen the latter and now had in his pocket a crudely drawn map obtained from the innkeeper.

They would be able to ride across country in many spots, stop about midway for the night and be crossing the border at Coldstream Bridge by midday tomorrow. Directly at the end of that bridge stood the toll house, also known now as the Marriage House. They'd be minus the blacksmith, and most probably any but a symbolic anvil, but the marriage would be just as binding. According to the innkeeper, half of Scotland was now licensed to perform marriages.

Only then would they proceed directly to Gretna Green, to confront Chelsea's family. Not that Beau was going to allow her within a mile of her brother and sister. No, they'd meet with Puck outside the village, and he would keep her safe as Beau rode on to meet with the earl.

Beau turned slightly in the saddle now to speak to Chelsea, as they were all but walking their mounts for a mile to rest them. "You like Puck, don't you?"

She looked at him quizzically. "Well, yes, of course. He's very likeable. And not half as silly as he'd like the world to think. Although he is silly. Young."

Beau laughed. "Young? He's a good five years your senior, I might point out."

"Oh, that doesn't signify. Boys stay silly much longer than girls. Probably because they're allowed to do so. Girls are set to growing up much earlier, being told to practice ways that will have them snapped up from the marriage mart their very first Season. By the time I was fourteen, I had learned how to manage a household, plan dinner parties and the proper protocol for placing the guests around the table, among too much more to mention. What was required of you at fourteen, Oliver? That you know how to spit without dribbling on your chin?"

"Actually, I think I was mastering how to swear like a sailor and whistle like a coachie. At fifteen, my father took me to the local tavern and introduced me to Lottie, who'd…educated most of the young lads in the area. That was supposed to make me a man, you understand. And why the devil do I tell you these things? Come on, the horses are rested enough."

"Yes, sir," Chelsea said, still grinning. "But first, is Lottie still at the tavern?"

"Why would you ask me something like that?"

"I don't know. I thought perhaps I should thank her." Her grin turned positively wicked. "Now come on, Oliver. We mustn't dawdle. We have a blacksmith to see in Gretna Green tomorrow."

He watched her spur her mount on, his mouth half open, although he didn't know what he could possibly have said to her in any case. In the end, he settled for muttering a line from Shakespeare he no longer believed he could give much credence: "'Men at sometime are the masters of their fate,'" and adding, "but clearly not right now."

Three hours later, believing they'd covered as much ground as they needed to in order to make it to Coldstream by midday the next day, he'd signed the inn register as Mr. and Mrs. Claridge for what he hoped would be the last time and asked that their belongings be removed from their saddles and taken up to their rooms. He also, when Chelsea pointedly nudged him with her elbow, ordered that tubs be immediately prepared for them both.

She nudged him again, and he ordered a late supper, to be served in Mrs. Claridge's chamber in one hour.

"Is there anything else, my dear," he asked, employing the weary tone of an aggrieved husband without much effort as they walked toward the stairs, "or am I released to visit the taproom for a mug of ale?"

"No, unfortunately not. I was simply practicing being a wife. Do you mind?"

He leaned down and gave her a kiss on the forehead. "In truth? No, I don't think I do. I think I should, but I don't. You're a frightening woman, Chelsea."

"Oh, well, that's good. I've always wanted to be—ah, there's my bag." She turned away without another word to him, following the serving maid up the stairs, telling her which bag belonged to her and already asking if she could have something in it pressed immediately, please.

He watched her until she'd gotten to the top of the stairs, at which point she stopped, turned to look down at him and said, "You may want to have that supper sent up in *two* hours, Oliver."

Beau thought about that statement for a moment, thought about how upset Chelsea had been about possibly leaving behind the purchases Puck had made and he had carried back to the inn that night…and then he went to hunt down the innkeeper and change his instructions, delaying their supper by *three* hours.

He should have said *four,* something he realized when he'd bathed and dressed and gone knocking on Chelsea's door.

Moments later he stood just inside Chelsea's assigned bedchamber and watched as she walked toward him, stopping a few feet away to hold out her arms and turn in a full circle in front of him.

It would seem the mischievous Puck had made one of his purchases in a shop catering to high-priced courtesans. He'd have to take very good care of his brother's estate while Puck was still in Paris.

Chelsea's new nightwear was white. But there, any comparison to *virginal* stopped and *blatantly sexual* began.

There was silk, yards and yards of sleek, flowing silk. There were areas of lace, sheer, and in the most interesting places. Thin satin ribbons crisscrossing her bosom, which was entirely bare beneath the dressing gown, and with a long, oval-shaped, cunning cut in the center of the flowing skirt, so that when she had walked toward him and the material moved, he could catch glimpses of her knee, her thigh…and higher.

Never in the history of the world had a woman wearing so many yards of material appeared to be quite so naked.

Her hair was down, the soft curls shining in the firelight, seven or more unbelievable shades of blond and gold, tangled in artful disarray.

Her eyes…those bewitchingly clear, gray-blue eyes. Part amused, part questioning…definitely hungry.

"It, uh, it took forever to figure out how it all went. The ties and things. At first I thought I had it on backward…but then I finally realized how it all works."

"It all works very well," he said, feeling a sudden need to swallow.

She lifted a hand to tug on one of the satin ribbons holding the dressing gown shut at her throat.

"No," he said, his voice more husky and pleading than imperious. "Leave it."

He approached her slowly, the anticipation nearly as good as what would come next, his body already hard and ready, his mind awhirl with possibilities.

He settled on one. There were more. But, then, they had all night…

A kiss. He'd begin with a kiss.

She lifted her mouth to his, a small smile curving her lips so that they were warm, welcoming. Sweetly, supremely sensual. Their tongues met, played, teased in ways that were more instinctual than calculating, practiced.

His hands went to her waist, and he picked her up, mouths still joined, her arms wrapped around his neck. He carried her to the table beside the fire and sat her down, insinuating himself between her legs.

Then moved his hands to more interesting places. His thumbs skimmed her nipples through the revealing lace of the dressing gown, the material slightly rough, just enough to arouse, to tighten, so that when he cupped her left breast in his hand and put his mouth to her, it was to feel the hard bud of desire through the material. She held on tight as he licked at her, took her nipple and the damp lace into his mouth, flicked her with his tongue.

She moaned, low in her throat. If he had been anticipating, so had she. They both knew what they wanted, and they wanted it now. *Now.*

He took her hand and guided it to her other breast, pressed her palm to the underside of it, put his thumb over hers and showed her how to move it over her nipple. How to please herself, even as he was pleasing her.

She didn't pull away. Within moments, she was squeezing her nipple between thumb and forefinger, coaxing it to bud for him. Only then did he shift, still cupping her left breast and taking it into his mouth as he had the other.

She knew. She knew what he wanted. Because what he wanted had become what she wanted. As he suckled at her, nipped gently at her, she began pinching and rubbing her left breast as he held it as if in offering to her…as she held her other breast, offering it to him.

He slid his hand between her legs, his stroking fingers matching the rhythm of his tongue, her own clever fingers. She threw back her head, nearly weeping in her pleasure, bucking against him as he took her higher, higher.

"Oh, God…. Oh, God. So…so good…"

She wrapped her arms and legs around him as he lifted his head and kissed her yet again.

He worked his buttons free, the urgency gripping him impossible to delay much longer. She was all heat, all fire, her legs wrapped tightly around him, her center open to him.

She was silk and lace, sleek and wet. Wild and wanton.

His.

He pushed himself into her, feeling her body pulsing with her pleasure, and drove into her deeply, again and again, until she tensed, hovered, suspended over the brink.

He moved one last time, and she cried out, clung to him as he exploded inside her, took what she gave, gave in return. Gave with passion, gave with need, gave with a certainty that he would never, could never, feel this way with any other woman.

She was his.

And he was hers….

THEY LAY on the bed, Beau's head in Chelsea's lap, and she fed him grapes, warning him not to choke because that was one story she didn't want to tell their grandchildren.

"If I choke right now," he told her between grapes, "there won't be any grandchildren."

She leaned down so that she could whisper the next words in his ear. "Now, Oliver, think about what we have been doing, and what you just said. How can you know that for sure?" Then she pounded him on the back as he jackknifed to a sitting position, coughing and choking.

"You did that on purpose," he said accusingly, wiping at his eyes with a corner of the sheet. "But, yes, I know it's possible."

"Lottie explained it all to you, I imagine," she said sweetly, putting down the bowl of grapes.

"No, you pernicious brat. Lottie showed me how to *avoid* such consequences. I simply can't seem to remember them when you're strutting about half-naked, seducing me."

She giggled.

He couldn't believe it. She was the most passionate, naturally sensual female in his fairly vast experience, and yet with that free, unaffected giggle she became at once young, innocent, playful. And, because she was also intelligent, funny, unexpected and kind, she was also the most dangerous woman in the world.

Beau looked at her for long moments and then said, "I begin at last to understand my father's dilemma."

"Pardon me?" Chelsea shook her head. "What are you talking about?"

"Nothing," he said, wishing he hadn't said anything. "No, not nothing. I said, am saying, that when a woman takes hold of a man, as you seemed to have done with me—don't look away—there isn't much she can ask that the man wouldn't give. To make her happy. To hear her laugh, see her smile. To *keep* her."

Chelsea's bottom lip trembled slightly. "Oliver, that was the nicest possible thing you could ever say to me. And the worst. I don't want to think that…that I have *wiles*."

"You'd rather think you're powerless to move me?" he asked her, laying her back against the bed, watching as her hair fanned out across the pillows.

"No," she said with her customary honesty. "But I'd like to believe I would never purposely *try* to…to move you. I really move you?"

He leaned closer to nuzzle at her throat. "Now I've done it, haven't I? Yes, Chelsea, you move me. Not to say that I wouldn't first ask *why* if you were to suggest that I cut off my right hand for you. But I'd probably consider it. That's also probably why women have never had to go to war. There's no need to take up arms when you can conquer with a smile, a look."

"Or with a bit of naughty nonsense that, now that I've worn it, probably means I will never be able to look your brother in the eye again."

"Yes, but that was why you insisted Puck go back to the inn to gather up our meager belongings, wasn't it? You'd brought the gown with you, planning to wear it for me."

"But not to employ it as a…a feminine wile."

He insinuated his hand inside the clever opening to draw lazy circles on her belly even as he began tracing a line of kisses down the side of her throat and into the sweet valley between her breasts.

"Well," she said, her voice slightly breathless, "maybe just a little…"

Beau chuckled against her skin and then raised his head to look deeply into her eyes. "I never do anything I don't want to do, Chelsea, and I haven't for a very long time. The difference is that now I want to do everything for you. I don't think you planned things that way, and God knows I didn't, but here we are."

"Oh, Oliver…" she said, reaching for him, "you'll do everything but say the words, won't you? Why don't you simply show me?"

Could he tell her that he was afraid to do that? Could he tell her that arousing her carnally was one thing; awakening her, teaching her, enjoying her, giving her pleasure. But if he truly, truly made love to her, made love with her, without the physical urgency, without the newness of it all, the teasing, even this gown, then he would be stepping beyond anything he'd ever done, anything he'd ever imagined.

He'd be giving not just his body, but himself.

"Chelsea, I—"

She put her fingers to his lips. "*Shh,* no, don't say anything. I don't want you to think you need to say anything."

He took hold of her hand and kissed her fingertips. "You were right earlier today. Men do stay silly much longer than women. Some of us remain silly for a very long time."

"Yes, but women are wise, Oliver. We can wait. Although I would very much like for you to look at me again the way you looked at me a moment ago. And if you could possibly consider kissing me…"

He kissed her. Close-mouthed and chaste. He spent a long time kissing her.

He rid her of the silk and laces. They were fine, for some other time. But not now.

Now he touched her, yes, but reverently. Slowly rousing her, worshipping her body, every inch of it. He kissed her eyelids, her hair, the crook of her elbow, the back of her knee. He ran his hands over her, following his hands with his mouth. Savoring each moment, each touch, each heartbeat.

Passion could be quick, hot, easily roused, swiftly sated. Physical pleasure.

Now he touched her with his mind as well as his hands and mouth.

He wasn't bringing passion to her body.

He was making love to Chelsea.

With Chelsea.

And he would never be the same…

THOMAS MILLS-BECKMAN, Earl of Brean, sat huddled close to the fireplace and a small brace of candles (and a lovely glass of not very inferior wine), reading Scripture from the prayer book that had been a gift from his own father, many years earlier.

It had been a long journey, both in time and in the mental ground he'd covered since they'd left London. He'd always known he wasn't a brilliant man. And yet now, for the first time in a long time, he felt comfortable with himself. He hadn't known he'd been uncomfortable, rather as if he'd had a toothache for so long that he only realized he'd had it when the pain finally stopped.

He'd never been particularly holy. Not even marginally devout. Not until he'd nearly died and made all those rash promises. He'd seldom opened this blackbound volume in the past two years—and never before that—although he often carried it with him now, as a sort of talisman, he thought. Francis had preferred that the earl limit his reading to sermons he, Francis, had penned—and Thomas had paid to have published.

He was shaking his head in amazement over one particular passage when his sister entered the private sitting room positioned between their two bedchambers, a glass of wine in her hand.

"You can't sleep, either, I see," she said, rather inelegantly plunking herself down on the facing chair. "And you're *reading?* E-gods, man, when did you take up that boring exercise?"

Thomas looked at his sister. He'd tried to like her, he really had. Tried for nearly five whole days. But it hadn't worked. He didn't much like himself, what he'd been for most of his life, what he'd turned into these past two years. He'd seen himself in some sort of mental mirror and had admitted to his reflection that he probably wasn't too bright. He most definitely wasn't kind, he was often deliberately mean, and he had a vile temper when he was goaded or too drunk. He didn't fight fairly—but then again, who in their right mind did?

But for all his faults, he still liked himself much better than he liked her. At least he knew who he was. She actually believed herself to be witty and even lovable.

"It's the strangest thing, Maddie. Everything sounds so different when I read the words for myself. Francis uses bits, snippets, in his sermons, to make his points, you understand. But when you see the *whole?*" He shook his head.

"Yes? When you see the whole—the whole *what,* Thomas?"

He closed the prayer book. Admitting to gullibility wasn't something he was eager to share with Madelyn. And when he thought about the money he'd poured into Francis's schemes and then compounded his losses by trying to recoup them with risky schemes of his own? That was even worse than thinking about how he'd nearly given his younger sister into the man's clutches. Madelyn had been lost years ago, but Chelsea might still be saved. No, he *would* save her. Chelsea had never much cared for her sister. That alone put her in his good books.

As a matter of fact, he probably should have listed Chelsea first in his litany of woes against Francis, but then again, Thomas knew he was not a perfect man. According to what he'd gleaned from his readings tonight, he simply had to *try* to be a better man. It wasn't all or nothing, good or evil. And, if by some chance there was some merit in Francis's beliefs, well, then he'd hedge his bets and at least *try* to become better. As in: better safe than sorry.

He'd sort out precisely *what* he'd try to be better at in the coming days and weeks. Probably by trial and error. Although he already felt fairly certain that once he tried keeping a mistress again that he'd cross that sort of sacrifice off his list. That, and abstaining from drinking strong spirits. And possibly loving one's neighbor as himself—nobody in his right mind would love any of his neighbors, especially the Dowager Countess of Loughborough, who lived next door at Number 23 Portland Place, and whose pack of yipping, yapping pug dogs she let roam free to bite at ankles and piddle on lampposts.

That was the answer: pick and choose. If a man tried to do *everything* good, all the time? He may as well be dead.

"Nothing. You wouldn't understand, Maddie. Suffice it to say that I've made some decisions. I've informed Francis that he is to be sent packing tomorrow morning, before I push on to Gretna Green."

"Oh, you did, did you? I'm glad to know you're at last seeing some sense. And will you now leave off those *horrible* funereal coats and cravats? I cannot tell you how you *embarrass* me with them. And how did the crow take the news? Badly, one could hope."

Thomas sighed. "I believe Francis suffers from the sin of anger. He called down God's wrath on my immortal soul. The fact that it has been a full three hours and lightning has not yet struck me tells me much about

Francis's true influence with the Almighty. When I mentioned that a little while ago, when he crawled back in here to ask that I reconsider, and I refused, he raised his hand to me."

"Oh, dear. And what did *you* do?"

"I hit him in the face with that chair over there. Several times," Thomas said, lifting his wineglass in a salute to himself. "The way I see it, Maddie, if Francis is right and I'm going to go to hell, I may as well enjoy the journey."

Madelyn raised her glass, watching him out of the corners of her eyes as she took a long sip of its contents. "And Blackthorn? Will you content yourself to merely taking a horsewhip to him again? You have to *know* he's defiled her by now. The man isn't *stupid.*"

"He's probably had her a dozen times by now." Thomas sighed. He'd hoped to wait until morning to tell her the rest, but she was here now. "As long as they aren't wed, I will take her back. She's bound to be thoroughly chastened by now, having to keep company with that uncouth bastard. I can always marry her off for a price, as we did with you."

"*What?* You and Papa thought I wasn't a…that is, Blackthorn *never*…he wasn't…"

"Your first? Yes, I know. But you were getting reckless, encouraging Blackthorn that way. I won't be in such a rush this time. I'll wait to see if she's going to whelp before I buy her a groom."

Maddie got to her feet. "Wait a moment, Thomas. You *knew* I wasn't a virgin?"

"Half of London knew," he told her, getting to his feet. "In fact, probably the only one who didn't was that fool Blackthorn, since he wasn't welcome at White's and never saw your name written down in the betting book, as I did the same morning he came to pay his addresses to you. 'J.S. wages W.R. a monkey he'll have a certain lock of hair from M.M.B. by fourteen June.' I raced home to wring your neck, only to find you'd sunk to seducing bastards. What would have been next, Maddie? The footmen? A chimney sweep?"

Madelyn paled as he watched, her eyes first going wide and then narrowing to slits, as if she had finally realized that she had lost some contest she'd felt sure she'd won. "That you should *dare* say such vile things to me. I've always *loathed* you, Thomas. I only *pretended* to like you. But it was only pity. You're *so* stupid."

"Yes, I know. I have done some stupid things, as well. I may have taken the whip to the bastard that day, but only because I couldn't take it to you—and only because I knew you weren't worthy of anything more than he is. I realize that now. You were lucky Papa and I could buy you a baron. No matter that Francis is wrong on so many counts, he was right about you. One way or another, you and your round heels are the cause of all of this. You can travel back to London with Francis in the morning. I've hired a coach, and that damn rocking horse is already strapped to its roof. See if you can make his life the hell you've made everyone else's. Goodbye, Maddie."

CHAPTER TWENTY-ONE

THEY ROSE BEFORE dawn, Beau having never returned to his own chamber, nibbled at the slightly stale bread and cheese they'd ignored along with the rest of the supper that had been delivered to the room, and were on the road to Gretna Green just as a watery sun was rising above the treetops.

This was it. This was the last day of their escape, their mad adventure, their—as Chelsea believed she would always think of it—journey of discovery.

This was the day they would marry.

This was the day they would confront Thomas and Madelyn and the horrible Francis Flotley.

Chelsea and Beau rode at a steady pace all morning, with their horses side by side, the roadway curving and rising, the air cooler here, the sun somehow brighter.

She was so anxious to arrive in Gretna Green. When she wasn't wishing they'd never get there, but could simply continue on the way they had begun, just the two of them, with the rest of the world and all its problems far, far away.

Her domineering brother. His strange, selfish mother. Society, who judged people on such superficial merits, so that Thomas Mills-Beckman was considered a gentleman and Oliver Le Beau Blackthorn as unworthy, beneath contempt.

She kept stealing looks at Beau from beneath her lashes, watching as, more and more, he turned from the perfect lover he had been last night to the tight-jawed man she had seen determined to protect his brother.

Right or wrong, he was going to protect his brother. Good or bad, he was going to protect his brother.

Beau, she thought, could give lessons to Thomas on what it meant to be a brother, what it meant to be a family. Good or bad, pleasing or a problem, family was family. You protected them, you defended them, you didn't judge, you didn't condemn.

Chelsea sighed silently. Which meant, if she also were to benefit from Beau's example, she would have to try very, very hard to not judge Adelaide Claridge.

"Where will we live, Oliver?" she asked him as they reined in the horses at a small crossroads and a series of fingerposts nailed to the trunk of a tree.

He'd pulled a folded scrap of paper from his pocket and frowned as he consulted it and the fingerposts. "Where would you like to live?" he asked in the tone of a person who probably wasn't going to pay much attention to the answer.

"Wherever you live, I imagine. It seems convenient," she answered, at last turning to inspect the fingerposts herself, in case he'd gotten them lost again...not that she'd say such a thing to him. At least not unless he wouldn't admit he was lost, because they should have been seeing signposts for Gretna Green by now, as it had gone past noon.

"I don't *live* anywhere, now that I think about it," he said, refolding the paper and slipping it back into his pocket. "I *reside*. Sometimes at Blackthorn, sometimes on the estates I oversee, sometimes in Grosvenor Square."

"Oh." Wasn't that strange. "Then I suppose I should ask you where you would *like* to live."

"Well, that I can answer easily enough. In your pocket," he told her, grinning rather evilly. "But, first, I suppose we ought to finally do what we rode all this way to do, and get married. Are you ready to be caught up in the parson's mousetrap, or at least with a toe stuck beneath his anvil?"

"They sound equally painful, and rather insulting to women, I would think, since I've heard it said that marriage is an institution created by females. But I don't see a sign pointing toward Gretna Green. Are you lost again, Oliver?"

He turned his horse to take the road heading off to the left, one that led down yet another rolling hillside, and she urged her mare to follow. "We aren't going directly to Gretna Green, Chelsea. As soon as we cross that bridge you can now see some distance ahead of us, we will be in Scotland, at a place called Coldstream. It has a very convenient establishment at the end of the bridge, I'm told. We can pay our bridge toll and get married at the same time."

Chelsea squinted as she leaned forward on her horse,

to see the bridge about a mile ahead, crossing a river she supposed made up a natural borderline between England and Scotland. "But...but Puck is waiting for us in Gretna Green. Isn't he?"

"Very nearly. He's reconnoitering while keeping safely out of the way of your brother and sister, and we'll join him there, but only once the deed is done. I didn't want us reciting our vows while constantly looking over our shoulders, in case they caught up with us."

"Once the deed is done," Chelsea repeated. "That sounds so...cold-blooded."

"Which is what I don't want our wedding to be," Beau said, sounding reasonable, or at least he probably supposed it did to his own ears.

"Do you think that if Thomas knows he's too late, that the *deed is done,* he will simply turn around and head back to London?"

"Do you?"

Chelsea shook her head. "No. Do you?"

"Truthfully? No, I don't. What I do know is that he can't be allowed to intervene before our vows are said. Once we're married, he can't drag you to the nearest blacksmith and insist you wed the reverend."

"You wouldn't let Thomas do that if you—" Her hands began to tremble so much that her mare, sensing her fear, began to dance as if ready to take the bit in its mouth and go for a run.

Beau leaned over and took hold of the mare's bridle, moving closer to Chelsea. "Look at me, Chelsea. Whether you are wife or widow, Thomas will no longer be in charge of your life, and Puck, your brother-in-law and therefore your guardian in my absence, will be there to make that clear to the Scottish authorities. I don't believe your brother would be so harebrained as to attempt to shoot me down, especially in Scotland, where the laws rather frown on such things, murdering brothers and fathers being very bad for business for the blacksmith parsons, I'd imagine. I truly don't think your brother will turn violent, not if I get to say my piece, but I had to prepare as best I could to protect you, no matter what happens later today. Do you understand?"

"No, I don't. If we're to be married without having to go to Gretna Green, why would we go there? Why can't we simply *do the deed* and immediately turn back to Blackthorn?"

"We have to face your brother sooner or later," he told her reasonably. "I'd just as soon get it done now, rather than at some place and time of his choosing. Besides, I'd rather face him and not someone he might hire."

"You actually think he might *hire* someone to harm you? That hadn't occurred to me. You've thought this all out, haven't you? You and Puck. And yet you waited this long to tell me?"

He smiled at her as the horses took their first steps onto the bridge. "Are you angry?"

She goggled at him. "Angry? I'm *incensed!*"

"Well, then, there's your answer. I believe I'm beginning to learn how to think as a husband."

"Well, don't flatter yourself, Oliver. It would appear

husbands think no more clearly than those who are not. You said Puck is waiting for us *near* Gretna Green. You intend to leave me wherever that is, with him, and confront Thomas alone, don't you?"

"At gunpoint if he has to, yes," Beau told her as they stopped in front of the toll house. "Now, are you ready to be married?"

She set her chin. "I don't think so, no."

"Chelsea…"

She looked at him, saw the concern in his eyes and relented. "Yes, I'm ready to be married to you. But if you somehow manage to make me a widow before the day is out, I'll never forgive you."

"You could stop scowling at any time, Chelsea," Beau said out of the corner of his mouth as they sat side by side on a bench in the toll house. "I think the man is beginning to believe I've coerced you in some way."

"You didn't trust me. You had me thinking one thing while you were planning another. This is not a good way to begin a marriage, Oliver."

"Please feel free to berate me. Later," he said, putting on a smile while trying to avoid Mr. Ramsey McHugh's concerned glances.

"I would say that I think you can count on that, yes. For now, could you please ask Mr. McHugh if he has a copy of the marriage ceremony? I believe I would like to take a look at the vows."

She was tipping up her chin again. Beau hadn't known her for very long, but certainly long enough to know that her tipped-up chin didn't bode well for him. "I would imagine they're typical of marriage vows anywhere. Said over an anvil, granted, but just as binding as if they were recited in St. George's."

"Yes, I suppose you're right. But I want to see if there is any mention of always being truthful to your spouse. Because unless it's a vow, then I may well spend the rest of my life wondering if you're only telling me things I wish to hear, and hiding those you know will have me looking at you like this—" she turned to glare at him "—and saying, *Oh, Oliver!*"

He laughed softly, shot a quick glance at McHugh and then whispered in her ear. "But I like the way you say *Oh, Oliver.* Especially the way you said it last night. *Ohhhhh, Oll-e-varrr.*"

She pressed her lips together tightly but couldn't hold back a smile. Or her soft giggle. "I do not sound anything like that."

"Yes, you do. Although sometimes you just purr."

"*Shh.* He'll hear you."

"Good. At least then maybe he'll stop thinking I've kidnapped you and am forcing this marriage, or whatever it is he's thinking. Excuse me a moment."

He got to his feet and walked over to where the rather fantastically mustachioed Ramsey McHugh was speaking to a couple who'd just moments earlier entered the building.

"I hesitate to interrupt, but my betrothed and I are in a bit of a rush. Will you be much longer?"

The man answered in a thick Scottish burr, which

made Beau suspect that the man was trying much too hard to be Scottish. "It will just be a little longer, laddie. Mr. and Mrs. McTavish are here now, so we're just waiting on my mother and my aunt Susan. Her little one, Mary, is sick with a nasty head. Sniffling and sneezing to send the birds from their branches. She'll be that sorry to miss this one. A real ladyship? We don't get many of those."

Beau looked to Mr. and Mrs. McTavish, who both smiled at him. Mrs. McTavish shyly waggled her fingers at him and blushed.

"Am I being obtuse? Why would we be waiting for your mother? And aunt, I think you said?" Beau was beginning to think Coldstream had been a mistake.

"For the wedding, sir. We don't get so many as what we used to, what with it being Gretna Green, Gretna Green, all over, as if it's the only town in Scotland worth eloping to, you understand. You're the first in a fortnight, and nobody wants to miss it." He leaned closer to Beau. "Truthfully, sir, there's not much else to do here in Coldstream."

"Oliver? Is something wrong?"

Beau walked back over to the bench and sat down. "It appears we're to have an audience," he told her, caught between exasperation and amusement. "Do you mind?"

Chelsea looked toward the small but now growing knot of people. "She's waving at me," she said even as she lifted her own hand and rather tentatively waved back, a small, nervous smile on her face. "Do you think I should go talk to them?"

"And say what in heaven's name?"

"I don't know. Perhaps I should thank them for coming?"

Beau pinched at the bridge of his nose. "Yes, all right. Why don't you go do that. Go play at hostess. I'll just sit here and yet again reflect on my sins."

"You could start with the one where you decided not to tell me what you planned for today," Chelsea suggested sweetly and then stood up and walked over to the group of—could they be considered *wedding guests?*

But thirty minutes later it was done. Beau wore a sprig of white heather in his lapel, given to him by Mr. McTavish, Chelsea clutched a small bouquet of some yellow flowers, McHugh rolled his Rs all over the vows, Mrs. McTavish not all that quietly snuffled into her handkerchief, Beau twisted at his signet ring until he could dislodge it from his finger and place it on Chelsea's finger—it promptly fell off—they signed the wedding register as Oliver Le Beau and Lady Chelsea Blackthorn, Chelsea had kissed all the women goodbye, and McHugh's mother insisted upon crumbling up what appeared to be a small and probably stale wheat cake and tossing the crumbs at them for luck as they exited the toll house.

In her hand, along with the small bouquet, Chelsea held a folded bit of paper carrying the addresses of her wedding guests, as she planned to send them all "something to thank them" once they returned to England. Oh, and she would tell everyone that Coldstream was a much better choice than Gretna Green, if they were of a mind to elope, that is.

Beau felt certain his headache would fade at some point but probably not for some time.

Not that he wasn't delighted to be married to this unique and wonderful woman. Because he was. Delighted, that is. But there was something about having been a carefree bachelor one day and suddenly married the next that might take a little getting used to. He'd been free. Not necessarily wild, but free. Now he'd been…domesticated. Almost overnight.

Still, the more he thought about it as they turned their horses toward Gretna Green, he knew he also felt complete now, even more so than last night…as if a part of him he hadn't known had been missing had finally been tucked into place. More people should do this—marry. The world would be a better place.

Now if he could only find a way to be rid of the wheat cake crumbs that had managed to insinuate themselves under his shirt…but then again, he knew he would soon be confronting the earl of Brean, and that a few cake crumbs were really the smallest of his problems.

CHELSEA SAT at the small table of the wayside inn, her chin in her hand, and looked at her husband. *Husband.* The word rather rolled off the tongue. Not as well as Mr. McHugh's Rs, but very nicely in any case.

"I'm very happy," she told Beau as he chewed on a bite of boiled potato. "And I've decided that you were right. I'm so glad we didn't simply attempt to beat

Thomas to Gretna Green and then just rush through some ramshackle ceremony. And now that the *deed is done,* there's really very little Thomas can do."

"He could shoot me," Beau pointed out reasonably. "I thought you'd been worried about that possibility."

"I wasn't, at the beginning, when first I suggested we elope. And then I was," she told him. "But now, suddenly, I'm not again. I think you should point out to him that you won't require him to hand over my dowry. It's rather large, you know. Things like that matter to Thomas."

Beau put down his fork. "Really? And should I then tell him I'll stop trying to bleed him dry so that he falls into despair and puts a pistol to his head?"

"You really do hate each other, don't you? You weren't, as you tried to tell me, merely *amusing* yourself. Were you?"

Beau seemed to consider her question for long moments. "I've despised your brother for a lot of years, and for more than one reason. But I think now we're even, more than even. He doesn't know what he's lost, and I'm amazed by what I've gained. I'm a very lucky man. God help me, I might even tell him that. We're both older now, hopefully wiser. There are no more scores to settle between us, not now."

Chelsea felt tears burning at the backs of her eyes. "You're being much too charitable, Oliver, and that could be dangerous. Let me go with you to meet with them. And Puck, as well. Don't go alone, please. There are three of them and only one of you. My brother can be volatile, especially if the peppermint means he's been drinking again. You suffered the blows, but I saw it all, remember? If he whipped you for daring to apply for Madelyn's hand, what will he do when he finds out we're married? Oliver—please."

"I'll think about it," he said, reaching across the table and taking her hand in his. "We can be there in less than an hour if we leave now. I imagine Puck will agree with you."

An hour later Puck did just that when they met up with him in an inn yard just outside Gretna Green, shortly after kissing Chelsea on both cheeks and giving her a brotherly hug. "I only agreed with his daft plan because I had the utmost confidence in your powers of persuasion, Chelsea." He then turned to visually inspect Beau, who was scowling at him, but not with any real heat. "You don't look any different. How does it feel to be married?"

"I'll let you know when we've been married for more than three or four hours, all right? How long have you been waiting here?"

Puck looked around him at the fairly uninspired scenery. "Long enough to be happy to see you, I suppose. Brean's here, by the way. But he's alone. He's camped just outside what I suppose is the marrying place—that's what's painted on the sign someone hung there, *The Marrying Place*. Well, the *Marying* place, as our anvil priest is probably not a scholar. But there has been a rather steady stream of hopeful young and not-so-young couples going in and out, so that's where Brean has planted himself."

Chelsea took hold of Puck's arm. "How does he look? Does he appear angry?"

"He's armed," Puck said, looking at Beau. "A dueling pistol, jammed into his waistband, his hand on the hilt as he stares down everyone who passes by. Personally, I think he's making quite a cake of himself, not to mention frightening the ladies. Oh, and he's got a bottle with him, although at the rate he was tipping it back, that's probably empty by now. I'd venture to say that if you stand more than three feet away from him, he'll miss you if he fires."

"And you're sure he's alone? No sister, no reverend, no coachman or grooms? No nefarious-looking thugs milling around, ready to pounce on me the moment he gives the word?"

"All bottle bravado," Puck said, nodding his head. "Say *boo* to him, and he'll most probably run away. Especially when you tell him she's already married. Should be fun, actually."

She, being Chelsea, had heard enough. "*Fun?* And you agree with him, don't you? All these days and nights, all the worry, all this dire business of me becoming a widow just as I've become a wife—and he calls it *fun?* And *you*—yes, you, *husband*—you've most probably been looking forward to this meeting. Haven't you?"

"I think she's got you there, brother mine. The perfect revenge. For the beating, for the rest of it. You said it,

Chelsea here said it, and that's what it is. If he doesn't get lucky and blow a hole in you, that is." Puck turned about to smile at Chelsea. "Not that he doesn't care for you, because he does. Otherwise he would simply have ruined you and sent you back. Right, Beau?"

Chelsea looked at Beau. Her husband.

"I'd appreciate it if you didn't *help* me anymore, Puck," he said quietly, returning Chelsea's look.

She began to count, silently, inside her head. One, Puck was probably right, in the beginning, so I'm not going to allow that to signify anything. Two, there was more between her brother and Oliver than she knew; Puck had just as much as said so. Three, she'd have the whole truth out of one of them at some point, but now probably wasn't the time. Four, somewhere between London and this place, everything had changed. For Oliver, for her. Five, a long coach trip with Madelyn had clearly served to unhinge her brother's mind in some way; he'd turned back to drink, and Francis Flotley was no longer stuck to him like a mustard plaster. Six, Oliver loved her. He might not call it love now, but he would, in time.

"It's all right, Oliver. Puck hasn't said anything that isn't true, or wasn't, at some point. Can we go see Thomas now? Because I *am* going. I doubt he's come all this way to give us his blessing, but I feel certain something has changed, and I want to know what it is. We'll take the coach."

Puck stepped ahead smartly and opened the coach

door, pulling down the steps and then backing away as Beau helped Chelsea inside.

"I'm sorry, Chelsea. I'm not usually obtuse. Beau? I'll take your Pegasus if you'd rather. At the moment, it seems safer."

"Get in the coach, you fool. I'm not going to hit you."

"It wasn't you I was worrying about," Puck said, grinning as he gracefully propelled himself into the coach. "Now, is there a plan? We probably should have a plan."

Chelsea turned her head to look at Beau. "I think it would be best if we apologized to Thomas," she said and then waited for him to explode. "We don't have to mean it, after all, and he really won't be expecting it."

"I don't believe he's in a forgiving mood. He has a pistol stuck in his waistband," Puck said. "I did mention that one niggling little problem, didn't I?"

"If I knew I was coming to see me, I'd have a pistol in my waistband, as well," Beau said as Chelsea slipped her hand into his. "But he's alone. *I* hadn't expected that. Puck, I want you to remain inside the coach. That seems only fair."

"Oh, yes, by all means, brother mine, you want to be *fair.* Are you out of your mind?"

"Probably. But I am armed, in a way," Beau said as the coach slowed to a stop. "Ah, and there he is, just as you described him. What in bloody hell is he doing?"

Chelsea pushed Beau back against the cushions and leaned across him, to peek out through the window of the coach. "He...why, I think he's flirting with that rather brightly dressed woman. Drink, and now loose women? And Francis Flotley nowhere to be seen?" Beau pulled her back onto the seat, and she turned to him in delight. "Do you know what it is, Oliver? I've been wondering, and now it's clear. Madelyn's made him desert his new devout religion. I told you she would make his life a hell. Oh, my sister-in-law will be *so* relieved!"

"He's seen you," Puck warned quietly. "Here he comes. You should get out, you're at a disadvantage in here."

"Stay with Puck," Beau said, kissing her cheek. Then he kissed her forehead, her nose, her mouth. He cupped her cheeks between his hands and looked at her for a long time, as if he might not see her again. "If I need rescuing by my wife, then you should have chosen another husband."

He hugged her, fiercely, and then turned to his brother. "Puck, you remember what we discussed. And if you have to sit on her, do it."

Chelsea tried to grab his arm. "But—"

Beau was already out of the coach, standing in the cobbled street, his hands well away from his body, the earl still a good ten feet away. Brean took another two or three steps and then planted himself.

"Where's m'sister?"

"My wife is in the coach."

"Oh, that might not have been brilliant. Concise, but not brilliant," Puck said, opening a side compartment in the coach and drawing out a pistol, resting it across his lap.

"Shh," Chelsea warned. "Thomas is talking."

"Why did she go to you?"

"Why did she run from you?"

Brean waved his arm as if to dismiss Beau's words. "I already know why she did that. I was wrong to try to force Francis on her, I know that now. But she had no right to disobey me."

"I think she'd disagree. Where is the Reverend Flotley, by the way? Chelsea tells me his mouth is always wet. I've wondered if she might have been exaggerating on that point."

Inside the coach, Chelsea shook her head at Puck. She hadn't exaggerated.

"I told you, it doesn't matter about Francis. It was the mumps, that's where the blame lies. The mumps and Madelyn. I see that now." He raised his voice. "Chelsea! I forgive you! I'm here to take you home!"

"I don't think you've been listening, Brean. Chelsea is my wife now. She stays with me. Your argument is with me."

"No. She can't be your wife. You just got here, remember?"

"There's more than one blacksmith shop in Scotland, Brean. You're too late."

The earl reached toward the pistol but withdrew his hand before he touched it. "I can have the marriage annulled."

"No, Brean, you can't. With luck, she's already carrying my child."

The earl's cheeks puffed in and out several times before he spat out, "You bastard!"

"Now, there's something Beau didn't know about himself," Puck said quietly. "It's such an easy insult, isn't it? You'd think the man would have more imagination."

Chelsea slapped his hand, to silence him. It was going well, she thought. Thomas was angry, but he'd not drawn his pistol. If he hadn't drawn it immediately, she doubted he ever would.

"It's over between us now, Brean. Settled. What happened the day I came to Portland Place…and what happened after that."

Chelsea saw her brother stagger where he stood. Not thanks to drink, but nearly knocked sideways by the words Beau had just spoken.

"Ah," Puck whispered beside her, "the coup de grâce. He has him now. I never doubted it. Not much, at least."

She didn't understand. Once more, she motioned for Puck to be silent. Something important was happening.

Thomas took a step back, away from Beau. "You know?"

"I've always known. That's why I came here today, to tell you that. And to tell you this. We're even now, quits. Stay away from Chelsea. Forget either of us exists. God knows we both want to forget you."

"I—I was young," the earl said plaintively. "My own father called me a coward. Using the whip like that. Me! His own son—a coward. He…he said the bastard was more the gentleman than I was. God, I hated my father. But not as much as I hated you." He moved his hand toward the pistol once more, and once again let it drop. "He said a *real* gentleman would have used his fists, knocked you down."

"You can still try to do that. I'd rather welcome it."

Inside the coach, Chelsea pressed a fist to her mouth, her heart pounding. But no matter how fearful she was, she couldn't look away.

"And maybe I don't blame you," the earl said, pushing his hands through his already mussed hair. "You went off to war, and I didn't do that, either. As the only son, the heir, I couldn't do that. But that didn't stop my father from pointing to you and saying at least the bastard loves his country. For all I knew, you'd kill fifty Froggies with your bare hands, and come home a hero. I'd never hear the end of it, not when m'father knew where to stick his pins. I was sick to death of you. Nothing shamed you, you never learned your *place.*"

"My place, I'll assume, being at the wrong end of a firing squad after you'd arranged it that I be found guilty of looting. And, failing that, simply being shot in the back while facing the French. I don't like you, Brean. Are you sure you don't want to try to knock me down?"

"For the love of God, man, don't *ask* him," Puck grumbled quietly. "Introduce the front of his nose to the back of his head."

"Puck—*shh!* You heard what even my father said— it's Oliver who is the real gentleman. Why didn't he tell me about any of this?" She sighed, shook her head. "Why am I not all that surprised to think Thomas capable of such cowardice and treachery?"

"Now who's making the noise in here? I want to hear what your brother has to say for himself. At the moment, however, he looks like he's just tried to swallow an apple in one bite. Come on, man, *say* something."

"No," the earl conceded at last. "No, I'm too drunk, and maybe my father was right..."

"So we're done here now, Brean? Really done?"

The earl closed his eyes. Nodded.

"Good. I doubt we'll be traveling in the same social circles, so we may not meet again. But I want to tell you something that might ease your mind. I love her. I love your sister with all my heart, and I will spend my life doing everything in my power to be worthy of her."

The earl looked at Beau, looked past him to the coach. "Why would I care about that?" he asked, his confusion genuine. And then he turned and walked away.

But Chelsea hadn't really been paying attention to anything from the moment she'd heard Beau tell her brother that he loved her.

She unashamedly wiped at her tear-wet cheeks. "Oliver loves me, Puck. He loves me."

Puck looked to her in some confusion. "Well, yes. I knew that."

Chelsea smiled through her tears. "That's not

important. It's important that Oliver knows it." She watched as her husband—her gentleman—turned and walked toward the coach. "Now, go away for a few minutes, please, Puck, because I think he's finally going to tell me."

EPILOGUE

THEY'D BEEN BACK at Blackthorn for nearly a week, and Puck had just departed for London, having decided to take up lodging in the Grosvenor Square mansion for what little remained of the Season. He said it was to do some reconnoitering on Jack's two friends before he approached them the following year with his pointed request that they assist him socially.

"I'd say I'll miss him, but I don't think I will," Beau told Chelsea as they watched the pair of coaches move off down the gravel drive. Puck did not exactly travel unencumbered.

"Oliver! That's a terrible thing to say about your own brother."

"Possibly. But with my parents currently playing at happy villagers in the cottage, we're finally alone. No one to ask why we never come down to breakfast. No one to make what he thinks are amusing remarks when we retire early. No one to walk in on us in the conservatory…"

"That could have been embarrassing," Chelsea said as they turned and headed back up the marble steps and into the entrance hall. "All right, I'll agree. We won't miss him. Are we going upstairs?"

He put his arm around her waist and led her to the stairs. "I think so, if you don't mind. We can celebrate Puck's departure."

"But we already celebrated the sun rising this morning," she teased, lifting up her skirts and running down the hall ahead of him to the large bedchamber that now belonged to both of them. There was an adjoining bedchamber, and that was supposedly hers, but she'd yet to sleep in the bed and probably never would. Edith said that wasn't proper, but then she'd winked at her.

Once inside the room, Chelsea stopped with her back to Beau, silently indicating that he could play at maid for her and undo the long row of buttons on her new morning gown. She could be more subtle, she supposed, even coy, but that was such a waste of time.

Besides, she had something to tell him, and she'd rather get it over with, as she'd been attempting to hide her reaction to the news all morning.

"Oliver?" she said as he opened the buttons one by one, dropping quick kisses on each new exposed area of skin. "I had a letter from Madelyn in this morning's post."

"And promptly dispatched it into the nearest fireplace, I would hope."

"No, I read it. She has disowned me. How did she say it? Oh, yes. Seed, breed and generation. All disowned. Can she do that?"

The last button undone, he turned her about to face

him. "I thought that was the prerogative of the head of the family. But I imagine she sees it as symbolic. I'm sorry, sweetheart."

"I don't think I am. Sorry, that is. There's more, Oliver. She also wrote that Thomas is back to his old haunts, drinking and whoring and gambling rather deep. Our elopement doesn't seem to have affected him at all, except that Madelyn says all of Mayfair is buzzing about the *stern thrashing* he gave you when he arrived in Gretna Green too late to stop the nuptials. Within an inch of your life, or so Thomas tells it. Madelyn wanted to know if that's true. So now it's my turn to say I'm sorry."

Beau smiled. "And here I was, feeling somewhat guilty—not much, mind you, but somewhat—because it was too late to somehow warn him about the investment he'd been neatly steered to last month."

"Investment?" Chelsea began backing up toward the bed, urging Beau with her by the simple expedient of tugging on his neck cloth. "More grapes?"

"Even your brother isn't so dim that he'd trust a scheme like that a second time. But did you know, Mrs. Blackthorn, that it is said there is gold to be found in the hills of Shropshire?"

She stepped out of her gown and climbed up onto the bed, to kneel there in her shift while she undid his neck cloth and shirt buttons. "Why, no, Mr. Blackthorn, I did *not* know that there is gold to be found in the hills of Shropshire. But that's because there isn't any, is there?"

"If there is, your brother will be a very wealthy man.

But I'm fairly certain that won't be the case. However, that's the last bit of amusement I'll be having at your brother's expense. He isn't worth the effort, to be honest. Are you going to be all day with those buttons?"

"Don't feel badly that you couldn't stop the scheme. My brother attempted to have you hanged for looting. He's a horrible, horrible man. No wonder he was so terrified of dying and being sent straightway to hell. There, all done. You can take everything off now and come to bed. Aren't we becoming proficient?"

"And one of us is becoming rather cheeky," he teased as he joined her, taking hold of her shoulders and lowering her onto the pillows. "How many times today have I told you that I love you?"

She reached up her hand to run her fingers through his thick blond hair. "Only three. But that's already once more than yesterday. Does it get easier, Oliver?"

"I don't remember why it ever was difficult. I think I knew I loved you the moment you kicked me in the ankle, the night we came here for the first time." He leaned in and kissed her. "Or maybe," he continued as he began untying the laces at the top of her chemise, "I knew I loved you when I saw that blister on your thumb and you lied, said you hadn't noticed it. No, that can't be it. I know. It was when I was helping as you leaned over that ditch, ridding yourself of that truly horrible meat pie. Or maybe—"

She put her hand across his mouth.

"Oliver," she said sternly. "I believe that will be enough."

He put his hand over hers, kissed her palm and then pressed it over his heart, which belonged to her in any case. "Yes, sweetheart, that's it. I knew I was in love with you when you called me Oliver."

"But…but that was the very first day."

He leaned down to whisper against her ear. "Yes, I know."

She turned into his arms. "Oh, Oliver…"

* * * * *

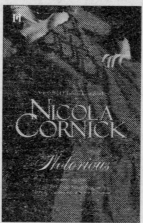

Her perfect life waits just around the corner....

**A smart, sexy new tale from *New York Times*
and *USA TODAY* bestselling author**

KRISTAN HIGGINS

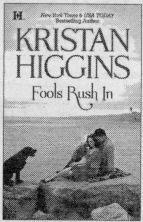

September 2011

Millie Barnes is *this close* to achieving the perfect life.
Rewarding job as a doctor? Check. Cute cottage of her very
own? Check. Adorable puppy? Check! All she needs is for
her former crush Joe Carpenter to notice her, and Millie
will be set. But perfection isn't easy—not when handsome
policeman Sam Nickerson is so distracting....

Fools Rush In

Coming soon!

REQUEST YOUR
FREE BOOKS!

2 FREE NOVELS
FROM THE ROMANCE COLLECTION
PLUS 2 FREE GIFTS!

YES! Please send me 2 FREE novels from the Romance Collection and my 2 FREE gifts (gifts are worth about $10). After receiving them, if I don't wish to receive any more books, I can return the shipping statement marked "cancel." If I don't cancel, I will receive 4 brand-new novels every month and be billed just $5.99 per book in the U.S. or $6.49 per book in Canada. That's a saving of at least 25% off the cover price. It's quite a bargain! Shipping and handling is just 50¢ per book in the U.S. and 75¢ per book in Canada.* I understand that accepting the 2 free books and gifts places me under no obligation to buy anything. I can always return a shipment and cancel at any time. Even if I never buy another book, the two free books and gifts are mine to keep forever.

194/394 MDN FELQ

Name	(PLEASE PRINT)	
Address		Apt. #
City	State/Prov.	Zip/Postal Code

Signature (if under 18, a parent or guardian must sign)

Mail to the **Reader Service:**
IN U.S.A.: P.O. Box 1867, Buffalo, NY 14240-1867
IN CANADA: P.O. Box 609, Fort Erie, Ontario L2A 5X3

Not valid for current subscribers to the Romance Collection
or the Romance/Suspense Collection.

Want to try two free books from another line?
Call 1-800-873-8635 or visit www.ReaderService.com.

* Terms and prices subject to change without notice. Prices do not include applicable taxes. Sales tax applicable in N.Y. Canadian residents will be charged applicable taxes. Offer not valid in Quebec. This offer is limited to one order per household. All orders subject to credit approval. Credit or debit balances in a customer's account(s) may be offset by any other outstanding balance owed by or to the customer. Please allow 4 to 6 weeks for delivery. Offer available while quantities last.

Your Privacy—The Reader Service is committed to protecting your privacy. Our Privacy Policy is available online at www.ReaderService.com or upon request from the Reader Service.

We make a portion of our mailing list available to reputable third parties that offer products we believe may interest you. If you prefer that we not exchange your name with third parties, or if you wish to clarify or modify your communication preferences, please visit us at www.ReaderService.com/consumerschoice or write to us at Reader Service Preference Service, P.O. Box 9062, Buffalo, NY 14269. Include your complete name and address.

ROM11

MICHAELS

77463	HOW TO WED A BARON	___ $7.99 U.S.	___ $9.99 CAN.
77433	HOW TO BEGUILE A BEAUTY	___ $7.99 U.S.	___ $9.99 CAN.
77376	HOW TO TAME A LADY	___ $7.99 U.S.	___ $8.99 CAN.
77371	HOW TO TEMPT A DUKE	___ $7.99 U.S.	___ $8.99 CAN.
77191	A MOST UNSUITABLE GROOM	___ $6.99 U.S.	___ $8.50 CAN.

(limited quantities available)

TOTAL AMOUNT	$ _____
POSTAGE & HANDLING	$ _____
($1.00 FOR 1 BOOK, 50¢ for each additional)	
APPLICABLE TAXES*	$ _____
TOTAL PAYABLE	$ _____

(check or money order — please do not send cash)

To order, complete this form and send it, along with a check or money order for the total above, payable to HQN Books, to: **In the U.S.:** 3010 Walden Avenue, P.O. Box 9077, Buffalo, NY 14269-9077; **In Canada:** P.O. Box 636, Fort Erie, Ontario, L2A 5X3.

Name: _____
Address: _____ City: _____
State/Prov.: _____ Zip/Postal Code: _____
Account Number (if applicable): _____

075 CSAS

*New York residents remit applicable sales taxes.
*Canadian residents remit applicable GST and provincial taxes.

™ www.Harlequin.com

PHKM0811BL